Darkness over Love:
A Writer's Workbook

Paul Monk

BARRALLIER BOOKS

First published in 2014 by Barrallier Books Pty Ltd,

Registered Office: 35-37 Gordon Avenue, West Geelong, Victoria 3220, Australia.

www.barrallierbooks.com

Copyright © Paul Monk 2014

National Library of Australia cataloguing-in-publication information:

Creator: Monk, Paul M., author.

Darkenss over love : a writer's workbook / Paul Monk.

ISBN: 9780992588045 : (hardback)

Dewey Number: A823.4

Set in Garamond Premier Pro 12/17 and Fragrance

Cover image: *She Grows Old 1* (1967)

Jörg Schmeisser

Un regalo para mi paloma blanca

Contents

Images

Fragments, Maze and Mandala
Jörg Schmeisser's image 005 from *Etchings* (1987)

Book One
Reflections on creating the story

'So we seek the artist who lets us approach ourselves purely, encounter ourselves. His novel gaze molds unrecognizable new shapes and moves like a swimmer, like a cyclone through the given ... How do we hear ourselves at first? As an endless singing to oneself, and in the dance.'

– Ernst Bloch *The Spirit of Utopia* (Berlin, 1923)

'Stendhal always considered Love *his principal work, because in it he had expressed his most cherished ideas, his most intimate beliefs, all that science of happiness to which he attached so much importance; above all because he had enclosed in it his most painful secrets about love. Perhaps he even preferred the book less for its theories than for the memories with which he had filled it. His personal experience has a preponderant part in it and the sense of the book would escape us, if we were unaware of certain circumstances of his life and of his love for Mathilde Dembowski.'*

– Henri Martineau *L'Œuvre de Stendhal* (Paris, 1951)

'A new project long occupied me, and has not ceased to do so, namely, the construction of the Odeon, a model library provided with halls for courses and lectures to serve as a centre of Greek culture in Rome. I made it less splendid than the new library at Ephesus, built three or four years before, and gave it less grace and elegance than the library of Athens, but I intend to make this foundation a close second to, if not the equal of the Museum of Alexandria ...'

– Marguerite Yourcenar *Memoirs of Hadrian* (Paris, 1951)

' ... art as a category of responsible experience, that sustains us by a reciprocating relation to life, belongs to the metabolism of our culture and possibly of all culture. It deserves to be protected with all our powers from those who would borrow its mantle to protect and ennoble displays of unredeemed depravity and violence.'

– Roger Shattuck *Candor and Perversion* (New York, 1999)

' ... Lionel Trilling claimed 'all prose fiction is a variation on the theme of Don Quixote', that paradigm-shifting Spanish inquisition into illusion vs. reality. I would argue further that this should be the lifelong goal of every intelligent person: to see through the polite lies promulgated by political, corporate, media and religious entities, the often irrational customs, beliefs and prejudices of one's social group ... to arrive at a clear understanding of the true nature of things.'

– Steven Moore *The Novel: An Alternative History, Beginnings to 1600* (New York and London, 2010)

Author's Note: How to Read this Book

Read this book slowly, sitting in a comfortable chair, with a glass of red wine at hand, would be my recommendation; unless, that is, the wine itself will put you to sleep. I hope you will find what I have written and rewritten deeply absorbing and, at many points, quite profoundly enjoyable. It is not, however, a light read and to make matters worse it isn't even finished yet. The key parts of it—the celebrated three notebooks of Fenimore Moneghan— are discussed at either end of this book, but they are missing from the heart of it. You need, therefore, to heed what you are told about them and use your imagination to fill in the (large) gaps for the present.

If you do not read it slowly and attentively, rather than foolishly skimming through it as if you will then either 'get' the thing quickly or spot the 'answer' or 'outcome' to a presumed plot, you will miss a great deal. The story, as it now stands, is coherent, but it isn't simple and there is by no means a simple 'answer' or 'outcome' to be spotted by the hasty reader. For the patient, meditative reader, on the other hand, there will, I believe, be rich rewards. Certainly, the greatest strength of the story as now framed (and what you have here is the framework) is in its numerous wry subtleties and ironies. See how many of these you can spot.

It isn't necessary to read the long essay at the front of the book before plunging into the story, if you are impatient to 'get on with it'; but I do recommend that you do so. I pondered placing the essay at the end of the book, but I decided, on reflection, to place it at the start because this book is all about the evolution of an intricate story intended—should my abilities and energies prove adequate to the task—to become eventually a far larger work of high literary art. The essay sets out how that ambition and the story as it now stands have gradually emerged from my personal background and belated efforts to become a serious literary writer.

You will find in these pages several different 'voices', though for the time being you will hear very little of the voices of either of the two principal protagonists (Fenimore and Margarita) or those of the numerous minor characters from around the world. That's because all these naturally belong in the gaping hole in the middle of the manuscript. They are chattering away off stage at the moment, as I keep working on the core narrative. Here and there in this book you will see quite a few of them mentioned and even quoted. There is a lot more to come. After all, as the essay makes clear, I am just starting to get the hang of this narrative writing game.

What you do have here are the editorial voices of N. Herman and Tom Emerson, a little of Fenimore and Margarita (in the Prologue and the four sections of Notebooks II and III that have been included), the delightful (I think) Cardinal Roberto Bolzano (in his long letter to the Pope) and a few others in minor roles (notably the strident voices of the Chinese security analysts and Anonymous manifesto writers). It is the commentaries by N. Herman and Tom Emerson to which you should pay most attention. In particular, don't skip over apparent details, such as Tom's footnotes in the Appendices. They may look purely marginal, but they are full of reading pleasure. They are also my own reflections on 'Fenimore' and what he has been writing.

Above all, remember that this is a private offering to elicit responses to a work in progress. Read it that way and try to appreciate how much careful thought has had to go into drafting and redrafting even what is here in order to have all the many 'moving parts' work in unison. Believe me, it has come a long way and only with these parts in place does the—still exceptionally challenging—work ahead now look as though it might be achievable. I hope you enjoy this current form of the emerging story in its own right and look forward to your feedback on what you do or do not either understand or, frankly, enjoy. There are Discussion Points at the end!

Fernando Pessoa: An Inspiration

"The boy king Sebastian led the Portuguese army into a slaughter in Morocco, in 1578. Since the royal body was not found on the battlefield, a national myth came into being, Sebastianism, which held that the hero lived on, in a mystic island, and someday would return as the Hidden One, and establish Portugal as the Fifth Empire..."

– Harold Bloom *Genius: A Mosaic of One Hundred Exemplary Creative Minds,* (2002)

Fernando Pessoa (1888-1935), was a Portuguese poet, writer, literary critic, translator, publisher and philosopher. He is widely regarded as one of the most significant literary figures of the 20th century. He is certainly one of the greatest poets in the Portuguese language. He also wrote in and translated from English and French. He emerged as a model for what I have done with this novel as I slowly came to realize what the novel was about and discovered its humorous inner logic and elegiac mood.

Pessoa's poems often carried humorous versions of 'Anonymous' as the author's name. He began using pen names when still quite young. Through a literary life that lasted only until his early death from cirrhosis of the liver at the age of 47, he used literally scores of *noms de plume*. He was an enthusiast for Hermetic and Gnostic myths, notably in the form of Rosicrucian mysticism—a subtle blend of Enlightenment rationalism, Christianity and pre-Christian myths. He brought to his writing, especially as it matured, that complex irony one associates with Hispanic and Lusitanian literature from the time of Cervantes to that of Garcia Marquez.

Harold Bloom wrote in 2002 that Pessoa was "at least three great poets". He was also the critic of those poets and he wrote the poetry and the criticism under different names. His own surname, Pessoa, *means* "persona" or "mask", which may be what prompted him to use masks for his authorship. It is possible, Bloom speculates, that the name 'Pessoa' derived from Jewish ancestors who had been forced to convert to Catholicism in order to survive. Pessoa's favourite pen name was Alvaro de Campos, a Portuguese Jew.

Though born in Portugal, Pessoa was raised in English-speaking South Africa before the First World War, when the British Empire was at its zenith. This, also, fits with Fenimore Moneghan in this novel being located para-geographically, at "the Ends of the Earth" at the zenith of the Pax Americana. Pessoa's literary culture, Bloom remarks, "was as much Anglo-American as it was Portuguese or—in Borges's case—Spanish." He only published one book of poetry, called *Mensagem* (*Message* or *Summons*), which is seen as an esoteric work of an almost Kabbalistic nature. He regarded Shakespeare, Keats, Shelley, Browning and Whitman as his precursors. He played at Gnosticism and Kabbalah, concludes Bloom, but was "a master of evasions."

Pessoa wrote:

> *With such a deficiency of literature as there is today, what can a man of genius do but convert himself, on his own, into a literature? With such a deficiency of coexistable people as there is today, what can a man of sensibility do but invent his own friends, or at least his intellectual companions?*

It is from a similar set of impulses, ultimately, that *Darkness over Love: A Complete Fiction* has arisen. Having invented Fenimore, I found it irresistible to make his story at once complete and yet buried within the interpretations of others and the confusions that this creates, without actually losing the clarity he brings to his own story. This led to the creation of Tom as the editor and rapporteur of Fenimore's privately written story—initially intended only for the eyes of Margarita—and then onto further elaborations which, I hope, will delight the reader.

The Evolution of a Story: An author's reflections on the creative process

Preamble

Darkness over Love: A Complete Fiction is a work in progress, but a work that has come a long way over the past five years. What I am now attempting is absurdly ambitious and may prove impossible. Yet the way it has grown unexpectedly from a very different beginning seems to me to be interesting in itself. It began as a cycle of poems. It has become an attempt to capture, inside a single story, an entire philosophy of life and reality; and to do so in a way that both works as a story and illuminates the nature of story-telling as such. It has been inspired along the way by many great myths and stories. It now aspires to become one in its own right. Whether I shall succeed in my ambition remains to be seen. Already, however, the experience of seeing this tale grow from its small beginnings into what it now adumbrates has been so intimate an exploration of the creative process that I want to set it down—before the verdict is in, as it were.

So, this essay is an author's reflection on the *creative process*, at what seems to be a crucial turning point in the evolution of this particular story. It is printed in this volume along with the existing design for and certain advanced elements of the story, under the title *Darkness over Love: A Writer's Workbook*, as a kind of bivouac on the ascent 'up the mountain' towards what I hope will be 'a complete fiction' in the not too distant future. That 'complete fiction' is quite deliberately intended to evoke, with varying degrees of subtlety, Homer's *Odyssey*, Virgil's *Aeneid*, Ovid's *Metamorphoses*, Dante's *Divine Comedy*, Boccaccio's *Decameron*, Cervantes' *Don Quixote* and a dozen or so great modern novels. But it is neither a mere pastiche of these taken together nor a shallow imitation of any of those classic works. It is, in the author's intention, an attempt to create a wholly new work that might achieve the status of a myth for the 21st century. It is, also, an absorbing and intensely amusing creative exercise in its own right. This is its story so far.

Schematically, the work has grown through the following stages:

2008   In March, I wrote a cathartic cycle of intimate poems called *The Neruda Variations,* based on Pablo Neruda's famous book of poetry *Twenty Love Poems and a Song of Despair*. Late that year, I began to attempt to transform *The Neruda Variations* into a prose script, under the title *Letters to my Muse*. It had no cover image and was not divided into three parts. It did, however, have a Prologue, an Epilogue and, rather curiously, twenty four chapters. It began with what was then an explicitly autobiographical reminiscence and reflection under the title 'Fragments of a Conversation.' It also had an Appendix which reproduced *The Neruda Variations*.

2009   I began to re-write the late 2008 script as a novel, adding the main title *Darkness over Love*, but keeping *Letters to my Muse* as a sub-title. The writing plainly grew organically out of the earlier cycle of poems, but as a development of them that had not been anticipated when they were written, or even when the first prose script was composed. It had an anonymous narrator, who was partly me and partly an ill-defined avatar of me. It was transparently autobiographical and lacked a clear story line. It had a gloomy cover image based on Bartok's dark opera *Duke Bluebeard's Castle* (see Annex, Image 1).

2010   I completed the first draft of *Darkness over Love: Letters to my Muse* with great enthusiasm, during a winter break down by the ocean; but I then asked myself a set of probing questions about what I was attempting to do and how narrative fiction works. I invented a name (Frederick Beresford) for the narrator and a rudimentary biography for him. After some thought, I relocated his apartment and enhanced it in several ways. I gave it the name 'Cos' and it began to evolve into a completely invented place. I changed the title of the story to *Darkness over Love: A Complete Fiction*. The cover image, however, remained the same.

2011   I completed the second draft of the novel, now called *Darkness over Love: A Complete Fiction*, by the spring (September) with many changes and significant textual improvements, but many of my misgivings remained. I began a third draft as the summer approached and made significant further changes. I rewrote the Prologue radically, entirely deleting the autobiographical thread and moving the setting to Toledo (Spain). I changed the narrator's name from Frederick Beresford (with which I had never felt entirely comfortable) to Fenimore Moneghan. The identity of his Muse became better defined and her character, as Margarita Henderson, much more fully developed. She now lived in the Canary Islands, in exile from her native land. Moneghan's dwelling place, 'Cos', ceased to be an apartment and became a large house. A substantial cast of other characters began to appear. The cover was altered dramatically from an image of gloom and darkness to one of light and space (see Annex, Image 2).

2012   After an intense summer of work on the third draft, I came to a halt, having realized that I was only now at the *beginning* of crafting a genuine story and that I had a great deal of thinking to do about the story itself, various back stories that underpinned it; characterization and the art of narrative fiction in general. It had become clear that many lines of the story needed to be thought through and the whole approach to story-telling given a lot of thought. I decided to take a 'sabbatical' for a whole year, in which I would give my time and energy over to research, reading and thinking about the preparation of the novel.

2013   Having moved the Prologue to Toledo and domiciled the Muse, Margarita, in Santa Cruz de Tenerife, I realized that I needed and indeed wanted to visit those places and get *inside the story*. I planned the journey for some months, then, in April, travelled to Spain (via Egypt and Israel) to explore the physical and social locations in which the narrator and his Muse first met and that in which she lived. I spent a number of days in both Tenerife and Toledo. Toledo I had briefly visited many years before. Tenerife was wholly new to me. The fortnight in Spain catalysed a fresh start, so that even before leaving that storied country I was already at work on a fourth draft.

A symbolic change at this point was the further alteration of the cover image, from a cosmological one to the interior of San Roman (see Annex, Image 3). This truly was getting inside the story. However, by mid-winter it had become apparent that there were still intractable problems with the narrative structure. In the spring and early summer I came up with a radically new one. I abandoned the incipient third and fourth drafts and reframed the story along new and much more imaginative lines. As I did so, I began to think more than ever about how the story would be *read* and to visualize key scenes in *cinematic* terms. Crucially, the new structure began dramatically and with a voice other than that of the supposed primary narrator.

2014   I undertook another journey; this time to the United States, Italy and the Aegean, to explore and animate various aspects of the new design. I spent five days in Boston exploring Harvard and Cambridge, where the core characters had met in the 1980s. I made exciting discoveries in Italy and Santorini. The new design was confirmed and a substantial draft of this account of the creative process since 2008 was written down in Santorini. For the first time, all the elements of the narrative appeared to cohere and the nature of the creative work ahead seemed, while daunting, a matter of craftsmanship that I felt I was mastering.

What follows is an account in reflective detail of the creative journey just schematically outlined. It is a reflection on both the creative process of storytelling in general and as it can be shown at work in the development of this particular story. Looking back, it is possible to see the elements of the story, the coherence of the narrative, the nature and even existence of characters and the significance of incidents slowly taking shape. It is striking, in that perspective, that the way these things happened was *not* a conscious or mechanical process. It was a rather *mysterious* process and very definitely an *evolutionary* one—one of mutation, adaptation, natural selection, the elimination of the unfit; the emergence of the new in 'ecological niches' that opened up often unexpectedly. The unexpectedness of new developments is what makes the experience and the outcome both full of surprises and fascinating to look back upon. I have found the journey extraordinary—though there is still a long way to go. I hope that you, the reader, will find my account of it—as well as the new design, which might be called the *fifth* draft—an interesting story in itself.

Genesis of the early manuscripts

This, then, is a reflection on the evolution of a story that I have been working on for a number of years and which may take some years more to complete. Its imaginative roots go back many years. Yet it seems to me only in the past twelve months or so finally to have begun to assume the strength and vitality of a 'true' story. Above all, it has only been in that twelve months that the exercise has become what I would call 'ludic', that is to say playful, self-aware, ironical and truly creative. There was no mistaking the point at which this occurred. It was the spring of 2013 and I had a cascade of insights about solutions to intractable problems with which I had been wrestling for a long time. I found myself bursting into laughter with sheer enjoyment of the creative experience and the relief of having solved those problems in so original a manner. It was at that point, more than at any previous point, that I realized what a fascinating journey of exploration I had been on and how far I had come.

All stories, but great stories especially, take time to evolve. This is clearly true of the ancient myths and legends. Often, they evolved over centuries or even millennia. It's true, also, of great novels of the modern era, whether the classics of nineteenth century realism, those of twentieth century modernism or the best loved children's fables. They evolve in the sense that their authors take time to develop them from the threads of inherited tradition and personal experience, through iterative refinement and linguistic invention. Goethe, though already a famous poet and novelist, worked on *Faust* all his life. Flaubert took years to write each of his great novels (at least six for *Madame Bovary*, for example) and even longer for the short tale *The Temptation of St Antony*, which he thought would never be published in his lifetime. Mikhail Bulgakov worked on *The Master and Margarita* for ten years and never saw it published, due to the hostile conditions in Stalin's Russia. Boris Pasternak took more than ten years to complete *Doctor Zhivago* and died a few years after it was published.

Long before I attempted to write a story of my own, I was fascinated by many great stories, especially the great myths which were handed down as part of our Western cultural heritage: the myths of the classical and pre-classical worlds and those in the Bible. My education in them, as it happens, was indifferent; so it was not until my adult years that I developed a more sustained and reflective interest in where they had come from. In the interim, I was fascinated by the enormously popular fable by J. R. R. Tolkien, *The Lord of the Rings;* and by its author's statement that "this tale grew in the telling, until it became a history of the Great War of the Ring and included many glimpses of the yet more ancient history that preceded it". As I grew older, this hint of how Tolkien had found himself caught up in a story that grew far beyond his initial expectations, led to an interest in the accounts of its origin and evolution through many drafts by the author's son, Christopher Tolkien. One of the books I read during my 2012 'sabbatical' was John D. Rateliff's newly published study *The History of the Hobbit*, a scholarly account of the evolution of Tolkien's earlier and much less accomplished, but still classic children's story. It shows a similar process, albeit on a far smaller scale.

In recent years, I have developed an ever greater interest in the nature of stories as such; in the nature of language and in the nature of humanity. We are a species made in important respects unique by language; we are the language animal. For that reason, chiefly, we live *inside evolving stories*—narratives constructed in language. We exist in a constant tension between the personal narratives that run in our individual heads; a barely coherent understanding of the cultural stories that govern our lives; strange literalism and even dogmatism in clinging to such stories; and (very occasionally) fabulous creativity in making new stories or remaking old ones. Delving into the subject as an aspiring writer, I came to appreciate how complex it is. I increasingly grew to understand how important it is to grapple with it, if we wish to come to grips with our own humanity. As we do so, whether spontaneously or under guidance, what we find is that the stories within which we live our lives are like a great onion with ring after ring: personal stories, family stories, community stories, urban stories, national stories, vast international stories, religious myths and, transcending all of them, the immense and unfathomably deep stories of life on Earth and of the cosmos within which our small and highly unusual world exists.

At every layer or level, the question of what is the *true* story rather than an illusory or actually mendacious one is apt to intrude upon our consciousness. At a certain point, the question even arises as to what one might mean by 'the true story'. This became a problem for me as a young man. I could not find a story within which I was content to live. Throughout a great part of my adult life, determined to ascertain the 'true story' of humanity, the Earth and the cosmos, I spent literally decades distrusting fiction, even where I loved it. It seemed to me that human beings succumbed to far too much fiction in the form of vacuous fantasy, foolish daydreams, religious faiths, dogmatic ideologies and so on. I longed to be free of all that. I studied philosophy, history and international relations in a determined effort to get to the bottom of what made the human world work the way it did and how it had come to be the way it was. My strongest belief, from my undergraduate years in the late 1970s through into my years working as a professional intelligence analyst in the early to mid-1990s, was that the world around me was plagued by confused fictions and false beliefs. The task of a serious person was to see through this mass of error to a true understanding of how the world worked.

Then, one day just on ten years ago, in the nature of great stories, I had a chance meeting with a wonderful woman. She arrived in my world out of her Hispanic one with almost no prior warning and brought with her a depth of character and a passion for both the life of the mind and the importance of the emotions that were an enormous gift to me. She and I became close and she very quickly concluded that what was imprisoned within my serious and labouring psyche was a story-teller who badly needed to be released from his inhibitions. She would call upon me to tell her stories, to sing her songs; and I would freeze up, as if struck dumb. Almost exactly six months after she had arrived, she wrote me the most beautiful note I have ever received. It was on a simple and tastefully selected birthday card, which I have kept ever since. It read as follows:

> *El verdadero regalo de este onomástico cumpleaños es mi ferviente creencia en tu capacidad creativa.*
> *Creo en ti, en nosotros y en la novela. Nos entregaremos a todo ello con humildad y pasión*
>
> *......*
>
> *[The real gift for this particular birthday is my fervent belief in your creative capacity.*
> *I believe in you, in us and in the novel. We shall engage in all this with humility and passion.]*

In the months that followed, she would say to me, "*Do you realize that we are living a story that has not yet been written?*" Without her, there is no question that *this* story would *never* have been written. If it comes to fruition, it will be because of her and my love for her. This interim volume is primarily a gift for her, on the tenth anniversary of her extraordinary card.

Yet despite all those hints and encouragements, years passed and there was no novel. There were other books, one after another—a book on the modernization of China, a book of sonnets written in the 1990s with art work and commentary, a study of industrial relations reform in Australia, a set of thirty essays on Western civilization - but there was inertia when it came to the specific matter of attempting to create a *new* story—whether fictional or the one that we were living and that had not yet been written. Believing that I had rejected her as a muse and as a companion, she went away after three and a half years. Only then and only little by little did the internal inhibitions and barriers to creativity begin to break down. Only then did a kind of story begin to form and find expression, but it was not a coherent story and it was certainly not the story that has since emerged. I found that setting myself free as a story-teller was a Herculean labour. Now, looking back some years, it seems to me that the emergence of a genuinely creative story out of a mass of memories, ideas and inchoate emotions has been an extraordinarily cathartic and expressive experience.

For a novel to be written, as of 2007, some kind of emotional dam needed to burst. That occurred, looking back, in the late summer and early autumn of 2008 with an outpouring of the most emotional and unstructured poetry I had ever written. I felt no sense, as I wrote the poetry, that I was attempting to write a novel. I felt desolate at the departure of a woman I loved very much and whom I felt I had failed. I attempted to express these feelings of both erotic and emotional failure, but also of enduring love and gratitude, in a cycle of poems which I called *The Neruda Variations*. Pablo Neruda was a great 20th century Chilean poet, acclaimed by some as the century's greatest poet in any language. My muse had given me, a couple of years before, a bilingual edition of the book that had first brought him acclaim: *Twenty Love Poems and a Song of Despair*. I now drew upon that book in an effort to give words to my own sense of love and despair. The poems as a set are never likely to be published; but several of them have been carried over, in more polished form, into the novel. They were without doubt an emotional catharsis and writing them set me free to attempt other creative work.

I shared the poems, soon after they had been written, with a small circle of acquaintances, but two of those I shared them with were my muse herself and a great male friend in America. Let me, for present purposes; simply refer to them as the Muse and the Friend. The Muse responded that she appreciated the poems, but she said that it was as if, in them, she had become a 'literary character' rather than her own self. This was, of course, inevitably the case and prompted mixed feelings on my part. I had wanted them to occur as direct communications; yet the idea that they had somehow generated a latent 'literary character' was tantalizing feedback. The Friend responded that 'the poems read like letters to your wife', which, of course, they essentially were—for the Muse and I had married within weeks of the card she gave me in late 2004. These two pieces of rudimentary, but sensitive feedback were, I would say, what *precipitated* the shift from cathartic, highly personal free verse to the first attempt at story-telling. It was some months before I put pen to paper (or finger to keyboard); but their feedback was a turning point. As the story took shape, two central figures in it would be inspired by the Muse and the Friend.

I had had a long and checkered love life before the Muse appeared in my world and a decade earlier had had vague thoughts of attempting a novel under the title *Letters to Foreign Women*. Nothing had ever come of that idea, but these were new circumstances and by late 2008 I found myself attempting, without any detached or thorough plan, to write a quasi-story with very strong autobiographical overtones, under the working title *Letters to my Muse*. The link in the chain will be immediately obvious. The nature of the process was also, especially looking back, very evident: the new manuscript was every bit as much a cathartic outpouring as *The Neruda Variations*; but in prose and in the form not so much of a single story as of a series of interlinked tales and half-fictionalized recollections. The emotional dam had well and truly burst, releasing a flood of ideas. After the deluge, however, I had to begin sifting through what it had swept downstream. Among the bewildering mass of detritus, I found the elements of a tale that I thought it might be both possible and worthwhile to write.

One of the great debates in the study of literature is about the extent to which novelists (or, for that matter, poets) draw upon their personal experiences in writing what they do. In other words, how much 'autobiography' is there, however camouflaged or reworked, in the novels of Tolstoy or Dostoevsky, Flaubert or Thomas Mann? I had long been somewhat interested in this question and there seemed good evidence that the lives of creative writers, especially the emotional impact on them of the dramatic events in their lives, gave them the material out of which they fashioned their novels; or at the very least the slant they gave to what they wrote about. Yet it was certainly not autobiography that they wrote in any obvious sense. It was literature. Little by little, I began to experience at firsthand how much skill and artistry is needed simply to tell a story, true or false, autobiographical or fanciful. But that realization was relatively slow in coming. It was preceded by an unleashed enthusiasm for creative writing, which generated a long manuscript (almost 450 pages), including many new poems and even songs, several new and wholly imaginary fables and a very free reckoning with a great deal of my past—addressed to the Muse.

From this earliest attempt to create a work of prose fiction, the urgent autobiographical and cathartic impulse was evident. The Prologue to the first manuscript, dated December 2008, was titled 'Fragments of a Conversation'. It recounted my first conversation with the Muse, on her arrival in Melbourne in May 2004. It began with the following paragraph:

> *Whenever I sit down in my own private space to compose my thoughts, I am reminded of the words Robert Bolt put into the mouth of Yuri at Varykino, in his screenplay for Doctor Zhivago: "Anna taught me to write at this desk." Those words come especially to mind now, as I sit down to write to you, because you sat at this desk and here we talked so much about writing and the life of the mind and the importance of the emotions. But above all, because, in the first conversation we ever had, if only to make conversation, I asked you, "If you had to name your all-time favourite film, what would it be?" and you responded, without hesitation, "It would have to be Doctor Zhivago." I was astonished. "Ah! It's also my favourite film!" I exclaimed. "I must have seen it fifteen or twenty times over the years." And so began our sharing of what life and meaning and poetry are all about.*

That opening and what followed from it endured through some two or three years of writing; only being supplanted when it occurred to me that the narrator was not me and that he had first met *his* Muse in Toledo, about a month before I first met mine.

In the winter of 2010 I completed the first full draft manuscript. I finished the writing in a fortnight down at an ocean beach house belonging to one of my younger sisters and her husband. Never before, even when writing up my doctorate, more than twenty years earlier, had I felt so totally engaged in the writing process. Each day I would rise before dawn, fix a coffee and a round of toast and get down to work, writing until about 3.30 in the afternoon, before going down to the ocean beach and walking along the grey, wintry sea strand until dark, which fell by about 5.30. Often, I would take with me down to the rocky ledges and outcrops by the shore a volume of poetry, chiefly Rilke's *Duino Elegies* or his *Sonnets to Orpheus* and read them aloud to myself, contained within the sound shell of the breaking waves and the winter wind. I would then come back, fix an evening meal and listen to music for some hours before retiring. I had never before had so intense an experience of immersion in the creative process. I had written a doctoral dissertation in the 1980s, poetry in the 1980s and 1990s, numerous essays in the 2000s and four earlier books, but this was different in both scope, depth and emotional commitment.

When I wrote the concluding lines to the draft Epilogue, I felt exultant. Such was my mood in that context that I deluded myself I had created a masterpiece. There seems no question, in retrospect, that that misjudgement was due to two things: the enormous emotional release that the writing had involved and the tacit sense that, within the manuscript, there were glimmers of a genuinely creative and sweeping story. It was only a few weeks later, with a cooler head and a little detachment, that I realized with considerable dismay how prolix, rambling and thoroughly unpublishable the manuscript was—very far, indeed, from being any kind of masterpiece. Yet I still felt intuitively that the effort had been worthwhile and that within the mass of stuff there on paper lay the elements of a story that I could write and wanted to complete. It stood to reason that, although I was in my fifties and had done a lot of writing, this being my first attempt to write a story of any kind, it would show all the defects of a lack of mastery of the genre. But it was there before me, like a rough cut lump of stone, urging: "Reshape me! Rework me! Bring me into being as a true *story*—which is to say, as a *complete* fiction!"

In the manuscript I had created, the whole quasi-story was narrated in the first person; but it wasn't clear whether that person was really meant to be me or someone else. I stood back from the manuscript and thought: this narrator has to have a name and a life *independent* of mine. I named him Frederick Beresford and he kept that name (and the rudimentary life story that I invented to go with it) for about two years; perhaps more. But on the cover of the first draft manuscript, I wrote a set of questions for myself, as the point of departure for a second draft:

> *Who is Frederick Beresford? What is his 'voice'? Why is he writing these letters? What are the inner and outer conflicts that drive the writing? Under what circumstances is he writing them? Over what period of time is he doing so? Why are they arranged in this precise sequence? Who, exactly, is M [his Muse]?*

The questions alone demonstrated how much work I needed to do to get even the basic elements of a story hammered out. Beneath them I wrote the following:

This draft is a block of marble, or at least of stone. But now the real work of the sculptor must begin.

Naturally, I thought I could do that work expeditiously, and that the writing would follow quite readily. I was very much in error. That, however, has been all to the good. The process of having to work *hard* at ambitious tasks forces us to challenge ourselves again and again. The creative breakthroughs that have occurred along the way have often been remarkable and certainly delightful. Not only that, but the evolving manuscript has been like a reflecting mirror in which I have seen myself transformed by refashioning what I project onto it.

The questions about Frederick and M were written down three and a half years ago. In the intervening years, I have had two major distractions. I have had to earn a living and I have been afflicted by what we generally call a running battle with cancer; with melanoma, to be precise. I say 'running' battle, but the problem was concentrated in my right leg, which was operated upon fifteen times over less than a decade. Perhaps, therefore, it would be more accurate to refer to the challenge as a 'limping' or 'hobbling' battle than a *running* one. There were also other writing commitments of a non-fictional nature, since I remained a fairly prolific writer of book reviews, opinion pieces for the press and essays for magazines. In 2008-09, I was also preparing and seeing into press a book called *The West in a Nutshell: Foundations, Fragilities, Futures.* That was decidedly *not* a work of fiction. It did contribute, however, to the slowly emerging sense of what 'Frederick' was up to—his mental world. In short, redrafting the story was very much a part time undertaking and returning to it after intervals often required considerable conscious effort.

Myth, story and writing

I have declared that I started with a very private cycle of poems and yet am now attempting to write a prose epic in the great tradition. Let's step back from my story for a moment to think about 'story' as such. This is important, because I have often found that, when I mention to people that I am working on a novel, they assume I am writing the kind of novel with which they are familiar; but to a disturbing extent that kind of novel is the kind I do not read and would see no point in writing. I am referring to what are generally known as 'airport novels' or 'pulp fiction'; the kind of popular and superficial novel that is the staple of the entertainment industry. I regard such books as the literary equivalent of junk food. There is some fascination to be had in seeking to understand why they sell in high volumes, but the explanation is not *far* to seek. They provide, as junk food provides, regular sugar, salt or fat hits, which are gratifying in the short term, but destructive of one's health over the long haul.

Call me a snob or a highbrow, but I am interested in good writing, in literature that enriches and nourishes minds and hearts. I am, for that reason, interested in the anthropology of good stories, going back deep into the origins of our common humanity—like the use of fire. In this regard, it's vital to remind ourselves that the *telling* of stories goes back, in our human lineage, long, long before the *writing* of stories. This is important, if we are to get into perspective the relationship between the fragments of story in our heads and the setting down in readable (to say nothing of widely read) form of stories that have not yet been written. We don't know when our human ancestors first became capable of making up and telling stories, but the capacity to do so would seem to be coeval with the emergence of language and to go back at least 100,000 years; perhaps much further. It seems to have emerged within our genome at about the same time as the capacity for symbolic art.

At the very beginning of his study of these matters, *On the Origin of Stories: Evolution, Cognition and Fiction* (2009)—written, as it were, just in time for me - Brian Boyd set a paragraph from Vladimir Nabokov's *Pale Fire*:

> *We are absurdly accustomed to the miracle of a few written signs being able to contain immortal imagery, involutions of thought, new worlds with live people, speaking, weeping, laughing. We take it for granted so simply that in a sense, by the very act of brutish routine acceptance, we undo the work of the ages, the history of the gradual elaboration of poetical description and construction, from the tree-man to Browning, from the caveman to Keats.*

In setting out to write *literature*, I became conscious of all this in exactly the way Nabokov might have hoped or thought we should all be. I suspect that *all* acquired skills and habits, like biological reflexes, recede beneath the level of conscious awe and appreciation fairly quickly; and then get taken for granted. There are enormous efficiencies in that. Yet Nabokov's point remains pungent. For this natural process (of becoming simply accustomed to things) impoverishes our wonder at what we are and at what we experience. It impoverishes, among other things, our appreciation of the miraculous character of *mimesis*—of art, written symbols and creative fiction. The poverty of most people's reading is a consequence of our culture's more general failure to instil and cultivate an appreciation of the miracle to which Nabokov was drawing attention.

Boyd's argument, in its simplest form, is that the capacity for story-telling has served adaptive functions for the human species. It has enabled us to provide shared understanding and 'just so' explanations to youngsters, in the form of folk wisdom, for tens of thousands of years. But more importantly, it has enabled us to *play* conceptually with possibilities in a way that no other animal is able to do. Stories enable us to instil in the minds of children various kinds of folk wisdom about what is right and wrong, pleasant and unpleasant, safe and dangerous in ways that direct experience would often not be able to do in a timely or enduring manner. The grammar of past tense, future tense, contingency, hope and possibility also makes it possible for us to imagine and compose endless variations on the apparently obvious and on the inescapably 'real' or natural circumstances in which we live. This is something other primates—to say nothing of non-primates - are evidently unable to do. Once grasped (in the manner of a stone tool) these capacities can make us truly Promethean in the reach and inventiveness of our minds—if they are creatively exercised.

Such lines of thought could take us down many long and winding roads. Here and now, I want to narrow the focus to a few reflections on the nature of the *great* stories that have long been acclaimed as the core stories of what is sometimes dubbed 'the Western canon.' Never mind, for present purposes, the 'post-modernist' critique of the whole idea of a Western canon as a Eurocentric obsession with Dead White European Males. There are more important issues at stake in simply pondering the evolution of storytelling itself. That process has nowhere been better exemplified or studied than in the case of the classics of Western literature, from the Greek myths to the Bible stories. I grew up as a Catholic and a good deal of my early adult life was preoccupied with trying to work out how to assimilate the Bible stories and Church history into a late 20th century experience of the world. But it was chiefly to the old epics that I turned or returned in recent years, when I wished to teach myself how to become a writer of 'classic' fiction. Since 2012, when I discovered it, a remark by Flaubert well over a century ago has hovered in my imagination: 'The novel awaits its Homer.' Little by little, I have come to dream of being that Homer of the novel—with the novel I am working on, *Darkness over Love: A Complete Fiction*.

The shadow of Homer has loomed over my writing now for several years; even before I stumbled upon that arresting remark by Flaubert. *The Iliad* and *The Odyssey*, committed to writing approximately 2,800 years ago, stand at the beginning of Western literature. There are far older stories, including written ones, from around the world; but these two stand out for their literary qualities and have had an enduring influence right down to our time. Why is this so? Three reasons seem evident to me. First, they are the earliest surviving major works rendered in the new *alphabetic* system of writing, which the Greeks had adopted (and adapted) from the Phoenicians just before Homer's time.[1] Second, they were based on centuries

---

1   For a brief and lucid introduction to the subject of the alphabet, see David Sacks *The Alphabet* (Hutchinson, London, 2003). The genius of the alphabet, he observes, was that it combined simplicity with precision. With just a couple of dozen letters, it could be adapted to express any sound in any language. It made literacy and the growth of expressive writing far more possible than older, less user friendly scripts had done.

of oral tradition within the Greek world that—in the absence of historical accounts of any kind—embodied the collective folk memory of the vanished world of the Bronze Age. Third, in writing down these traditional stories, Homer exhibited a singular mastery of the *art* of storytelling that has rarely been bettered.[2] I knew all this before I re-read Homer in 2012, but I had never reflected deeply on any of those three considerations before that sabbatical year. Doing so by reading both *The Iliad* and *The Odyssey* again, pencil in hand, was a richly self-educative process.

The 18th century English poet Alexander Pope once wrote:

Homer makes us hearers and Virgil leaves us readers.

Homer wrote as a bard, rather than a versifier. He set himself the task of putting into the new, flexible, pronounceable alphabetic writing the great oral traditions handed down from centuries past and encrusted with verbal and historical anachronisms and allusions to things grown unfamiliar. *The Iliad* and *The Odyssey* in the original Greek bear countless signs of this root in traditional orality. In modern translation, much of that is scoured away or else eludes the naïve reader who knows nothing of oral cultures or recitals. Yet even in the classical world, the fact that they had been written down gave them a fixed and durable form that they had never had before. They thenceforth dominated competing oral accounts. They were no longer simply a tenuous oral tradition. They had become 'Homer'. Almost for the first time, the power of great writing and of authorship to impress itself on a culture as if on wax was demonstrated.

Virgil wrote *The Aeneid*—the attempt to crystallise the link between the downfall of Troy and the origins of Rome - eight centuries later. By then, alphabetic literacy had become vastly more common. Whole libraries of written works had come into being in many genres, both fiction and non-fiction. Homer wrote at the end of the Dorian Dark Age, between the literate civilisation of the Aegean Bronze Age and that of the classical Greek Iron Age, which most Westerners loosely identify with 5th century BCE Athens.[3] Virgil wrote at the beginning of the Roman principate

---

2   It has been argued by specialists that, in fact, the epic poems we attribute to 'Homer' show linguistic traces suggesting that they date back long before the alphabet and may first have been composed as early as a thousand years before that, in the high Bronze Age around 1800 BCE. See Adam Nicolson *The Mighty Dead: Why Homer Matters* (William Collins, London, 2014). While the detailed arguments involved are fascinating, the key point simply reinforces my observation here that the great stories evolve over time. Nicolson's argument is that 'Homer' evolved over a far longer period of time than is traditionally allowed and, in the process, became both a rich linguistic puzzle and a powerful evocation of human experience with enduring resonance.

3   One of the anomalies in Nicolson's argument about Homer is that he suggests the Homeric legends date back to 1800 BCE and were, therefore, in circulation in a literate Bronze Age civilization for many hundreds of years before the collapse of that civilization around 1200

of Augustus, following the fall of the Roman Republic and the epic of Antony and Cleopatra. The centuries between the two great epic poets had seen the rise and fall of classical Greece, the epic of Alexander's march across the Persian world, the creation of the Library and Museum at Alexandria by the Ptolemies and the Roman conquest of the entire Mediterranean basin. The great Library and Museum at Alexandria was founded almost three hundred years before Virgil's time and, though damaged in Caesar's expedition to Egypt in 48 BCE, it endured as long as the Roman Empire lasted; still being used by Platonist scholars in the late fifth century CE.

Homer had had only oral traditions and the alphabet to work with. Virgil had Homer, histories, literary criticism and the written work of numerous other poets to draw upon. Yet, from the point of view of an aspiring writer of an original epic tale, it is very striking that neither Homer nor Virgil *invented* the tales they told in their epic poems. Homer's story had come down to him in various forms over centuries of retelling. What he had to do was set it down in writing in a particular way. We do not know how or why he decided to set it down in the particular form that he did; or how much of that form was his own literary genius. Virgil was even better placed than Homer in terms of source material. The legend that Aeneas had fled from the sack of Troy to Italy to found a new Troy and that Rome had sprung from his labours went back at least two centuries before his lifetime. Moreover, it wasn't merely an oral tradition. It had been set down in hexameter verse by the proto-historian Ennius in his *Annales* long before Virgil was born. And during the years in which Virgil was writing, a flourishing literary culture in the Roman world was turning out history, poetry and translations of the Greek classics; Rome's first public libraries were being established and wealthy magnates were becoming patrons of promising writers.

Virgil, in other words, was a member of a culture far more literate than Homer's; and even more than Homer, he also had the materials, the plot, the characters, even the telling of his story ready to hand. He simply had to tell it *better*, in his own inimitable fashion. And long before he set out to do this he had obtained a good education and become an accomplished poet. As I attempt to invent an epic tale, I am more than ever conscious of the advantages these great poets had, as well as of the mastery of language and narrative that they exhibited in using the materials they inherited. What they did might be compared with Shakespeare taking stories from Plutarch,

---

BCE, to say nothing of the revival of literacy around 800 BCE with the Greek adoption and adaptation of the Phoenician alphabet. Yet he nowhere explains why they were never, apparently, committed to writing in the old Linear A or Linear B scripts of the earlier culture. The more conventional theory has always been that the catastrophic end of the Bronze Age included events that grew into the legend of the fall of Troy and that archaisms were handed down from that era for centuries before Homer, a single poet in the Aegean, took the various stories and set them down in writing, without correcting or removing old trace elements from the distant past.

such as Antony and Cleopatra or Julius Caesar, or from Raphael Holinshed's histories of England and turning them into stage plays. I have found that it is far more difficult to put together a story that has *never before been written*. And, if Virgil had advantages on account of his literate culture, a writer today faces the reality that there is an overwhelming superfluity of writing of all kinds. Any new offering seems dauntingly likely to be lost in the mass of printed matter forever pouring off the world's presses; to say nothing of the relentless immediacy and anarchy of electronic media.

Nonetheless, I am drawn irresistibly to attempting to write this story which has never before been written. Moreover, I am conscious, in doing so, that I am prompted by a Muse in a very real and personal manner. And this gives me a strong sense of affinity with Homer and Virgil, each of whom began by invoking his Muse, or *the* Muse. We can only tentatively infer Homer's beliefs from the manner of his depiction of the gods and of human motivation and action. In Virgil's case, it isn't clear what he actually believed the Muse to have been. He was educated as an Epicurean and presumably had a sceptical view of the traditional Greek pantheon. Yet we can assume that the Muse, for Homer and Virgil alike, was at the very least a traditional way of attempting to acknowledge the mysterious creative process that sets inspired ideas and their expression free in the brain of the poet.

The opening lines of *The Iliad* pivot on the words:

> *Begin, Muse, when the two first broke and clashed*
> *Agamemnon lord of men and brilliant Achilles*

The Odyssey famously commences:

> *Sing to me of the man, Muse, the man of twists and turns,*
> *Driven time and again off course, once he had plundered*
> *The hallowed heights of Troy*

And here is Virgil, eight centuries later:

> *Wars and a man I sing—an exile driven on by Fate...*
> *Tell me, Muse, how it all began...*[4]

The Muse here, clearly, was imagined as a more or less divine being, embodying the intense sensations of 'flow' experienced by the bard or poet in bringing their stories to life.

To an extent that does not seem to have been true of Homer or Virgil, I have had a very personal Muse. She had said to me in as many words:

> *Do you realize that we are living a story that has not yet been written?*

She had sung to me, as it were, of her fervent belief in my creative abilities and in the possibility of a novel. Then, as though she had been a handmaiden or emissary of the ancient Muse,

---

4   All three citations are from the excellent recent translations of Homer and Virgil by Robert Fagles: *The Iliad* (Viking Penguin, 1990), *The Odyssey* (Viking Penguin, 1996) and *The Aeneid* (Penguin, 2006).

she left me and the more traditional process had to be drawn upon to transmute the ideas, memories and exemplars available to me into a written story of the novel kind she had had in mind. Having poured out a first draft, I could now see, I thought, that she had been correct. The problem was that the story itself was inchoate, *never having been told before, much less written*. In any case, the possibility of the novel, I could now see, was very much in using that unwritten story as a point of departure for a written story, for a *novel* story, rather than to simply tell the 'story that has not yet been written'. A liberating insight slowly came to me: that being part of a story that has not yet been written, one is free to be the *author* of that story and not to merely set it down as if someone else had in fact already determined exactly what it should say.

As I contemplate the evolved manuscript, I find myself asking, as perhaps only a sometime student of the classical world would do: *How did Homer and Virgil do it?* How did they take stories that were in common circulation and turn them into powerfully written versions of those stories that became imprinted on the imaginations and cultures of millennia? Not that they had had any idea, as they completed their work, that this would be the outcome. Homer, assuming he was an individual who gave final form in writing to the oral legends, can surely have had no inkling of the place his work was to occupy in Western civilization. Virgil worked on *The Aeneid* for ten years, but when stricken by fever at the age of fifty and realizing that he was about to die, he instructed his literary executors to destroy the unfinished work. He was still not content with what he had written. His self-annihilating instruction was overruled, however, by the Prince—Augustus— which is why two millennia of people have been able to read *The Aeneid*.

The literary judgment of the Prince was a judicious one. *The Aeneid* shaped Latin literature and rhetoric for centuries to come and has influenced poets for many centuries more. My interest lay and lies in how Virgil had been able to do this, for all his own misgivings. I wrote that he and Homer "became imprinted" on future ages; but this is an anachronism. There was *no* printing in Virgil's time, to say nothing of Homer's. Moveable type and printing presses would not appear in the West for almost 1,500 years after Virgil's death. Homer and Virgil *wrote* and revised in longhand and their works were similarly *copied by hand*—for century after century, before printing presses secured their more abundant and reliable reproduction. So, rather than saying that Homer's and Virgil's masterpieces became *imprinted* on the consciousness of millennia, it would be more accurate to say that they became *inscribed* there. The ambition of strong writing, I believe, is still to somehow achieve that. But doing so has become formidably difficult now, because we are swamped by printed and electronic matter, which is generically and undiscriminatingly dubbed 'information'. This reality necessarily haunts literary writing in our time and has been doing so now for at least half a century.

That Homer and Virgil wrote their masterpieces in long hand gives a more personal sense to the effect that they have had. A living hand wrote *The Aeneid*, transcribing musical, evocative, compelling uses of the Latin language brought alive in the mind of Virgil by the Muse. That writing, that use of language, then entered into the wider use of Latin for centuries. The very sense of what Latin—or any language—could express was *altered* by that writing, much as it is claimed that Shakespeare's writing extended and deepened the sense of what could be expressed in English or accomplished in writing itself. So, again, the question presses itself upon me: '*How did he (Virgil) do this?*' Even the mechanics of his process of composition remain obscure to us. We have no drafts, no record of how he set about conceiving, designing, sketching or revising his masterpiece. I like to imagine Virgil's wealthy patron, Maecenas, keeping the poet's personal papers and drafts for some years and reflecting on the creative process; but I know of no evidence that this occurred. The only version of *The Aeneid* that Virgil appears to have left us was that single unfinished manuscript.

Even had Maecenas kept Virgil's working papers, they would have perished within a generation or so. He died a decade after Virgil and no classical library would have had copyists spend their time reproducing the rough drafts of a work already in circulation. It isn't even clear that Virgil would have wanted them to do so. But we have records of that nature for a wide range of great modern authors and it can be highly instructive. For the classical authors, however, we have no such thing. It is as if all the great pioneers of poetry, drama, history and philosophy simply wrote their works, as Ben Jonson remarked of Shakespeare, without blotting (that is, correcting) a line. This is impossible to believe. But the finished works are so impressive as to make the author engaged in drafting feel daunted by comparison. I have had continually to remind myself that even the greatest artists have had to draft and revise and develop and polish their lines. The best evidence for this, perhaps, is Virgil's dissatisfaction at the end of ten years of labour on a book which, had he been writing it effortlessly, might have been completed in twelve months.

While strenuously engaged in my own drafting and revision, I have experienced at first hand a truth that the great Jesuit scholar Walter J. Ong articulated more than thirty years ago: writing is consciousness-raising.[5] It makes possible an externalization, review and revision

---

5   Walter J. Ong *Orality and Literacy: The Technologizing of the Word* (Routledge, 1982). Ong's opening paragraph is arresting and ought to draw any intelligent person into reading the rest of his little book: "In recent years, certain basic differences have been discovered between the ways of managing knowledge and verbalization in primary oral cultures (cultures with no knowledge at all of writing) and in cultures deeply affected by the use of writing. The implications of the new discoveries have been startling. Many of the features we have taken for granted in thought and expression in literature, philosophy and science,

of the thinking process itself in ways totally unavailable to the illiterate mind. It gives to thought and expression possibilities of extension, plasticity, artfulness, objectivity and durability that are lacking in oral cultures. I have discovered that it is one thing to read that these things are so and to accept that they are probable. It is quite another to find yourself immersed in a writing project which has the direct and powerful effect of bringing them home to you at a highly personal level. Yet that is what has happened to me in the work on this novel, in a way of which I was never before so conscious, whether writing poetry or prose. The realization of what was happening—that my own consciousness was being raised by my own writing—not only made the project more fruitful; it fed back into the project. It deepened my sense of what the novel was about and of what it could accomplish, if I could write it well enough.

Only very recently have neuroscientists discovered and been able to explore what has been dubbed 'neuroplasticity': the remarkable capacity of the human brain to *reorganize and reshape itself,* as it learns, or copes with a challenge. Among the discoveries that have flowed from this are fresh insights into the way that literacy—reading and writing— physically reorganizes the brain; but also that the very invention of letters and writing stems from deep structures in the brain.[6] We must assume that the emergence of literacy, but above all the highly creative exercise of it, reshaped the brains of the great writers of the ancient world. But they lacked any science of neurons and necessarily placed different and vaguer interpretations on their experiences. Being aware of the science while going through at least the early stages of a major creative literary exercise has been a remarkable experience. As much as anything else, it has led me to want to set down these reflections; simply to register something of what I have seen and felt happening along the way.

It will be apparent from these remarks that, quite apart from my long under-developed personal skill at writing narrative fiction; the process of composing an ambitious literary work has been slowed down by my fascination with questions of history and theory that would seem to have nothing to do with the immediate story-writing task. Yet the two interests are intimately linked. For, in attempting to write a work of literature, I have not only found myself, like Odysseus, driven time and again off course after I had plundered the immediately available raw material; but have found the process of inquiry and revision deeply formative of my sense of myself, both as a person and as an aspiring artist.

and even in oral discourse among literates, are not directly native to human existence as such but have come into being because of the resources which the technology of writing makes available to human consciousness. We have had to revise our understanding of human identity."

6   Stanislas Dehaene *Reading in the Brain* (Viking, 2009)

Moreover, the novel, at least as it has evolved over the past few years, through successive drafts, is ultimately *about* the relationship between truth and fiction; between the acts of reading and writing and the nature of interpretation and action in the 'real' world—the world of animal instincts and biological life and death within which the strangeness and 'magic' of human language and literacy are embedded.

For these reasons, my digressions to study the nature and origins of story-telling and of human literacy itself are not only germane to the work of conceiving and writing a work of fiction on a substantial scale; they are, perhaps, the 'real' story, as well as being the roots of what will, I hope, surface, *as* a story in the ordinary sense of the word. The allusion in the previous paragraph to the opening lines of *The Odyssey* was, of course, deliberate for just this reason. That epic is only superficially about Odysseus returning to Ithaca, central though that idea plainly is to the dramatic structure of the poem. Rather, as millennia of readers have intuited ever since Homer's work was first circulated, it is about the wider world within which Ithaca is situated and the many and various challenges with which it confronts anyone who ventures out into it. It is about life as adventure and journey. It is about the pitfalls of fortune and the importance of wily intelligence in coping with them. It is about the very nature of human experience and the very art of story-telling. The 'digressions', the being driven time and again 'off course' are the heart of the story.

Odysseus became, through Homer's artful story-telling, the most enduring archetype of the human being born into a world of social stratification and endemic warfare. He is thrown towards death in the aftermath of the prolonged war at Troy by the impact of storms at sea and the anger of the gods. He seeks some form of home-coming in a world of wild seas, monstrous dangers, beguiling temptations, love, feasts and comradeship. This, of course, is in fundamental respects *the human condition*—writ large; or more precisely *written at all* and imaginatively. Whether or not we have had adventures remotely as challenging as those of Odysseus, we are almost all able to see in them the nature of human life. That startling fact and the wit of Odysseus that is shaped or revealed along the way, is the true story of *The Odyssey*. The telling of it in such a way as to have made Odysseus the representative for all of us was the genius of Homer. So if one wishes to become a great story teller it is necessary to attend to both what the true story is that one is telling (full of digressions) and how such stories are told—or written.

Hard thinking about the craft of story-telling

The present story is my own attempt, very self-consciously - at least since I sat back and seriously contemplated the first and second drafts—to write a literary 'classic', a modern

Odyssey for the 21ˢᵗ century. The raw material, as my earlier remarks suggest, has its roots in studies and experiences going back a lifetime. They are, as it were, my equivalent of the oral traditions inherited by Homer, or the *Annales* of Ennius inherited by Virgil. Just as those great poets invoked the Muse as the source of their capacity to turn these sources into a new and enduring poetry, I was prompted by my own Muse to attempt this with my own interests, memories and emotions. As I wrote, revised and reflected, it increasingly seemed that there was a more ancient Muse at work; because I began to feel as though I was *discovering* the story rather than deliberately writing it; that the logic, the music, the depth of the story was being *given* to me just to the extent that I gave myself over freely to the creative process—which is my secularized way of describing what Homer and Virgil referred to *as* the Muse.

Quite early on, though only after I had written a complete draft and was well into a second, I realized two things: unless one is very practised, very skilled at story-telling, doing it does not come easily. It is an art and, at the literary level, a very high art indeed. The composition of a long and literary story, I saw, demands design and revision, like any major undertaking. I conceived the idea that this had to take place in three stages: structure, content and voice. By the end of the first draft I actually had a rudimentary structure, the core elements of which have endured—although the radical restructuring that took place in 2013 has reduced that early structure to a mere foreshadowing of the inner core of the story. There was also a lot of content and this was amplified (and modified) in the second draft. There was, however, I realized to my consternation, *almost no feel for voice*—the character and motives even of the narrator, to say nothing of other characters in the story. That I lacked the capacity to bring out free, well-formed and independent voices was my starkest realization and the most instructive at that stage.

That fact in itself had a profound set of implications both for my capacity to tell stories and for my sense of myself as a human being. I also realized that my central concern, only implicit in the first and second drafts, was the actual *relationship* between truth and fiction. It struck me that the reason, certainly *a* reason, why I had been unable to respond in earlier years to the call of my Muse to tell her stories and sing her songs was that something in me had, over decades, become *resistant* to fiction itself. This had actually *disabled* me, in a crucial way. Once I saw the disordered, cathartic draft in front of me, external to me, I was able to see its disorder and its content as precisely that *within* me which was in need of therapeutic revision and creative refashioning. If oral traditions and written myths are what have held tribes and cultures together, I saw that the creative labour entailed in bringing a coherent story out of that mass of bits and pieces was necessary for my own mental coherence and 'happiness'. It was necessary if I was finally to make sense of my own existence; where making sense refers not merely to a quick intuitive process, but to a thoroughgoing and demanding *autopoiesis*—an actual fashioning of sense and reshaping of the self.[7]

My problem was twofold, therefore. I wanted more or less whimsically to create a work of high quality fiction; but I had serious misgivings at a deeper level, about fiction *as such*. Having realized these things, in the early summer of 2011-12, I could see that my narrative theme had to be the tension *between* fiction and reality; but also that, like Virgil, I had to learn from a master (as Virgil had learned from Homer) or more than one (adding Ennius and others). Having, by that stage, reached the beginning of a third draft, I had actually begun to hear voices coming to life within the story and discovered the identity and voice of the narrator, though still only faintly. I took a year off from writing to study the art of narrative fiction and to reflect on how I was going to go about shaping my materials into the kind of book I dreamed of completing. I could not see my way forward clearly, but I resolved that I wanted to navigate past any and all obstacles to get to my own literary Ithaca.

---

7   It was in reading Evan Thompson's *Mind in Life: Biology, Phenomenology and the Sciences of Mind* (Belknap Press, Harvard University, 2007) in 2011 that I learned about the concept of *autopoiesis* and saw its relevance to what I was doing and to what was emerging as the philosophical outlook of my narrator (then Frederick Beresford). Perhaps the key passage was the following: "There is a basic formal organization of life, and its paradigm and minimal case is to be found in the single cell. A single-cell organism is a self-making or self-producing being. Self-production is different from reproduction: in reproduction a cell divides in two; in self-production, a cell continuously produces itself as a spatially bounded system, distinct from its medium or milieu. What is remarkable about self-production is that every molecular reaction in the system is generated by the very same system that those molecular reactions produce. Some years ago, the neurobiologists Humberto Maturana and Francisco Varela drew attention to this circular, self-producing organization and called it autopoiesis." (p. 92).

I found myself at once reminded of two passages in *Doctor Zhivago*, clearly written decades before the work of Maturana and Varela, to say nothing of Evan Thompson. The first is a quite famous one, in which Yuri Zhivago rebukes the Bolshevik Liberius Mikulitsyn for his crude opinions about how the Communist revolution will 'remake life': 'The remaking of life! People who can reason like that may have been around, but they've never once known life, never felt its spirit, its soul. For them existence is a lump of coarse material not yet ennobled by their touch, in need of being processed by them. But life has never been a material, a substance. It is, if you want to know, a continually self-renewing, eternally self-recreating principle, it eternally alters and transforms itself, it is far above your and my dim-witted theories.'

The second passage, only seven pages later, depicts Yuri observing a brown speckled butterfly with wonder and insight. In his reflections, Pasternak wrote, '...Darwin met with Schelling and the passing butterfly with modern painting, with impressionist art. He thought of creation, the creature, creativity and mimicry.' These two passages had long since impressed me. They now assumed deeper significance and fed into my aspiration to create a narrative in which that synthesis of 'Darwin and Schelling', as it were, could find expression. At the centre of the picture, from that point forward, was the concept of autopoiesis.

Did I do well to take a 'sabbatical', instead of simply toiling on with the writing—or perhaps giving up, with the judgement that I did not have it in me to finish the work? The sabbatical, I believe, proved its worth. In those months, I read or re-read many, many things. Among them was *Don Quixote,* which I read for the first time. I learned why it is such a classic. I discovered that Cervantes, too, and perhaps pre-eminently, had been fascinated by the relationship between truth and fiction. I learned that he had done many things and written many things without gaining recognition or financial success before he wrote *Don Quixote.* I found, in his novel, the wellspring of the celebrated 'magical realism' of the modern Hispanic world. I went on to read *One Hundred Years of Solitude* and *The General in His Labyrinth,* by Gabriel Garcia Marquez; *The War of the End of the World* and *The Notebooks of Don Rigoberto* by Mario Vargas Llosa. I appreciated why both authors had been awarded the Nobel Prize for Literature. I read a first class biography of Garcia Marquez and absorbed the enormous, almost bankrupting labour that went into the writing of his first novel.[8] I re-read the remarkable short fables and the literary essays of Jorge Luis Borges.

I read all these things chiefly because my Muse is Hispanic. I was seeking to explore her world and to find a way to write a story that would be able to come alive inside that world. But I also read other things, both concerning fiction and concerning the themes that appeared to lie beneath the surface of my draft writing. Apart from re-reading both Homer and Virgil, more attentively than ever before, I read Boccaccio's *Decameron,* as a primer in story-telling. But, as I was increasingly coming to see that the narrator was at work on a major philosophical treatise about scientific truth and the future of civilization, with the tension between truth and fiction playing out in his relationship with his (Hispanic) muse, I also read works of

---

8   Living in Mexico City, Garcia Marquez and his wife, Mercedes, struggled to survive in thoroughly Bohemian conditions as he tapped away for years at his type-writer. When he finally had a manuscript he was prepared to send to a publisher in Buenos Aires, they had to pawn almost their last household possessions to pay for the postage. As they left the post office, Mercedes said to him, "Hey, Gabo, all we need now is for the book to be no good!" Gerald Martin Gabriel *Garcia Marquez: A Life* (Bloomsbury, 2008, p. 312). Such are the uncertainties of writers and their mortal muses. The book was *One Hundred Years of Solitude.* It was a runaway best seller, made Garcia Marquez instantly famous and launched his career as an acclaimed novelist.

It is arguable, as Gerald Martin observes, that he would have been immortal even had he never written another novel. Yet his own reaction to its acclaim was strange. He lost interest in it, expressed boredom with it, accused journalists of asking stupid questions, described the book as superficial and declared that its popularity was due merely to a set of writer's tricks. His problem was that he was haunted by a Leninist conscience, if that is not a contradiction in terms. He believed, at the end of the day, that politics was all important and that, as he angrily expressed it to a fellow writer, it would not matter if they (presumably the radical revolutionaries of his imagination) "hanged all of us writers." I may have had my reservations about literary fiction, but I have far stronger ones about the fiction of Leninist revolution.

cosmology, biological evolution and philosophy. The reading was very wide-ranging, yet very purposeful and it all cohered around the emerging logic of the story. Naturally, there were points at which I came to think I was attempting something quite impossible; yet something enchanting, something existential always drew me on.

I had this notion that the narrator was wrestling with the deep philosophical problems that had beset Edmund Husserl and Martin Heidegger, in the 1920s and 1930s, about the relationship between scientific truth and human experience. I immersed myself, therefore, in Heidegger's unfinished masterpiece *Being and Time* (1927) and Husserl's unfinished and posthumously published *The Crisis of the European Sciences and Transcendental Phenomenology* (1938). I realized, moreover, that the narrator and his overseas colleagues had formed a hedge fund and participated in shorting the mortgage market and Wall Street banks in 2005-08. I therefore read books about the origins of the Global Financial Crisis and particularly Michael Lewis's classic *The Big Short*. Pasternak had been a big influence on me, so I re-read *Doctor Zhivago* very closely and appreciated it, also, for the first time, although I had loved the story for thirty years. In other words, the story, still to be properly delineated, was getting very complicated indeed—far more so than legends of the Bronze Age or the origins of Rome.

Throughout those months, I kept notebooks and I can now see in them how the elements of the story and the nature of the art of narrative were constantly in ferment and slowly working themselves out. One of those elements was the architectural design of the narrator's habitat: 'Cos'. I met an architect by chance at a lunch talk by the economist Ross Garnaut about China, in 2011, and struck up a friendship; based, in part, on his interest in the idea of the novel. We conceived and he drew ground plans for what began as a modern apartment; but evolved into a larger and larger residence. My journal from that time shows me trying to squeeze the growing amplitude of the story into the cramped, realist confines of an ordinary dwelling place. In 2013-14, Cos broke away from its realist moorings altogether and soared into the realm of myth. Well before then, my architect friend had pulled back from drawing designs, waiting perhaps for the picture of Cos to become more settled in my own mind and within the story; but the dialogue with him about it had been both highly stimulating and enormously useful in disciplining my sense of space and design.

By early 2013, it had become clear to me that the narrator would be a polymath with global connections and reputation, bent on synthesizing the extraordinary findings of the modern sciences into a philosophical 'guide of the perplexed' for the early 21st century—a treatise in the tradition of the great medieval Jewish sage Maimonides, whose three volume *Guide of the Perplexed*, written in Egypt in the late 12th century, remains a classic of Judaic and philosophical thought.[9] This was an undertaking of superhuman, if not quixotic proportions, of course. It was plainly beyond my own abilities, but perhaps even beyond those of a fictional character endowed with advantages I did not enjoy. He would, I decided as I went, have a company called Peripatetica Decision Architects, dedicated to rational analysis, critical thinking and myth-busting, which ran, among other things, a seminar called the Conspiracy Theory and Cognition Workshop. His muse, Margarita, would be immersed in the world of music and dance and would urge upon him the idea that, whatever their truth claims, human beings live by their capacity to *dance*; as well as inside the *songs* that give them an emotional sense of orientation and meaning.

These elements seemed to hold some promise, but I had not solved the problems of a dramatic structure or narrative style that could hold a reader's interest—though several readers of the first drafts generously informed me that even these did, in fact, hold their interest. I had, by then, transformed the Prologue from an almost purely autobiographical recollection of my first meeting with the Muse to a wholly fictional first meeting by the narrator and Margarita in Toledo, in April 2004. I had imagined, also, that at that point in time, Margarita was living in exile in Tenerife, had created a business there in music therapy and was living with or near a lover by the name of Anactoria Lopez, an archaeologist. What I went looking for in Tenerife and Toledo was nuance, voice, colour and the tangible feel of the story. While my Muse had declared to me that she and I had been *living* a story that had not yet been *written*; I felt that I had begun *writing* a story that had not yet been *lived*. I went to Spain to live it, or at least to get a better sense of how it might play out in 'real life'; how it might look and sound.

That was an inspired step to have taken, as it turned out. Moreover, it had even deeper roots in my relationship with my Muse than *The Neruda Variations*. The Alcantara, the old Arabic stone bridge over the Rio Tajo, the river that swirls around Toledo on three sides, had been the dominant metaphor in my first poem for her ('Ancient Bridge'), in July 2004. Before traveling to Toledo in 2013, I had written many poems as part of the creative unfolding of the novel; one of which was 'Dance me on down from Toledo', a fine poem, I think, and a considerable advance on 'Ancient Bridge', both stylistically and thematically. In important ways, it was the further development of that poem. My three days exploring Toledo, playing out and enhancing the scenario in the third draft Prologue, felt like sensitively touching the physical boundaries between truth and fiction. Similarly, my five days on the balmy island of Tenerife, enabled me to discover where Margarita lived and worked, what she experienced and remembered, where her archaeologist lover lived and worked; and what resources there were for a music therapist both to enjoy music and to run a business. All this brought Margarita's character to life and animated a crucial part of the story.

---

9   For a lucid introduction to Maimonides, see Moshe Halbertal *Maimonides: Life and Thought*, Princeton University Press, 2014, especially chapters seven and eight, which are specifically on the Guide of the Perplexed and the various interpretations to which it has been subject over the centuries.

In Toledo, for example, having written into the third draft that the narrator and Margarita met in a small restaurant on the far side of the Alcantara from Toledo, called La Cubana, I had to explore La Cubana itself and establish whether this made sense and exactly how they met and where they sat. This worked beautifully, as did the iterative exploration of how they walked up through the old city to the religious sanctuary and contemporary museum of San Roman. That it should be their goal is decided within the story by Margarita; but San Roman embodies a great deal culturally. It also points both to their *romance* and to the novel (*roman*) within which all this is occurring. Fenimore in fact remarks, when they stand before the entrance to San Roman, 'I imagine this building's Roman right down at its foundations.' The pun on *Bildungsroman* (the novel of education and worldly experience) will surely be lost on most readers, but is there for the canny to detect. It was, in the full sense of the word, a fabulous experience doing these things.

Then, from Toledo, I travelled to Cordoba and Granada, extending my reach into elements of the story only evoked in conversation or poetry. The latter, in particular, is central to the poem 'Dance me on down from Toledo'. I needed to see it and to establish with greater exactitude the allusions to geography and to the Alhambra that the poem offered. Cordoba and Granada are also where Margarita is going from Toledo, when she and the narrator meet. I already had the notion that the two would part outside the Teatro Cervantes in Buenos Aires years later; she walking off down *Libertad* (Freedom) St and he being left to return to his hotel—down *Cordoba* St. I was richly rewarded. So rich a haul of colour and insight did I gain, in fact, that I did not want to return from Spain. I wanted badly to go to Mallorca, like Robert Graves in the 1930s, and just write.

On my unavoidable return, I thoroughly rewrote the Prologue. I briefly imagined, in fact, that the momentum I had gained would enable me to charge ahead with the revision of the whole story. In that respect, I was in error. I ground to a halt again over the problems of plot, character and voice. I had, in the interim, renamed the narrator Fenimore Moneghan and believed I had satisfactorily at last created the basis for his encounter with Margarita in Toledo and their mutual enchantment. But why and to whom was he *narrating* this story? To Margarita? Why would he do that, rather than simply communicate by conventional and contemporary means? How did this narrative relate to his work? Why would it ever have appeared in print— even inside the fictional world, never mind in the current world of commercial publishing? How could the voices of other characters credibly be brought into play if Fenimore was the sole narrator?

These questions dogged me throughout the winter of 2013 and I saw that they were fundamental and could not be waved aside. They were, in fact, structural problems; problems of narrative technique. What I realized, as early as July that year, was that I could not move the story forward unless I solved them. The solution came to me in the spring of that year. But before describing how it came to me, let me step back a little to reflect on some other elements of the evolution of the story. These have more to do with content than with structure and they show how the capacity for story-telling as such was evolving, even as I wrestled with fundamental problems of narrative design and voice. It is only looking back and only because I have kept an archive of drafts and notebooks that I can see how these things did evolve; but in retrospect the evolutionary process is remarkably clear and, from the point of view of the creative process itself, rather interesting. Things were constantly going on 'beneath the surface' of which I was barely conscious. When they coalesced and surfaced as insight, they would astonish me.

Poems, fables and the piecemeal emergence of a real story

One of the few features of the first and second drafts that I do *not* now look back on with embarrassment is the emergence within them of several entirely original fables, which are likely, in a modified form, to survive into the finished story. These include a fable about Santorini, Minoan Crete and the downfall of Atlantis; Manntezuma's tale of the epic of the pre-Hispanic Americas; the Tale of Raneb and Nefesh (originally in a now deleted chapter, 'In the House of Memories', in Part II; now the second chapter in Part III) and the fantasia about Cleis Scamandros (originally in the final chapter, of Part III, 'Intimate Disclosure'; since radically reframed and renamed). In the third draft another such tale arose: the opera libretto 'Karl and Paula', which also, I believe, has considerable promise. These apparent digressions from the (very loose and ill-defined) central narrative were the first signs that a skill at *narrative itself* was beginning to develop.

Similarly, there was a great burst of poetic creativity from comparatively early in the piece, which produced a much greater variety of poetry in mood and style than any that I had written before. The Friend, when I put this to him on a visit to America in April 2014, declared at once, 'I agree!' *The Neruda Variations* had probably prepared the way for this creativity, by reanimating both my emotional life and my freedom to express myself in verse. But what was striking was the manner in which the poems arose within the context of the story that was emerging. Whereas *it* was emerging only in baggy, ill-shaped form, *they* were emerging 'fully-formed from the head of Zeus', as the old Greek myth says of Athena. There were long poems and short poems, serious ones and funny ones; poems in strict metre (even a villanelle, which is a very demanding metrical and rhyming form that I had never so much as attempted before) and others in more relaxed rhythmic forms with slant rhymes or various relaxed rhythms.

Of the three tales in the early drafts, the Tale of Raneb and Nefesh has been the one that has assumed the greatest prominence in the evolving story. As the reader will see, the primary editor of Fenimore's notebooks, Tom Emerson, finds particular significance in this tale. He adds an appendix about it to his privately printed edition of the Notebooks for the Academy of Lynxes. But mention of that edition and of Tom Emerson takes me well ahead of the present narrative. There was no Tom Emerson in the early drafts, although he was loosely prefigured. There was, also, no Fenimore Moneghan and there were no Notebooks. By the time Tom Emerson arose as a key figure in the story, the Tale of Raneb and Nefesh had long been written. Built into it was the element he singled out as so striking about it: that it seemed to have a special place in the relationship between Fenimore and Margarita. That special place and its articulation are what changed from one draft to the next, from something largely incidental to something deeply romantic and completely fundamental.

The change even in the title, from the first draft's *Darkness over Love: Letters to my Muse*, to the second draft's *Darkness over Love: A Complete Fiction* was an early symptom of the mutation in the narrative and where it was trying to go. There were seven chapters in each of the three parts of the first draft, but eight in each part of the second. This, also, was a symptom of the story's sense of direction. It was *longing to emulate Homer*, for there are twenty four 'books' in *The Odyssey* and from the second draft on there have been twenty four 'sections' in the novel— but also front matter and end matter which book-end the odyssey in question. Similarly, the Prologue in the second draft was still, as in the first draft, the heavily autobiographical 'Fragments of a Conversation', but in the third draft it leapt half way around the world and won itself enormous freedom from that constraint. This leap of freedom was symbolized, also, by the radical change in the cover image. At the same time, the internal fables were assigned clearer places in the narrative and the poems and songs likewise started to discover where they belonged within the evolving story. All this was before the revolution in narrative structure in late 2013; but that revolution would enormously strengthen those earlier changes and add many, many others to them.

Psychologically, the pivotal chapter in the first two drafts was certainly Part I chapter 5, 'In Bluebeard's Castle'. At that stage, the whole idea of 'darkness over love', as well as the grim cover image, derived directly from two sources: Bartok's opera *Duke Bluebeard's Castle* (1911) and George Steiner's cultural essay *In Bluebeard's Castle* (1971). A great deal of the dramatic shift in the story over successive drafts looks, in retrospect, like the relentless processing of this root mood and its transformation into a larger and more universal vision. That processing was nudged in a more generous direction by the remark of my Muse, from a distance, that the second draft, like the first, remained "very gloomy". In other words, the darkness was too dominant. It is probably worth pausing, therefore, to explain the Bartok and Steiner roots of the darkness and how, little by little, my sense of perspective on what I was doing evolved, until the castle was blown away into the immense radiance of the Sombrero Galaxy (the new cover image for the third draft)[10], even as the narrator's dwelling place was transformed from a conventional apartment in a real city into the mythic and symbolic 'Cos' at 'the Ends of the Earth'.

In 1910, the Hungarian playwright Bela Balazs produced a stage play called *Bluebeard's Castle*. His contemporary, the composer Bela Bartok, became familiar with it just after its completion and it appealed to him very much, because it suited his emotional state—one of desolate loneliness. He was an intensely gifted musician, but had failed to establish an intimate relationship with either male friends or female companions in the years before 1910. He had undergone a personal crisis on account of this. He recognized that what Balazs had done was to take the old, dark Hungarian folktale about the Bluebeard who murdered his wives, one after another, in his bleak castle, and transform it into a dramatized metaphor of the loneliness and eternal secrecy of the psyche that even the deepest love cannot reach. Inspired by this artistic rendering of something he felt so deeply himself, he wrote his brilliantly intense and sombre opera. I first learned about this opera when reading Steiner's book, in about 1975, and had for decades after that taken it very much to heart. It had informed and perhaps warped my own love life.

As Judit Frigyesi remarks, in *Bela Bartok and Turn of the Century Budapest* (1998):

> *Unlike Bartok, Balazs had a natural inclination to think and talk about emotional mat-ters. And though he had no more success than Bartok in finding a companion, he was able to look at his experiences as a workshop for exploring, as an artist, the nature of life and art. The longing to be understood and the failure of communication—experiences Balazs, too, lived through very intensely—gave the impetus for a global conception of life and art as a 'mystery play.'*

Having become fascinated by the play, Bartok created his own, more profound and enduring version of the tale and put it to music. In that tale, the castle is the symbol for the psyche of Bluebeard and all that takes places on stage, to music, is a psychodrama within that bounded and hermetic self: the lonely psyche. As Frigyesi concludes, the opera is "the drama of the eternal condition of love, the impossibility of fulfilling and resolving the infinite yearning for

---

10   The image is a breathtaking photomosaic put together from the astonishing imagery harvested by the Hubble Telescope. It is everything about the staggering scale and awe-inspiring beauty of the cosmos – and the fact that the physical sciences have enabled us to start exploring all that. But beneath the techniques of the sciences and the facts themselves, of course, is the question of human intelligence itself and why we have reached for the stars in this manner. See the Annex to this essay: 'Successive Cover Images of the Early MSS'.

intimacy." We all know that so terribly often intimacy fails or atrophies, but that it should be *impossible* is a daunting thought. I had long been familiar with that thought before I read Frigyesi's book and before the Muse entered my castle.

Those unfamiliar with Bartok's opera will need to find it for themselves if they wish to absorb its complexities and subtleties. The key motif, however, is that Judith, the fourth woman in Bluebeard's life, enters his castle, finding it dark; and vows to bring light and warmth into it. She perceives that there are seven great sealed doors within it. That was the precise image on the front of the first and second drafts of the novel.[11] She insists that Bluebeard give her the keys to open them, one after another. He is ambivalent about allowing her to do this and becomes more and more resistant as she proceeds. Before the seventh door, finally, he begs her to desist, to love him and leave the door closed. She will not, but insists on the key and opens the final door; only to see behind it the three women who had already passed through his life and to find that, having opened the door, she was now doomed to join them behind it. When my Muse and I realized that she had entered my life much as Judith had entered Bluebeard's castle, the stage was set for her to flee and for me to seek a way to overcome my Bluebeard complex.

Frigyesi argues that Bartok's opera is open to various interpretations, as all good art is. Long before reading her book, I had been fascinated by the opera and in some ways captivated by it. What deepened the fascination was my reading and re-reading of Steiner's *In Bluebeard's Castle*, over many years, until it became one of the most heavily annotated books in my library. The book was not a reflection on love and loneliness. It was a reflection on science and civilization in the nuclear age. Steiner borrowed Judith as a symbol for what he saw as the human insistence on understanding the natural world, even at the peril of the human future itself. He wrote at the height of the Cold War and the nuclear arms race, when genetics and information technology were just beginning to blossom as sciences. Steiner's forebodings were another, complementary, form of darkness, reinforcing the first. Both were central to the mood in which I undertook the early drafts of the novel. The question was how to create a story that adequately gave expression to them—or just conceivably found a way to transcend them.

The key passage in Steiner is at pages 105-06 of his little book, culminating in the last four sentences, which I have underscored for this reason:

> *The pursuit of the facts, of which the sciences merely provide the most visible, organized instance, is no contingent error embarked on by Western man at some moment of elitist or bourgeois rapacity. That pursuit is, I believe, imprinted on the fabric, on the electro-chemistry and impulse-net of our cortex. Given an adequate climatic and nutritive milieu, it was bound to evolve and to augment by a constant feedback of new energy. The partial*

---

11   See Annex, image one.

> *absence of this questing compulsion from less developed, dormant races and civilizations*
> *does not represent a free choice or feat of innocence. It represents, as Montesquieu knew,*
> *the force of adverse ecological and genetic circumstance. The flower child in the Western*
> *city, the neo-primitive chanting his five words of Tibetan on the highway are performing*
> *an infantile charade—founded on the surplus wealth of that same city or highway. <u>We</u>*
> <u>*cannot turn back. We cannot choose the dreams of unknowing. We shall, I expect, open*</u>
> <u>*the last door in the castle even if it leads, perhaps because it leads, onto realities which are*</u>
> <u>*beyond the reach of human comprehension and control. We shall do so with that desolate*</u>
> <u>*clairvoyance, so marvellously rendered in Bartok's music, because opening doors is the*</u>
> <u>*tragic merit of our identity.*</u>

This is integral to the sense of 'darkness over love' that gave the novel its name from the outset. How is one to love if intimacy is impossible, the human world is on a perilous trajectory from which it cannot turn back *and* it is virtually impossible to get a clear perspective on that trajectory, its origins and prospects? The novel began as my attempt to find a way to *express* this—prompted by my Muse—but what it evolved into was something else: a way to think one's way *through* all this.

Steiner argued, at the very end of his book, that:

> *...we stand at a point where models of previous culture and event are of little help...At most*
> *one can try to get certain perplexities into focus. Hope may lie in that small exercise.*

But of course, it is not a *small* exercise at all. Nor had Steiner spelled out what kind of 'hope' he had in mind: for what and for whom? All the same, the perplexities of which he wrote have burdened me all my adult life. There is no doubt that they lie deep beneath the surface of the very attempt to write a story about the fate of the Earth and the nature of intimacy, called *Darkness over Love*. Grappling with them and trying to reduce them to order and clarity in prose as an *act* of love is what the project is all about. And working on it has forced me back, again and again, into the greatest myths handed down to us: the descent into the Labyrinth to confront the Minotaur, the labours of Hercules, the epic of Odysseus, the descent into the Underworld and the sacrifice and resurrection of the god of harvests and spring.

The attempt to transcend both Bartok and Steiner was right there in that first draft. It is the strongest part of that original draft of the Bluebeard chapter. The narrator (then without so much as a name and for practical purposes indistinguishable from the author) declares that it is precisely in a powerful *reinterpretation* of Bartok's opera that he will find liberation from the darkness of solitude in his castle and a capacity to love his own Judith (M). He will then welcome the light and warmth that she brings within his castle walls. Virtually none of the actual writing in that draft will survive into the evolved version of the story, but this declaration was a crucial step in getting to the root of what was *psychologically driving* the writing. It was an early symptom of how I was slowly freeing myself to transcend more 'automatic' or driven writing and discovering a capacity for ludic art and imaginative exploration. But *slowly* was the key word. If the perplexities I am endeavouring to get into focus were less serious or less complex, perhaps the progress would have been faster and the darkness less forbidding.

The opening lines of Part I, chapter 7, in the *second* draft, 'Out of the Cave', show the first glimmerings of several ideas that will become far more pronounced as the story develops. The narrator has in this draft, for the first time, been given a name and identity separate from that of the author: Frederick Beresford. He is deeply preoccupied with Bartok's opera and Steiner's book. But here we see that he is also a devotee of the symphonies of Gustav Mahler (something perfectly consistent with the Bartok and Steiner attachments—and not true of me until that point) and that he is at work on a book about the *cognitive foundations of Western civilization* and the challenges it faces. This brought together the fact that I had, indeed, long had an interest in this subject; that I had had a book published in 2009 (*The West in a Nutshell*) that was, in some respects, a first attempt to put those matters into perspective; and that I was seeing the dramatic tension between the narrator's gloom and the brightness of his Muse as centring somehow on his attempt to write such a book.

There is also the first passing mention, in this chapter, of cave paintings, which would assume a vastly more important place in the story later. Ephemeral though the mention of cave art is in the second draft, elements of the later use of the trope can be seen already: the appreciation of the antiquity and universality of human artistic endeavour; the link between cave paintings and the development of symbols for writing; the metaphysical puzzle of the relationship between images on cave walls and reality, classically set out in Plato's 'Cave Simile', in his great treatise, the *Republic*. It was only in the winter of 2011, when the second draft was more or less finished, that I read Jean Clottes' *Return to Chauvet Cave* and, in a few electrifying moments, had a transcendent vision of what could be done with the specific story he tells about the 32,000 year old paintings there. This was a particularly illuminating example of how a discovery, as if by chance, could throw wide open to creativity a rudimentary idea that I had had earlier in the piece. Like the Tale of Raneb and Nefesh, the idea of cave paintings would begin as an incidental or whimsical aside and slowly grow into a central metaphor and narrative trope in the novel.

My journal records that on 9 July 2011 I wrote:

> *A further two months have elapsed with not so much as a note! I've been busy. But now I turn*
> *back to the creation of the book of my life. Many thoughts have enriched my approach to the*
> *book in that time, but the immediate task, this coming week, is to press on with completion of the*

> *second draft—starting with chapter XXII 'Singing in time'...I am reading Jean Clottes' <u>Return to Chauvet Cave</u> and have discovered a priceless detail which will definitely slip into 'Out of the Cave': the great art work at Chauvet was done between 32,000 and 30,000 years ago, then there was apparently no human presence in the cave for several thousand years. But around 26,000 years ago a young boy, holding a torch and accompanied by a dog, walked deep into the cave, casting his eyes over the art on its walls. Astounding discovery!*

What I could do with this astounding discovery took time to realize. Ultimately, however, the idea of the art works concealed for thousands of years and then becoming the purely private discovery of a young boy, by the flickering light of a Palaeolithic torch and accompanied only by a dog, would contribute powerfully to the very heart of the story, to the idea of what art is and to my understanding of the nature of a written work and its relationship to the *reader*.

Curiously, towards the end of that chapter, there occurs for the first time the idea that Frederick and M meet by chance in Toledo. In this early form, their encounter is not something that actually happens. It is a wholly imaginary encounter that Frederick conjures up in trying to think through the nature of intimacy and M's significance for him. In the third draft, this idea would leap into its dominant place in the Prologue, as the way in which the two *actually* first met. That Prologue, with the title 'You had come from Tenerife', in turn foreshadowed the radically revised fourth draft Prologue, written after my visit to Toledo (and Tenerife) in April 2013, and renamed again, as 'The Ascent to San Roman'. But in the winter and spring of 2011 none of this had been foreseen. All that existed were the lines, buried towards the end of the last chapter of Part I:

> *Let's imagine ourselves in a hotel in Toledo. We've met by chance on the ancient bridge, fallen into conversation, become fascinated by one another, spent a long afternoon strolling the old cobbled streets of the city and becoming acquainted over coffee and wine in its salubrious corners...*

In the July 2004 poem 'Ancient Bridge', I had imagined the Alcantara as the place where my Muse and I had met. In Frederick's new version, the scenario was simply the lead-in for a reworked version of one of *The Neruda Variations*, 'Cave and Woman'. In other words, the *evolutionary* artistic process can be seen at work here from the 2004 poem[12], via the original 2008 outpouring of cathartic verse (*The Neruda Variations*) all the way to the fully delineated Prologue composed after the journey to Toledo in 2013.

The very next chapter of the second draft (Part I, chapter 8 'Reckoning with Lorca') opened with an explicitly autobiographical trope, which would, in the third and subsequent drafts rise to become a central motif of the slowly cohering story:

---

12   See Poem #7 'Cave and woman' in Appendix C.

'Tell me a story, Federico!', 'Sing me a song, Federico!' These were among your most frequent and endearing refrains...But again and again your beautiful requests would somehow strike me dumb...

M became Margarita long before she became Margarita Henderson y Mendoza, music therapist, resident in Tenerife, musical protégé and political critic of Jose Antonio Abreu and El Sistema, principal of Capirote Therapies, scion of a wealthy land-owning and oil managing Venezuelan family and lover of the Argentinian archaeologist Anactoria Lopez. All that came to me only later. Yet we can see here that the root idea, the seed of it all, was the request by the Muse for story and song from the author/narrator. From this, again, we can see how raw, rudimentary and uncertain were the first attempts to generate a story out of the flotsam and jetsam of dishevelled autobiography—and how wonderfully the creative process somehow transformed that detritus into things altogether more interesting and fruitful.

Perhaps the most notable things to come out of chapters 9 and 10 in those early drafts were two poems: a villanelle - the first villanelle I had ever attempted to compose - called 'The Poet's Bell' and a long poem called 'The Bell and the Choir'.[13] There was more beauty and polished craftsmanship in each of these than in either of the prose chapters. Each actually pointed to what I was trying to accomplish in the novel as a whole, but was still woefully far from achieving: the expression of certain ideas in a beautiful form, a poetic structure that would lend coherence and musical resolution to the whole world of my ideas and feelings. The evidence was quite plain that I was more at ease crafting verse than crafting a story. I needed to work harder at the skill of story-telling. When I survey those early drafts, I realize that I have been attempting an *absurdly ambitious* story, vastly more sweeping and complex than had ever been attempted by Homer or Virgil, or for that matter Cervantes or Flaubert—and that I wanted it to be 'musical'.

It wasn't even clear that this cosmic story could be put together at all. The poems still seem to go to the heart of the undertaking, looking back; but everything else was in bits and pieces. In chapter 11, 'Some Silurian Nureyev', there is what seems to be the first hint of the later emergence of the Academy of Lynxes, with the mention (or invention) of two characters called Jack Fremont and Tom Benjamin. But, having introduced them, the chapter at once digressed into a long soliloquy on the Egyptian antiquities holdings in New York's Metropolitan Museum of Art, before wandering all over the philosophical landscape from Dante to Darwin and Kant to Nietzsche. It reads like a kaleidoscopic, free-associating ramble through the history of ideas. Plainly, I was letting all these things tumble out onto paper, in a meandering effort to sort out my own thinking. The material was, perhaps, interesting in its own way; but any story-line was notable for its absence.

---

13   'A Poet's Bell' is #16 in Appendix C. 'The Bell and the Choir' is #28

As an author, I now look back on draft material like this with dismay; asking myself with incredulity, "What was I thinking?" Even more distressing is the thought that, whatever I was thinking, my prose was simply not of an acceptable standard—even though I had been writing prose and winning a lot of praise for my efforts over many years. Of course, what I hadn't been doing was writing *literature*. Yet, here again, looking back it's possible to discern what I certainly could *not* see at the time or for years afterwards: the underpinnings of Fenimore's philosophical concerns, his books and his treatise, his longstanding friendship with the other members of the Academy of Lynxes and the implicit threat posed by his work to organized religion and dictatorial ideology in the 21st century. Little by little, over the following few years, poetic discipline, structure and narrative cohesion would begin to take such raw materials and make something more coherent out of them—a story.

Part II, chapter 12 of the second draft 'So that you will hear me', broke new ground[14]. It took its very title from one of *The Neruda Variations*, so the 'bloodline' or genetic lineage is unmistakable. What it exhibited was the soul-searching question: 'has any of this been other than a soliloquy: me ranting and raving like a solitary and perhaps somewhat unhinged individual?' While the title came from Neruda, however, the real inspiration came from a beautiful book by William Waters called *Poetry's Touch: On Lyric Address* (2003), which I seem to have owned since 2004, but only read in about 2011. As I was in the habit of doing in those early drafts, I simply downloaded my own thinking through the fingers of Frederick Beresford:

> *What led me to open* <u>Poetry's Touch</u> *just now, after neglecting it for almost five years* [the chronology of the implicit story being slightly different than that of the author's life]? *Not a conscious strategy, but something that has been growing within me slowly for some time. I find increasingly that I need insistently to reflect on lyric address in general, but especially in the context of my attempts to address you lyrically without striking a false note. No-one tried harder than you to stir this within me and draw my attention to it. Yet it's only now, long after your leave-taking, that I find myself caressing this book as a treasured possession and aching inwardly to hear what it is saying to me.*

These lines, of course, still adhered to the autobiographical bone. The mind that wrote them remained quite unfree, as a creative writer, to bring forth a story for others. But they pointed in the right direction and perhaps the later idea of Fenimore's private Notebooks, as an attempt to communicate *uniquely and completely* with Margarita, can be glimpsed here for the first time.[15]

---

14   'So that you will hear me' is Poem #23 in Appendix C.

15   The manner in which the story plays out, of course, provides a far from simple resolution of the Bluebeard trope, but that is all part of the design.

Lullabies, Messages in Bottles and the Shaping of Gifts

Waters' lovely book includes a reflection on Rilke's poem 'Lullaby'. It is echoed in a passage in the first and second drafts which has long since been culled, because it was clearly part of the author's 'digestive process' rather than part of the story. However, as an element—an enzyme, as it were—in the development of the story, it is worth recalling from oblivion, even if only briefly. Rilke's poem inspired my own (which is to say Frederick's and then Fenimore's) 'Lullaby for Junius'[16]. It reads:

> *Some day when I lose you*
> *Will you be able to sleep*
> *Without me to whisper over you*
> *Like a crown of linden branches?*
>
> *Without me to stay awake here*
> *And put words, almost like eyelids*
> *On your breasts, on your limbs*
> *Down upon your mouth?*
>
> *Without me to lock you up*
> *And leave you alone with what is yours*
> *Like a garden thickly sown*
> *With mint balm and star anise.*

This poem, accompanied by Waters' perceptive commentary, raised the question that every poet and every novelist actually has to be able to answer—to say nothing of every lover.

In the old manuscript, this was how I/Frederick understood that question:

> *How do I address you in such a manner that you can see yourself, can live inside what I write; and not experience it as merely someone else sounding off without actually understanding you?...I feared to love you, for fear of losing you. Now, however, as my love for you grows, it is overshadowed by the thought that the more love I give you, the more you will lose when...*

There is something at work here that fertilized a good deal of the otherwise rather barren volcanic soil of which the nascent story consisted at that time. I think Waters encouraged me to think more and more about all the subtleties and ironies in attempts at intimate communication, which was to pay dividends sometime later. He wrote:

> *...by its nature, a lullaby targets someone who is meant to hear but not entirely to heed what is said. It's not that anyone else is meant, nor that one is singing to oneself; and yet a real lullaby is sung in the hope that its listener will turn her back on the utterance and leave the speaker and his words, at the last, unheard and alone...*

---

16   'Lullaby for Junius' is Poem #30 in Appendix C.

These lines, I suspect, connected synaptically with the images from the Chauvet Cave, when I read Jean Clottes' fabulous book later that year (2011) and thereby generated what was to become an absolutely central motif in the story. Just as I was spell-bound by the idea of the young boy walking through Chauvet Cave with his torch four or five thousand years after it had been abandoned by the painters; so was my imagination captured by the image of Rilke's lullaby singer crooning softly over his beloved, or a child while she fell asleep. There were fantastic intimations in both these cases of the nature of the author and the relationship between the author (of image, utterance or script) and those who see, listen to or read what is put out there. How, I wondered, did my own writing or the writing I was attributing to my narrator, seem, sound or look in this kind of perspective? How did I *want* it to look?

Reading Waters was fruitful in other respects. For example, he relates that Rilke's muse, Baladine Klossowska, for Christmas 1920, gave him a French translation of Ovid's *Metamorphoses*. When she left him in November 1921, at a time when he seemed to have lost his poetic inspiration, she left pinned to the wall opposite his writing table a picture of Orpheus sitting beneath a tree surrounded by animals, as he played a stringed instrument and sang. This was a scene straight out of Ovid's fabulous epic poem. Rilke spent that winter hibernating. Then, in a frenzy of inspiration, in late February and March 1922, he completed his long-stalled *Duino Elegies* and wrote the whole of his acclaimed *Sonnets to Orpheus*. I had read a lot of Rilke while writing the first draft of the manuscript. But these passages from Waters deepened my appreciation of Rilke's creative process—and of the remarkable fertility of Ovid's writing, two thousand years ago. They also struck me as bearing an uncanny resemblance to my own experience and the composition of *The Neruda Variations*.

The discovery about Rilke, of course, prompted me to re-read (more than one translation of) Ovid's *Metamorphoses* and, in the process, to realize that what my narrator was attempting, in some sense or other, was to compose a *Metamorphoses* for the 21st century; or rather to compose something which in my rendering of the story would echo both Homer, Virgil and Ovid—among other things! But how would someone *do* that? The very idea raised all the key questions about poetry and culture, truth and fiction, fable and science that have dominated intellectual debate in the modern world for centuries. It took me quite some time to realize that Ovid was actually an early case of someone trying to get certain perplexities into perspective in Steiner's sense. This was my own *underlying* quest. What made Ovid more than usually stimulating was that he seemed to be attempting to get a sense of perspective that was not just a matter of a vast, impersonal account of what was so; but rather *a renewed way of being* in the light of the changes that had occurred since the creation of the world and the rise of the 'modern' human order (the Roman Empire)[17]. This, of course, was the kind of story I was trying to write.

Waters contributed to my thinking about what I was doing in other ways. Not only Rilke, but other poets, notably Osip Mandelstam and Paul Celan, were brought sensitively to my attention by his reflections. Both were Jewish and both fell victim to the brutal politics and terrors of the mid-20th century. Mandelstam perished, a dissident, in Stalin's GULAG in the late 1930s. Celan (unlike his family) survived the Holocaust, but committed suicide in 1970, drowning himself in the Seine. Several key citations from the thoughts of Mandelstam and Celan struck home at that time and, along with the strands of Rilke's poetry and the Chauvet Cave, fell into the more and more polysemic cluster of ideas that was forming within my subconscious around the restless question: *What is my narrator up to? What is he trying to accomplish?* That he was, by this point, on the page and therefore outside me made it both easier and more compelling to pose the question in this third person form. Asking what *he* was trying to accomplish was easier than asking endlessly what *I* was trying to accomplish.

When Mandelstam was still young, in 1913, before the catastrophe of war, revolution and terror had turned Russia upside down, he wrote:

> *At a critical moment, a seafarer throws into the ocean waves a sealed bottle, containing his name and an account of his fate. Many years later, wandering along the dunes, I find it in the sand, read the message, learn the date of the event and the last will of one now lost. I had the right to do so. I did not open someone else's mail. The message sealed in the bottle was addressed to one who would find it. I found it. That means, I really am its secret addressee.*

Suppose, I thought at the time, one disagreed with Mandelstam, or was more hopeful than his seafarer. Would it not be possible to communicate with a specific beloved in an inimitable manner and *not* simply throw a bottle overboard? Here we see the idea of Fenimore's beautifully hand written Notebooks very slowly beginning to germinate. But once more it is starkly clear that there was no such pre-planned project and no instant flash of inspiration that brought it into play.

Waters also introduced the seminal thinking of Celan, himself an admirer and translator of Mandelstam, with two striking epigrams that struck even more deeply into my brain than Rilke or Mandelstam. He quoted Celan as having written, first:

---

17   Two poems in Appendix C spring directly from this root: #32 'Ovid's Metamorphoses' and #33 'Orpheus among the Stones'. At the end of *Metamorphoses*, Ovid reflects on the philosophy of Pythagoras, as he understood it, and seems to make a plea for such values to be adopted in place of the harsh ones that predominate in the Roman Empire of his day. Perhaps this is one reason why his work, especially the *Metamorphoses*, remained a perennial favourite throughout the Christian centuries, following the downfall of the Roman Empire.

> *Poems are headed towards something. Toward what? Toward something open, inhabitable, an addressable you, perhaps; an addressable reality. Such realities are, I think, at stake in a poem.*

Not only poems, I thought, but stories, or art work of any kind. Then Waters added the following from Celan:

> *Craft means handiwork, a matter of hands. And these hands, in turn, belong to just one person, that is to a unique and mortal soul searching for a way with its voice and its dumbness. Only real hands write real poems. I cannot see any basic difference between a pressing of hands and a poem.*

There seems no doubt, looking back, that this last passage, in particular, made a deep impression. The opening lines of the very next chapter suggest as much in exclamatory manner. From that point the core idea of a 'shaped gift', something crafted by hand and headed towards someone (Margarita) became more and more pivotal to my thinking—although, of course, it had been implicit in the project from the start.

The opening to Part II, chapter 13 'Other autumns loom', in the early manuscript, reads:

> *That quote from Paul Celan, with which I finished my last letter to you, fell like a stone, down, down into the well of the past and memory; until it slipped, with the most distant sound, into the cool darkness of deep waters...Of course! Poiesis—crafting or making—began with stones! The art of chiselling shape and purpose and beauty into objects goes back long, long before language, to say nothing of writing. Like prokaryotes giving off oxygen, our remote ancestors gave off creative intentionality. Like oxygen accumulating in the atmosphere in the Archaean epoch, creative intentionality accumulated in the human genome until, with the appearance of our species on the Earth, both art and technology, both planning and story-telling became possible. Everything else, everything we think of as 'world history' is the cultural 'Cambrian Explosion' that followed—and its aftermath.*

If anything signifies the first mutation that was gradually turning Frederick Beresford the rambling letter writer into Fenimore Moneghan the crafter by hand of stylized Notebooks that he longed to press into the hands of his beloved, this is probably it.

But something else happened at that same juncture which exhibited both humour and irony regarding any such project: the composition of the wry poem 'Nutcracker Man'[18], with its reflection on the emergence of creative intentionality millions of years ago in the hominid genome—and the scepticism of practical females about the creativity in question. This, as it was to turn out, was also the germ of a later major line of development—indeed one that might be said to have taken over and transformed the mood and significance of the entire novel by the early summer of 2013-14. But that was latent in 2010-11. The keynote is still one of a longing for intimacy and the desire to create something beautiful for the loved one. This is expressed, again, much better in the verse than in the prose. The poem 'Consuela, my love' captures

---

18   'Nutcracker Man' is Poem #2 in Appendix C.

the mood most precisely, with its nostalgia for a lost romance and its hopeful acceptance of the possibilities of mutual freedom to meet *and part* again.[19]

But more notable, because it stands out from that background mood, is the reworked *Neruda Variation* 'Leaning into the long afternoons'[20], which, in its playful exuberance and celebration of beauty, gift giving and freedom of spirit, clearly signifies the changing direction of the story writing that is going on. The following lines from that poem, far more ludic than the earlier mood of the manuscript or for that matter the original poem by Neruda, point upwards to what will burst on the scene in the third draft: a much wider and more passionate cosmology and a rejuvenated sense of what can be created inside the story:

> *Out there in the wide, turbulent currents*
> *My nefesh swims and dives*
>
> *It sights and brings high to the light to show you*
> *Sparkling, many-coloured things of beauty*
>
> *It revels and frolics, like a dolphin of the deep*
> *In the green and the blue of your regard*

Again and again, looking back, I am struck by the fact that it is in the poems, much more than in the prose, especially at this stage in the process, that the mutations, insights and felicities of expression first surface.

This is further underscored by the appearance in that same, long chapter of the first authentic *song* in the book, even if it is still embedded in a rather chaotic mass of stone and cannot, therefore, stand out to its greatest advantage. The song is 'Thanks for the thread, Ariadne.'[21] It's whole mood is one of exuberant play, deep gratitude, liberation expressed with jazz-like jauntiness in language and rhythm. The narrator, still tied by a highly visible umbilical cord to the author, is signifying with this song that he believes he has—thanks to his Muse—found his way out of the Labyrinth, which might also be identified with Bluebeard's Castle. That rings out from the song with reverberant clarity. Yet it remains unclear what is happening inside the supposed story to have the narrator feel this way. Clearly, it was more a subliminal sense in the author that he increasingly believed he was finding his way and enjoying the creative process, than a logical statement by the narrator that he had emerged from his own labyrinth or castle.

Part II, chapter 14 'In the House of Memories' (in the first and second drafts) suffers from all the deficiencies in prose style and construction of those that preceded it. However, it was in this chapter that the Tale of Raneb and Nefesh first appeared. It is the only part

---

19　'Consuela, my love' is Poem #27 in Appendix C.

20　'Leaning into the long afternoons' is Poem #24 in Appendix C.

21　'Thanks for the thread, Ariadne' is Poem #29 in Appendix C.

of that chapter likely to survive in the long run, but it has grown and grown in significance through successive drafts. The genesis of the tale is a little difficult to reconstruct now, but it seems to have arisen at the confluence of several quite disparate ideas or influences. There was clearly the background memory of the Muse asking in vain for stories and songs. There was her love of the story-telling segment in *Out of Africa* and *The Tales from the Arabian Nights*. There was Philip Glass's contemporary opera, *Akhnaten*. There was a broader interest in ancient Egypt and archaeology. There was a reading of Robert Alter's translation of and commentary on the Psalms. There was a reading of Daniel Levitin's *The World in Six Songs*.

But where did the *synthesis* come from that led to the original tale? That's the central question of the creative process. Conversely, the sheer mass of background material prompts the question, how could all this be put into a novel without making it unreadable? Leaving aside that last question, the Tale of Raneb and Nefesh was notable because it was the first genuine fable to arise from within the early drafts. It was not a poem and it was not a lecture on science or history or an autobiographical rumination. It was a romantic tale in its own right, with its own characters and plot and even its own internal poetry. It exhibits for the first time a sharp and confident break from what might be dubbed the 'autobiographical undertow' of the early drafts and a leap into narrative fiction. Moreover, as it unfolded, the story got bolder in conception, until it produced the fantastic idea that Levitin's theory of six basic types of song had been instantiated and understood in the early third millennium BCE in Old Kingdom Egypt—and transcended with a seventh song.

The link with the Muse's request for story and song is, of course, clear and unmistakable. This will give it what will later become its special place in Tom Emerson's account of the thinking and writing of Fenimore Moneghan. As I reworked the fourth draft and then the set to work on a fifth, this became ever clearer to me. Finally, it led to my decision to separate the seven songs of Queen Nefesh from the main text and to have Tom discover them during his researches into the work of the deceased (or vanished) Fenimore. The separation of the songs into an Appendix made several things possible, including Tom's unearthing, in Fenimore's immense library, the Vivarium, of a copy of Daniel Levitin's book, *The World in Six Songs*, given to him by Margarita in Cairo itself some years before. He reads her dedication inside the cover of Levitin's book and exclaims that here, written in her own language and her own hand, is evidence that the mysterious Margarita really existed and was not merely a figment of Fenimore's fertile imagination. He also finds Fenimore's incomplete reflections on the seven songs and includes them in the Appendix, along with a few observations of his own.

There is no need, in an essay of this nature, to reflect on each successive chapter and draft of the story. It is sufficient to note that the two creative tendencies—a newly discovered facility for original fable-writing and an increasing freedom of mood and exuberance of spirit in versifying - were the signs that something was bubbling away beneath the surface. The sketches later in the manuscript for the Tale of Manntezuma (the epic of the pre-Hispanic Americas), Humboldt on the Orinoco, the irreverent 'Macondo Mambo', poking fun at the politics of Gabriel Garcia Marquez, the Tale of Archimedes, the various death scene sketches drawing on Russian literature and poems and the first draft of the Epilogue, all show more and more signs of story-telling technique coming to the fore. The novel as a whole, despite the rough architectural design put in place quite early on, was obviously jerry-built and needed a thoroughgoing overhaul. Yet the examples I have cited and others besides show that, even within that rather shoddily painted and furnished mansion, in a manner of speaking, there were—for some strange reason—numerous rather fine pieces of sculpture. Since 2013, I've pulled them out, demolished the old mansion, cleared the site and begun to rebuild.

The Preparation of the Novel

Often we see, hear or read things that make an impression upon us, but whose deeper influence only takes place subconsciously, over time. My journal records that, on 24 February 2011, long before I completed the second draft, I wrote the following:

> *In Readings yesterday...I stumbled upon a newly published book by Roland Barthes called* <u>*The Preparation of the Novel*</u>*. How truly fortuitous, I thought, that it should appear in English now and just before I prepare to revise the Paris chapter of my book. Barthes died on 26 March 1980. This book wasn't published, even in French, until 2003 and in English only this year, by Columbia University Press. It consists of a set of lectures Barthes gave in 1979 on the very idea of preparing to write a novel.*

Naturally, I bought the book and read it very closely, though not until April and May. Both my copy of the book, with its extensive annotations and underlinings; and my journals bear witness to that fact. Yet this was a full year before I decided to take a 'sabbatical' to reflect more deeply on my own preparation of the novel. I would say, looking back, that Barthes' deeper influence on me really only began to become evident *two years* after I read it—in the journey to Spain and the thinking that followed it, later in 2013.

It seems that at the very end of his life (though it was not evident to him at the time how close the end was), Barthes—arguably the greatest French literary critic of his time—contemplated composing a novel, as a kind of writing experiment, but also as a vehicle for self-expression. He wanted it to be, he wrote, his equivalent of Dante's *Vita Nuova*, but it initially took the form of a diary in which he deliberated on whether or not it was possible for a diary itself to become a work of art. At the time of his death, a page was found in his typewriter (this being before the invention of word-processors or Word). It was headed 'One always fails in speaking of what one loves'. It was a fragment of a work in progress about Stendhal, the great early nineteenth century French novelist. Stendhal's most fragmentary and personal book was simply called *Love*. That was a book to which I had made close reference in the very first draft of my own novel, invoking Stendhal's unrequited love for *his* Muse, Mathilde Dembowski. That allusion was later cut, yet it is still echoed in the late poem 'Cleis Scamandros'[22]—an inconsistency that will require attention as I work on the fifth draft.

According to the editor of Barthes' lectures, Nathalie Leger, Barthes thought that the novel—"that uncertain form, the material of remembered as much as of desired speech"—was the only art form capable of expressing 'the truth of affect', whereby meaning is revealed and undone. He was fascinated, she says, by the metaphor of the labyrinth and thought that the quest for the novel can only culminate in a melancholy and luminous world of apparitions. Reading this, I was astonished at how closely it spoke to my own state of mind and writing. The translator, Kate Briggs, in turn, reveals that Barthes did, in fact, sketch out a plan for a novel of his own, but it was only a schema. She wrote:

> By the end of the 1970s, apparently, everyone knew that Roland Barthes was writing
> a novel. It was not until 1995, however, that the facsimiles of Barthes' eight page plan
> entered the public domain. When they did...the general feeling was one of disappointment:
> What? Only eight pages? Only eight pages, amounting to eight variations on the same
> sketched outline of a prospective novel?

I was fascinated by this - and heartened, of course. The greatest literary critic of his time had set out to write a novel, but over quite some years had created, on paper, no more than a series of rough sketches for what the novel would be about. For all my floundering, I reflected, I had done a good deal better than that.

Briggs went on, however:

> The preparation of the novel is evidently something distinct from the fact of writing one:
> rumour may have had it that Barthes was writing a novel, but...this was not the case...as
> Barthes stresses repeatedly, working out how to go about writing a novel is really far from
> obvious: it is hard-going, difficult, all-consuming and often a source of pain and distress.

I found it a great source of relief and consolation to read these lines, after a summer of difficult and all-consuming work on my own novel and it has remained a source of encouragement to me ever since. She went on to remark that Barthes' personal writing project actually took the form of a *teaching* project addressed to his students (and now to all those of us who read the lectures). 'Do you desire to write a novel? Are you embarking on the journey of attempting to create a literary work?', the lectures implicitly ask. Then this is what you will go through. This

---

22   'Cleis Scamandros' is Poem #35 in Appendix C.

is how your precursors, who created enduring works of literature in the modern era, prepared themselves and what they went through to accomplish their works. Yet again, I felt, a great thinker and writer had written very much for me.

Barthes felt that the insistence on *objectivity* and 'correct' or 'scientific' ideology in the twentieth century was more and more *stifling the subject* and with it the very possibility of literature in the traditional sense. I found myself intrigued by this line of argument, if only because the emerging design for my own novel was that its narrator himself insisted on the importance and primacy of objectivity and was resistant to the very idea of writing a novel. Just as I was pondering all these thoughts, one deeply engaged reader of my work wrote to declare that he believed the second draft had "come an enormous distance from the first". My journal entries suggest that I felt the same way. Looking back, I am more struck by the *similarities* between the two and my lack of radical progress. But that only made the reading of Barthes all the more interesting and important, both at the time and in retrospect. Certainly, between the first draft and where things now stand, I *have* come an enormous distance.

Drawing extensively on the private journals and letters of such writers as Flaubert, Tolstoy, Proust, Kafka and Camus, Barthes commented that the preparation of a novel "is actually composed of repetitions, back-trackings, uncertainties, mistakes". This was, naturally, my own experience and I felt increasingly that Barthes had designed and delivered his course of lectures specifically for me. Moreover, he wrote that he associated his own project, his would-be *Vita Nuova* in the manner of Dante, with:

> *A House or, failing that, what I'll call the cavernous apartment = out of the way, enclosed.*
> *I know of one: peaceful neighbourhood, plus courtyard and back garden and very big*
> *room with a window: grandeur and seclusion; shelter (Mallarme)*

These lines would perhaps have made my hair stand on end, had I enough hair for it to do so. Even in the second draft, this was precisely what I had, with the collaboration of my architect friend, been seeking to bring into 'existence' within the confines of the novel. These very characteristics were driving the gradual emergence of Cos and would govern its breakout from the strictures of realism into a symbolic and mythic abode characterised by precisely the "out of the way grandeur and seclusion" of which Barthes had written. I found this somewhat uncanny, but it can only have helped my creative process.

I was still absorbing Barthes' lectures at Easter 2011. They drew me on, encouraging me by showing that everything I was attempting fitted well within what the great critic saw as both the task and the nature of such writing. He wrote and I transcribed these lines into my journal:

> *To write, according to my desire and in my experience, at least, is to see the book; to visual-*
> *ize the book: on the horizon—the book.*

And:

> *Reading is a metonymical activity, an all-consuming activity: you're gradually pulling the entire continuum of culture toward you, as into the sea at high tide. You plunge into the imaginary of culture, into the chorus, the polyphony of a thousand other voices to which I add my own: a book (in truth, not all books, unfortunately: let's say a book that 'takes') is like a loose thread...*

Or again:

> *...almost all the writers' lives are organized around a central crisis...that serves as the point of departure of the triumphant, regenerated Work...*

I felt so implicated in all this, so described by it all, that I felt strongly vindicated in what I was attempting to do—and more prepared than ever before to work at it until I got it right—in order precisely as Barthes had written, to *pull the entire continuum of culture toward me.*

There was so much of this nature in the reflections of Barthes. I found them startlingly relevant to what I had already been going through. So much so that I am tempted to describe his lectures as a 'second bridge' from where I had started to where the story finally began to take root. The 'first bridge' was the Alcantara in Toledo, which, as I have written, antedated in my poetics even *The Neruda Variations* and which surfaced in the second draft, then took a prominent place in the Prologue from the third draft. But this second bridge was a bridge to the idea that I was, as I had hoped, writing—or striving to write—*entirely within the classical literary tradition.* I would go so far as to say that reading Barthes' lectures gave me the resolution to pause for a year in 2012 and take more serious stock of what I was doing and how I was going about it. Certainly, he had made me realize that the central themes of what I had already put on paper were literary in the best sense. What I had to do was keep the Work, the Book, in view on the horizon and press forward.

Like Nabokov, in *Pale Fire*, Barthes expressed bewilderment and sorrow at the decline and even dying out of literature. They both thought the world of letters was declining into a kind of dull, anti-poetic flatness of 'universal reportage' and anti-traditional ideology. Barthes openly blamed the student upheavals of the 1960s, fingering 'May '68' and not the catastrophes of the Second World War as the tipping point, the 'mutation of sensibility'; although he stated that Proust was perhaps the last great writer who had been 'totally integrated into the canonical concept of literature'. Surely, I think, Thomas Mann was such a writer; but he was one who sensed that he lived in a literary and cultural *fin de siecle*—as his novels bear witness. By sheer coincidence, the year after Barthes died, in 1980, I wrote my History honours thesis, in 1981, on the student rebellions in France of May 1968. By no coincidence at all, I had had a deep and unfulfilled longing from an early age to find a way to become integrated into the great tradition and to become a great writer. Barthes' lectures were now spelling out for me, why this had been so difficult for me, what was at stake and, to some extent, how to proceed.

He wrote at one point:

> *This course is so fundamentally 'archaic' that, in a sense, its object—that is, the notion of the Work—no longer has any currency in the field of letters. It would appear that those who write produce (or) want to produce books; but what's disappeared is the intentionality that characterizes the Work as a personal monument; a mad object that the writer is totally invested in; a personal cosmos-stone that the writer constructs over the course of history...*

Very often, I had felt that what I was writing, what I was attempting to create, was in just this sense 'archaic'. I would go so far as to say that one of the sombre psychological drives behind the work itself and the titling of it was a deep-seated sense of futility. The novel, if I could complete it and get it published, would be a monument, 'a mad object' that I had been totally invested in. Yet it would be a monument as a tombstone is a monument. It would give expression to the fact or belief that pulling the entire continuum of culture toward oneself and writing within the canonical idea of literature was a quixotic quest; a hopelessly anachronistic and eccentric thing to do. Only since 2013 have I had a more hopeful sense that it might be more than this.

Ironically, as Barthes pointed out, this very sense of my situation as a writer put me in the company of the 'heroes' of the great modern novels, since 'the novel is about a hero at odds with modern society because the times are out of joint'. Logically, he went on, the hero must succumb, which makes him a tragic hero. I felt the current pulling me in this direction for personal as well as literary reasons long before I read *The Preparation of the Novel*. Even in the first draft, the narrator dies (or is clearly about to die) in the Epilogue. Reading Barthes strengthened my understanding that what was happening here *transcended my personal experience* or psychological disposition. It placed me precisely within the literary tradition that I admire. What remained to be done, of course, was to separate myself sufficiently from the novel as a piece of craft work that I could create a literary figure who embodied that transcendence better than I ever could as a real individual. That was the *task* of literature, as Barthes himself had put it. That was the *preparation* that was required, if one was to write an authentic novel.

Finally, Barthes laid passionate emphasis on the need for *poetic language* in literature. What he derided as the language of 'universal reportage' appeared to be based, he speculated, on the notion that language should merely be the *neutral instrument for conveying information*, with no substance or resonance in itself. There was no room in such a requirement, he commented for artistic archaism and allusion, for any sense of the origins of things, for any ritual or liturgy in the use of the tongue and the teasing of the mind. There was only room for a language of immediacy with no conscious roots in the past; what he called 'an absolutely secular language'. Such a usage of language, he argued, eliminated the individual writer and replaced such individual forms of expression with a kind of collective sameness of both sense and sensibility. I need hardly say that reading these remarks, also, I felt utterly at one with Barthes and vindicated in the fact that the best parts of even my first draft had consisted precisely of poetry—poetry, moreover, which the Friend has since agreed is the best I have written.

Barthes took a stand against this 'secular' and anti-poetic trend. He invoked Mallarmé[23]—who had declared that everything in the world was made to end up in a book—in insisting that in genuinely literary writing there is *no sharp boundary between poetry and prose*. Great prose, Mallarmé had declared, *is* verse, because so long as there is stylistic effort there is versification. Indeed, there is, in literary work, no such thing as prose: there is the alphabet and then there are verses that are more or less closely knit, more or less diffuse.[24] The prose of any 'luxurious writer' counts, in fact, as 'broken verse'. This year I have been reading Proust's *In Search of Lost Time* and have discovered that no novel better illustrates this argument of Mallarmé's. Barthes commented that taking this stand was not to say that novels must consist of 'hidden alexandrines' (alexandrines being iambic lines of poetry with six 'feet' or twelve syllables); only that literary writing is enriched by 'ellipses and formulae', poetical and incantatory, that set it 'radically, voluntarily and gloriously' apart from 'brute, immediate, social language'. What a sigh of relief and contentment I exhaled on reading this.

On Easter Sunday 2011, having written all these lines from Barthes into my journal, I concluded:

> *This, decidedly, is what <u>Darkness over Love</u> is all about. The only question is: Can I accomplish this? I believe I am getting there in the second draft.*

My remarks in the foregoing pages about the second draft will have made plain that, in retrospect, I would say I was only 'getting there' in the most preliminary and uncertain way. Barthes' concluding observations about the challenge to literature in the late twentieth century suggest that the problem was not only my own underdeveloped or inadequate literary abilities,

---

23   Stéphane Mallarmé (1842 – 1898) was a French literary figure famous for his use of language in anything but a common or neutral manner. He was a leading figure in the poetic Symbolist movement and inspired not only writers but artists and various other kinds of revolutionaries in the half century following his death.

24   Mallarmé was a mystic of human experience and remarked at one point, though I have not been able to trace this quote to its source: "It is the job of poetry to clean up our word-clogged reality by creating silences around things." Clearly, by silences he did not mean a retreat from language, but a regeneration of it through the spurning of banal and clichéd writing and demotic speech.

but that knowledge (the sciences) since Leibniz[25] and the writing of fiction since Proust had both become so complex as to be 'unmasterable'. In other words, the thing he longed to be able to do or see others do, he was inclined to suspect was *no longer possible*. This, of course, linked his perspective, in 1979, with Steiner's concerns of only a few years before, to which I have drawn attention and which I had first read in the mid-1970s.

Yet even in the great writing that his lectures drew upon, Barthes observed, there was something of this overwhelming challenge—and it had been met:

> *Before the world, the Writer, such as I've tried to imagine him, someone who devotes himself to the Literary Absolute...feels himself to be both a truthful (he sees the truth) and an impotent witness.*

To which he added:

> *What is the Tragic? = to come to terms with your Fate in such a radical way that it gives rise to a freedom; for to come to terms with is to transform; nothing can be said, accepted, if it isn't bound up with a labour of transformation.*

All this, I would say, having been transcribed in my journal, worked its way deep into my psyche. It formed subtle and hidden synaptic links with what I had read in Cervantes, in the Latin American novelists, in Waters' remarks about Rilke, Mandelstam and Celan; in my reflections on the significance of the paintings in the Chauvet Cave. And, in due course, it enabled me to transform the early drafts into a very different, much stronger, clearly delineated story-line; a far more realistic attempt at achieving the 'Literary Absolute' and building a monument—yet one that was still (as shown in this present Work) a *preparation* of the novel.

Upheavals of Thought in the spring of 2013

Having confidently re-written the Prologue on my return from Spain in late April 2013, I had both run into unanticipated health problems and intractable literary problems by late June. The health problems were uncanny. In the manuscript as it existed at that time, I had written a scenario in which the narrator (just then emerging as Fenimore Moneghan) had returned from a world journey (in late April or early May 2010) to discover that he had

---

25   Gottfried Wilhelm von Leibniz (1646 – 1716) was a German mathematician and philosopher, who developed calculus independently of Isaac Newton and was one of the most prolific inventors in the field of mechanical calculators. With René Descartes and Baruch Spinoza, he was one of the three great 17th century advocates of rationalism. He was an extraordinary polymath, doing original work in both physics and technology, while putting forward ideas that later proved influential in philosophy, probability theory, biology, medicine, geology, psychology, linguistics, and computer science. He wrote works on philosophy, politics, law, ethics, theology, history, and philology.

an aggressive metastatic cancer. In May 2013, following what I thought would be a routine PET scan, I discovered that the melanoma that had been plaguing my right leg for eight and a half years had finally broken out into my torso—in the groin and near the heart. In other words, I had a metastatic—though not apparently aggressive—cancer. Life seemed to be imitating art. I felt a new sense of urgency in attempting to complete the novel; but I found that the way forward was blocked, or at the very least still labyrinthine.

This was registered in my journal, where I wrote on 18 August:

> *I have to get back inside the story and that begins with imagining Cos and…not allowing my boldness of imagination to be cramped by a tawdry realism. I am Prospero on his island and must weave magic to have my way against the powers that have confined me there. Cos is my Fenimore's palazzo and I am immersing myself in Angheli Zalappi's Palazzi of Sicily to stir my imagination.*

Three nights later, there was a kind of break in the dam, though I had no idea what a flood of ideas would follow. On the morning of 21 August, I wrote:

> *I have had a remarkable night…I could not sleep. I was obsessed and depressed by the impasse with the novel. For three hours I tossed and turned despondently…However, my brain performed a conceptual miracle. What had been troubling me was the idea that Cos has become too large and its library too unwieldy and that there was no way to tell this story of erudition and philosophy in a publishable, much less an entertaining manner. I was gripped by the fear that critics would describe the whole thing as an overblown case of wish fulfilment, egotism, narcissism and fantasy.*
>
> *Then something synaptic and analogical took place. I realized that it had all to be exactly that—a fantasy—but of the contemporary kind. It is a blend of The Matrix with Borges and Bulgakov. This frees me up. Inside the matrix, which might well be Fenimore's head (drawing upon Lieberman's The Evolution of the Human Head) anything is possible. A physical realism becomes irrelevant…The brain is the most extraordinary thing. Yet the elements it had to work with are clear enough…The impressive thing is that my emotional and intuitive brain needed time and energy to come up with insights of which my conscious and anxious brain was bereft. There is still, of course, all the work in the world to do. But I feel liberated and reanimated.*

A week later, I recorded that the same energy which had liberated my attitude to Cos had begun to run right through the structure of the novel. So much so that I once again deluded myself into thinking I had finally got the structure right:

> *Today has been…my best day ever of work on Darkness over Love…I have completed a comprehensive structured synopsis of the entire story, which vindicates the sense I formed in Spain that I could see my way through the whole tale having got inside it while in Tenerife and Toledo…This is what I had sensed and hoped all along could be done. I may well be able to put the final touches to this form of the book next week, over a few days. It

has been extraordinary experiencing the sequence of strain, doubt, emotional exhaustion, retreat, rest, reflection and breakthrough over the past four days. This has been a triumph of creativity over self-doubt.

But confidence ebbed and flowed. On 2 September, I wrote:

Having created the dramatis personae and extracted the fables yesterday, I sat back dismayed by the poor quality of the existing draft. That is actually the second draft for the most part, because the third never got beyond chapter four and some work on a number of other chapters or passages; and the chapter structure has now changed in any case. For practical purposes, the story writing is only now beginning. Everything up to this point has been very rough, experimental drafting work.

Without tracking the ebb and flow of confidence over the weeks and months that followed, I want to register that still, in the early spring last year, I was plagued by doubts concerning the fundamental architecture of the novel and the nature of the story I was trying to tell. Then, with surprising suddenness, that changed.

It's curious the tricks memory plays, of course. If I had been asked, without benefit of checking my journal from late last year, when the breakthrough came, I would have said without hesitation that it was in September. But the journal makes it very clear that that was not so. Throughout October, in fact, I was still wallowing in detailed set pieces for various chapters, especially a long and excessively detailed sketch for a visit to Germany by Fenimore in 2000, as he begins to contemplate building Cos. It was only at the very end of October and early November that a wholly new idea came to me—and transformed my feeling about the story from introverted earnestness and gloom to laughter and a sense of exuberant and even wicked creativity. I had, of course, begun edging in this direction much earlier and especially with the beginning of the third draft. But at no point until late last year had a truly ludic perception of the Work as a whole gripped me or fallen into place.

To appreciate what exploded into being at this point, it is necessary to recapitulate how the architecture of the story had slowly changed. Having begun as a relatively unselfconscious and autobiographical piece of writing, the narrative had become a journal kept by an increasingly well-defined character. Quite early in the piece the idea had been raised in the Epilogue that this journal would be sent by the dying narrator to a great American friend, with a request that he arrange for a deluxe, printed version to be made and given as a parting gift to the Muse and to a small circle of friends. The character of the Muse, the friend and the small circle of other friends all developed further. In particular, the small circle of friends became the Academy of Lynxes. They had all met at Harvard in the mid-1980s and had formed a common vision, staying in touch for many years afterwards.

One of them, originally named Jack Fremont, but by the fourth draft renamed Irad Kripke (and radically changed also in character), had set up a hedge fund at the turn of the century, around the same time that the narrator started to design Cos. The vision for Cos had changed from an apartment (draft 2), to a house (draft 3), to a mansion (draft 4) (all in Melbourne, Australia) and finally into a quasi-magical abode at a transcendent and mysterious location called 'the Ends of the Earth' (draft 5). His company at the Ends of the Earth, Peripatetica Decision Architects, had been shown to run a special professional seminar called the Conspiracy Theory and Cognition Workshop. His American friend, Tom Emerson, meanwhile, had been described as the author of a book called *The Bow of Odysseus* about terrorism and the state in the 21st century. And the hedge fund, even before Irad Kripke appeared, was declared to have made a great deal of money shorting the mortgage companies and Wall Street banks in the lead-up to the 2008 financial crisis.

The question, of course, was how to weave all this together into a coherent narrative of even a picaresque kind. The first step was seeing that Fenimore was not simply writing a private journal. He was writing (alongside it) a treatise about truth, science and civilization which would have earth-shaking implications for the world of organized religion and political ideology. He had written serious books before and had a global reputation among serious people. It was known that he was working on a book about science, religion and philosophy, so a number of powerful parties were quietly taking an interest in what it might say. The second step was seeing that Fenimore's untimely death, long foreseen in the development of the story, would trigger a chain of events that he had never foreseen—any more than I had. Several things contributed to this: confusion among the uninitiated between his treatise (which he never gets to finish) and his Notebooks (which are kept secret, because they are private); the windfall gains made by the hedge fund in 2008; and the involvement of Tom Emerson in international security affairs and counter-terrorism.

The sense that these things must all flow together was late in coming to me. Once it did, however, it released a flood of new ideas. It became apparent that, even as he and the other members of the Academy plan to create a foundation through which to channel the several billion dollars their hedge fund made in shorting Wall Street banks, Fenimore has a catastrophic and unexpected break with his Muse; and at the same time falls critically ill. *In extremis,* he rounds offs his final Notebook and sends a set of three such Notebooks to Tom (by surface mail, because these are handwritten manuscripts, not electronic documents), asking that he prepare a private, deluxe printed edition for the Academy of Lynxes. He then disappears, sailing out to sea on his yacht *Aletheia* and vanishing. The boat is later found, but not his body. In all the circumstances, rumours begin to spread and these become conspiracy theories. I delighted in the realization that the unforeseen and uncontrollable consequence of Fenimore's disappearance and apparent death is an outbreak of just the kind of conspiracy theories that the Peripatetica Conspiracy Theory and Cognition Workshop was designed to 'deconstruct'.

But I then saw that this was only the beginning. Tom proceeds to prepare the private printed edition and writes both a Foreword and an Afterword to it. In other words, as the editor of Fenimore's Notebooks (which are three in number), he becomes a second order, even a higher order narrator. This was refreshing. It enabled me to break out of the rather restricting single narrator structure and, of course, gave me a voice that could provide an account of what happened to Fenimore and how the plague of conspiracy theories came into being, as well as explaining directly how the book itself had come into being. At this point, therefore, Tom really started to come to life. Through his eyes, I was actually able to look at the nature and history of the Notebooks themselves differently. It was only with this angle of vision that I finally saw what they were: a work of art in stylized longhand, written on fine paper in leather-bound notebooks. They were Fenimore's ultimate 'poem' for Margarita. They were a 'shaped gift' in a lineage that could be traced all the way back to hand axes 1.5 million years ago and which fully met the desiderata of Mandelstam (the message in the bottle cast into the sea) and Celan (about a poem being a work of the hands).

These were exciting aesthetic breakthroughs, as well as narrative devices that for the first time started to make sense of the whole elaborate saga. But it then became clear to me that a further step was necessary. After all, how did this fastidiously edited private volume, created by Tom Emerson for the Academy of Lynxes, find its way into *your* hands, reader? And if it was only some kind of private journal addressed to the Muse and meaningful to a small circle of Fenimore's friends, why would you be interested in reading it? Besides, what had become of all those conspiracy theories? Were they mere harmless nonsense, or did they have consequences? *Of course* they had consequences, I realized! This is a *novel*! Fenimore's work was 'dynamite'; his disappearance mysterious; the billions made by the hedge fund were an acute source of jealousy and suspicion in a time of anger and upheaval; and Tom's work drew both these things into the world of terrorism and political violence. Hadn't I long since foreshadowed something like this, by writing even in the first account of the narrator and his Muse meeting in Toledo (in the new Prologue for the third draft), that they met very soon after the Madrid bombings and the publication of *The Bow of Odysseus*?

Now the pieces really began to fall into place. It emerged that among the parties that had taken a quiet, observant interest in what Fenimore was up to was the Vatican. We all know that there is a market for conspiracy theories involving the Vatican and that its rich history and secrecy readily lend themselves to such things. The challenge was both to come up with an original conspiracy theory and to make it one that conformed with the serious purposes of the novel, rather than a fatuous one of the kind made so popular by Dan Brown in *The Da Vinci Code*. It was at this point that I first met Cardinal Roberto Bolzano and was given a guided tour of the history and contemporary thinking of the Holy Office. I say 'met' him because he simply appeared in front of me one day, as I pondered the possibilities and dilemmas of story-making, and confided in me that he had made a special journey to the Ends of the Earth to meet Doctor Moneghan, at the bidding of the Pope, and that this visit had had unforeseen consequences.

What consequences, exactly? He was a little vague about that at first, but I did a little investigating and discovered that, following his visit to the Ends of the Earth, he had written a fairly long, Eyes Only letter to the Pope about Cos, Doctor Moneghan and the implications for the Vatican of what the good Doctor was writing. This was innocuous enough in itself, but after the announcement in mid-2010 that Fenimore Moneghan had vanished and was presumed dead and after conspiracy theories began to flourish—and after Tom, having custody of the private Notebooks of Fenimore (rumoured to be the controversial treatise), had set up base at a villa in northern Italy—the Pope asked Bolzano for an updated memorandum on the matter.[26] Now, it so happened that Bolzano, although a close confidante of the Pope over many years, had been a CIA asset for even longer. And here, as they say, the plot began to thicken. For he passed a copy of this updated memorandum to the CIA Station Chief in Rome, Martin Rienzi—and from there, the intelligence world being what it is, things got out of hand.

In one of the rapid cascades of ideas that occurs only once the internal logic of a situation has worked itself out, I now saw that the CIA Station Chief had dispatched Bolzano's memorandum to CIA HQ, Langley, with a covering cable that placed it in the larger context of CIA relations with the Vatican and assessments at the Station as to where the Vatican was heading under the then Pope—Benedict XVI. The two documents taken together were then copied by a Chinese mole inside the US intelligence system and supplied to the Ministry of State Security in Beijing. Having always been paranoid about the CIA and the presumed American strategy for bringing about the downfall of the Communist Party, the gnomes of the MSS (perhaps, it is hinted, supervised by the since disgraced head of state security, Zhou Yongkang) prepare a briefing for the Politburo. It declares that these documents betray a covert operation involving the CIA and the Vatican, in which Fenimore, Tom and the other members of the Academy of Lynxes are alleged accomplices or actual agents of the CIA.

---

26   See the full text of this letter in Appendix D, as presented by N. Herman of Brandom House, New York.

By this stage, I was on a roll and a whole new dimension to the story had begun to unfold. For it transpired that, just as the Chinese had moles inside the CIA, so the CIA had moles inside the Chinese Communist Party. The MSS briefing to the Politburo was, therefore, supplied back to Langley, where analysts read with astonishment of the interpretation placed on the Bolzano letter and the cable from the Rome Station by the minions of Zhou Yongkang in Beijing. But even as they puzzle over that interpretation, the set of three documents is lifted from their system by the 'hacktivist' federation, Anonymous. Already persuaded that vast conspiracies are afoot within the US Government, Anonymous takes a similar line to the Chinese. They draft a memorandum roundly denouncing the CIA and the Vatican for conspiring to do away with the liberties of all Americans (and anyone else who has them) in the name of law, order and 'true religion'. But whereas the MSS briefing was classified and shown only to the Politburo; Anonymous make a YouTube video of their manifesto and put it on-line.

The internet and the new social media being what they are, this sends speculation, conspiracy theory and confusion into over-drive. Far away from Langley or the suburban covens of Anonymous, the allegations about the CIA and the Vatican draw close interest at the headquarters of the Iranian Revolutionary Guard Corps in Tehran and among the heads of Hezbollah in Beirut and the Beka'a Valley, Lebanon. From being a matter of fastidious private artwork and philosophical reflection, shared among a small circle of scholarly friends, the work of Moneghan has now become a matter of global and malevolent conspiracy theory. But the members of the Academy of Lynxes, deeply immersed in their researches and in their plans to use the windfall gains from the hedge fund to create a philanthropic body dedicated to reason and the delineation of public goods (called the Amor Mundi Foundation), fail to perceive in what danger all this has placed them. As they prepare for a gala event at their Italian villa to celebrate the private printing of Fenimore's Notebooks and the setting up of their foundation, with (I imagine) the brindisi from Verdi's *La Traviata* playing exuberantly over a public address system wired up for the party)[27] a Hezbollah truck bomb careens through the villa's open gates and across its gardens, crashing into the side of the villa and blowing both them, the villa and the original Notebooks sky-high. Well...almost all of them.

Not all of them were there. It seems that at least two of them had escaped the bombing. One of those, Bianca Ruggiero, who had been detained in Rome at the time and so escaped

---

27   Why the *brindisi* from Act I of *La Traviata*? Three reasons occur to me: that Villa Barberini had originally been built for a wealthy Italian who loved Verdi's operas; the villa was, in any case, set in northern Italy; and Virgil died in Brindisi (Brundisium) before he could complete *The Aeneid*. Obviously, the soundtrack for a cinematic take on *Darkness over Love* could do this – or use other music. This is simply a musical motif that occurred to me at the moment of composition.

the attack, then took her copy of the printed version of Fenimore's notebooks to a New York publisher, seeking the publication of a commercial edition that might put an end to the mad speculation which had seemingly triggered this shocking violence. Since the bombing had taken global interest in what the French dailies had long since dubbed *l'Affaire Moneghan* to new heights, the publisher agrees. Even as the commercial edition is being prepared, however, Bianca Ruggiero and her staff in Rome are attacked in broad daylight and murdered—except that it isn't clear that this attack was carried out by the same party that destroyed the Villa Barberini. And who is the unidentified member of the Academy of Lynxes said still to be on the loose? The drama has been brought to fever pitch. The sense of danger and mayhem is acute. It all surrounds this obscure manuscript, which, you, the reader, now have in your trembling hands. That's not a bad story-line I thought. And it's a world removed from where I started five or more years ago. In fact, it was a world removed from where I had stood only weeks before.

But it didn't stop there. The implications of these ideas reverberated right through the existing manuscript, from its core ideas to the style in which it was written. They galvanized it. Everything now took on the possibility of becoming more dynamic, more electric, more challenging and dramatic. First, however, I had to put all these new ideas in order and in place. That meant actually writing the letter from Cardinal Bolzano to the Pope, the CIA Station Chief's cable from Rome to Langley; the MSS briefing for the Politburo and the Anonymous manifesto. Those documents, like Tom's Foreword and Afterword and other editorial remarks about Fenimore's work, were exciting, because they were not only creative exercises in themselves, but they each offered a fresh perspective on both Fenimore and the central axis of the story-line. Moreover, I found that I was able to write them quickly and with confidence, because the narrative logic of what they were and how they had come into existence seemed crystal clear.

But who was the publisher to whom Bianca went, in the northern summer of 2014, after the terrible explosion at the Villa Barberini—the Italian villa, in Lombardy, where Tom had been editing Fenimore's papers and the other members of the Academy had been gathering? Had Bianca survived to tell her tale, perhaps she would have written an Introduction to the book, lamenting the deaths not only of Fenimore but of Tom and her other colleagues. She, however, had also been assassinated—in her offices in Rome, with colleagues and security guards. Therefore, the Introduction had to be written by someone else—an editor from the publishing house. It was at this juncture that I encountered the beguiling figure of N. Herman, literary editor for the publishing firm Brandom House, New York. She offered me a whole new voice. She offered to write a trenchant Introduction to the book, with the title '*Darkness over Love*—the True Story'. This had a profound appeal, given that I had long since called the novel itself *Darkness over Love: A Complete Fiction*; and given that the work of Fenimore was now wreathed in conspiracy theories as in clouds of smoke.

Who, however, was 'N. Herman' and why just the initial? There had been an underdeveloped backstory since the third draft about Fenimore having had a lover in the mid-1980s by the name of Nathalie Morton, with whom he had had a falling out. She, a graduate in Fine Arts from Vassar College, had hoped that he would go to Wall Street after his Master of Arts in Law and Diplomacy and make a fortune in merchant banking, while she lived an aesthetic life. When he chose, instead, to undertake a PhD in philosophy at Harvard, she went her own way, later marrying a bond trader by the name of Bruno Herman. So, I think 'N. Herman', writing from a cottage in Poughkeepsie, New York (where Vassar College is located) was, initially, as fate would have it, *Nathalie* Herman nee Morton. She had ended up by sheer coincidence becoming the editor of the private journal Fenimore had intended for another woman altogether and the teller of the horrific story of what had happened to Fenimore and all his circle. I pictured her as a sort of Mary McCarthy figure and was unsure of her attitude toward Fenimore (or Bruno) by the time the editing took place. After all, thirty years had passed since she and Fenimore had shared a romantic summer, travelled the Veneto and then gone their separate ways.

As I pondered these questions, a fresh insight came to me. Wasn't it possible that *Darkness over Love* was 'a complete fiction' not because I, the author, say so; but because N. Herman had *made up the whole story herself?* This turned the idea that she was 'really' Nathalie Morton on its head. In reality, as it were, Nathalie Morton was a character in a story made up by N. Herman, of Poughkeepsie, New York. This would mean that the overall architecture of the book would now become a story written by a man (me) about a woman (N. Herman) who makes up a story about a woman (Bianca) who brings her a manuscript prepared by a man (Tom) based (supposedly) on the private Notebooks of an intimate friend of his (Fenimore), who had addressed them exclusively to a woman he loved (Margarita). This looked like enormous fun and a splendid challenge; but could it all hang together? Could it work as a narrative structure? By the beginning of December 2013, I had persuaded myself that, in principle, it could—and that this new structure was a great deal more promising and intriguing than any of the story-lines I had had before—insofar as I had had one at all.

The problem, of course, was that I now had a great many more 'moving parts' to coordinate and yet I had still to resolve the problem of how to write the core story in a readable and engaging manner. The second of these problems will be an exacting process that will take a lot of time, patience, creativity and discipline yet. There can be no doubt about that. The first one, on the other hand, resolved itself or has been resolving itself with surprising facility.

The great advantage of having 'complicated' the narrative in this manner is that it has given me more and more and then again more critical perspective on and narrative distance from the character at the heart of the story, Fenimore Moneghan. He had originally (as the first draft anonymous narrator and then as Frederick Beresford in the second draft) been altogether too close to the autobiographical bone. Now others were editing his work, commenting on his work, had participated in his work, were telling the story from their different angles. The sense of liberation this gave me from myself and within the narrative was unmistakable. I felt, at last, that I had some real *leverage* in moving the story along. It had become 'dialogical' in Mikhail Bakhtin's sense and this set it free to become literature.[28]

The second notable gain from these breakthrough developments (what I have loosely called the fifth draft, of late 2013) was that, for the first time, I found myself actually *laughing* (with amusement, joy and fascination) at the twists and turns in the plot, the dark ironies in the way things turn out, the manner in which my characters had serious and thoughtful perspectives on what was happening in their worlds, but failed utterly (each in their own way) to foresee the consequences of their own actions. It wasn't that all these things were comical in a merely slapstick manner. That was not my intention. Rather, it was that the story had really taken on a life of its own that had nothing specifically to do with my life and was making it possible for my imagination to play with the realm of possibilities, the logic of action, the whole box and dice of thought, intention, confusion and consequences with which dramatic literature is concerned. I was liberated, in other words, from the straitjacket of my personal credibility and preoccupations. Instead, I had catapulted myself into a kind of conversation with the reader about the antics, pathos and relationships of a whole cast of imaginary characters that had sprung to life. Where had they come from? Well, that is *the* question regarding the creative process, isn't it?

A third and very concrete gain from all this was that the working out of how the conspiracy theories arose and impinged on the fates of the core, meditative characters enabled me to do

---

28   Mikhail Bakhtin (1896-1975) was a remarkable Russian literary critic who somehow survived the Lenin and Stalin catastrophe, in which so many creative figures perished, and still managed to write works of originality and insight that have endured. The key books bearing on the idea of the 'dialogical' are *Problems of Dostoevsky's Poetics: Polyphony and Unfinalizability* and a set of four essays on the theory of the novel published under the title *The Dialogic Imagination: Chronotope, Heteroglossia*. I first read Bakhtin's work as an undergraduate student of modern history. The fruitfulness and insightfulness of his ideas only really struck home to me decades later, as I attempted to write serious literature myself and had to find my way to the kinds of polyphony and 'heteroglossia' that were required of dialogical writing – that is to say, writing in which more than one voice and perspective can be discerned.

what the great Latin poet and friend of Virgil, Horace, had long ago declared must be done in an epic: start the story *in medias res*—in the middle of the action. Neither Homer nor Virgil begins from a sedate start and slowly works his way through a story chronologically to its conclusion. Rather, they plunge us into the scene of action and then, at intervals, while slowly approaching the denouement of their stories, take us back to earlier episodes to fill in the *back* story and keep us engaged by variety and reflection. This is, quite literally, classic story-telling. Not all novelists proceed this way, of course, but variations on the theme are surprisingly common. Whether in terms of a dramatic, perhaps violent act, a crucial scene setting or the retrospective recollection by a narrator of some event that calls for a retelling of the story in question, a great many novels do this. They do it in order to seize the reader's attention from the outset and justify the recounting of the detailed, often meandering story that follows.

In short, after five years of writing, pondering, revision, despondency, invention, travel and further revision, I have finally come up with what seem to be the elements of a possible story. It is, I would like to believe, a story that might hold the reader's attention, that would be genuinely original and creative and that would be sufficiently free from the detritus of my own life that I could play around within it with a clear conscience and in a genuinely ludic mood. I now have a full and engaging cast of characters, a rather original narrative structure, a mass of incident, a world full of colour and poetry; and it is all my own to play with. This will not be merely the retelling of some familiar fable or the imitation of some classic. This will be a story that has never yet been written. It will also be a story that will enable me to work with all the concerns I have had for many years and to make something out of them with my own hands. It will be a story that will enable me to emulate Fernando Pessoa and generate my own literature and my own circle of intellectual friends. It will be a story that will enable me to become my own Homer and Virgil. It will be a story that, with its poetic spirit will evoke Ovid and with the Irish-sounding name of its central character, will enable me to create my own *Ulysses.*

In sum, it finally looks as though, in both design and content, if completed, it could take its place as a true original—as my Work, in Roland Barthes' sense. It is now, most definitely, the Book on the horizon. Of course, assuming it gets published as the novel I am preparing, it would inevitably be subjected to all manner of critical interpretations. I could not resist, therefore, given the narrative latitude for doing so, the temptation of *pre-empting* at least some of them. The vehicle for doing this readily presented itself. As the editor of the commercial edition of the private version of Fenimore's Notebooks prepared by Tom Emerson, N. Herman had the latitude to comment on what it all means—especially, of course, if she had made up the whole thing herself from start to finish. She does this, I realized, in a Postscript to the book. Not only does she naturally have some thoughts of her own along these lines, but insofar as she is (secretly) the actual author of the entire thing, she decides to toy with her readers and add a whole ludic element to her creative fiction. One of her devices is to point out that she sent the pre-publication galley-proofs out to a number of scholars to gauge their responses both to the Notebooks and to the 'true story' that had enveloped them. This turned out to be a delightful exercise all on its own, in ways that, as with so much else, I had neither planned nor foreseen.

It transpired that, among the people to whom she sent the galley-proofs, was a literary scholar in California, called Lilith Zohar. That was a little bit of mischief all on its own. The Zohar is a foundational text of Kabbalistic (or Cabbalistic) thought. According to medieval Jewish tales, rooted in ancient Babylonian myths; Lilith was first wife of Adam, before the creation of Eve from one of Adam's ribs. She left Adam, refusing to become subservient to him, and mated with the Archangel Samael. Lilith responds by telling Herman that she intends to convene a conference the following year on the whole subject of Moneghan's writings, their meaning and the significance of the violence they have generated, as well as his mysterious disappearance and apparent death. Abstracts for papers have been pouring in and a common theme is the Cabbalistic interpretation of the Notebooks or Tom's editing of them; as well as reflections on the 'death of the author'. This Postscript definitely has a future, I think. A refined—but not necessarily final—version of it is included in this volume. It is, without doubt, the most 'Pessoan' part of the novel.

Consistent with this crowning touch to the narrative structure, I invented a little dedication to the book by N. Herman. This is a detail that is likely to be overlooked entirely by most readers; while even those who notice it will almost certainly fail to realize its significance. It is written in Italian and reads:

Una piccola storia per il mio mostro, Bruno, che si è macchiato di tale delitto

Since few readers will be able to understand Italian, the meaning of this will elude them. Even those who do are unlikely to translate it with sufficient subtlety to see what it points to. Its correct translation is:

A little story for my monster, Bruno, who has made such a killing

It is written in Italian, because he, Bruno, is a second generation Italian American. He has made a killing in the idiomatic sense that he has made a pile of money. She has written this 'little story' ostensibly to entertain him. But, of course, given how wily she is in the whole creative exercise, one would be unwise to assume that she means this in any simple, obvious or self-deprecating sense. In fact, my most secret idea of all is that she has written the whole thing as a kind of warning to her 'monster' Bruno that she is Lilith and may well desert him in his Garden, despite the 'killing' he has made, because there is a freer and more interesting life elsewhere—teaching art and classics at New York University and writing imaginative fiction, for example; while keeping a comfortable country getaway up in Poughkeepsie, not far from Vassar College, where she did her college degree in fine art many years before. That, at least, is how the story emerged for me as I played more and more with its elements and their possibilities. There! You are in on the secret.

Mimesis and reality

As I have remarked in passing several times, a question that I have pondered for many years and which deeply concerns Fenimore is the ancient philosophical question of the relationship between truth and fiction; between reality and interpretation; between what is so and what the poets say about it; between what is true about the world and the nonsense and superstition that fill human heads. This concern hobbled me in attempting to write a novel, at least to begin with. I had a bad conscience about making things up; not least making things up about myself. And, well before I realized that Margarita Henderson y Mendoza was a music therapist who ran a company called Capirote Therapies in the Canary Islands, I had imagined M or Margarita, the narrator's Muse, as challenging him to write a novel instead of a serious philosophical treatise about truth and civilization. After all, she taunted him, even supposing you can pin down 'the Truth' in some universal, objective sense, what on Earth would you expect people to *do* with it? People live inside stories and you have to give them a new story that they can live inside; one that will engage their imaginations, she argued.

That idea was at work, at least inchoately, in the early drafts. Then, rather fantastically, I discovered that Margarita's real calling was *song*, rather than novel writing. I think the root of this idea was a book I read in 2005 by Stephen Mithen. It is called *The Singing Neanderthals: The Origins of Music, Language, Mind and Body*. He argued that a kind of singing antedated grammatical speech. It is a fascinating book. But it was only when (or perhaps some considerable time after) I read the work of Daniel Levitin, that Margarita's true vocation began to dawn on me.[29] That gave a novel twist to the story, as it were. Arising from several sources, it enabled me to make sense of the fact that the narrator, from the outset,

---

29   Daniel Levitin *This is Your Brain on Music: The Science of a Human Obsession*, Dutton, New York, 2006; and *The World in Six Songs: How the Musical Brain Created Human Nature*, Dutton, New York, 2008. My own note, inside the cover of the latter, states that I bought it on 17 September 2008 to help with "composing *Letters to my Muse*". It isn't clear, however, that I read it at once. What is striking is that it came to my attention so very early in the evolutionary process and that in jotting down that note I referred to the manuscript or idea for a Work not as *Darkness over Love*, but simply as *Letters to my Muse*. That particular book, partly for this reason, has found a unique place in the story, as related by Tom Emerson in his Appendix B.

wrote poems for Margarita and eventually songs. It gave an added nuance to the tension both in their relationship and in Fenimore's thinking about what he was doing. When I further stumbled upon the theme of the work of hands and the shaped gift, the question of the Notebooks was solved and I no longer needed to trouble myself so much about whether or not Fenimore was writing a novel. Eventually, of course, the miraculously mischievous N. Herman took over that role from him. All this freed me up enormously to play—in all seriousness—with the matter of truth and fiction. N. Herman's Postscript exhibits that playfulness at its very best, I believe.

Yet both as an author and as a human being, I remain deeply fascinated by the philosophical questions mentioned above. How is it that, as conscious beings and language animals, we *make sense* of the world and of ourselves? How do we *represent reality* in such a way that we can effectively grapple with it? What is the role of art and poetry, or fiction generally in that process? These questions have puzzled the most intelligent and reflective human beings for thousands of years and not least in the modern world, as scientific knowledge has grown enormously— though popular confusion seems hardly to have diminished. It remained a central part of my purpose, as all the developments described above gradually unfolded, to use the novel as a means for exploring these questions. The challenge, as Margarita had seen from the outset, was how to do so in such a way that the book would be readable and even enchanting to as many literate people as possible—and, at a pinch, even as something that might be read aloud to those who were actually *not* literate - in the ancient, almost pre-Homeric manner!

During my 'sabbatical', in 2012, one of the many books I deliberately took the time to read, for reasons that should be obvious in the light of this essay, if not otherwise, was Herman Broch's novel *The Death of Virgil* (1945). It is a long, modernist novel, which features many passages of 'stream-of-consciousness' prose that are barely intelligible. It is a challenge to read and yet a boldly experimental attempt to come to terms with two things: the state of mind of the great poet on his death-bed, despairing that, at the age of 50, he has not completed his planned masterpiece as he had hoped; and a sceptical reflection by Broch himself on the very nature and utility of poetry or of fiction in general, including his own.

Very early in the novel, Broch has Virgil agonizing over this second question:

Nothing availed the poet, he could right no wrongs; he is heeded only if he extols the world, never if he portrays it as it is. Only falsehood wins renown, not understanding! And could one assume that <u>The Aeneid</u> would be vouchsafed another or better influence? Oh yes, people would praise it because as yet everything he had written had been praised, because only the agreeable things would be abstracted from it, and because there was neither danger nor hope that the exhortations would be heeded; ah, he was forbidden either to delude himself or to permit himself to be deluded...

Thinking this way can inhibit even the attempt to write poetry or fiction. It did do so, in my case, for many years. But I found myself irresistibly drawn to the challenge, despite my misgivings and the discovery of my shortcomings as a writer.

On reflection, I believe there were two main reasons for this. Both have to do with the paradoxically clarifying effects of writing or attempting to write fiction: it throws into ever sharper relief the relationship between truth and fiction; and it compels the author to see himself and his cast of mind and limitations reflected in the fiction that he writes. It is my opinion that these two features of the process of writing have been at the heart of the matter since writing systems were first invented and that they are the chief reasons why good writing, even more than good reading, is "consciousness-raising", in Walter Ong's sense. In my sabbatical year, reading Ong's *Orality and Literacy*, I was struck by his remark—so obviously true of what I had been engaged in attempting—that:

> *Writing is a solipsistic operation. I am writing a book which I hope will be read by hundreds of thousands of people, so I must be isolated from everyone...*

This is the paradox one experiences in attempting to write a serious novel, but at the end of the day, perhaps, any book. If you are attempting, as I am, to write a book that would somehow sum up and mimetically master reality, this is even more so. The solipsistic nature of the exercise can induce an acute sense of vertigo and eccentricity. That alone makes progress difficult.

Of course, I began by trying to off-load the solipsism, as it were, onto an avatar of myself, a narrator, who was writing letters or what became notebooks. This, however, as Ong was well aware, only brought out all the more clearly the curious epistemological and psychological contortions that are entailed in undertaking such an exercise:

> *Even in a personal diary addressed to myself I must fictionalize the addressee. Indeed, the diary demands in a way the maximum fictionalizing of the utterer and the addressee. Writing is always a kind of imitation talking, and in a diary I am therefore pretending that I am talking to myself. But I never really talk this way to myself; nor could I without writing, or indeed without print. The personal diary is a very late literary form, in effect unknown until the seventeenth century. The kind of verbalized solipsistic reveries it implies are a product of consciousness as shaped by print culture. And for which self am I writing? Myself today? As I think I will be in ten years from now? As I hope I will be? For myself as I imagine myself or hope others may imagine me? Questions such as this can and do fill diaries with anxieties and often enough lead to discontinuation of diaries. The diarist can no longer live with his or her fiction.*

This last line mirrors, of course, exactly and by no coincidence, the denouement I have in mind for the romance between Fenimore and Margarita. She tells him outside the Teatro Cervantes, in the second last chapter, "*I can no longer sustain this fiction.*" That is rendered all the more charming by the possibility that the whole story of their romance has been made up from start to finish by N. Herman and is, therefore, 'a complete fiction'. It was a necessary stratagem on my part, however, to be able to step back from the fiction and take stock of what I am doing with it.

I found Ong's work endlessly instructive as I wrestled with the most basic problems of narrative structure, narrative style and dialogue between imaginary characters. As he wrote, some thirty years ago:

> The way in which readers are fictionalized is the underside of literary history, of which the topside is the history of genres and the handling of character and plot. Early writing provides the reader with conspicuous help for situating himself imaginatively. It presents philosophical material in dialogues, such as those of Plato's Socrates, which the reader can imagine himself overhearing. Or episodes are to be imagined as told to a live audience on successive days. Later, in the Middle Ages, writing will present philosophical and theological texts in objection-response form, so that the reader can imagine an oral disputation. Boccaccio and Chaucer will provide the reader with fictional groups of men and women telling stories to one another, that is a 'frame story', so that the reader can pretend to be one of the listening company. But who is talking to whom in <u>Pride and Prejudice</u> or in <u>Le Rouge et le Noir</u>, or in <u>Adam Bede</u>? Nineteenth century novelists self-consciously intone 'dear reader', over and over again to remind themselves that they are not telling a story but writing one in which both author and reader are having difficulty situating themselves...

I have made my own attempt to solve this problem by inventing the elaborate, multi-layered narrative structure that takes the reader into a labyrinth in which truth and fiction are refracted through at least three different prisms. This leaves the problem of interpretation of the fiction and immersion in the 'reality' of the story quite *novel* and, I hope, charming in its aesthetic rigour.

In pursuit of this vision, in April and May 2014, I undertook, as noted above, a journey to a number of the locations central to the narrative as it was emerging ever more clearly: Austin, where Tom Emerson dwells in his walled estate of Treehaven; Harvard University, where the Academy of Lynxes fellows met long ago, to find out where they had lived, studied, met for coffees and taken strolls; Venice and the Veneto to see them with the youthful eyes of Fenimore and Nathalie; Sabbioneta, to find the Villa Barberini and imagine its awful destruction in the northern summer of 2014; and finally Santorini, where Fenimore flees, in desolation, grieving at the loss of Margarita, filled with memories of the exotic Cleis Scamandros, whom he has met in Istanbul, and pondering the gigantic volcanic caldera that gives the ancient island its character and which lies at the very root of the Platonic legend of the downfall of Atlantis. He does so unaware that a kind of volcanic eruption is going on *within* him even as he gazes out to sea: the aggressive metastasis of a cancer that will, apparently, kill him—or would have done so, had he not pre-empted it by, as he expresses it in his final line, embarking on *Aletheia* and going where *Nun* (the ancient Egyptian god of the ocean) will find him.

One of the most striking places I visited while on that journey was the Palazzo Te, just outside Mantova, (the Mantua of classical Italy and the birthplace of Virgil), in Lombardy. The Palazzo Te was designed and its construction and interior decoration supervised by Giulio Romano, the greatest pupil of Raphael and a contemporary of Andrea Palladio, in the mid-sixteenth century. It was built for the Gonzagas, the aristocratic dynasty that ruled Mantua from the early fourteenth century until the beginning of the eighteenth. It is quite 'Palladian' in its symmetry and the human scale of its design. Its interior walls are covered in an astounding variety of frescoes evoking the great legends of classical Greece and the histories of Italy. As I contemplated its design, with its successive gardens, its rounding colonnade and its secret grotto, it struck me that what I was constructing as the architecture of the novel had something of the same character. I hope that this book, which is intended to exhibit and foreshadow the completion of the novel, will show you that this is so and impress you architecturally, as the Palazzo Te impressed me.

The most obvious manner in which I have set out to make the novel resemble the Palazzo Te or a Palladian villa is by having Fenimore write the whole of his Notebooks in what Tom dubs 'octavos'—uniform eight line paragraphs. None of the early drafts so much as hinted at this. It was an idea that occurred to me only when I was in northern Italy in the northern spring of this year. It is, of course, wholly consistent with the central idea of the Notebooks being a hand crafted gift on Fenimore's part, but it is an idea distinctive in itself and in need of at least a little explanation. While Tom speculates at one point that Fenimore's stylistic conceit might possibly have been intended to make the Notebooks as a whole into a kind of epic philosophical poem linking his work all the way back to the first great philosopher in the Western tradition and one of the most famous of the Pre-Socratics, Parmenides; he finds no direct evidence for this claim in Fenimore's own words.

We know from internal evidence that Fenimore was at work on a philosophical treatise of a serious kind and that the Notebooks were quite separate from it—or at least both Tom and N. Herman tell us so. The problem is that we cannot be quite certain we can rely on the testimony of either of them, for different reasons. In any case, the internal evidence of the Notebooks implies that it is not only Parmenides who provides a possible antecedent for Fenimore writing an 'epic poem'. In Notebooks I and II (though it is not evident in this version of the story, to be sure), it becomes clear that Fenimore's view of reality is strongly 'materialist' and that he sees the famous philosophical poem *De Rerum Natura* (On the Nature of Things) by the 1st century BCE Roman poet Lucretius as a precursor to what he is doing philosophically—dispelling superstition and setting out the nature of things for the confused and misguided. And Lucretius was an Epicurean, committing to verse the atomism of Democritus and Epicurus, who had developed their ideas as a critique of the cosmology of Parmenides.

Neither Parmenides nor Lucretius, however, wrote in octavos. Nor did any of the other epic poets alluded to in the Notebooks, most obviously Homer, whose presence is signalled from the beginning of the Prologue with the references to Tom's book and Fenimore's reflection that one of the passages from *The Odyssey* cited by Tom seems to him to prefigure what he himself is doing. The octavos are, in other words, an original device for the composition of a prose poem and Fenimore at no point explains why he adopted this particular form. The use of it, however, imposes a poetic structure and discipline on his prose and, even more clearly, an architectural style on the appearance of the Notebooks. This is accentuated by the fact that every section of the Notebooks has exactly sixty such paragraphs and that the Notebooks have an internal symmetry: a Prologue offset by an Epilogue, three Parts and eight sections in each Part. As Tom remarks, it seems inconceivable that all this can have been written in long hand with a fountain pen without very careful drafting. Yet he could find no draft manuscripts or signs of correction within the Notebooks.

The effect of all this, I hope, if I can successfully write the rest of the Notebooks as I have planned, should be aesthetically very striking in its own right. In reworking the early drafts into this form, even for the present volume, I have found that it imposes a delightful discipline on the use of language in just the manner than writing poetry does. Each paragraph, each octavo, becomes like a stanza and the sixty have to balance and complete the part of the story that is at stake in each section of the novel. I've been very pleased so far with the improvements that this has brought to the pre-existing prose. Whether readers will delight in it or find it tedious remains to be seen. Certainly, one of the things it does is inhibit the creation of standard realist dialogue between characters. But given that Fenimore is writing reflections intended as an object of art for Margarita's contemplation, this does not seem to me to be a serious objection. The challenge is to keep the octavos themselves and the book, section by section, sufficiently colourful, engaging and varied that readers are drawn deeper and deeper into it on its own terms.

Proust and the Cave Simile

Architecture is one thing, but the writing of narrative prose is another. Perhaps because Roland Barthes had described Marcel Proust as the last of the great writers fully embedded in the literary tradition, I decided late last year finally to read Proust's legendary masterpiece *In Search of Lost Time*. I grew up knowing this famous novel as *Remembrance of Things Past* and as 'the greatest novel never read'. Its sheer length tends to be inhibiting: six volumes and a total of some 4,650 pages in the best English translation.[30] Who, these days, has the stamina to read so much? How did Proust, a man plagued by ill health chiefly to do with his lungs, ever find the stamina to write it?[31] Besides, Proust's prose is 'notorious' for its inordinately long sentences and lack of any evident story line, other than the narrator's recollections of his past and aspirations to become a writer. This last theme is, of course, a delicious irony in the whole Work; not least because at the end of the sixth volume the narrator, actually called Marcel, concludes that he finally feels ready to *start* writing his novel.

However, as the architecture of my novel fell into place, I decided at last to read Proust's masterpiece. I have, as of this writing, reached the middle of volume three and from the very start of the first volume I have been astounded and enchanted by his prose. When Barthes wrote, in 1979, citing Mallarmé, that literary prose is, in fact, poetry and that without the poetry it becomes bland 'universal reportage', he clearly had Proust in mind, perhaps more than any other writer, as the exemplar of such deeply poetic prose. The subtlety, variety and expressiveness of Proust's writing continually takes my breath away. Again and again, I find myself wondering, how did a man afflicted by acute asthma and increasingly confined to his bed in his later adult life, find the emotional and physical energy to write this astonishing epic of poetic prose? How did a man chronically short of breath—a condition that finally put an end to his life when he was not much more than 50 years of age (like Virgil)—conceive of and repeat to himself finely constructed and eloquent sentences that often run to fifteen, twenty or even thirty lines?

Whereas reading the long, but not nearly as long novels of the Marquis de Sade quickly becomes boring and grotesque, the master work of Proust is endlessly enriching, astonishing and absorbing. If this was, as Barthes would have it, the last hurrah of the great literary tradition,

---

30   Marcel Proust *In Search of Lost Time*, 6 volumes, translated by C. K. Scott Moncrieff and Terence Kilmartin and revised by D. J. Enright, the Modern Library, New York, 2003.

31   After writing a number of things in which the development of his ideas can be traced in the 1890s and 1900s, he began work on what was to become *In Search of Lost Time* in about 1908. The first volume, *Swann's Way*, was published in 1913. The second volume, *Within a Budding Grove*, was published in 1919, the First World War perhaps having delayed its appearance. That volume won him great acclaim, including the prestigious Prix Goncourt, France's top literary award. The third volume, *The Guermantes Way*, followed in 1920; the fourth, *Sodom and Gomorrah*, a year later, suggesting that they had all been banked up awaiting editing by the end of the War. The fifth and sixth volumes (*The Captive* and *The Fugitive*, followed by *Time Regained*) did not appear until after his death. He died at just past the age of 50, like Virgil, in late 1922. The remaining parts of his work appeared in 1923, 1925 and 1927. In all probability, therefore, he had written some 4,500 publishable pages in the space of not much more than ten years from 1908 – a prodigious achievement by any measure.

then it was a climax well worthy of the entire tradition going back to the classics of the ancient world. There have, of course, been countless novels since, and one could make a case that the best of them, including the novels of Joyce, Mann, Broch, Hesse, Garcia Marquez and Vargas Llosa, to name only half a dozen, still belong in the great tradition. There is, however, a whole other way to look at the situation; one still consistent with the core insights or claims of Mallarmé and Barthes. That is to see the four and a half thousand pages of *In Search of Lost Time* as the lineal descendant, over thirty thousand years and more, of the paintings in the Chauvet Cave and to feel stunned at the immense progress in the human capacity to generate meaning using signs. This is what Nabokov, as much as Mallarmé or Barthes, had in mind; and the lack of astonishment at which he lamented in *Pale Fire*.

That is what interests me more as both a writer and a thinker than the academic question of whether anyone after Proust rose to an acceptable standard. It is what induces Fenimore Moneghan to reproduce those very Ice Age paintings in his Hall of Frescoes at Cos and to have depicted on the ceiling above them a set of images of the life cycle of the Earth itself and the legendary, but perfectly real, Pleiades constellation, set against the brilliance of deep space. At Cos, as if emulating the remarks of Barthes, he sought to pull the entire continuum of culture toward himself, as into the sea at high tide. You will see the extent to which this is true within the pages of this book. The plan is to articulate it with as much poetic prose as I can generate in the months and possibly the years ahead. Proust is an inspiration in that respect, but the challenge is to create a narrative style of my own and the elements of that have begun to emerge in the past few months. Ultimately, I would like to create a literary work of art that has the architectural beauty of a Palladian villa or of the Palazzo Te, with a prose that has the same kind of linguistic and imaginative impact on readers—whoever they might be—as Virgil has long had and as Proust has had for those who take the time to immerse themselves in his great novel.

Being and Time

Why would I aspire to something so apparently unattainable? During my sabbatical year, I read a remarkable book by Wade Davis called *Into the Silence: The Great War, Mallory and the Conquest of Everest.* It is the true story of the attempt by George Mallory and various companions to scale Everest in 1921, partly as a way of trying to transcend the horror and personal losses of the First World War. They did not succeed. Having failed at the first attempt, they returned to try again, in 1922, and only reluctantly accepted the advice that they use oxygen masks at the upper levels of the huge mountain. They failed again, though they got higher. Undaunted, they returned for a third attempt, in 1924. After a monumental effort, most of the team waited at the highest base camp, while Mallory and a young protégé by the name of Sandy Irvine attempted to reach the summit. They seem to have got to within 800 feet of their goal, but then fell to their deaths. The mountain would not be conquered for another thirty years and the bodies of Mallory and Irvine would not be recovered until the early years of the present century. I at once conceived the idea that attempting what I have set out to do is tantamount to attempting to scale a literary Everest and that Mallory was a figure to admire and to emulate.

Does that mean I expect to fail and to die without attaining my goal? Given the scope of the project as well as my health problems over the past decade, those possibilities can hardly be denied. Indeed, they are surely, on the balance of probabilities, more likely than the chance that I will succeed. Yet we admire Mallory for what he attempted and for how close he got to his goal. Many, of course, could not comprehend why he and his companions would attempt so perilous and improbable a venture. Among them was the Dalai Lama. Likewise with what I am attempting—except that Mallory had a world-wide audience for his epic venture, whereas mine is known only to a small circle of friends and may remain so. Nonetheless, I feel more inclined than at any point since my project began to try to press on to the summit and I see this volume as my base camp thousands of feet up the Himalayas, but still many thousands below the pinnacle that I can see in the distance. The further I have gone, the more I have felt that this project is what my whole life is about. It is an existential project and, whether I succeed finally or die trying, it means more to me now than anything else that it is within my means to attempt.

This is less a matter of eccentric obsession than of philosophical conviction. I remarked earlier that, as part of the preparation for the novel, two years ago, I studied Martin Heidegger's *Being and Time*. For all of Heidegger's errors of judgement and offences against moral rectitude in enthusiastically joining the Nazi Party in 1933 and endorsing the purge of Jews from the universities—including that of his mentor Edmund Husserl—he wrote a fascinating and thought provoking book in the late 1920s, in which the central idea was that, as conscious beings, our existence is defined by the fact that, from the time we are born we are *thrown towards death*. The response of most people, he argued, is to shut their eyes to this, to seek distractions or to cling to beliefs that flatly deny the reality of our personal finitude. The authentic human being, he argued, looking this existential reality in the face, finds that if viewed straight on it gives life its savour and urgency. He declared that the important thing, if you wanted to be both authentic and fully alive, is to *make a creative project of your life*. It might readily be objected that this is rather difficult for a good many people, except in a comparatively mundane sense. Yet it seems available to me. Should I not take the option?

This book, or more precisely, the Work that it points to, *is* my existential project. Given that I am thrown towards death and could at any time be precipitated towards my actual physical demise, the project takes on growing meaning and urgency as time passes. My thinking, my reading, my travels, my attempt to control my time and bring as much energy and commitment to this project as I can are all governed by this. But it goes deeper. Ever since I read about the Chauvet Cave I have been seized of the fact that the paintings there were created with no inkling that our civilization would ever come into existence; were looked upon thousands of years later by a boy who had no inkling who painted them; and then were sealed up and seen by no-one at all for more than 25,000 years. Yet they were there. They were *there*, irrespective of the fact that no-one knew of them for that humanly enormous period of time—*a thousand generations*. They were a reality in the cosmic scheme of things, as the great beasts of the remote past, long since extinct and reduced to a few fossils, were and *remain* a cosmic reality. So, I thought, will be what I write, regardless of its fate in the marketplace. That is a motivation, a point of view, utterly at variance with the standard notion that one writes to entertain a passing multitude of contemporary common readers. Just possibly, I shall succeed in doing both, but my priority is to paint my own Chauvet Cave.

Conclusion

It remains only to say that what you will see in this book does not include all the hundreds of pages of material that went into the early drafts. That material has been archived and very little of it will survive in the finished story. It has served its purpose. It has enabled me to conduct trials and experiments, to make mistakes and false starts; to invent characters and then reinvent or abolish them; to draft scenes, compose poems and songs and fables; but above all to put enough down on paper that I could see how radically it needed rethinking, reordering, revision, improvement and better dramatization. Little by little now, perhaps accelerating as I find my rhythm and grow in assurance, I intend to fill in the gaps that the following design still leaves: to colour the rooms with frescoes, as it were, and to fill them with Renaissance furniture and musical instruments and all the appurtenances of a complete fiction. If you have enjoyed this essay and if you find the design that constitutes the remainder of this book fascinating, you will, I feel sure, wish me luck as I set out on the next stage of the ascent up the literary Everest.

As you can see, the Dramatis Personae at the beginning of this volume includes quite a cast of characters. Yet only a small number of those characters appear in the parts of the book included in this volume. The key personalities—N. Herman, Tom Emerson, Fenimore Moneghan and Margarita Henderson y Mendoza—are firmly in place. There are brief references to a few of the others, such as Bianca Ruggiero, Irad Kripke, Mr Bojangles, Ariel

Kurzweil and Donald 'Tarski' Finch, and there is the cameo role of Cardinal Roberto Bolzano, through the text of his long letter to the Pope, in Appendix D; but almost all the others remain names only at this stage. They will enter the stage in Part I, for the most part, as Cos comes to life, the team at Peripatetica Decision Architects is shown at work and the back story about the Academy of Lynxes is sketched in. All that is still to come and will, I hope, get written in the course of 2015. I am especially eager to write the section of Part I called 'Cave Paintings', about the Hall of Frescoes. And, of course, there is a great deal awaiting us in Part II, in which life on Earth itself is explored against the backdrop of the shorting, by Iced Rowanberry Investments, of Wall Street in the lead-up to the financial crisis of 2008.

Will anything that has been committed to hard copy in this volume be revised as I continue working on *Darkness over Love: A Complete Fiction* in the months and perhaps years ahead? It is quite possible that will happen, given that the story has been evolving considerably in the twelve months during which this present form of it has taken shape. They say that there was an Ur-*Faust*, an early draft of the epic poem by Goethe, before he committed to print even the first version he was reasonably happy with; and still he kept revising it and adding to it for decades afterwards. They say that Shakespeare revised *Hamlet* several times before he died. I don't know what state *Doctor Zhivago* or *The Master and Margarita* were in after five years or how much revision Pasternak and Bulgakov engaged in in the following five years in which each worked on his masterpiece. All I know is I am very ambitious for this book of mine and that this version of it is only the first version in which I have felt enough confidence to put it between covers and in front of a few readers. Given life and health, I hope to become ever more creative and masterful in my use of language and my skill at story-telling from this point. Failing that, you will have, in this book, at least an indication of what I aspired to achieve—and so will I, come what may.

Nomikos Villas

Santorini

12 May 2014

Annex:
Successive Cover Images of the Early Manuscripts

Interior of Bluebeard's castle from the Bartok opera
2009-12, (First and second drafts)

The Sombrero Galaxy from the Hubble Telescope

Interior of San Roman, Toledo
2013-14 (Fourth and fifth drafts)

Dramatis Personae

The denizens of Cos

Fenimore Moneghan – érudit and heir to an industrial fortune in plastics, the proprietor of Cos

Bo Zhangliu (Mr Bojangles) – Fenimore's aide and librarian

Othello Nyerere – the gay Tanzanian lover of Mr Bojangles and Fenimore's driver

Axel von Darmstadt ('Apollodorus of Damascus') – architect of Cos

Theo Forrest – botanist and landscape architect, designer of the exterior grounds of Cos

Denis Icmalius – craftsman of the furniture at Cos

Pablo Daley – artist, painter and interior designer, creator of the Hall of Frescoes

Ariel Kurzweil – Fenimore's technology adviser and database manager

Malvine Steinschneider – Fenimore's housekeeper and cook

Vera Burbage – thespian and impresario of the theatrical productions at Cos

Qiu Xiaoli – Chinese dissident in exile, guest of Fenimore and collaborator on the China project

Margarita's circle

Margarita Henderson y Mendoza – music therapist with a business called Capirote Therapies based at Tenerife, in the Canary Islands

Anactoria Lopez – Argentinian archaeologist and lover of Margarita

Ycario Henderson y Mendoza – oil executive and father of Margarita

Alfreda Henderson y Mendoza Gonzalez – Margarita's mother

Fernando Henderson y Mendoza – Margarita's brother who works at UBS in Zurich until the global financial crisis hits Europe and costs him his job

The staff at Peripatetica Decision Architects

Donald Finch ('Tarski') – head of research and methodologies

Eleni Tsalanidis – head of training; convenor of the conspiracy and cognition workshop

Andreas van der Heijden ('Fault') – head of software design and development

Marcus Feinstein ('the Marquis Fucking Einstein') – business development manager

Jacob Goldman – assistant to Marcus

Sarah Tonnies (Serotonin) – training assistant to Eleni

Nora Pinhas (Norepinephrine) – research assistant to Eleni

Giuseppe 'Gus' Brancusi – lead consultant

Other consultants, software engineers, support staff

The members of the Academy of Lynxes

Thomas Emerson – specialist in law and strategic studies, editor of Fenimore's notebooks

Monica Sventitsky – cosmologist and theoretical astrophysicist

Irad Kripke – doctor of medicine and founder of the hedge fund Iced Rowanberry Investments

Bianco Ruggiero – evolutionary biologist; specialist on human cranial and cerebral evolution

Poseidon Wang – environmental historian and Chinese American polymath

Suzanne Baker – professor of languages, linguistics and comparative literature

Yusuf Erdogan – Turkish archaeologist of the ancient Middle East

Amartya Menon – economist and financial analyst at the IMF

Dambisa Mbeke – historian of epidemiology and pandemics

Other characters in the tale

Cleis Scamandros – Greek heiress, friend of Yusuf Erdogan, classical scholar, specialist on the lost songs of Sappho

Andrea Tsai – friend of Fenimore's and staff member of the Taiwanese office at the Ends of the Earth

Cardinal Roberto Bolzano – official of the Vatican's Congregation for the Doctrine of the Faith, who visits Cos to investigate Fenimore's work

Catriona Campbell – Fenimore's girlfriend in his undergraduate years, whom he left behind when he went to Boston for graduate studies

Nathalie Morton – Fenimore's girlfriend at the Fletcher School, a Fine Arts graduate from Vassar College, who abandoned him to marry a banker and bond trader

Bruno Herman – the Wall St bond-trader whom Nathalie marries in place of Fenimore

Weili Wu – Fenimore's mistress in Beijing in the late 1990s, who vanishes in 1999

Father Polycarp Irons SJ – Fenimore's Jesuit teacher of Greek and Latin at St Ignatius Loyola College, at the Ends of the Earth.

Immerwahr Denker – philosopher and psychologist at Marburg and friend of Axel's

Mignon Denker – daughter of Immerwahr, eight years old in 2000, twenty three by 2015

Dante Denker – son of Immerwahr, five years old in 2000, when Fenimore visits Marburg

Giuliano Pippi – Italian interior designer and friend of Axel's

N. Herman – Poughkeepsie based editor for the New York publishing firm Brandom House, to whom Bianca Ruggiero comes after the Hezbollah raid on and destruction of the Villa Barberini and the death of Tom Emerson

Lilith Zohar – Professor of Hebrew and comparative literature, Stanford University, convenor of the 2016 conference on the life and work of Fenimore Moneghan.

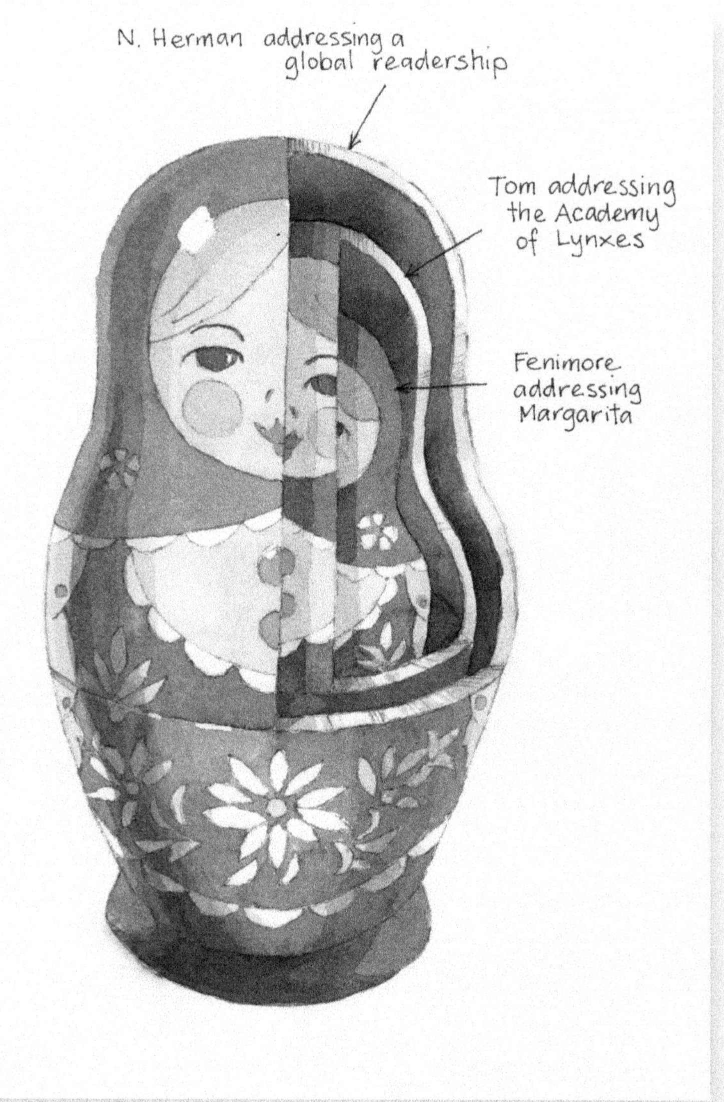

Babushka Doll.
Image by Catherine Gordon.

Book Two

The manuscript as it stands

Darkness Over Love:

The True Story of Fenimore Moneghan
and
The Amor Mundi Foundation

Edited by N. Herman

BRANDOM HOUSE

Published by We-are-the-ones-who-say-'we' Non-Fiction Press

New York and London

© 2015 Amor Mundi Foundation

Printed in the United States of America 9 8 7 6 5 4 3 2 1

The Villa Barberini as photographed by Bianca Ruggiero before the catastrophe of 2014

Una piccola storia per il mio mostro, Bruno, che si è macchiato di tale delitto

Introduction
Darkness Over Love – the True Story

That this manuscript has found its way into print at all is truly remarkable. Powerful and hidden forces strove to make that impossible. Those who had custody of it were hunted down and killed by terrorists in the midst of rampant speculation about what secrets it contained and what those custodians were plotting. As many readers will be aware, there were two dramatic terrorist incidents in Italy over the past year and a half; the first in Lombardy, the second in Rome. The first, on Midsummer Eve last year, involved a massive explosion at a rural retreat called Villa Barberini, outside the small northern Italian town of Sabbioneta, on the Po. Nine people were killed by a truck bomb, which obliterated the villa and incinerated the bodies. Among the dead were international law, counter-terrorism and strategic affairs specialist Thomas C. Emerson and a number of other members of a mysterious body called the Academy of Lynxes. In that explosion the original copy of the present manuscript, the page proofs of the first, private edition and many other papers were destroyed.

Responsibility for the attack on Villa Barberini was claimed by the so-called Party of God (Hezbollah), which issued a press release declaring that the manuscript in question was "the work of Satan" and its authors and custodians "enemies of Allah and the Prophet". Six weeks later, this publishing house was approached by a woman who appears to have been the last surviving custodian of the private edition of the manuscript, which had been printed early in the spring of last year and distributed among a very small circle of friends. She asked would we publish it, so that, as she expressed it, "there might be an end to the speculation, paranoia and terrible violence that have, without just cause, come to swirl around it." We carefully reviewed the manuscript and, after detailed discussions with her, decided that publication might well help to achieve those things. We were determined, also, to defy the terrorists, in the name of law, civil society and freedom of expression. The book you have in your hands both embodies those ideals and has been published in defence of them.

We had not long completed the page proofs, in the late fall of last year, when the second terrorist attack occurred. In broad daylight, a team of masked individuals broke into the offices of the newly established Amor Mundi Foundation on the Via dei Cappellari, Rome. As if to advertise their ruthlessness, they murdered the two security guards posted at the building in the wake of the Villa Barberini incident, then shot three Foundation staff before brutally beheading the woman who had brought this manuscript to New York: Professor Bianca Ruggiero. Having committed this atrocious deed, they placed her head on the top of her own desk and spray-painted in black letters across the wall behind her in English the slogan OCD: Operation Completely Decapitated. The significance of the initials OCD will be clear to anyone who has been following the case in the press. The reader new to it will find them explained below. Disturbing as the attack on Villa Barberini had been, this subsequent assault was even more unsettling, because no-one claimed responsibility for it.

Meanwhile, investigations by Italian police and Interpol had been unable to confidently establish the identities of all nine fatalities at Villa Barberini. Our sources inform us that they were able to identify four members of the Academy of Lynxes and a possible fifth, as well as two and possibly three catering staff who had been at the premises. Considerable speculation has been sparked about whether this means that one or even two members of the Academy survived the assault. It is understood that there had originally been nine members (other than Fenimore Moneghan), of whom Professor Ruggiero had been one. The assassins in Rome may have believed that, in killing Ruggiero, they had eliminated the last of the Academy of Lynxes. It now appears that at least one of them escaped the hit-squads, but which one is either unknown or being suppressed by the authorities. That individual is now believed to be in hiding; whereabouts unknown. We ourselves, at Brandom House, live under the shadow of these events. We have faced threats of extreme violence and have had to take extraordinary security precautions.

How has all this come about? In some ways, the manuscript itself sets the record straight and we will allow it to speak for itself. That is the point of publishing it. But we feel that it will be a public service to provide just enough of the back story for readers to appreciate what they have in their hands. For the terrible violence that has been visited upon fifteen people and two properties has only been the climax of a story that began about five years ago and has its roots much further back again. The turning point seems to have been the disappearance and presumed death, in June 2010, of the polymath and author of the original manuscript, Fenimore Moneghan. He had been at work, we understand, on a philosophical treatise of remarkable scope, which was intended to make possible a "consilient" or unified understanding of the sciences and human experience. It would, supposedly, have laid down a foundation for a future human civilization transcending all the old religions and dogmatic ideologies.

The present book is *not* that treatise, which he did not live to complete. This is vital, because much of the madness which has taken place appears to have been premised on the assumption that the present manuscript was, indeed, that controversial treatise. We make no comment here as to whether the original project was a good idea, or whether it could have succeeded in its aims. The fact is that Moneghan died before he was able to finish it. What has become of his papers remains a matter of some confusion, not least because of the destruction of the Villa Barberini and the ransacking of the Rome offices of the Amor Mundi Foundation. The death or disappearance of the entire inner circle of those best acquainted with Moneghan's work has made it exceptionally difficult for us to get to the bottom of what the Paris dailies have long since dubbed *L'Affaire Moneghan*. What we do know is that, while working on the treatise, Moneghan kept a set of personal notebooks, in which he reflected on the meaning of what he was trying to do. He seems never to have anticipated how dangerous the undertaking would prove to be to those around him.

The notebooks were not merely jottings or a purely personal meditation. They seem, in fact, to have been addressed to a mysterious woman by the name of Margarita Henderson y Mendoza, who was unknown to all Moneghan's associates. Moreover, they were *written*, not typed, according to Professor Ruggiero. Indeed, they were written with a fountain pen, using a stylized Chancery script, on very fine quality paper, in three deluxe notebooks bound in calfskin. We can only conjecture as to why their author chose to set his thoughts down in such an arcane manner. Our conversations with Professor Ruggiero and her colleagues, before they were murdered, as well as certain indications within the notebooks themselves, suggest that it was because he did not intend that they would ever be published. Rather, he intended to make a personal gift of this private, beautifully hand written three volume manuscript to Margarita when his real work, his great treatise, had been completed and published. We cannot be sure, however; because Moneghan never confided in anyone about Margarita or the notebooks while he lived – except the original editor of the manuscript, Thomas Emerson.

Emerson set down some of his thoughts on the subject in his remarks as an editor, but since he is now dead, we have been unable to inquire further as to the personal knowledge he had. We have been left, therefore, to draw our own conclusions. Moneghan may eventually have revealed the existence of Margarita and the nature of his private reflections to all his colleagues, once the treatise was completed and his public work under way. We cannot be certain. But his hand was forced by developments which violently disrupted whatever plans he had. There seems to have been a sudden and unforeseen rupture with Margarita in the late spring of 2010, early in a long journey that Moneghan had undertaken around the world. He completed that journey, then returned to his abode at the Ends of the Earth, but was taken ill. He wrote a last entry in the third of his notebooks, sent them to Thomas Emerson in Austin, then disappeared. Official inquiries declared that he was dead, but his body was never found. This immediately began to give rise to rumour and speculation, first in his own part of the world and then around the globe. All that was known with apparent certainty is that his boat had been found offshore, while he himself had vanished without trace.

The emptiness of that boat has been the subject of endless conjecture. But that conjecture was fuelled by vague awareness of what he had been working on and swirling reports that an unspecified secret manuscript had been spirited away from his dwelling by members of his circle and was being used by them as part of a vast, ambitious and shadowy project. There was, in fact, such a project: the creation of the Amor Mundi Foundation. Those killed at the Villa Barberini and on the Via dei Cappellari were all involved. It is now clear that's *why* they were killed. But to understand the nature of their project and its relationship with this manuscript, we need to take you back quite a few years – to Harvard University in the mid-1980s. It was there and then that many of the victims of these acts of violence met Fenimore Moneghan. They were all brilliant students of the modern sciences, in diverse fields. They met by chance in cafes and at lectures and privately formed a circle of philosophical friends with a convergent vision. In 1986 they decided to call themselves the Academy of Lynxes.

The original Academy of Lynxes was founded in Rome, in 1603, by a certain Federico Cesi. It was the first academy of natural sciences to exist in Italy and a seed-bed for the scientific revolution in Europe. Cesi named it after the lynx, an animal whose acute vision, he thought, symbolized the piercing observational powers that science requires. Among its early members was Galileo. In fact, he became its leading light and the other members of the Academy defended him against the Roman Inquisition, when he came under attack for having apparently defied and offended the Pope in the matter of the new cosmology. But the pioneering body did not long survive Cesi's death in 1630. It seems to have closed its doors in 1651. The name was exhumed in the 1870s, with the creation of the modern Italian nation state and the abolition of the Papal States. It became the new national academy of Italy, encouraging excellence in both the natural sciences and the liberal arts. This seems to have been what prompted the Harvard circle to use the name privately, over a century later.

Moneghan recalls this story in the first of his notebooks. We were able to check some of the details with Bianca Ruggiero and her colleagues last year. All ten of the "lynxes" completed their studies and went on to outstanding careers in different fields – ranging from economics and finance to literature, from cosmology to archaeology and from evolutionary biology to philosophy. But they kept in touch with one another, bound together by what Professor Ruggiero described to us as "the Ionian Enchantment" – the idea, dating back to the first Greek philosophers and natural scientists 2,500 years ago, that a comprehension of the integral nature of reality and of humanity's place in the cosmos is possible. They would meet at intervals; often, it seems, in New York. There they would talk, as they had in their student days, about the state of the world and the relationships between their fields of knowledge. There seems to have been little more to their association than the Ionian Enchantment throughout the 1990s. Then things changed in two ways.

Just before the turn of the century, led by one of their number called Irad Kripke, they set up a hedge fund, called Iced Rowanberry Investments (IRI). Around the same time, Moneghan, who had spent much of the 1990s working in China, announced to the others that he intended to withdraw to dwell at the Ends of the Earth and write a "guide of the perplexed in the 21st century" – a philosophical treatise of sweeping scope and ambition. These two developments do not seem to have been intended, in the beginning, to have anything to do with one another. But they converged from 2005, when Kripke analysed the sub-prime mortgage bonds that were being sold in such large quantities by Wall Street. IRI (whose advisory board consisted of all ten members of the Academy of Lynxes) decided to short the bonds. The hedge fund handled the matter adroitly and, in 2008, collected several billion dollars on its short strategy. The group then decided to use this windfall to create something they called the Amor Mundi (Love of the World) Foundation.

Plans for the setting up of the Foundation were initiated, it seems, in 2009, but were still in the early stages when Moneghan disappeared the following year. As rumours about the Foundation spread, his disappearance became the subject of ever more speculation. The other members of the circle appear to have regarded it all as obviously wrong-headed and simply ignored it. Little did they realize that they had attracted the attention of powerful interests, who were increasingly peering covertly into their philosophical world. They were being watched, it seems, as early as 2004, long before the hedge fund windfall or Moneghan's disappearance. What pushed suspicion to dark places after 2010 was the rumour that a secret manuscript existed. According to one theory that circulated on the Internet, it was a blueprint for the fulfilment of all the storied purposes long attributed to the Illuminati – a short-lived association of Enlightenment intellectuals, which has been the object of dubious "global takeover" conspiracy theories for more than a hundred years.

There *was* such a 'secret' manuscript, of course. It is the manuscript you have in your hands. But it is very different from what rumour and conspiracy theory made it seem. It was, in actual fact, the three private notebooks of Fenimore Moneghan, not his treatise and not the blueprint for a takeover by the fabled Illuminati. Thomas Emerson had the hand-written notebooks in his possession from 2010 and was quietly editing them for printing and distribution solely among the small circle of old Harvard friends – as Moneghan had apparently requested before he died. *That* is why it had been kept 'secret'. It had never been intended to become a public document – unlike the planned treatise, which Moneghan fully intended would be published and which he clearly hoped would make an enduring impact. Confusion about the relationship between the *reported* (but unwritten or at least never completed) treatise and the *unknown* (because private and personal) notebooks seems to have been the root cause of all the confusion. Emerson, who had himself done consulting work in the 'secret world' of intelligence and security, unwittingly fuelled that speculation by respecting Moneghan's privacy and taking his papers to the Villa Barberini, in late 2011.

That move, innocent and natural when you understand the true story, triggered a train of events of which Emerson himself was almost certainly unaware, right up until the time of his death. He was unaware of it because it was taking place for the most part in the shadows. In retrospect, it appears that secret surveillance was being conducted at Villa Barberini and perhaps in Rome, by more than one intelligence service. Secret memoranda were being written in the centres of power concerning the supposed purposes and work of this small circle of people. It is extraordinary to realize that, while they quietly went about their academic work and mourned the death of their friend, they were the subject of surveillance by several secret services. This became startlingly evident in late 2013, when top secret memoranda were hacked by the anarchist group Anonymous and published on-line. We have reproduced them here (in Appendix D), in order to show, by juxtaposition with the actual text of the 'secret blueprint', how utterly tangled things can become in the minds of conspiracy theorists – wherever they are in the greater scheme of things.

At the centre of all these startling and tragic developments stands the figure of Thomas Emerson. Like the billions made by IRI in 2008 and the secrecy surrounding Moneghan's writings, his work as a consultant on international security affairs, after the Islamist assault on New York in 2001, seems to have contributed to the tragic denouement to the whole story. It was to him that Moneghan turned, in the early northern summer of 2010; asking would he arrange for the printing of a private edition of his notebooks for members of the Academy. As we can see from Emerson's own Foreword to that edition (reprinted in this book), he ran into immediate problems owing to the unfinished state of Moneghan's treatise, his voluminous private papers and his considerable estate. The situation was further complicated by the claims of Moneghan's company, Peripatetica Decision Architects and Moneghan's personal staff at his compound at the Ends of the Earth. Those problems began, not surprisingly, with disputes about the fate of Moneghan himself and then about his fortune and very substantial property.

Emerson's determination to honour Moneghan's request that the notebooks remain confidential and circulation of them be confined to the members of the Academy occurred in the midst of considerable ambient tension. Brandom House was informed by Bianca Ruggiero that it was Emerson's inability to reach an understanding with Peripatetica and Moneghan's staff about the disposition of Moneghan's papers which prompted him to propose that the Academy purchase the Villa Barberini. There he moved the Moneghan archives and prepared his deluxe edition of the notebooks, giving them the title *Darkness over Love.* He explains in his own Foreword why he chose this title. In the light of what subsequently happened on account of this labour of love on his part, the very choice of title seems sadly ironical. We hope that the publication of the present book will help to dispel the forces of darkness that gathered around the incipient Amor Mundi Foundation; and even make possible a revival of its work in different hands.

The leaked memoranda and the actual manuscript, including Emerson's Foreword, Afterword, and other editorial work on the notebooks, which includes three Appendices, speak for themselves. We do not intend, therefore, to indulge in extensive editorial comment, other than this Introduction and a Postscript. The leaked memoranda, when seen together, show graphically how strangely the story morphed in the course of secret transmission and interpretation. They constituted a burning fuse that led, via Tehran and the Beka'a Valley, to the explosion at the Villa Barberini and perhaps the savage attack in Rome. We deplore those acts of violence. Our motto at Brandom House, especially here at the non-fiction press, has long been 'making it explicit'. We have attempted to honour that in this unusual and disturbing case, by publishing both the manuscript which caused so much unwarranted speculation and fear; and the series of documents which show how a conspiratorial mind-set was able to convert private and even poetic reflections into a wholly fictive global conspiracy.

Preparing this book for publication has been by turns exhilarating, exhausting and even terrifying. As an editor, I am haunted by the realization that almost everyone associated with the story told here has died under violent or mysterious circumstances, or gone into hiding. This is all the more unsettling when one considers the beauty and innocence of what the manuscript contains. Or so I have preferred to believe. Yet, as I put the finishing touches to it, I cannot suppress a reluctant sense that, in their own subtle way, these pages *are* actually explosive – if I may be forgiven that expression in the circumstances. They may not be the treatise that Moneghan hoped to write, but they do show the nature of his thinking and spell out a view of the world (including a wholly original Credo)[32] that points to what the Amor Mundi Foundation was apparently being designed to work for in the world at large. There are without doubt many powerful interests in the world that stand opposed to any such agenda.

We can also see, moreover, in a way that may actually have been obscured in a formal and philosophical treatise, not only what Moneghan had come to believe, but why he had inquired

---

32   See Appendix A, as included in the original print edition by Thomas C. Emerson. – NH.

at all and how his inquiries gave meaning to his life. Those who know little cosmology will find here, it could be said, all that they might wish to know about the cosmos and humanity's place in it. Those who have wondered what life is and how it came about on this Earth will find in these pages a luminous and coherent explanation, not in the dry language of formal science, but in the animated language of a man seeking to communicate his thinking to the woman he had come to love in a transcendent manner. It is this combination of rare erudition with poignant intimacy that we believe sets these pages apart even more than their 'explosive' philosophical message. Those qualities persuaded us that, quite apart from the inclination to defy terror in the name of freedom of expression, we should publish this book as a work of literature and thought in its own right.

It remains to say a few words about the burning fuse that led to the acts of terror which shattered the vision of the Academy of Lynxes. The Anonymous manifesto brought out into the open the secret interest of powerful organizations in Moneghan's work. In late 2013, that notorious organization released a YouTube video on the Internet denouncing what it described as the secretive creation by the CIA, in collaboration with the Vatican, of a covert operation on an unprecedented scale to undermine freedom of religion and exert control over the future not just of Western civilization, but of human civilization as a whole. It went viral and sparked or gave further oxygen to a series of extravagant conspiracy theories that swept through the web and the blogosphere like a firestorm that winter. It was the petri dish in which the terrorist plots fermented. It is a disturbing piece of work, exhibiting a thoroughly paranoid – indeed, quite unhinged - cast of mind. A transcript of the full text is reprinted, as indicated earlier, in Appendix D.

Its derivation of a conspiracy to build a new Universal Empire out of the sign over the gates at Cos as related in Cardinal Bolzano's letter to the Pope is surely proof enough of how irrational these 'hacktivists' had become by 2013. That it was accompanied by a sound track from the famous Schubert/Mahler composition 'Death and the Maiden' only makes it the more unsettling in the circumstances, especially to those of us who met Bianca Ruggiero before her horrific murder. It seems that the video was both watched and taken very seriously in Tehran by the Grand Ayatollah Ali Khamenei and his circle, then passed on to their clients in the Beka'a Valley. What has not been released into the public sphere is the actual train of thought that led to the Hezbollah decision to exterminate the Academy of Lynxes as 'servants of Satan'. But after reading the Anonymous manifesto, which leaves nothing to the imagination, it hardly seems necessary; since any number of psychotic or obsessive individuals or groups might have watched and listened to that video and then decided, based on it alone, to commit atrocious acts of violence.

The Anonymous YouTube production was preceded and partly inspired by a secret report to the Chinese Politburo. That report reads almost as strangely as the Anonymous manifesto. It was written in the summer of 2012 by a very senior officer in China's enormous state security system and addressed to the Politburo (the top leadership body or cabinet) of the Communist Party. There are suggestions that it may even have been written by then state security supremo Zhou Yongkang, or someone very close to him. Ironically, in 2013, he was himself to be accused of conspiring to stage a *coup d'état* in China in league with the flamboyant and populist Bo Xilai. In any case, the report reprinted here was the leading piece in a trio of documents illicitly obtained by Anonymous from the bowels of the American intelligence system, in the fall of 2013. The Foreign Ministry in Beijing at once denounced it as a fraud and a slander and suggested it was part of a CIA plot to weaken the Chinese government. As it happens, the report itself is full of just such claims and testifies to a mindset deeply infected with paranoia and conspiracy theory. It also reveals that the Chinese intelligence services had been spying on Moneghan and his associates for years beforehand.

The text reproduced in Appendix D is, of course, the Anonymous version of a CIA translation of a Chinese response to a CIA commentary on a secret Vatican document originally written in Latin. However, China specialists we spoke with at Columbia University assured us that the text of the Chinese report has the ring of authenticity. They showed us that it uses language common to many such documents that have come out over the years and bears a considerable similarity to leaked Chinese state security documents from the time of the Tiananmen massacre of 1989. In a strange process of circularity, it appears that a Chinese mole inside the CIA had supplied his handler with a copy of the Agency's spring 2012 cable about *L'Affaire Moneghan*, attached to a copy of Cardinal Bolzano's letter to the Pope, only for these same two documents – now marked up by at least one Chinese hand – and accompanied by a copy of the memo to the Politburo, to be leaked *back* to the CIA from one of its moles inside the *Chinese* state apparatus.

No-one has disclosed who that mole was, although press stories in the second half of 2012 reported that a CIA mole at a very high level within a top think tank of China's Ministry of State Security had been arrested in Beijing. It may have been that mole, since executed, in all probability, who supplied the CIA with the report. It may, however, have been another mole within the Ministry of State Security, one of the members of the Politburo itself, or perhaps a trusted aide or family member of one of them. The recent large-scale purges and disturbances in China under Xi Jinping, in the name of a drive against corruption and the drastic recentralization of power, have caused many casualties and it has become more difficult than ever to discern patterns of alignment and allegiance in the Communist Party's hierarchy. It was out of that fraught political state of affairs that the leak, or re-leak originated.

The markings on the report, when it arrived back at Langley, are a significant indicator of how the mind of a Chinese Communist Party conspiracy theorist works. The cable from the CIA Station in Rome has circlings and exclamation marks at a dozen places, most heavily around "SECRET ARCHIVES INQUISITION", "OP COG STRONGLY [RPT STRONGLY] CONFIRMED", and "MONIES – EST. 3BN US$ - ZURICH/LICHTENSTEIN". The letter from Cardinal Bolzano to the Pope which was appended to the cable has similar markings wherever there is mention of 'OCD' or the Jesuits. It is as if certain ideas or phrases leapt to the mind of whoever was reading these documents in Beijing, reinforcing phobias and prejudices of long standing. Those key words plainly fed into a pre-existing narrative; while all manner of remaining detail was overlooked or regarded as "code" for something other than what it says.

The Anonymous scribes, of course, having a full-blown narrative of their own, took this and amplified it even further. They seem to have had little concern about China, but to have focused solely on the evidence that the CIA and the Vatican were in secret communication regarding 'OCD' and 'true religion'. That they were also writing approvingly about Emerson, Moneghan and the Amor Mundi Foundation – with its estimated $US3 billion in bank accounts in Zurich and Lichtenstein – had the dire effect of directing venomous hostility at the Academy of Lynxes. It was as if a small team of medical researchers had been working hard to come up with a vaccine for a virulent and lethal disease, only to be attacked and murdered by a band of madmen who were suffering from precisely that disease, while ignorant of its causes, its symptoms or any way to cure themselves.

One has to admit that the details are the stuff of classic conspiracy fiction; but these parties responded to them as if they themselves were inside a Cormac McCarthy novel, rather than operating in the real world. Hezbollah, of course, has never done anything else. The new ISIS movement in Syria and Iraq is clearly even more unhinged and deluded. In any case, the much-travelled, snow-balling set of documents found its way to Anonymous and the MSS's pathological judgments, amplified by the hacktivists' wild-eyed view of the world, infected the Internet. This whole series of leaks and their consequences was surely an epic case of what the CIA's own chief of counter-intelligence at the height of the Cold War, James Jesus Angleton, used to call "a wilderness of mirrors", or a monumental case of "Chinese whispers." In an era in which "leaks" have become torrents, in which figures like Bradley Manning and Edward Snowden have been able to release hundreds of thousands of classified documents, this little trio of papers might seem inconsequential. Yet this 'inconsequential' leak ended up causing the deaths of more innocent people than all the leaks of Manning and Wikileaks or Edward Snowden combined.

The CIA cable itself is a curious document. For sheer, almost impenetrable compression it quite beggars belief. It takes some careful deciphering. However, it is important to bear in mind that a number of the things which jumped out at the conspiracy theorists are true: relations between the Vatican and the CIA *do* go back to the very beginnings of the Agency. The Chinese security report is at least correct on this point. Moreover, Avery Dulles, the nephew of 1950s CIA supremo Allen Welsh Dulles, *was* a graduate of Harvard University, a convert to Catholicism and a Jesuit priest and theologian, based in New York, who died in 2008. He *was* made a Cardinal by the Vatican in the last years of his long life. Our understanding, also, is that Cardinal Roberto Bolzano, who wrote the report from within the Congregation for the Doctrine of the Faith, had been a CIA asset – and informant – for many years. His contact with the CIA is said to have begun in the late 1970s, in the context of the kidnapping and murder of Italian Prime Minister Aldo Moro by the Red Brigades, led by Mario Moretti. Bolzano was only a young monsignor at that time, working in the archdiocese of Turin.[33]

We understand that Bolzano became a protégé of the future Pope, Joseph Ratzinger, not long after he was recruited by the CIA. Ratzinger, a leading figure at the Second Vatican Council between 1962 and 1965, rose through Church ranks thereafter and was appointed Prefect of the Congregation for the Doctrine of the Faith (CDF) by Pope John Paul II, in 1981. The reader may or may not be aware that the CDF was long known and is still informally known as the Holy Office. Its headquarters in Rome are in a palatial building in Vatican City simply called Sant' Uffizio – Holy Office. The Holy Office was originally established in 1542, by Pope Paul III to grapple with the serious challenge confronting the Catholic Church due to the printing press and the Reformation. Its full title was the Supreme Sacred Congregation of the Roman and Universal Inquisition. Its task was "to maintain and defend the integrity of the faith and to examine and proscribe errors and false doctrines". That is where Bolzano had been working for many years by 2009. Again, the conspiracy theorists pounced on this kind of thing and read into it things which are by no means necessarily the case.

It was this institution with which Giordano Bruno (1548-1600) and Galileo Galilei (1564-1642) collided, because of their commitments to a new cosmology. Readers are more likely to be aware of Galileo than of Bruno, but both were seminal figures in the beginnings of the 17th century scientific revolution. Bruno is especially interesting, because he is often seen as more a magus – absorbed in mysticism and the arcane secrets of the Hermetic tradition – than a scientist. Yet as Bruno scholar Hilary Gatti (a colleague of the late Bianca Ruggiero, at the Universita di Roma La Sapienza) has pointed out, he was fundamentally interested in the new heliocentric cosmology of Copernicus; the idea that there were many worlds in the cosmos,

---

33   We have not been able to establish whether it was Martin Rienzi, the 2012 CIA COS in Rome, who recruited him; but our sources inform us that Rienzi was on his first foreign tour of duty at that time - in northern Italy. NH

of which ours was only one; the revival of ancient atomism; number theory and the possibility of investigating, measuring and mapping anew the shape of the natural world.[34] He was burned alive by the Roman Inquisition on the Campo dei Fiori in 1600. Galileo was confined under house arrest some thirty years later – also for advancing the heliocentric theory of the cosmos. He had been, as we explained in the Introduction to this book, a founding member of Federico Cesi's Academy of Lynxes, after whom the 'Academy' that Fenimore and his friends formed in the 1980s had been named.

Bolzano's quite long letter shows that the Vatican's interest in Fenimore Moneghan dated back long before the dramatic events of the recent past. It seems to have been rooted in a major project that had been going on in the Vatican for twenty or thirty years. Bolzano refers to it as *Opus Civitas Dei*. Translated into English, that Latin name means literally 'Work (or Task) City of God'. But we infer that 'opus' here should be interpreted as it is in regard to a *musical* opus, hence the opus itself is 'City of God'. This, plainly, is the source for the CIA file name OP COG, which looks like *Operation* City of God. It seems clear that, from within the Vatican, Opus Civitas Dei had to do with a quiet but fundamental effort to rethink Catholic Church doctrine for the 21st century. The term 'City of God' alludes to the great treatise on meaning, truth and history written in the early fifth century CE by St Augustine of Hippo: *The City of God against the Pagans*. But the initials OCD were to have a most unfortunate consequence, once filtered through Chinese, Anonymous and Hezbollah interpretations.

Going on internal evidence, the Vatican project was only very indirectly connected with what Moneghan and his colleagues were doing. That connection, however, is important to understand, if the recent course of events is to be comprehended at all. Opus Civitas Dei (which, for shorthand purposes we shall refer to from this point simply as OCD, to distinguish it from the CIA's acronym 'OP COG') seems to have been the brainchild of a circle of thinkers within the Catholic Church supported by Pope John Paul II and possibly led by Cardinal Ratzinger, when he was Prefect of the Holy Office. It involved opening up the secret archives of the Holy Office, clearing up and actually acknowledging the misdeeds of the Catholic Church over the centuries and setting a new course for the 21st century – carefully, thoughtfully, conservatively and at a Vatican pace, but nonetheless quite deliberately. This is a remarkable discovery in itself, given the widespread view that, under John Paul II and then Benedict XVI, the Vatican retreated into a conservative and anti-modern shell of pre-Vatican II authoritarian Papism. But the election of Pope Francis in early 2013 may point to things of which few, if any outsiders had been aware.

----

34   See Hilary Gatti, *Giordano Bruno and Renaissance Science*, Cornell University Press (1999). – NH.

It seems that Cardinal Bolzano actually studied the writings of Fenimore Moneghan as part of his OCD work and went so far as to go to meet him in person in July 2009. That interest appears to be related to something which occurred not long after John Paul II had become Pope and before Joseph Ratzinger became the 'Grand Inquisitor', in 1981. In 1979, the historian Carlo Ginzburg, a specialist on the Inquisition, wrote a letter to the new Pope, appealing to him to open up the secret archives of the Inquisition to scholars like himself.[35] Ginzburg made no bones about the fact that he was both of Jewish descent and an atheist. He did not get a response for almost twenty years. When it came, he was astonished, because he had forgotten that he had actually written the letter in the first place. Meanwhile, in 1980, he had authored *The Cheese and the Worms*, a book about the persecution and burning by the Inquisition in northern Italy of a simple man called Domenico Scandella. The response, in 1998, was an invitation from the Grand Inquisitor himself to attend the *opening* of the secret archives of the Inquisition. It seems that Cardinal Ratzinger had been, for years beforehand, the chief advocate of taking this unprecedented step; something for which he appears to have been given little credit.

Bolzano apparently spent many of those and the following years working on a broad scholarly front to re-examine the history of the Inquisition and its implications for the role of the Catholic Church in the new millennium. That re-examination and reflection were at the heart of OCD. They entailed a painstaking effort to transcend the Vatican's long war against modernity without surrendering the ancient claims to revelation, Roman authority and Platonist transcendence on which the Church was built. The penitential procession through Rome on Ash Wednesday 2000 by Pope John Paul II, with his apology for the errors and misdeeds of the past, including those of the Inquisition; may well have sprung from OCD. It is even possible that the unheralded retirement of Pope Benedict XVI (Ratzinger) in early 2013 may also have been motivated by OCD. What is certain is that Bolzano's contact with Moneghan had *everything* to do with OCD.

All this puts in a different light the references to OP COG in the CIA cable. The CIA may have larger strategic objectives and close relations with the Vatican going back decades; but Bolzano's letter is not about plotting between the two. It is possible that the CIA saw the Vatican as simply a 'cog' within the wheels of its own strategic plans, but the Vatican,

---

35   The story of Ginzburg is covered in a book which was published, as it happens, in London and New York, in 2012-13, even as the cable from Rome was being written and then leaked, along with Bolzano's confidential letter. By the time it came out in paperback, the mischief was far advanced, with rather grim consequences in Italy. The book is Cullen Murphy's *God's Jury: The Inquisition and the Making of the Modern World. –* NH.

for its part, clearly had plans of its own. What we see in the letter is the work of a deeply reflective and learned Catholic cleric reporting with surprising sympathy on the fate of a thinker every bit as independent of the Vatican as Carlo Ginzburg. It's striking that there had been a meeting of minds at all. The clue may lie in Bolzano's own forthcoming work, *Bellarmine and Bruno*. Cardinal Bellarmine, a brilliant and highly educated man, was the Grand Inquisitor who tried and condemned Giordano Bruno in 1600. He is said to have agonized for years afterwards about his failure to persuade Bruno to renounce his heretical beliefs that the Earth orbits around the Sun and that the cosmos contains countless other worlds – to say nothing of Bruno's belief in the materialist doctrine of atomism.

Bolzano's letter is clearly that of an individual haunted by the figure of Bruno and by the whole legend of the Inquisition – which he has lived, on a day to day basis, for many years. Even before he met Moneghan, he had come to view him as a kind of present day Bruno, but one whose purposes and insights the Church ought to acknowledge. He hoped Moneghan's Catholic background and Jesuit education would provide common ground. He went so far as to liken him to the famous Jesuit Pierre Teilhard de Chardin, who strove throughout the first half of the 20th century to reconcile Catholic doctrine with the realities being revealed by modern evolutionary biology and cosmology. This is all the more notable given that Moneghan does not seem to have been attempting a reconciliation of science with Catholicism, but a transcendence of all the old religions. Bolzano drew attention to the long suppressed and denounced work of Teilhard and emphasized that it had been embraced by Joseph Ratzinger since the late 1960s and by Pope John Paul II from the beginning of his reign. We seem to be close to the central thrust of OCD here, but surely not at the doors of a sinister plot.

Bolzano originally, as he says, wrote a letter to the Pope in the late northern summer of 2009, after visiting Moneghan at the Ends of the Earth. But what he gave the CIA in early 2012, on a drive through the Alban Hills to Castel Gandolfo, was an updated version, requested by the Pope in late 2011, as *L'Affaire Moneghan* started to become an international news item. Moneghan had vanished, declared dead, and Emerson and the others had just set up the planning headquarters of the incipient Amor Mundi Foundation at the Villa Barberini. It looks like little more than a file update in the wake of these developments. His original brief, it seems, had been simply to assess what significance, if any, Moneghan's work might have in terms of the Vatican's OCD. The update added the fairly banal observations that Moneghan was deceased, the Amor Mundi Foundation had been created based on a very large sum of money obtained on Wall St by him and his colleagues and that the Foundation had set up base at Villa Barberini. There is no indication that he knew of the private journals Moneghan had kept, or that he had been in direct communication up to that point with Thomas Emerson or other members of the Academy.

I must not conclude these remarks without commenting on the strange coincidence that the rural refuge in Lombardy chosen by the Amor Mundi Foundation in 2011 was called the Villa Barberini. I say strange coincidence, because the only Grand Inquisitor – strictly, since the Second Vatican Council, Prefect of the Congregation for the Doctrine of the Faith - whose tenure exceeded that of Cardinal Ratzinger (1981-2005) was Cardinal Francesco Barberini, who held the office from 1633 until his death in 1679, almost twice as long as Ratzinger. Bolzano, of course, was perfectly aware of the coincidence when writing his letter to the Pope. Alas, he actually thought that the choice was evidence of sympathy for the Vatican and this remark in his letter seems to have contributed to the conspiracy theories that then erupted in Beijing, among the anarchists of Anonymous and, fatefully, among the mullahs in Tehran and their Hezbollah confederates. How could he have foreseen that his casual remark about this uncanny coincidence would be seen by all these fanatics as evidence of a nefarious conspiracy?

The Barberini were an Italian family of merchants who arose in Tuscany and Rome in the sixteenth century. They made a vast fortune in the seventeenth century, when Maffeo Barberini became Pope Urban VIII. He was infamous for his nepotism and made two of his nephews, Francesco and Antonio, Cardinals. Francesco he appointed Grand Inquisitor. The Barberini coat of arms was three honey bees and it was said sardonically in the seventeenth century that they sucked all the honey they could out of the Papal State while the going was good. When they removed ancient bronze beams from the celebrated Roman Pantheon to reuse the metal in St Peter's and for Papal guns, some anonymous wit quipped:

Quod non fecerunt barbari, fecerunt Barberini

(What the *barbarians* did not do, the *Barberini* did.)

After their accumulation of wealth through corruption and extortion, they became hereditary aristocracy in the time honoured European manner, inter-marrying with the Colonnas – a much older aristocratic family from the Alban Hills, which boasted a Pope two hundred years before the Barberini and numerous other Papal offices before and since.

But the Barberini, like the Medici, were also great lovers of the arts and liberal scholarship. They were, in almost every respect, classic figures of the 'Babylonian' Catholic Church against which the Reformation was made and were quite unreconstructed when it came to corruption and patronage on a grand scale. They were also doctrinally cautious, in the spirit of the Counter-Reformation and it was they who sought to keep Galileo in check in the last years of his life – not least because Maffeo had been personally offended by Galileo's attitude towards him. When the Chinese Communists and the anarchists at Anonymous learned about the Villa Barberini being the secluded place at which the new Foundation was being planned, they seem to have regarded this – almost on its own – as enough to draw dark conclusions about 'OP COG', the CIA, the Vatican and the Foundation. And it's not as if the Barberini connection was all they had to work with. The highly compressed language of the CIA cable, as we have seen, lent itself to paranoid interpretation at a number of places.

Yet the Villa Barberini does not have anything to do with the Barberini family. It was built for a wealthy businessman, Giovanni Battista Spinola, in the late nineteenth century. Spinola was a lover of art and opera, especially the compositions of his much-admired near contemporaries, Giuseppe Verdi and Giacomo Puccini. He rather whimsically gave his rural retreat the name Villa Barberini for no other reason than a fascination with the Italian past. He died not long after the First World War and the villa passed through various hands before being acquired almost a century later, in somewhat dilapidated, but still graceful condition by the ill-fated lynxes. How could he have guessed the terrible end that would come to his villa in a different age, in part, because of his love of opera? Bolzano's unawareness of these facts had consequences which he cannot have imagined and which must now haunt him every bit as much as the ghost of Bruno. He is reported since to have withdrawn to a Jesuit establishment – the location of which we have not been able to ascertain - to complete *Bellarmine and Bruno.* He could not be reached for comment.

N. Herman
Poughkeepsie
New York
March 3, 2015

Darkness Over Love:
The Notebooks of our Late Friend

Edited by Thomas C. Emerson

Photograph of Fenimore Moneghan's three Notebooks taken by Tom Emerson at Treehaven in 2010 - as reproduced in the original printed version.

Contents

---

36   This is the full table of contents of the Notebooks of Fenimore. Only a few sections are as yet in acceptable draft form in his famous octavos: the Prologue four sections and the Epilogue. They are included in what follows. - PM

Foreword: After Many Delays

Here, at last, after many delays, is the promised printed text of the three Notebooks sent to me by Fenimore before he died. It has taken me far longer than I had hoped to present them to you in this form, as he requested. Given the complications caused by the circumstances in which he disappeared and the complexities entailed in handling the settlement of his estate, it has taken me the better part of four years to accomplish the task. As you all know, we were beset by an absurd rash of speculation and suspicion from the late summer of 2010, which aggravated the already sensitive work of preparing this private manuscript for strictly limited circulation. The more so because I wanted to present it not only faithfully, but in an aesthetic form that would in some measure do justice to the fastidious and stylized manner in which Fenimore had written the originals. I hope you all find the finished book satisfying in these respects.

We few, who were privileged to have been the friends of Fenimore, were always aware of his restless energy, his voracious quest to understand everything and to draw together the many shards of human culture in the world we inherited at the end of the 20th century. As I remarked at Fenimore's untimely obsequies, from the first conversations I had with him, at the Fletcher School in 1982, I always felt electrified by his conversation. Never one to take his advantages for granted, he sought uncompromisingly to turn them to creative and profoundly humane ends. It was, perhaps, his incandescent vision, as much as anything, that first brought us together in Cambridge from 1984. Alas, in the midst of his culminating labours, he was cut down. He sent to me his three Notebooks when he faced the stark realization that for him the door to the future was about to slam shut. He requested that I print and bind them within a single volume, as I have done here and give each of you a copy as a gift from beyond that door. Those were his words; those were his intentions.

But before I could read his request or his Notebooks, he went through that door and shut it behind him with such decisive swiftness that even I was caught by surprise. For those of us who have known him from our youth, his untimely passing is a loss beyond measure. We held such high hopes for his creative contribution to our collective labours for many years to come and mourn his loss. What he means to each of you personally will in some respects remain irreducibly a private matter and, in that respect, each of you will take different things away from the reflections preserved between these covers. They are not merely a set of diaries recording his progress with the treatise he was working on for the last five years of his life; though initially

I thought that that was perhaps what he had sent me. They are much more and could not have taken their present form had he simply written his thoughts and reflections sequentially over several years. He clearly gave a great deal of thought to the writing, looking ahead as well as backwards. He was not writing this for himself, but for the eyes and understanding of another, about whom more presently.

The original, as you all know by now, consists of some seven hundred and fifty pages of polished prose, laid out in a cursive Chancery hand produced with a high quality fountain pen and in a unique style. As I type these lines, I have them at hand and still marvel at the sheer intricate artistry involved in generating them. You have all seen them by now and know that Fenimore created the Notebooks in this manner as a set and as an object of art. In fact, there is a sense that he created them as a kind of epic poem. That has to be why they are written in regular eight line paragraphs. Each one is perfectly formed, like a stanza of verse, without distortion of the meaning or disruption in the flow of the thinking they embody. It seems inconceivable that this was done spontaneously. The fact that, even as he created the Notebooks, he was writing poetry of considerable variety and sophistication, may have led him to decide to rework an earlier version of his reflections in the current form. But I have not been able to find any earlier drafts among his papers. Searching for something on these lines was something I took some pains in doing, but to no avail.

I still find it impossible to believe that he wrote 750 pages without some form of drafting and revision. Certainly, however, in what I received, there were no corrections of any kind (except one or two in what has become the Epilogue, written it seems with unaccustomed haste; when he was both ill and on the verge of existential decisions), despite the fact that there were remembered conversations, reflections on profound matters, outpourings of feeling, imaginary tales and even the outline for an opera libretto (in the third Notebook). I did find some evidence of drafting, but it was not of material included in any of the Notebooks. It was something supplementary to them, which I have published here in Appendix B. It consists of the Seven Songs of Queen Nefesh – clearly related to the fable in Notebook III. You will all recall my mention of this fable in the talk I gave at our gathering here just under a year ago. Even then, I had the sense that it held an unusual place in the whole work. It was only some months later that I made a chance discovery which put it – and the question of drafting – in a whole new light.

As every one of you is aware, I had arranged for the removal of Fenimore's personal papers and archives from Cos to the Villa Barberini, in the winter of 2011-12, after rather tense negotiations with the staff at Cos, especially Ms Kurzweil, Fenimore's erstwhile archivist and database manager. Collating and reviewing this enormous mass of material was a task that consumed a great deal of my time in 2012. One of my chief goals was to find, if I could, earlier drafts of the extraordinary finished work I had in hand within the Notebooks. In that I was unsuccessful, as I reported last year. However, very late in the piece and when I had almost given up the search, I came upon a printed manuscript in a ring-binder titled 'Assimilative Commentary on Robert Alter's Translation of the Book of Psalms'. This seemed to me an astonishing digression from the central concerns of Fenimore's treatise. In The Vivarium[37], as I knew by then, there had existed a heavily annotated copy of Alter's book, published in 2007. There was a strong alignment between the annotations and the commentary. But it was an unanticipated, almost one would say misfiled item in the folder that seized my attention.

When I was leafing through the many pages of commentary in the folder, a sheaf of loose leaves fell out of it. On them were several hand-written pages in prose and the lyrics of what at first glance I took to be seven of the Biblical psalms. On closer inspection, however, I quickly realized that they were psalm-like poems or songs, of Fenimore's own crafting. Unlike the Notebooks, they showed signs of correction and development, which made somewhat difficult the task of determining the final form he might have wished them to take. What was remarkable, however, was the realization that they belonged with the Tale of Raneb and Nefesh and were clearly a working draft for the actual lyrics of the songs alluded to in the fable. Writing them would seem to have been an afterthought on Fenimore's part, or perhaps an early experiment that he had abandoned. It was impossible to be sure, since there was no dating on the pages or even the folder. I have included them as an Appendix[38] because of their intrinsic interest and because the prose pages accompanying them point to something I had thought privately before then: that this tale was unusually close to Fenimore's heart.

As you can see, there are two other Appendices in the finished book.[39] I have added these at my own discretion, because they do not form a part of any of the Notebooks. However, they clearly form an important part of who Fenimore was and give expression to what he believed and how he saw human existence. The first is his Credo; something which we all knew was evolving over the past twenty five years, as he sought to hammer out a set of beliefs

---

37   The extraordinary private Library at Cos, of which the Ms (Ariel) Kurzweil to whom Emerson refers here was – along with Bo Zhangliu - evidently the chief custodian. – NH.

38   See Appendix B. – NH.

39   Emerson is, of course, referring to his own three Appendices. Brandom House have added two further Appendices, in the interests of setting the true story in its full context. There are, in consequence, five Appendices in all, alphabetically listed as A to E. – NH.

that were consistent both with the revolutionary findings of the natural sciences and with the human experience of being in the world. In an important sense, this was why he chose to study philosophy all those years ago rather than take his prodigious intelligence to Wall St to make a fortune. I came from a Unitarian background and he from a Catholic one. What I see in his Credo is a strong updating of the radical reform of Christian theology that Michael Servetus, the first Unitarian, attempted almost five hundred years ago and for which he was burned at the stake in Geneva – not by the Catholic Church, but by Jean Calvin and the Protestants. In my judgement – and I trust you will all agree – this book would not be complete if the Credo was omitted.

The other Appendix is a set of poems that I found among Fenimore's papers. I have made a few brief remarks at the beginning of the Appendix about their character and hesitate to say more here; for once started it almost seems necessary to write an entire separate book of exegesis of what is in those poems. They cover so much ground, yet they circle around three central themes, I believe: the nature of cosmic reality, the nature of human love and the nature of mortality. Each of you, when you have this book in hand and read them, will have your own responses to different poems, different lines, one or another of those three themes. In a sense you will each write your own book of exegesis on the body of verse that Fenimore left behind him. It will be your own very personal, ongoing conversation with him. And, of course, there is a sense – one which strongly governed my decision to include the poems in the book – that the Notebooks are Fenimore's own exegesis on his poetry. *They* are his greatest poem. All the others are, I suspect, simply essays in the craft, written as ancillary exercises while he crafted the epic poem we have inherited.

You can well imagine how astonished I was to discover what the three Notebooks contained. I could only with difficulty believe that Fenimore had created all this while apparently so utterly absorbed in cosmology, biology and profound questions about the nature of being itself. I had always thought that the beauty of truth was his great and all-consuming passion. Here I found something else. You will see, within, that he was, indeed, absorbed in his scientific and philosophical work. Yet from the time that he encountered Margarita or at least from the time when he commenced the first Notebook, he seems to have been drawn ever more deeply into attempting to express what it all meant in relation to *her* - above and beyond what it might have meant to any of the rest of us. This was his attempt to articulate his *private* world of meaning, within the classical architecture of his aspiration to make clear the foundations and implications of universal truths.

I read the Notebooks through for the first time consumed by memories of my friend, fascinated by the figure of Margarita and astonished at the deep secret Fenimore had kept. I read them a second time with closer attention to the astounding range of thoughts Fenimore had poured out in them in so personalized a manner. Then I read them a third time, overwhelmed by a sense of the personal journey and final tragedy of Fenimore and Margarita. It was some time before I could bring myself to tackle the relatively mechanical task of converting the handwritten manuscript into a typescript. In between those three readings, little by little, I unearthed the poems, the Credo, the songs, dispersed among his papers – almost as if confuting the fascinating and clearly troubled argument he advances in the poem 'A Poet's Bell'.[40] Reading them, as I discovered them, induced me to re-read and rethink many passages in the Notebooks and provided rich materials from which to attempt, at least, to reconstruct and comprehend the tragic end to Fenimore's life – above all, it's astonishing and seemingly arbitrary suddenness.

I have edited the Notebooks as lightly and faithfully as I was able. The fact that they had arrived in the post after Fenimore died, made it impossible for me to confer with him on matters of detail or even dating. That he had kept them secret from everyone, even Margarita, made it impossible to check with others what he may have meant at one point or another. That he wished only our circle to read them required, it seemed clear to me, that I withhold even their very existence from all others. As I put these finishing touches to the manuscript, I remain sure that this decision is not only consistent with Fenimore's wishes, but our own privacy and freedom to enjoy this gift untroubled by intrusion from the outside world and those who never knew our friend. The plague of irrational conspiracy theories that has proliferated since his death only confirms this judgement. Rational argument is one thing, but it would be a travesty to allow the fools who have indulged in such speculation and ignorant fantasy to desecrate these pages. What we will put out into the public domain in due course will be the considered work of the Amor Mundi Foundation.

From internal evidence I have been able to deduce that the Notebooks were written at staggered intervals over a period of just over three years, from the northern spring of 2007 until – in the case of what appears here as the Epilogue – shortly before his death in the early summer of 2010. The clearest evidence is the reference in the Prologue to events that did not occur until 2005 and 2006. But they must have been in preparation well before that, I believe. They are at times radically retrospective, taking him back to our days together at Harvard and even earlier; to say nothing of his digressions into history and deep time. But he starts with his first encounter, in the northern spring of 2004, with Margarita. That life-changing event

---

40   Poem 16 in Appendix C. – TCE.

stands at the beginning of the first Notebook, but I have given it separate and distinct status, as a Prologue, because it is so significant to everything that followed. Margarita enchanted Fenimore in a way no other woman had, but she also challenged him as no other had done. Her freedom of spirit took his breath away and came at last to shape his whole sense of who he was not merely as a man, but as a being. That shaping is what we see in these pages.

Her world was that of music and dance and she seems insistently to have urged him not only to think of the importance of those things to humanity, but to tell her stories and write her songs and recite poetry for her. Little by little, that is what he began to do. There was, however, a remarkable tension in their relationship, because his passionate desire was to see truth whole, without illusions and to delineate as clearly as possible the relationship between truth and method on the one hand and the flourishing of human civilization on the other. To begin with, the tension between them was like that which naturally and stirringly characterizes a dance between a man and a woman. It was by turns playful, ironical, humorous and passionate. But as time passed she came almost to possess him, which is surely what made her choices six years later so destructive of his equanimity. His late poem 'Fusion'[41] plainly gave expression to his longing for her. But at just that point, she had decided to go her own way.

It is very important, however, to understand that Margarita's choices were by no means the only thing that played a role in bringing about Fenimore's abrupt self-destruction just under four years ago. The decisive factor, very clearly, was his discovery that he had a highly aggressive metastatic cancer that would kill him and could at any time cripple him. He might, under other circumstances, have believed he could grapple with that challenge, or at least put off the end. His emotional exhaustion surely explains why that was not his judgement or preference. It is, of course, remarkably difficult to diagnose with confidence why someone you love chooses to end their life. Even if there have been warning signs, we tend not to see them. We prefer not to see them, as a rule. In Fenimore's case, it is only looking back that we can guess what combination of emotions and reflections catapulted him over the edge – for one cannot, I believe, talk merely of tipping. These Notebooks are not those of an individual with suicidal tendencies.

When he collapsed at Treehaven on the first evening of the climate conference four years ago, I assumed – knowing nothing of Margarita and nothing at all about the cancer – that he was simply exhausted from his travels. Then I thought that perhaps the grim news reported by so many presentations at the conference and the evident fact that global consensus for coherent action was nowhere in sight may have precipitated the collapse. After he had rested for a couple of days and the conference was largely over, we sat in the library and he began to

---

41   See Poem #31 in Appendix C. – TCE.

tell me about Margarita. I was so stunned at his confession of a secret guarded closely for six years that I could have collapsed myself. Slowly, over several days, between long rests and on strolls around the gardens, he related to me the barest outlines of what you will read in this book, culminating in a shattering moment in Buenos Aires which seems to have struck him like a bolt of lightning from a blue sky.

Since this is covered with exquisite reflectiveness and poetry inside this book, I will not attempt to summarize the story here. Having worked on the Notebooks and poems for so long, however, I believe I can see some warrant for two alternative interpretations of his actions. The first interpretation would be that he was suffering from a growing sense of the sheer overwhelming difficulty of what he had undertaken; not so much intellectually as socially. He was climbing with extraordinary tenacity and skill in his effort to reach the summit of a philosophical Mount Everest, but appears slowly to have come to doubt that his work would make any difference at all to the ingrained prejudices and irrational proclivities of the mass of humankind. I would not go so far as to say that he despaired, but I do believe that this gnawing doubt sapped his energy; to the point where, slipping violently on the combination of emotional upheaval and medical catastrophe, he fell from the cliff face to his death.

The second interpretation is that, in a sense, his death, his self-immolation, was not an act of exhaustion, nihilism or abandonment, but actually a kind of improvised consummation. Confronted by a stark set of circumstances, he had what he thought of as an epiphany and flung himself forward into death, rather as Empedocles, long ago, cast himself into the volcanic crater of Mount Etna. When he sailed out into the oceans at the End of the Earth on his yacht to end his life; he did not do so because he had given up on the world or on his work; however much it may appear so to those who have not known him, conversed with him – and read his Notebooks. He chose, seeing that the end was about to take him, to take the end freely and in his own manner. Did he fall, then, or did he leap? I suspect that he leapt, but there were conditions which prompted him to do so and we may think of those conditions as a kind of fall.

For what it is worth – and you will reach your own conclusions in due course – I believe he saw this gesture, this leap into oblivion, as a great act of acceptance of his human thrownness towards death and his subordinate place in the grand scheme of things. He did not resist reality, but embraced it with open eyes. What he did was an act of humility and sacrifice. He was declaring that he had done what he could and now others must do what they can, since this is the way of all things. In sending his Notebooks to me, he was saying that it is for us now to pick up the torch and run the next lap, or climb the next rock face. He would not have chosen this end if he could have freely shaped his own destiny, but seeing what confronted him, he stepped into it with unflinching calm. That, at least, is my own interpretation of the enigma of his passing.

Fenimore always had a love of literature and poetry, as you all know. We would all recite poetry from around the world at our first youthful gatherings. He would often remark how fascinated he was by the figure of Robert Oppenheimer, who was so gifted a scientist, so troubled and articulate an ethicist, so effective and patriotic a manager of a perilous and controversial program – and who loved language and poetry as the core of his very Jewish humanity. I think Fenimore was haunted, in a way, by Oppenheimer's deeds and his fate. He would recite Oppenheimer's reported exclamation at Alamogordo, when the first successful test of an atomic bomb was conducted, quoting the *Bhagavad Gita*,

> *Now I am become death, destroyer of worlds.*

That is the context in which Fenimore saw and experienced poetry, I think. It is also the context in which he saw the modern physical sciences. It is the context in which we must all read the poems he wrote in his final years and his long, integral prose poem, which filled three privately crafted Notebooks.

I would say that in the pages that follow we see a mind striving with all its power to bring together the great Table of Law which he saw as the procedures of the hard sciences with the expressive and intimate nature of lived humanity. Many fine human beings at least gesture at this lofty goal, but somehow Fenimore could not settle for gestures only: he aspired to actually *solve* and demonstrate in his own life the great questions of truth and meaning that have preoccupied the greatest minds for millennia. It was, surely, too much to attempt. Yet the very endeavour was heroic and somehow necessary. Perhaps, also, the failure was necessary. In any case, he fell from high up on the rock face of that forbidding mountain and out of his knapsack, you might say, fell his Notebooks. They fell to us and it is for us to make of them now what we will.

He had, of course, won a global reputation among the cognoscenti for his two published books. Each exhibited an astringent and keenly analytical mind at work. To see so determined and unsentimental a thinker attempting to communicate with a beloved muse and to blend the worlds of fact and imagination is profoundly moving; the more so because we knew the man but never knew the woman. He chose, or rather they chose to keep their intimacy a secret from all the world, even from us; not because there was anything scandalous about it, but as far as I can ascertain wholly and solely because they wished to preserve inviolate the freedom, privacy and tenderness of their conversation. Then something went very wrong. Other than the indirect reflection of that conversation that we find in these Notebooks, nothing will ever be heard by others of what passed between them. Theirs was a rare and poignant liberty – rare in soaring above mundanity and banality;

poignant in its ultimate fragility and its catastrophic ending. I will save my remarks about what went wrong for an Afterword, since here I wish to dwell chiefly upon the Notebooks themselves.

Once I had removed the non-digital parts of Fenimore's archive to the Villa Barberini, while securing custody of his massive digital databases, I spent something like a year perusing the catalogue of his papers. I had known for many years, as all of you have known, of his interest in and precocious schoolboy's facility with both classical and modern languages; his passion for the physical sciences and German as an undergraduate; his studies in economics, law and diplomacy at graduate school, where I first met him in the early 1980s; his doctorate in philosophy and study of Chinese at Harvard. That he should have taken up learning Chinese while doing his doctorate was only one more indication of his irrepressible energy. The range of his interests and writings, therefore, made the perusal of his papers at once an all but overwhelming and quite exhilarating task. I took the time, also, to read properly for the first time both of his published books: *Continental Drift* and *The Horsemen and the Abacus*.

This is not the place to catalogue the scope of the work he had done on what was to be his third and culminating book, or his plans for completing it in the next few years. You all have some sense of his earlier work; perhaps none of you more so than Poseidon[42], who worked with him in China for considerable stretches. We know that what he had embarked upon after leaving China at the turn of the century was to have brought all these interests and studies to a crowning fruition in a book which he saw as finally addressing the great questions raised in their unfinished works of the 1920s and 1930s by Martin Heidegger's *Being and Time* and Edmund Husserl's *The Crisis of the European Sciences and Transcendental Phenomenology*. The challenge, of course, was not only to address the questions they had raised, but to answer them in the light of the stupendous advances of the natural sciences since the late 1930s. Above all, as Monica[43] and Bianca know, he intended to place the condition of humanity in the context of the clearest possible understanding of contemporary cosmology and evolutionary biology.

Fenimore set out to trace the evolution of the understanding of cosmology, biology and ontology in human civilization and their relationship to the ecological and existential dilemmas now confronting humanity. He had, in the first decade of this century, laid out the ground work for this *magnum opus*. I have read through the draft outlines, which will be kept in manuscript form at the Villa Barberini, until or unless we choose a different headquarters for the Foundation. They are the designs for his formidably ambitious Work; a work which, ironically, of course, remains unfinished. It is evident from his meticulous preparation that he

---

42   Poseidon Wang, a Chinese American member of the Academy of Lynxes. – NH

43   Monica Sventitsky, a brilliant astrophysicist and member of the Academy of Lynxes. – NH.

appreciated the scale and scope of what he had undertaken. Yet his plans now exist only as - and must remain - little more than an elaborate architectural drawing. In the pages of this book we see him not so much setting out his arguments, but addressing his beloved from within the world of understanding that he was developing elsewhere.

We have the outline and are making plans to see whether we as a team may be able to find a way to complete it. It may have been with some hope of this that he decided to offer us his Notebooks. Certainly, as I read them and edited them, I could not help but feel a current pulling me in that direction. When you have all had a chance to read this book, there will be time to discuss its relationship to his outlines for the greater work and also the vast database he and his staff at Cos assembled, over the years in which he worked on it. Our collective world view has, since the 1980s, aspired to reach the horizons that Fenimore was touching when he died. There is a good deal in these pages that will surely stimulate us to work towards a synthesis, following in his footsteps – or to create our own synthesis, differing in some possible ways from the one he was close to putting together. I do not think that he would have objected to that. Our conversations within the Academy of Lynxes, I'm sure you will all agree, were always exploratory and open-ended over the many years of our association.

Fenimore often spoke of his treatise as *A Guide of the Perplexed in Our Time*, or *A 21ˢᵗ Century Guide of the Perplexed*. In this he was clearly borrowing from the famous Maimonides, as we shall see him telling Margarita when they first meet; but that isn't the title of his Notebooks. Indeed, they had *no* actual title. The finished treatise was to have had three major divisions:

    I.   Cosmology

    II.   Biology

    III.   Ontology

I was, for that reason, briefly tempted to give the three Notebooks these headings. They happen to roughly coincide in the chronology of their composition with his work on the design for the three divisions of his book. However, it was quite evident from the personal nature of the Notebooks that this would not do at all. This was not some kind of rough draft for the treatise, but a phenomenon *sui generis* which drew upon and drew into itself almost the whole continuum of human culture. It needed a title of its own.

On reflection and in the light of the tragic denouement to the relationship between Fenimore and Margarita, I chose titles for both this edited volume and the three main parts of it which seemed best to express the content of the book as a whole and those three component parts. Likewise the titles of what appear here as chapters or sections. The original Notebooks lacked such titles and section headings. As you all know and have seen, they are simply entitled Notebooks I, II and III and are written in a continuous script, broken only by paragraphs and page breaks. It was as if he could not come up with a title at the beginning and did not care to at the end. Yet there were blank spaces where such titles might have been written into the manuscript. Fenimore simply did not fill in those blank spaces. The abstract nature of the Notebook 'titles' left me pondering what had caused Fenimore to leave such sparseness and emptiness in the framing of his object of art, but I do not have an answer to that question.

After much deliberation, I have called the volume as a whole *Darkness over Love*. That seems an apt summation of the material it contains and also of the secrecy under which Fenimore and Margarita conducted their relationship, to say nothing of the tragic manner in which it ended. The three parts of the book are titled 'Darkness', 'Over' and 'Love', in some measure because this seemed an effective way to use the words in the main title; but also because these three words appeared to me to sum up the development of Fenimore's thinking and creative output in the successive Notebooks. I hope you will all agree that I have chosen well. There was the option of leaving the blankness as it was, but this seemed to me to be an arid way of preserving Fenimore's work. It is, after all, a *memento mori* and the titles, therefore, might be seen as our tribute to and recognition of what he has given us.

In Notebook I, written during his intense work on cosmology and the enigma of dark matter and dark energy, the theme of darkness recurs again and again, contrasted with the bright light and energetic work going on at Cos. In Notebook II, he was at work on the nature of life on Earth, the evolution of the human species and the nature of human knowledge, but he can be seen passing over from immersion in his own work to ever greater relatedness to Margarita as the centre of his *own* life. The word 'over' here denotes transcending and moving above or across. This is how he saw the evolution of life on Earth, but also the effect of Margarita on his own thinking and way of being. In Notebook III, written during his breakthrough work on ontology and phenomenology, we see him being swept up into a deeply poetic love for Margarita – which then crashes to earth tragically.

Since the foundation of our circle a generation ago, astounding developments have taken place. Civilization is now confronted by great dangers every bit as daunting in their own way as those of the Cold War, during which we all grew to adulthood. Yet it is on the cusp, also, of unprecedented possibilities. In passing this volume to you, I recall our conversations in the 1980s about the Ionian Enchantment, the Library of Alexandria and the idea of a scientific civilization for the 21st century. Since the turn of the century, we have concurred in calling this vision consilience – following the work of Edward O. Wilson, who even taught a couple of us at Harvard twenty years before.[44] This vision and a shared horror at the totalitarian catastrophes and ecological excesses of the 20th century brought us all together in Fenimore's rooms on Tremont St, opposite the little synagogue, for those unforgettable soirees. As you read these pages, you will be reminded of all that; but will also see how broad and sweeping Fenimore's mind had become and how the synthesis, the synoptic understanding we all long for, was shimmering in his mind's eye.

Fenimore was an ardent lover of the symphonies of Mahler and musical orchestration lay at the heart of his love for Margarita. This is evident in his response to her insistence that one's *own* song must express the *inner* orchestration, the lived knowledge, the life wisdom one has acquired. Nowhere exhibited in Notebook I; this influence slowly surfaces in Notebook II and all but takes over in Notebook III. The cadenced prose he crafted, as well as the incidental poems and songs we now know he was writing on the side show a philosopher striving to give personal expression to the *meaning* of his objective knowledge – the emerging philosophical system that he dubbed 'cellular phenomenology'. Perhaps he would have preferred to complete his treatise; but what we have here – what he has given to *us* - was written with the preferences and sensibility of *another* in mind. Read on, friends. In the fullness of time and in the idyllic peace of rural Lombardy, we will take our understanding further. It will inform the philanthropic work we plan to undertake through the Amor Mundi Foundation – for the love of the world.

Tom Emerson
Villa Barberini
March 15, 2014

---

44   Edward O. Wilson's *Consilience: The Unity of Knowledge* was published by Knopf, New York, in 1998. - NH

The statue of Miguel Cervantes at the top of Calle Cervantes, Toledo.
This is a photograph I, Tom, took on a visit to Toledo in 2013 to revisit the site of Fenimore and Margarita's first meeting. The statue did not exist when they visited Toledo in April 2004.

Prologue: The Ascent to San Roman

This much I remember of our first meeting. What will you remember? I was seated in the northeast corner of the dining room at La Cubana, in an ecstasy of reflective solitude, after a morning strolling around the full circuit of the old walls of Toledo. The place had only just opened for lunch and not another of the immaculately laid, white-covered tables was occupied. I'd ordered a generous flagon of sangria and a platter of honeyed aubergines and sat back from a shaft of spring sunlight at ease. Angling in from the north across the Tajo, through the sturdy, rustic drapes of that delightful little establishment, it cast a lamp-like beam of illumination onto the cover of Tom's freshly minted book, which I'd placed in front of me for prandial perusal.

That's when you made your entrance, as splendidly and unexpectedly solitary as I was. Just as I opened the cover of *The Bow of Odysseus*, to re-read the opening pages, a voice from behind the curtain to my right, a feminine one among those of the waiting staff, caught my hearing. Within the instant, my peripheral vision was captured by a womanly figure sweeping between the drapes into the dining room. In a notably graceful sequence of moves, it danced a few feet past me, took in the emptiness of the room, swivelled and glanced in my direction. My reverie was broken. The eyes which, at that moment, looked into mine, were one of those rare, luminous pairs that seem both to see into one and also open into another blue-green world of unguessed depths.

Of course, it was yet to be revealed to me that the eyes belonged to you. Nor was that at once revealed. Having glanced at me and caught my eye, you turned once more and, with what was clearly a dancer's grace, glided to the far end of the dining room, the opposing corner and took a seat symmetrically placed with regard to mine, in your own beam of spring sunlight. I remember, or so my memory informs me, glancing at the wall clock to your left at the moment you seated yourself. It was 12.35. Naturally, I have to correct the memory's tendencies to picture that old clock, in retrospect, as a surrealist Dali melting off the wall; and to embroider your appearance with later impressions. But these were certainly my first impressions of you.

With these elementary observations, I returned to my planned reading; the sangria and aubergines not having yet arrived. It was no ordinary reverie you had just stepped into that afternoon. I was in the midst of the last of three days in Toledo; having left Mr Bojangles in Madrid to discuss with the academics at the Autónoma details regarding the publication of our paper on the internet and dissent in China. He would fly back to the Ends of the Earth separately. My break in Toledo was about the famous role of the city, a thousand years ago, as a centre of learning, libraries and translation of the Greek classics from Arabic into Latin. It was about religion and science: Judaism, Islam, Christianity - and the question of a new synthesis.

My purpose, of course, was given a sharper edge by the fact that the Madrid train bombings by Muslim fanatics, killing and wounding some 2,500 people, had occurred just a month or so before I arrived. I'd come from New York, bearing with me Tom's timely book on terrorism, law and the 21st century state. He'd given a copy to me and each of the other members of our old circle, on its publication. Work on it had begun just before 9/11. He completed the manuscript as the war in Iraq erupted, in March 2003. Its publication a year later had been quite an event; not least because Tom had advanced a contentious and ambitious new theory of the state, concerning which there were many questions, both at launch events and in the international press.

The linkages between what I was flying to Madrid to say and the core themes of Tom's book were profound. The history I was in Toledo to ponder was a also crucial aspect of the prehistory of all these things. I spent two days absorbed in the art work and museums of the city, but walked that morning from my hotel outside the El Greco Museum, in the heart of the old Jewish quarter, down to the San Martin Bridge, then right around the beautifully restored and landscaped perimeter of the old Arabic walls. The whole idea of walls, of boundaries and borders, of privacy and sanctuary, was on my mind and the numerous cypresses, standing like the guardians of memory and reflection around the walls of Toledo; made a lasting impression.

This city, I reflected, had a remarkable history. It had been here long before the Romans conquered Spain. It was conquered by the Arabs a thousand years after that; then reconquered by Catholics four centuries later again. It had been for centuries the city of three cultures of 'The Book': Judaism, Christianity and Islam. I was thinking of the more common dogmatic and sectarian quarrels between these religions. I was dreaming of writing a book that, in a single vast sweep, would lay bare the anachronism of the old religions and set the foundations of a wider, deeper, more humane vision for civilization in the 21st century and beyond. It was to be a book that would synthesize the labours of countless scholars and scientists: a great book of consilience.

Throughout my circumambulation of the great stone walls, from San Martin to the old Arabic Red Gate and around the eastern perimeter, I was deep in conversation with my chosen precursors: the Pre-Socratics, like Parmenides, brooding on his dark sphere, and Democritus the atomist, the laughing philosopher; the Hellenistic scientists, pioneers of method; and the moderns, from Galileo to Hubble, who opened up the cosmos to our eyes. Not that anyone would have seen them walking with me that morning. Yet we conversed animatedly on the origins of method; the crisis of learning in the downfall of the classical world; its revival; the very nature of science and the human place in the cosmos: all that and the significance of Toledo.

We came to the Alcantara, that ancient bridge over the Rio Tajo, which now holds personal meaning for you and me, shortly after noon. Looking over it, I saw the place to seclude myself for an hour or three with sangria and Tom's book. I'd brought it with me in my knapsack. I excused myself politely from my eminent company and crossed the bridge to La Cubana and there you found me within the half hour. What brought you there? I've always been an outsider; loving learned company, but enjoying above all the quiet seclusion conducive to passionate study and reflection. La Cubana beckoned as a haven where I might simply sit with my thoughts and my friend's new book. You, at just that point? That, of course, was a different story altogether.

That story and our chance meeting at La Cubana are generating this writing. Yet at that precise moment, I would never have anticipated any such thing. Once you'd seated yourself and I'd noted the time, I returned to Tom's book; re-reading the lines from Homer that he had set at the start, explaining his title: two long passages from Book XXI of *The Odyssey*. They seemed to imply that the great bow of Odysseus, which Odysseus alone could fire, stood for the capacities of the state to cope with terrorism. Odysseus challenged the insolent suitors at Ithaca to wield that mighty bow, but he alone could do it. He then turned the bow on them, slaughtering them all in his sealed halls. Was this, I wondered, Tom's prefiguring of war in Afghanistan or Iraq?[45]

Tom had promised to explain his use of Homer over a lunch at the Knickerbocker Club, after the launch. But Irad and Amartya had entirely usurped the conversation that day, by raising their prognostications about the derivatives trading frenzy and the emerging condition of the US housing market. Amartya was writing a paper on the risks that the derivatives represented to the American economy. Irad was talking of the implications for our new and thriving hedge fund.

---

45   Fenimore's reconstruction of my citations from Homer was about right. The challenge that faced Odysseus in his halls is intended to represent the challenges that I see facing the constitutional order of the democratic states with the rise of 21st century terrorism. The bow stands for the fact that only the United States has the right combination of global interests, resources and trust to lead the democracies against this new danger. Only it can draw this bow. There is also the inheritance of a global role as a gift from an older generation, so that the bow signifies both the role as well as the means for exercising that role. What I did not wish to evoke is the revenge story, the slaughter of the suitors at the hall in Ithaca in an orgy of violence that calls to mind early Clint Eastwood or Charles Bronson films—very emotionally satisfying, but not my point. Unfortunately, as war unfolded in both Afghanistan and Iraq, especially from 2004, the violence there led altogether too many of my readers to assert that slaughter was what I had in mind. - TCE

We didn't return to Homer before I flew out from New York. It was left to me to ponder, flying via London to Madrid, but I had many other things to think about – including the violence in Madrid - and gave the matter only superficial thought before sitting down to lunch at La Cubana.

Half a dozen lines in the middle of the first long passage in his epigraph drew my mind well into the Homeric world of weapons and the mighty dead, but also brought to mind by association of ideas the place I was building and the work I have embarked upon. 'That great weapon', runs the fabled verse in Fagles' strong English, 'King Odysseus never took it abroad with him, when he sailed off to war in his long black ships. He kept it stored away in his stately house, guarding the memory of a cherished friend and only took that bow on hunts at home.' These lines seemed to me, sitting in that Spanish sunlight, to link together not only the fabled world of Bronze Age warfare with our times, but Ithaca with my new built Cos; Homer with the Work I had in mind.

I was in the midst of such ruminations on time past and projects afoot when the sangria and honeyed aubergines arrived beside Tom's book. I poured myself a glass of the refreshing fluid, but had hardly done so when you rose from where you'd sat and walked with studied deliberation back towards me, your gaze fixed on me, seeking my attention. There were still no other diners in that curtained space, so that the movement could not be mistaken for any more general motion in the room. Even from the Halls of Ithaca my attention was drawn to the fact of your approach. The moment you stood before me, introducing yourself, was one of those in which time dilates and memory is mesmerised. You entered my world at that precise point.

I don't believe I responded at once to what I take it was a suggestion that we eat together. I think I was transfixed by your eyes, but also by the timbre of your voice, which had a songlike quality to it. The figure standing before me - perhaps because I had just been meditating on Homer – seemed to me, I swear, at once to be that of a classical sculpture come to life with stylishly coiffed dark blonde hair and curves softened by an understated, but self-possessed mode of dress. You could have been the avatar of a goddess. Melete herself – the Muse of meditation – had come to my table, I thought. Though I'd entered La Cubana to seclude myself and read, I don't recall feeling your presence as an intrusion. I put aside Tom's book and gave you a seat.

My memory fails me regarding our first words, but I have a vivid image of you holding a glass of sangria in your hand, from which I infer that I must not only have invited you to sit, but have offered you also a glass of the red beverage. Indeed, I must already have requested a second glass from the waiter. I remember a perfectly formed white hand curled around the sangria as you shook your mane of shining hair and pronounced your name, 'Margarita'. The syllables on the page don't do justice to the sound from your lips; the sunlight glistening on your glass and that hand. The Hispanic trill was unmistakable: Mar-gah-rri-tah I heard; and it re-echoed in my mind and danced on the end of my tongue as I repeated it: Mar-gah-rri-tah, Margahrritah, Margarita.

How do first conversations go such that we might recall them in ways that aren't banal? So much depends on mood and memory that the words themselves elude us or come back to us with resonances that it would take an accomplished writer to capture on the page. But this much, stripped of all atmospherics, is what I learned in the first moments of our conversation at La Cubana: you lived in the Canary Islands, at Santa Cruz de Tenerife; and had come to Madrid a few days ago with a friend, who was giving a paper on the indigenous Guanches at a conference about the archaeology of the Canaries. You'd taken the opportunity to visit Toledo because you were in the field of music and wished to visit the famous Rodriguez guitar workshops in the city.

You pronounced my name, which, of course, I'd offered well before learning of your origins or purposes, with a lengthening of the first and a softening of the third syllable, so that it came out sounding like Feign-i-moor. The syllables seemed to fascinate you and move around on your palate being savoured very much as the Spanish trill in Margarita rolled around on my tongue and in my imagination. Over more than one glass of sangria, you circled back to a curiosity about where my name had come from, as if it said something about me that you wanted to play with or at least explore. Feign-ee-moor Mo-nee-can was the way you pronounced it and I disclosed, at last, that it had come from my parents' decision to name me for romantic frontier adventure.

Your head tilted at this discovery. I recall the moment more than its exact point in the conversation. 'My parents called me Fenimore because they loved the idea of their son reading romantic fiction. They gave me Walter Scott, James Fenimore Cooper, Robert Louis Stevenson, Rudyard Kipling, Edgar Allan Poe and such things. They called me Fenimore after Cooper. Do you know his novels?' 'Of course,' you breathed, '*El Ultimo Mohicano, The Last of the Mohicans*, is almost as famous as the novels of Mark Twain.' 'Yes, well', I must have commented, since the point comes up so commonly with regard to my name, 'my father used to say he hoped I would not end up becoming the last of the Moneghans.' As things stand, there's a good chance I shall.

But Henderson y Mendoza! Where had that name come from? That was a subject over which to savour honeyed aubergines to begin with and then almost forget to eat or drink, lost in fascination at the exotic genealogy, which far outstripped my family tree, or that little and recent branch of which I was more or less aware. Your family tree turned out to have a long history in Venezuela, the Caribbean and the American isthmus which, by your account, went back almost to the conquest in some lines and came forward via sugar, indigo, coffee and oil to the politics of the present time. English Hendersons and Spanish Mendozas are only the most recent and only the paternal line of the story. Commodities and political upheavals have been the substance of it.

How much did I learn that day and how much in the years since, especially during the days at Cos, in which we shared so much; during long afternoons two years ago in Vienna and Budapest; or above all, more recently in Yucatan, during afternoons at Maya sites or on Cancun nights scrolling through our memories and seeking the deeper contexts of our dreams? I can't record what was spoken. I can only draw upon it now as source material for creating something in writing that will fix in place my recollection and interpretation of things; my sense of how my world looks to me through the prism that you have become since that first conversation in Toledo. For I am a truth-seeker; but through you the world has become colour and meaning.

Colour and meaning and sound! For the culmination of your account of Hendersons in Jamaica and Mendozas in Colombia and at Maracaibo has been your personal story of music and El Sistema, of the orchestras brought into being by the genius of Jose Antonio Abreu and the accolades heaped upon him in recent years; of your apprenticeship in this great hope for changing lives; your vision of music therapy; your search for insight into music and the human brain; and your disillusionment at last with Abreu, because of his failure to stand up to the demagoguery and dictatorship imposed on your country by Hugo Chavez and his Castroite political movement. However far you confided in me that day, the theme took me back years.

I fear I've detached my recollections too far from the setting in Toledo. The sangria and aubergines would have long been finished before I learned all that I've just so briefly summarized. As I recall, we ordered paella mixta, various salads and Spanish wine, as you whirled through a first colouration of your past, while inquiring equally – in the chaotic manner of such exchanges - what had brought me to Toledo. What would I have said at such a point? The idea of the great library and the transmission of ancient knowledge must have been my theme. The fact that there in Toledo Western Europe had begun to recover the Greek classics, Aristotle not least, through Arabic copies of them being translated into Latin by often Jewish scholars. Yes?

Did you know of the great caliphal library at Cordoba, built at the height of Muslim rule in Spain, I must have asked. I mused, I feel certain, since this was and is so central to my worldview, on how that library, the greatest of its time, had been inspired by the legendary Library of Alexandria, which itself had been inspired by the private library of Aristotle, in Athens. After Berber fanatics sacked Cordoba and destroyed the library, I might have said, unaware of whether you knew these things, the Emir of Toledo built a new library in emulation of that at Cordoba. Aristotle's personal library, the Library of Alexandria, the great library of Cordoba and the emir's library here in Toledo form a direct line of descent, was my core idea.

'Why come here to think about all that, when the library vanished long ago?' you challenged me. 'Well, of course, I didn't come here expecting to find the library. I'm building a library with this history in mind. I came down from Madrid to muse on that history. It's more a meditation than an investigation. I believe science, with its breathtaking new possibilities for civilization, was first born in Greece; but it had to be reborn in modern times. It was lost in between, due to the ignorance and carelessness of human beings. The rebirth began here, to some extent. Our own civilization is jerry-built and in serious danger of collapse. The library I am building is inspired by the idea that we need a renovation of scientific civilization - if we are to avert catastrophe,' I said.

Did I actually say all that over our paella mixta, salads and wine? 'So,' you might have murmured, 'are you an academic philosopher or historian; perhaps the administrator of a university or of a public library?' 'I'm none of those things,' I parried. 'I have academic contacts and am financially secure. I can afford to do things without feeling concerned about making a living. The library I'm building is my own; as private as that of Aristotle; but up to date. You must know the work of Jorge Luis Borges?' You looked at me as if to ask, 'What do you take me for?' 'I have always been fascinated by his story 'The Library of Babel'. I'm building what you might think of as the Library of anti-Babel – a library I intend to use to rethink human civilization at the foundation.'

'So,' you ventured, perhaps wondering what manner of eccentric you had encountered, 'you wish to be a modern Aristotle?' 'Actually,' I would surely have responded, 'my models are more recent. Have you heard of Maimonides?' You shook your head. 'He was born in Cordoba, almost a thousand years ago. When the ruling house at Cordoba was overthrown by fanatical and narrow-minded Muslims who persecuted the Jews, he left Cordoba for Egypt. There he wrote a book called *A Guide of the Perplexed*. It was written in the form of a letter to his most prized student - in three volumes. In them, he tried to set out as clearly as possible what was true about the cosmos, what was true about being and God and what was the best way to live in the world.'

'And you are setting out to do something like this?' you asked; the astonished look returning to your features. 'More or less,' I must have said; 'but Maimonides is not my only model. About five hundred years later, in Holland, another Jewish thinker wrote two books that inspire me. His name was Benedict de Spinoza? Have you heard of him? The Rabbis detested him, as did the Catholics and Protestants, because he argued that their dogmatic and sectarian ways of interpreting the Bible were unsound. He was shunned within his own Jewish community as a heretic. His *Theological-Political Treatise* demonstrated that true religion required a toleration of theological dissent and a republican form of government. Those were revolutionary ideas then.'

'Was he imprisoned?' you asked. 'No, but he could only publish anonymously, if at all. The second book of his that I admire, his *Ethics* was not published until after his death. Both books were condemned by church and synagogue alike. Reading them was forbidden for centuries by the Catholic Church. But they were read by thoughtful and free-thinking people and over time they persuaded more and more people to demand tolerance, humane reforms, the advancement of science and responsible government.' 'How did he die?' you wanted to know. 'He was fascinated by optics and used to grind lenses for eye glasses, telescopes and microscopes. Tiny fibres from the glass accumulated over the years in his lungs and finally destroyed his health.'

'What a pity there was no miracle cure for such a disease in those days!', you exclaimed, shuddering sympathetically at the idea of Spinoza's lungs being destroyed by glass. 'Well, miracles were precisely what Spinoza suggested we not rely upon", I replied a little sardonically. 'But medical science had only just begun to feel its way into the body. Dissection was still widely frowned upon and physiology primitive. Even now, there is a vast amount we don't know and many things we still can't remedy.' 'Well, in any case, he died centuries ago. Why is he a model now?' 'Do you think that the work of religious tolerance, the advancement of science and the establishment of sound government are all done and dusted?' I asked with some sharpness.

'Fenimore!', you exclaimed with growing familiarity, 'of course I don't! I simply meant, don't you have more recent sources of inspiration?' 'Well, of course! But we started with why I'm in Toledo! Another inspiration is the early 20th century figure Edmund Husserl; a philosopher of science who lived in Germany. He died in 1938, just as the Holocaust was getting under way.' 'You mean he was Jewish, too?' 'As it happens, yes', I responded. 'There have been many eminent Jewish thinkers over the centuries. Jews place a great emphasis on education and literacy; and living as a minority among Muslims and Christians, they were heterodox outsiders. That meant they were rather better placed to see things differently and think more critically.'

'Husserl interests me as a human being', I went on, 'but it is his last book that most fascinates me: *The Crisis of the European Sciences and Transcendental Phenomenology*. He was pondering the crisis of the European sciences a decade before Oppenheimer's team at Los Alamos succeeded in making an atomic bomb. I've believed since school days that the world faces a kind of existential crisis and that the sciences are both problem and solution. They talk about 'Faustian bargains', but as we peer into the void, most of us don't really want to play Faust and accept that we've sold our souls to the Devil. I'd like to try completing Husserl's work. Of course, both the natural sciences and the crisis of our civilization have gone ahead by leaps and bounds since he died.'

'So', you asked, pouring each of us a fresh glass of wine; 'this book you were reading…Is it about these matters? What is it called?' You peered at its title the wrong way up, translating it for yourself aloud, '*El Arco de Ulises*. This is not about the philosophy of science, I assume. Is it literature? Is it about Omeros and the world of legend?' 'Actually it's about terrorism, law and strategy. It's a new book by a great friend of mine. The allusion to Odysseus is for poetic colour. The book itself is not poetic. It is about the kind of thing that happened in Madrid a few weeks before you or I got here – the terrible train bombings – and what it makes sense for us to do in response to such incidents. That's Tom's field. The book has just been released in New York.'

We had already pushed back our plates and glasses, satisfied with the meal. We spoke a little about Madrid and the bombings and the war in Iraq and realized that we had discovered a rapport, an interest in one another that would outlast the meal. You suggested we head out from La Cubana and walk up through the heart of the city. The best part of the afternoon lay ahead; especially given the long light of spring in Toledo. 'Where do you suggest we go?' I asked. 'San Roman', you volunteered, as if it had been on the tip of your tongue. 'It's an old museum at the crown of the hill, past the Cathedral and the Church of San Juan de Bautista. It was a church long ago, then a mosque, then a church again. It's now a little museum. You don't know of it?'

The ascent and the destination sounded eminently attractive, given my background interests; but I was drawn chiefly by the idea of being with you in the ascent through the old city; attracted to beguiling the afternoon with more of the conversation we'd been sharing. I slipped Tom's book back into my knapsack, we cleared our bill and you led me out through the rustic anteroom and quaint little bar of La Cubana, across the road and onto the evocative Alcantara. Given all that has happened since, that bridge now has a special place in my memory. It has become a bridge of dreams. From the moment we stepped onto it, I became in a sense one of your clients on the Canary Islands: you began there to strum the strings of my being and call me to therapy sessions.

We were half way across the bridge when you asked, looking at me with those keen eyes of yours, 'So, when this book you are writing is finished, what effect will it have?' My gaze, like yours, had been sweeping from east to west in a wide arc, following the curl of the Rio Tajo around the southern walls of the city, resting back and forth upon the sight of the medieval bastions, the Alcazar and the Cathedral. 'An author should be modest about his work',

I began. But you were not about to let me get away with that. 'I'd be content if a small number of highly intelligent people appreciated it – perhaps even one exceptional reader', I said. 'But how would that help to solve the great crisis of civilization you believe in?', was your sceptical response.

'Have you heard of Immanuel Kant?', I asked. Your vague expression showed that his name was not exactly familiar. 'He was a great thinker in the 18th century. One of his earliest but still most impressive books, written when he was only thirty years old, was his *Universal Natural History and Theory of the Heavens*. It laid out a coherent theory of everything and also anticipated by a century fundamental discoveries of astronomy and geophysics. Imagine being able to do that! Thirty years later, he wrote an essay called *Idea for a Universal History with Cosmopolitan Intent*. Now sixty, he expressed disgust and pessimism at human behaviour in general, but still boldly imagined a future in which the full development of human reason would gradually transform civilization.'

You were still staring at me quizzically. 'If I could write a book that was a present day combination of those two works by Kant, I would feel I had done extraordinarily well', I offered. You asked, 'What form will your book take?' 'I intend', I began, as we crossed the road, 'that it will be a philosophical treatise. But in the essay I just referred to, Kant wrote that it would actually be a strange project to write a book about how civilization would have to develop if it was to end up becoming truly rational. He thought that such a book would probably have to be a novel. I've long been struck by that idea of his, though I hadn't given much thought to it for a while. Your question brought it back to mind. Of course, I don't intend to write a novel.'

We stood, by then, before the horseshoe arch on the far side of the Alcantara through which lay the ascent into Toledo and on up to San Roman. I looked at the old gateway flanked by its two slender cypresses and found myself reciting spontaneously and silently to myself the words from the Gospel of Matthew, "Narrow is the way and strait is the gate that leads to eternal life and there are few who find it.' A Catholic education embeds such phrases in you for life. But you led the way straight through the gate. You took me right, then around and up to the left to where I could see ahead of us a broad flight of steps. 'These steps take us up to the Paseo del Carmen', you declared boisterously; and all but leapt up the stairs, as one who knew the way ahead.

The Paseo del Carmen was a cul-de-sac, ending at the stairs. You took me across it a little way to a smaller set of steps, flanked by cypresses in the same manner as the horseshoe arch below. You urged me up these. As we emerged into a plaza, with an old building to our right, you turned to me and announced quietly, 'This is the Plaza de la Concepcion. That', you added, pointing to the building on the right, 'is the old Convent of the Conception; though I don't know how many conceptions have taken place there.' With a light-hearted laugh you led me onward and upward. 'We go to the left up there', you said, pointing across the plaza and, for the first time touching my hand, practically took hold of it and led me over the open space – the place of conception.

It was when we came to the end of the alley leading left out of the plaza that you paused and announced triumphantly, 'This is the Calle Miguel de Cervantes. It will take us up to the Zocodover, the main city square.' Cervantes Street! That sounded like something one would encounter in many a Spanish city, such was the writer's fame and the country's pride in him. But I had no memory of it, whether from the past few days or my brief visit to the city with Nathalie long ago. 'Our way lies up here and across the Zoco', you declared, like an enthusiastic tour guide. 'You seem you know the place like the back of your hand!' 'I've been here before', you conceded. 'My hotel is just beyond the Zoco. I came down here to La Cubana three hours ago."

As we strolled up the fairly steep gradient of Cervantes you made a remark which, I think, will always stay with me; like so much that day, but even more so, given what followed. You were walking right beside me now. 'Do you remember', you asked me, 'that wonderful passage in *Don Quixote* in which Cervantes tells us that he found the history of Don Quixote de la Mancha right here in Toledo, in the Alcana marketplace, as a manuscript in Arabic, being sold off as scrap paper? He was so excited that he bought the whole manuscript and hired a Moor – since he could not find a Jew ready to hand – to translate it for him into Spanish.' I was caught out and confessed a little sheepishly, 'Ah, well, actually, I never got around to reading *Don Quixote*.'

You seemed more incredulous at this than at what I had read. You looked, waiting for me to grin and acknowledge that I was fooling. 'How can you not have read *Don Quixote*?', you finally asked, slowly, as if each word was struggling to find its due weight. 'That is impossible! You are a highly educated man! It is the greatest novel ever written; the fountainhead of all modern fiction; certainly of what we like to call realismo magico in Latin America. It has been the inspiration for so many great writers: Jorge Luis Borges, Gabriel Garcia Marquez, Octavio Paz, Mario Vargas Llosa...Where have you been that you have failed to read it?' 'I actually haven't read many novels of any kind since I was an undergraduate', was my response. That was the sober truth.

You paused for some time, absorbed in your own thoughts, as we completed the climb to the top of Cervantes. As we were about to climb the steps under the large arch that opened into the Zoco, you halted and said with a kind of passionate vehemence, 'There should be a statue of Cervantes here, looking down the road, so that everyone who is as uninitiated as you will infallibly see him as they pass and will be forced to take his monumental existence into account!' I was astounded.

'Right here, you think?', I asked, looking around and gazing back down the street. But you were moving. 'Come with me!', you urged passionately. 'There's something I want to show you! It's a few hundred metres from here, across the square and down El Comercio.'

The following ten or fifteen or twenty minutes, perhaps it was half an hour or more, were a blur of crowds and souvenir stores, cafes and marzipan shops, accompanied by somewhat light hearted banter as you quite purposefully, though not without pauses or distractions, led me to the destination you had in mind. There came a point where we found ourselves in a little plaza with narrow streets feeding into it from four different directions, one leading more or less straight ahead, one heading off to the right and climbing up, another falling away to the left and descending. You moved a few steps across it and pointed. A sign read 'Plaza de los Cuatro Calles' – Plaza of the Four Streets. Your point was lost on me until you made your next move.

You moved another few steps, turned away from me and pointed up at a smaller sign, a kind of plaque high up on the wall of what at ground level was a small pizzeria. You read out what was written there, translating it into English for my benefit: 'Here, in the epoch of Cervantes, began the Alcana Market'. You turned back to me expectantly, glowing with a kind of fervour. I was, in fact, quite struck by this little plaque, given what you had said. So right about here was where Cervantes claimed to have found the manuscript of *Don Quixote*. That moment now blends with you reading the celebrated passage to me aboard *Aletheia*, off Cos, six months later. 'You cannot leave this city ignorant of *Don Quixote*', you confided. 'Let's find a cafe and I'll tell you more about it!'

We referred to a street map and discovered that the best way from there to San Roman lay down to the left, past the Cathedral. No sooner had we turned down that way than you spotted a café on the corner - La Malguerida de la Trinidad, sporting a welcoming sign which read 'Cocina abierto siempre' – 'Kitchen Always Open'! Captivated by its convenience and the sign, we declared in unison, 'Let's sit in here!' It had a small circle of overstuffed chairs just inside the window and, to our good fortune they were unoccupied. I thought we'd pause there for a brief drink and a passing conversation about Cervantes. I failed to allow for your passion. When we walked out, a bottle of wine and a story-laden deepening of intimacy later, two convivial hours had elapsed.

My recollection of those two hours is somehow far less exact than that of the hours preceding them; I suspect because instead of being immersed in my own thoughts I was plunged into listening more and more to you, attending to you, delighting in your skills as a raconteur, your infectious laughter, your account of the uproarious and yet deeply humane and poignant comedy of Don Quixote. I remember you saying, as we sat down and ordered a bottle of Tuscan Chianti,

'You must know something of Don Quixote. Tell me everything you know about it!' 'Well', I offered, 'I know he was notorious for tilting at windmills; had a squire called Sancho Panza and suffered from romantic delusions.' 'Go on!', you urged. 'That's pretty much it', I confessed.

Even now, after all the other impressions I have formed of you, I can see indelibly etched in my mind's eye, the somehow painterly chiaroscuro of you, seated in the chair closest to the window, shaded by the dim interior, but with the afternoon light from outside illuminating the left side of your face. You rolled your eyes and gestured generously and humorously that my ignorance on the subject was simply incredible. Then, as the wine was served and we settled into the mood of the place, you set us both afloat – rowing or hoisting the sail, while I sat back to enjoy the ride – on the wide sea of Cervantes, with far more tales of his hilarious misadventures than I had ever heard before. Clearly, the novel was an intimate part of you. Now it drew me in its wake.

Something I had never picked up, in all my travels and wide reading, was that *Don Quixote* consists of two novels, written a decade or more apart. In the first, which was intended to be the full tale, Cervantes related the follies of the knight of La Mancha that have long since been proverbial, including that of his mistaking windmills for giants and charging at them on his bony steed, Rocinante, despite Sancho's observation that they really looked like windmills to him. Why did he do these things? Well, you explained, he was a gentleman of independent means who had a library full of romantic novels about chivalric knights. His imagination became so full of these that he felt it would be better to be a knight errant than decline into dotage on his country estate.

I seem to remember thinking, but cannot recall saying, that I was, in a sense the antithesis of Don Quixote. I was retreating from the possibility of exploits in the public world to a library; and moreover a library full of serious and scientific books, not brain-addling romances. But you were off and flying. You related many of the adventures in Part One, but declared that the real genius was in Part Two; written to give their comeuppance to imitators and pirates of Part One. In Part Two, Don Quixote discovers that an account of his exploits has been published and people everywhere recognize him as the famous Knight Errant of La Mancha. Given his reputation, this leads them to play tricks on him or play up to his delusions for their amusement.

The hilarity grew as Don Quixote and others speculated about who would write an account of this second set of adventures. I lost myself in you, in laughter, in Chianti and Quixote. Yet, as the afternoon drew on, there came a moment when you drew our little boat gently into the bank and remarked, 'Perhaps it's time to climb up now to San Roman. Listo?' 'Can you lead the way from here?'. And so we set off on the third leg of our ascent to San Roman. My mood was now quite buoyant with tales of the Knight of La Mancha, wine and laughter. The way upward, in consequence, became a dream of winding streets, a fantasia in a maze of alleys, apparent dead ends, historic sites; but above all the sound of your singsong voice leading me on, enchanted.

The next distinct memory I have is arriving at the umpteenth cobbled street and hearing you say, into my ear from close at hand, 'We are almost there!' I looked up and could make out, in the late afternoon light, against an azure sky, up a final slope, several classic Toledo cypress trees looming above a low hedge and among them what appeared to be a statue. You led me directly to the front of the statue and announced, 'This is Garcilaso de la Vega, one of the greatest romantic poets of sixteenth century Spain. He died young, in the country's wars with France.' You led me to a seat nearby, in the midst of the arbour, and we sat once more, for I know not how long, talking poetry and the romantic imagination. You were becoming the embodiment of Toledo for me.

My own work and preoccupations drifted away from me in those hours. The longer I spent with you, the more content I became to accompany you wherever your whim led us. And it led us, after our oblivious interval seated among the cypresses at the foot of the great sixteenth century poet, finally to cross the plaza, turn around a slight corner and find ourselves, at last, at the low door to the old church and mosque of San Roman, now the Museum of Visigothic History. We gazed at it. I recall remarking somewhat abstractedly, 'I imagine this building's Roman right down at the foundations.' I don't think you heard me. You were, presumably, lost in your own reflections and your own interpretation of the situation and of the novelty of our rapport.

In any case, the state of mind in which I passed through that door and the effect of being in your company must surely account for what followed. For the precinct was quite unremarkable in some respects, compared with churches, synagogues or museums with which either or both of us were already familiar. Yet the very smallness of the interior, with its high rounded arches and its smaller, higher window-like apertures above them in triplets, opening onto the darkness of the beamed, Romanesque ceiling, took on the aura of a privileged and intimate space into which you had taken me. Looking back now, I suspect you had both known this and given it thought before suggesting we go there. Perhaps, however, it had simply been an intuition on your part?

We walked slowly and quite wordlessly around the few exhibits. Then you stepped away from me into the centre of the quiet space, turned and murmured, looking not at me but up into the ancient arches and at the darkness of the ceiling: 'This is the empty space of possibility where a new music can be composed!' I don't know how long we lingered there, contemplating that extraordinarily abstract idea, but those words have stayed with me and now infuse my memory of San Roman. They demonstrated that you must have been responding to much of what I had said to you earlier in the afternoon, quite as much as seeking to draw me into your own world. Yet your declaration was spoken clearly out of your world and into mine. What new music, then?

Your words blended into our long descent from that summit, guided by I know not what compass or agreement, until we found ourselves at my hotel, the Pintor El Greco; seated at one of those small black tables in the courtyard between the lobby and the restaurant. You recited a poem about exile, written, you said, by Abd al-Rahman, the Muslim conqueror of Spain long ago. The night air of spring in Toledo made the history of el-Andalus come to life for us and we fell to sharing the fantastic tale of the man known among his Muslim contemporaries as al-Dakhil – The Emigrant – and as The Falcon of the Quresh, greatest of the servants of the Prophet. This he was called by his mortal enemy, the Caliph al-Mansur, in reluctant admiration.

Fleeing al-Mansur, who slaughtered his family and sent assassins after him the length and breadth of Muslim North Africa, al-Dakhil drew an army to him and carved out a new empire in Visigothic Spain. He took the old Roman city of Cordoba and made it the most splendid city in the West. He built a great mosque and a great library. Outside the city's walls he built a garden called Rusafa after the place where his family had been murdered. You let slip that you'd be travelling on to Cordoba, but also Granada – seeking the music. Then you quoted with fervour Nietzsche's maxim, 'Sin musica, la vida seria un error (Without music, life would be a mistake)'. There and then, finally besotted, I longed to take you to a private and carnal place.

But at that very moment your mobile phone rang. The conversation that followed was in Spanish and the rapid patois of friendship. I gathered that your friend in Madrid had called. He or she had arrived in Toledo. Your disposition was to rendezvous. While chagrined at the abrupt end to the conversation, I made a dignified retreat; asking whether you would care for an escort to your hotel. That wouldn't be necessary, you replied. I walked you only to the yard outside the hotel, where the bronze bust of Samuel Levy barely gleamed in the dusk; and there bade you farewell. I offered you my card and declared how lovely it had been to have had your company for the day. You gently embraced me, then turned and disappeared into the gathering darkness.

After breakfast the next morning, I found a message from you at the front desk: *Gracias por el dia. Read Cervantes! Margarita.* There were no contact details. I breakfasted alone, headed back to Madrid and took the night flight. "One day conversation" might usefully now enter my lexicon alongside the familiar "one night stand", I decided. But I was wrong, I soon realized, to think of el dia in that way. It remained indelibly imprinted on my memory and imagination. When you emailed declaring *I am coming to the Ends of the Earth for a music therapy conference in October. Would you like to meet again? I would like to see your library. Margarita,* memories of that day bathed your lapidary sentences in the afternoon light of Toledo. It would not be a one day conversation, after all.

You wanted to see the library and the precincts of Cos. The timing was good. Cos had been completed a few months earlier. We were hard at work stocking the Vivarium and the Mahlerium, landscaping the grounds; finishing the frescoes. By October the library would be looking splendid in its architecturally classical layout; richly stocked in its Aristotelian abundance and bibliographic order. An arrangement was quickly agreed. You would come as my guest for ten days. So it was that you arrived at the Ends of the Earth one morning in the southern spring of 2004, from Tenerife via Madrid and Dubai, on Emirates; bringing with you as a gift the new translation of *Don Quixote* by Edith Grossman. And we began again the ascent to San Roman.

Pyramid at Tenochtitlan at its acme.
Image by Catherine Gordon.

The Fall of Tenochtitlan

Your Neruda sang that he was 'here to tell the story' of the Americas. Do you recall? He invoked 'precipitous tunnels of shady Venezuelan peacefulness', almost as if such peacefulness in what had been the New Andalusia was his Muse. He evoked the Rio Orinoco as a flow of the 'timeless hour' before the conquest and prayed that he might enter its 'baptismal darkness.' He did all this, he wrote all this, of course, half a century before Chavismo and has been praised for his poetry. Yet he was an admirer of Stalin and that monster's henchmen; which we cannot forget. Nor is there now peacefulness in Venezuela, by any means. But catastrophes come in many forms and here I want to draw different lines to those of that poet of fecund imagery.

My concern, having traced the evolution of both cosmos and life, is with the trajectory of science and the collision of worlds. How has it become possible, out of cosmos and life for mind to emerge and to conceive abstract entities, to generate theories and to test them in ways that transform reality? That is my concern and how can I sing of that? All those arguments that I have advanced to show that such abstraction and theory took a unique leap among the Hellenes, only to be stifled by Roman empiricism and empire, point to the flowering of the rational mind, but ever so briefly and among ever so few. And even then, catastrophe – as with the theory of atomic fission – leapt forth on pragmatic limbs from within the chrysalis of pure thought.

There is, the troubled mind reflects, a straight line – or, more precisely, a *curved* line - from the Grecian deduction that the Earth must be a sphere to the destruction of the ancient America extolled by Neruda in his *Canto Genérale*. That curve leads from Eratosthenes' calculation, in historic Alexandria, of the *circumference* of the spherical Earth to the discovery of the Americas by Columbus and the catastrophe of the European conquest of two continents they called the 'New World'. It occurs to me, from a certain angle, as being like the arc of a shell or perhaps of a nuclear missile. The curve was conceived without the slightest imperial intent. Yet it launched a missile: an intercontinental ballistic one - with multiple, independently-targeted re-entry vehicles.

Rehearse the core insight of the hominid as scientist observing the heavens. Aristotle, drawing upon two hundred years of primary natural philosophy, deduced that the Earth was immobile and at the centre of the universe. In these respects, the 'master of those who know' was in error. However, he believed on firmer grounds that the Earth is spherical, not flat – or any other shape. He set down his grounds in Book Two of *On the Heavens*. How else, he asked, would eclipses of the Moon show the intervening Earth, adumbrated on the lunar surface, to be curved as it does? Yet that was a simple observation compared with the cast of mind of Eratosthenes, with his trigonometry and his mathematical demonstration of the Earth's actual circumference.

Even Aristotle, however, a century before Eratosthenes made his great deduction, wrote, in that same treatise, *On the Heavens,* that "...one should not be too sure of the incredibility of the view of those who conceive that there is continuity between the parts of the Earth about the Pillars of Hercules and the parts about India, and that in this way the ocean is one. As further evidence in favour of this, they quote the case of elephants, a species occurring in each of these extreme regions, suggesting that the common characteristic of these extremes is explained by their continuity." He never guessed – that master - that there was a *discontinuity* and that there were no elephants in the vast continents that lay between the Pillars of Hercules (Gibraltar) and India.

He thought, many decades before Eratosthenes, that the Earth was *much smaller* than it is. It took acute observation, an ingenious experiment and trigonometry on the part of Eratosthenes to calculate correctly that the circumference of our world is 25,000 miles. Cristoforo Colombo, when trying to persuade Queen Isabella of Spain to finance an expedition across the Atlantic to India, used the Aristotelian estimate. He claimed and possibly believed that the Earth was much smaller than it actually is and that he could reach Japan (Cipango, he called it) by sailing about 3,700 kilometres farther west than your Canary Islands. The experts knew better. They had inherited Eratosthenes' proof. Yet none advanced the idea of continents in that extra space.

Do you see, therefore, that none of them, any more than the Greek scientist, *intended* to take the form of a ballistic missile with destructive MIRV warheads launched into a pristine ecology and unknown cultures. Colombo declared he could sail to Cipango and Cathay while avoiding the Turkish Empire. The experts declared against him, arguing that he had greatly underestimated the distances involved, so that the expedition would cost too much and surely fail. Both King John of Portugal, in 1485; and Queen Isabella heeded the experts on both counts. CC tried to drum up interest in Venice, in Genoa and in England, with equal lack of success. *None* of the powers that be conceived greedily of new worlds and the prospects of genocidal plunder.

Yet all that came about – as if by some strange and ineluctable fate; as if in a Greek tragedy, rather than as a consequence of Greek geometry. 1492 was – as everybody is uneasily aware – the year that the bell of fate tolled in the Spanish courts. Ferdinand and Isabella had literally just conquered Granada, destroying the last Muslim stronghold in Spain. Flushed with that conquest, they gave the insistent Colombo a fresh audience in Cordoba, in the Alcazar Castle. That signified, after almost 800 years, the triumph of the Cross and the Sceptre over the Falcon of the Quresh. The epoch in which we met, evoked by all that is Toledo, was at an end; but the seeds of Cervantes had been planted and the fuse lit of the Madrid train bombings by al Qaeda in our own times.

Isabella, on the advice of a priest, once again rejected Columbus's overture. What presentiment had that priest that persuaded him to urge against the explorer? It seems improbable that the priest believed there were untold millions of heathens awaiting forced conversion in a New World, or extermination for their sins in the name of a wrathful God. It seems even less probable that, guessing such things, he was seeking to avert the course of fate. In any case, Isabella again rejected the proposal. CC was departing Cordoba, believing he would never be able to put together his visionary expedition, when King Ferdinand intervened. A royal guard brought the missile engineer back to court; his proposal was endorsed and fate proceeded.

Ferdinand would later claim credit for 'discovery' of the Caribbean islands. Given the slaughter, slavery and poverty created there, he might reasonably have disclaimed responsibility; but there were wealth and glory to be had and the slaughter was taking place far away. The Spanish Crown and Colombo, followed by his descendants for almost three hundred years, would engage in legal disputes over entitlements to wealth from the Americas. The way was opened by Ferdinand; of that there can be no doubt. Without his regal patronage, the missile would neither have been assembled nor launched. Ponder that, as Neruda might have written, 'before we return to the sea, whence our sorrows come.' For CC moved in that Eratosthenean arc across the wide sea.

Colombo, harbinger of those sorrows, arrived in what we now call the Bahamas in October 1492. He found the natives peaceful and friendly. Ominously, he remarked that their lack of weaponry of any effective kind meant that he could easily conquer them with just fifty soldiers and govern them entirely as he saw fit. Such is the human use of human beings. Such is the manner in which the eye, lighting upon prospects of the easy satisfaction of imagined appetite, triggers the voracious behaviour of elementary life. So it was, from the dense life of the Cambrian seas, that predation first arose; generating in time monsters of prodigious size and astonishing variety; yet never such as we have proved to be and seldom more than there. There monsters feasted.

It might occur to you, in a quiet moment on the volcano of Tenerife, that the gross inequalities, the wrenching urban squalor and rural destitution, the countless callow caudillos and men on horseback who have plagued your continent were all the spawn of that casual remark by Cristoforo Colombo, first impact of the missile, all those years ago – 1492. Did Hugo Chavez with his 'socialism for the twenty first century' sprout, then, from the shores of Barbados? Not from those shores, no. We need to be more precise than a poetic turn of phrase would have us be. He sprang, in lineal descent, from those fateful words of Colombo and the world of destruction and domination that they brought into being. They declared the Greek tragedy had begun.

You've often asked, in finer cities than Caracas and more cosmopolitan settings than Santa Cruz de Tenerife, 'What can be done about the drift to dictatorship in my beautiful country?' Isn't it possible to orchestrate something or to play a benign Pied Piper and lead your people to a peaceful and prosperous state? Responding out of darkness or obliquely, due to immersion in my science, I remember recommending that you study the tribulations of Bolivar – as if that would solve your problems. On another occasion – either at Luxor or as we strolled the ruins of Chichen Itza – I urged upon you the memoirs of Nadezhda Mandelstam, *Hope Against Hope* and *Hope Abandoned* – in which the partner of the poet wrote of Stalin and the travails of Russia.

You are full of gentleness and music and therefore recoiled in dismay from the very title 'hope abandoned'. You insisted I offer something clear and fine. Neruda was fine, if not clear, but was a man of the Left, praising that very Stalin and his executioner Vyshinsky of whom the bereaved, but resilient Nadezhda had written. And how much difference did his cantos make, in general? Or Abreu, whose great project among the disinherited and unmusical you embraced with all your heart: what of his music? Has it enabled the barrios to rise above the demagoguery of Chavez or the soaring violence of Caracas? I would declare, 'Embrace reason and science!' But at that refrain, a dark chord sounds on the piano of my mind and evokes Ferdinand's terrible missile.

Didn't I say to you, strolling down the Unter den Linden in the freedom that has regrown since the Stasi's end in 1989 that you stand in a tradition going back to Plato? He believed, to be sure, that music is enormously important and that when you change the music of a society 'the city walls shake'. Yet his primary commitment was to reason and the apprehension of abstract truth. He declared to his disciples that, having 'received a better and more complete education' than the common run of mankind, it fell to them to move among the unenlightened, beset by obscurity and delusion, and to draw their minds towards the light and the good. You have despaired of doing so in your country. That is understandable. Plato, likewise, felt thwarted in his time.

You may think that, in referring back to Plato, a hundred years before Eratosthenes, I have chosen to avoid the subject of what occurred when Ferdinand's MIRV exploded in the New World.

That's not so. I am simply circling around the conundrum that even our best efforts to exercise reason and induce the mass of humanity to do likewise – or to play as members of an orchestra, as Abreu preaches – have run into difficulties. There is so much that we need to get into perspective. Besides, if the MIRV sprang from the reasoning of Eratosthenes, one might argue that the Catholic Church sprang in considerable measure from Plato's reasoning and his vision of the ideal republic governed by a Nocturnal Council of the wise. We still debate all this.

If you stepped back into your 'Bolivarian' New Andalusia, your Venezuela, even armed with impeccable doctrines and an international reputation, you'd be following in Plato's footsteps to Syracuse. His aim was to turn the tyrant Dionysius II into a 'philosopher-king'. When that failed, he became the mentor of Dion, nephew of the tyrant, who overthrew his uncle and tried to establish a republic on Plato's principles. It made him so unpopular that he was murdered. Plato had to flee for his life, so his epistles, written chiefly after this, might themselves be titled 'hope against hope and hope abandoned'. Yet he did not abandon hope. He *wrote*, hoping his writings would have long effect. Did their blending with Roman priesthood and Judaism justify his hope?

The fallout from CC as MIRV has been devastating and the recovery is far from complete. Why do you think Pablo Neruda was a Communist; or Gabriel Garcia Marquez a friend of Castro? Why do you think Isabel Allende lived in exile for years after 1973? Why did Mario Vargas Llosa write with such poignancy about *The War of the End of the World* and *The Real Life of Alejandro Mayta*? What do you know of the *matanza* in El Salvador in 1932, the *violencia* in Colombia in the 1950s, the right wing terror in Guatemala between the 1950s and the 1980s, the brutal purge of the Left by Pinochet in Chile from 1973, the dirty war in Argentina in the mid-1970s, the horrific death squad slaughter in El Salvador again in the 1980s? But these pale against the horrors of the Conquest.

How do we compute the numbers and why do they matter? *Sube a nacer conmigo, mi amor. Dame la mano desde la profunda, zona de tu dolor diseminado*, your Neruda wrote: Rise up reborn with me, my love. Lend me your hand out of the depths from which your sorrows grow.[46] The great French historian Fernand Braudel, in the opening chapter of his three volume work *Civilization and Capitalism From the 15th to the 18th Century*, concluded that the Spanish conquest 'brought a colossal biological slump to America', with the native population collapsing by around 90% in the sixteenth

---

46   Fenimore is here, again, alluding to Neruda's *Canto Genérale*, Part II, poem 12; but he has translated it for himself. The original is addressed to a 'brother', not a lover. The metaphorical brother was the vanished Inca. Fenimore uses the poem to address his own canto to Margarita, a child of Venezuela and the Orinoco. – TCE.

century. There is our mind-numbing *profunda*. Nothing in the long history of Eurasia, from the Atlantic sea coast to Cipango can compare. Nothing else in human history comes close.

The percentage itself is dumbfounding, but would count for less if there had only been very small numbers of 'Americans' before CC hit Barbados. However, their numbers cry out from the depths and while uncertain, seem to have numbered many millions and in all probability tens of millions. Linda Newson, in a paper on the depopulation of Nicaragua in the sixteenth century, estimated the native population of Central America, before the Spanish conquest, at six million. If her figures were correct, then Central America alone – excluding Mexico's estimated twenty to thirty million pre-Hispanic inhabitants – saw a Holocaust almost as horrific as that which Hitler perpetrated in Europe. Yet even Mexico's population fell to about one million in that time.

To this must be added the Caribbean, where, as the poet declared, 'the butchers razed the islands'. Mexico and, of course, the whole of the southern cone, not least the Inca lands of Ecuador, Peru and Chile; the lands of the Amazon basin and far Patagonia were all alike swept by the scythe of disease, murderous steel and men on horseback bearing guns. North America, too, was razed, in wide areas of the south east and south west, a century before the Puritans arrived at Plymouth Rock. The Puritans and those who followed were, nonetheless, another wave of missiles. They cleared the north east with smallpox and guns until ancient tribal lands of light footprint and chronic border wars had become New England of the dissenting and exiled churches.

What did I say of Plato and the Church? Father Bartolome de las Casas, rare saint of the New World holocaust, bore witness to the slaughter and the plunder. Not that others didn't. His, however, was a moral outcry, not an historical commentary only. He attempted, over many years, to minister to the afflicted in the razed islands and within the hinterland of the Orinoco, along the coastlands of that strangely named 'New Andalusia', where music and dancing suffered with the reckless depredations of the German mercenaries. He laboured and went down like Father Gabriel in *The Mission* – counting ineffectually the toll of the Conquest, while ineffectual decrees of the Spanish Crown and the Papacy papered over the obliteration of whole unknown cultures and native communities.

The man of God watched helplessly as the soldiers of the Spanish Crown and freebooters out for every kind of loot 'grabbed suckling infants by the feet and, ripping them from their mothers' breasts, dashed them headlong against the rocks'. He wrote that the marauders in the Caribbean 'slaughtered anyone and everyone in their path, on occasion running through a mother and her baby with a single thrust of their swords. They spared no one, erecting especially wide gibbets on which they could string their victims with their feet just off the ground and then burn them alive thirteen at a time, in honour of our Saviour and the twelve Apostles, or tie straw to their bodies and set fire to it.' Does this sound like the blood-lands of Eastern Europe under the Nazis?

There was no precedent for the scale of epidemics which the Spanish arrival unleashed upon the Americas. The diseases, starting with smallpox, to which the natives had no resistance, decimated the New World populations, even before Spanish marauders marched or rode inland and set about putting them to the sword, burning them alive, impaling them, hacking off hands and feet, setting wild dogs on them, hanging them, starving them, putting them to forced labour in mines, deporting them in droves as slaves. It has been estimated by credible and careful demographers that there had been eighty to a hundred million copper-skinned human beings in the New World by 1492. It was 90% of *this* number who perished in the decades that followed, down to 1600.

According to Las Casas, the despoliation of Venezuela in the 1520s was even more barbaric than the depredations in Mexico, Central America or Peru. Larger than Spain itself, he later wrote, Venezuela was inhabited by a people docile and peaceful, in a land abounding in natural riches. Does this sound familiar? Of course, Las Casas knew nothing of oil and its uses. He was referring to animal, vegetable and precious mineral. He claimed that a population of four or five million – a fraction of the current population - was all but annihilated by German mercenaries, hired by those granted use of its wide and helpless lands. 'Granted', you understand, by the Spanish Crown. And who 'gave' it to the Crown? Ah, well, the Pope, of course: the Borgia Pope in Rome.

The ravagers of Venezuela, Las Casas claimed, showed themselves to be 'fiends with their capacity for inventing diabolical and ever more sadistic methods of mass murder.' Disease, starvation, social collapse and slave labour, of course, killed far more of the population than outright violence. Fra Bartolome had occasion to reflect with particular regret on the fate of Venezuela. He had attempted for some years to establish a utopian society, where natives could peacefully co-exist with Spanish colonists. He built a hospice and school at Cumaná, now a beach resort for the bourgeoisie. It ended in bitter failure. His own Hispanic colonists, against his explicit instructions, went slave-hunting among the islands, triggering retaliation and seaborne war.

Were they 'overmen', the *ubermenschen* or supermen of Nietzsche, those conquistadors who brought guns, germs and steel to the Americas along the arc calculated by Eratosthenes? They were like Mongols in Central Asia three hundred years before; or like the proverbial Huns marauding across the Roman world a thousand years earlier, reaching the Brenner Pass; where the Pope – of all people – daunted Attila and he turned back. Yet Nietzsche at his most visionary invoked the crossing by Colombo of the unknown. We have shared and I have marked as shared that last aphorism in his *Daybreak*, proclaiming as 'aeronauts of the spirit' those who, like brave birds go 'where everything is sea, sea, sea', seeking India and risking wreckage against infinity.

There is the true arc of the human spirit, one longs to declare! Questing across uncharted seas; guided by mapped projections, abstract hypotheses and uncertain intuitions. All our great teachers and precursors, like exhausted migratory birds, have at last alighted on some desolate rock or fallen into the unending sea, he wrote; and so it well may be for you and me. 'But what of that?' he challenged. Others, stronger than us, will fly further. Why, however, in this direction, where all suns til now have sunk into the sea? Are even we hoping to reach an India? Is that why we risk being wrecked against infinity? His metaphor is the unexpected disclosure of new worlds. Yet that metaphor contains and can never be rid of the fate that befell those worlds. Do you see?

Long before we met, from a base deep within the walled enclaves of that New England of dissenting churches of which I wrote above, I journeyed south into the heartlands smitten long before by the first conquistadors. It was a time of brutal 'small wars' in Central America. A colleague from Boston was going on field work to Mexico City to interview political exiles from El Salvador and Guatemala. I chose to undertake the inquiry with him. Staying at the Hotel Maria Cristina, in Colonia Cuauhtémoc, I met a woman whom I shall refer to as the French Colonel's Daughter. She was French Vietnamese and was up in Mexico City from Acapulco, where she was working. Between political interviews, she and I became acquainted and spoke of many things.

Her father had fought in the early phases of the French war in Indochina. He had fallen in love with her Vietnamese mother while fighting the Viet Minh. She was born in the French stronghold of Vung Tau, in 1950, but raised in the Paris of De Gaulle. She embodied the history of revolution, counter-revolution and failed utopias. There was so much to talk about and, besides, she was beautiful. We went out to the great Olmec ruin of Teotihuacan on the day of Saturn and climbed the Temple of the Sun, from the summit of which one has a sweeping view of the wide and fertile valley in which that great city flourished long ago. We walked further down the Avenue of the Dead and ascended the two thousand year old Temple of the Moon to gain perspective.

There we talked of Tenochtitlan and the fate of the Aztecs, under the bright sun. When the Spaniards marched up into the Aztec dominion from Vera Cruz and Tlaxcala in 1519, they were astounded by what they saw and above all by Tenochtitlan. It was more orderly, one of their number later wrote, and also better designed, more opulent and beautiful than anything he or his companions had seen in Europe. Those men had, between them, seen Madrid and Paris, Rome and Constantinople, Venice at its apogee with its famous canals and Genoa of the ships. Yet this

Aztec city, built upon a lake, with bridges and causeways linking it to every shore, surpassed all those in its architectural elegance and specific wonders. She knew these things and we conversed.

Yet the Aztecs were late-comers to those parts and relative barbarians. They imposed themselves by conquest upon the natives. They were, in their own inimitable manner, Nietzschean overmen, dominating the *untermenschen* or 'under-men' of the hinterlands. This brought them their nemesis, since the under-men allied with the Spanish conquistadors to bring them down. When they had entered the valley of the lake, two hundred years earlier, however, the Aztecs themselves had been astounded by Teotihuacan, which they called 'the city of the gods'. It was already ruined and abandoned before they arrived from the north; though perhaps it still had a little more of its primal splendour than when she and I gazed upon it thirty years ago, in the Cold War years.

A measure of how it may have looked, before the stucco and paint and other ornamentation eroded wholly from its awesome stones, is the roofless ruin of the High Priest's House – a labyrinth of courts, store-rooms, dining halls, kitchens, sleeping quarters and small chapels. We could almost have been in an Egyptian ruin; or in Knossos of the Minoan Kings. Such ruins, as you know, are scattered across Mexico, especially its more southerly regions, and not least on the Yucatan peninsula. They are the remains of agrarian civilizations that arose in the Americas as far back as 7,000 BCE. Teotihuacan itself was relatively late, not early, in the history of the Americas and Tenochtitlan of the Aztecs was the last pinnacle of that history – before the Holocaust.

It was from Xicotenga, lord of Tlaxcala, that Cortes received the most detailed intelligence assessment of the condition of the Aztec empire, before he marched into central Mexico. It is recorded that the Spaniards were 'all astonished at the courtesy and mildness' with which Xicotenga and his lieutenants addressed them. Xicotenga informed Cortes that Montezuma, the Aztec emperor, could field an army of one hundred and fifty thousand men. The Tlaxcalans had had to fend off such armies throughout one hundred years of war with Tenochtitlan. 'How is it, then', asked Cortes of the tall, well-built and dignified lord of Tlaxcala, 'that with so large an army they have never entirely conquered you?' And Xicotenga spoke of the tidal flow of wars.

The key, declared Xicotenga, to the constraints on Aztec power, was the resentment of the undermen pressed into its service and their lack of spirit in fighting for their overlord. Cortes might have thought, at such a point, of how the Greeks outfought the Persian masses, from Themistocles to Alexander, for similar reasons'; but perhaps he did not. In any case, the rede of Xicotenga was that all the peoples subdued by Montezuma and harvested for bloody human sacrifices, were very hostile to the Aztecs and gave the Tlaxcalans warnings of impending invasion, enabling them to prepare their defences well. The inveterate ally, however, of dread Tenochtitlan was the very ancient Cholula, a day's march from Tlaxcala and deemed treacherous.

Cholula was an index of Mexico before the conquest, being at the trading hub of the Mexican heartland. It had been continuously inhabited for almost three thousand years by the time Cortes intruded upon its world-in-being. It was immensely older than Tenochtitlan and had a great sacred pyramid that was the largest such structure anywhere in the Americas. In fact, it was the largest pyramid by volume anywhere in the world, measuring 400 metres on each side and sixty six metres in height. New emperors of Tenochtitlan would be crowned by priests from Cholula, like Charlemagne being crowned Holy Roman Emperor by the Pope. The urban precinct alone had one hundred thousand inhabitants. Its textiles and fine pottery were widely prized by others.

Xicotenga and his court told Cortes further about Montezuma's provincial garrisons, his vast wealth, his tribute system, his palaces and his many women. They spoke of the formidable fortifications of Tenochtitlan, from long familiarity in war and peace. They specified the depths of the lake at different points and how the Aztecs had built their bridges and causeways for access and for urban defence. The houses within the city were themselves small fortresses, Cortes was informed, with flat roofs and parapets, so that they could be defended by small forces. They described Chapultepec, its spring, and its aqueduct; the Aztecs' weapons and their tactics in battle. These last they showed Cortes in pictures painted from history on sisal cloths.

There in Tlaxcala, the Spaniards were informed that, long ago, there had been giants in the Mexican world, whom the ancestors of the Tlaxcalans had had to subdue and exterminate. This was a folk tradition not only handed down but based on the evidence of bones. They brought before Cortes, to his amazement, the femur or thigh bone of one such imaginary giant. It measured more than five feet in length. The Spanish chronicler recorded that they all were so astonished by this bone that they 'felt certain there must have been giants in that land'. Yet we can say with greater confidence that the bone will have been that of a dinosaur or perhaps a great Pleistocene ground sloth, not that of a human being. Their folk legend has become our science.

Even in Tlaxcala of the mild and courteous councillors, however, the Spanish testified that they found not casual, but institutionalized cannibalism. The chronicler declares that there were 'wooden cages made of lattice-work, in which men and women were imprisoned and fed until they were fat enough to be sacrificed and eaten.' Horrified by the practice, the foreigners took it upon themselves everywhere to break open the cages, freeing the victims. Whenever they entered a city, he declared, their captain's first order would be to break open such cages full of human sheep. Cortes rebuked the Tlaxcalans for their cannibalism and they promised to reform; but they would resume the practice as soon as Spanish vigilance was averted, so he wrote.[47]

Cortes declared he would march to Tenochtitlan, Montezuma having already sent him emissaries bearing gifts and offers of hospitality. Xicotenga warned him by every means to put no faith in the emperor and to prepare himself and his small force for a war to the death against that Lord. Advised by Cortes to make peace with the them, Xicotenga replied that no treaty with the Aztecs was worth the sisal it was painted on, for enmity was too deeply rooted in their characters and they never kept faith, whatever they promised by way of agreements. If you fight them, as you will, he said, leave none alive, neither young nor old, but destroy them utterly. He spoke, in short, like the Hebrew God invoking the ban regarding the Canaanites in the land of promise.[48]

You would hardly guess from the general tone of the chronicler's narrative that the wholesale slaughter and death from epidemic which followed the Spanish arrival in the Caribbean and in Mexico was already well under way by 1519. His refrain is that Cortes everywhere treated the native chieftains with respect, issuing only the solemn injunction that he had come in the name of his majesty the King of Spain to save their souls. They must, he insisted, give up their worship of idols, their human sacrifice, their cannibalism and the practice of sodomy. The paradox that such 'wicked' peoples had built such flourishing cities and sophisticated cultures seems to have made little impression on the chronicler, even looking back on their destruction long afterward.

---

47   The chronicler to whom Fenimore refers here is clearly Bernal Diaz and his historical memoir *The Conquest of New Spain*. His copy in the Vivarium is dated April 1976 and is heavily annotated. It includes the original editor's observation that Diaz did not set down his account until the 1550s, when he was living on an estate in Guatemala. This was long after the events he describes, but he completed the work because he felt other accounts had not been accurate and that a faithful record of what had taken place was necessary. – TCE.

48   'Fenimore alludes here to one of the most notorious features of the Old Testament – the command given by God to the Israelites to exterminate the entire population and even the domesticated animals of whole Canaanite cities, beginning with Jericho. He does not, for some reason, pause to point out something which I know he was aware of from no later than 2001, when we discussed the subject in the context of the 9/11 calamity. The late twentieth century archaeological evidence from extensive excavations in Israel demonstrates that what the Book of Joshua describes never took place. Not only did Jericho not fall, walls and all, to a Hebrew conquest – since it was not a walled city at the time, but an abandoned site – but there was no sweeping conquest or genocide at all. The story presented in Deuteronomy and Joshua is a theological fiction of a most unsettling kind, made up centuries later to stir up feelings of religious solidarity and exclusivity among the people of the small and beleaguered Kingdom of Judah, in between the Assyrian destruction of the northern Kingdom of Israel (721 BCE), the crushing of King Josiah's army by the Egyptians in 610 BCE and the looming threat of the Babylonian conquest of 589 BCE. He and I spoke of the relevance of the dark legend of 'the ban' (the injunction to commit genocide) in regard to ideas of jihad and also counter-insurgency. – TCE.

Cholula, wrote the chronicler, was situated on a plain and surrounded by many other towns around it. He does not say villages, but towns and he names them: Tepeaca, Tlaxcala, Chalco, Tecamachalco, Huexotzinco 'and a great many more'. The land, he declared, was rich in maize, peppers and other vegetables as well as in the maguey from which they brew their wine. He praised their ceramics of red, white and black clay, painted with various motifs and noted that they supplied the provinces of the Aztec empire with these wares. As for the great city of Cholula itself, he wrote that it had 'many lofty towers, which were the temples and shrines in which they kept their idols' and that they held religious services 'like novenas' before one such.

Here Montezuma attempted to have them trapped and massacred, by arrangement with the lords of ancient Cholula. Cortes, however, discovering their plot, set upon them with his Tlaxcalan allies and turned the tables, in a massacre that became proverbial. Not, however, a genocidal one, since Cortes called his Tlaxcalan dogs of war to heel short of that and sent word ahead to Tenochtitlan that he had had some troubles in Cholula, but was coming in peace, nonetheless, to the Aztec capital. His reputation as some kind of magus now became enhanced and growing apprehension marched ahead of his small army into the heart of Mexico. Among his priests and idols, Montezuma took counsel about how to check the advance of this dangerous stranger.

The Aztec greeted the Spaniards, treating them with the greatest outward courtesy and showing them his magnificent city. According to the chronicler, the order and opulence it exhibited were alike breathtaking. He noted the riches of Montezuma's court, the extraordinary order and cleanliness of the whole urban layout. He bore witness to wonderful botanical gardens featuring many varieties of flowers and sweet-scented trees; fresh water ponds with inflow and outflow pipes; myriad species of small birds nesting in arbours; and the cultivation of numerous medicinal and useful herbs. Everything was built of stone and plaster, he observed: baths and walks, enclosures and rooms like summerhouses where the 'wicked' Aztecs danced and sang.

Not least, this man of Castile, who died a landlord in Guatemala, described in detail the great public market-place of Tenochtitlan. 'We were astounded', he wrote, 'at the great number of people and the quantities of merchandise and at the orderliness and good arrangements that prevailed, for we had never seen such a thing before…Some of our soldiers who had been in many parts of the world, in Constantinople, in Rome and all over Italy, said that they had never seen a market so well laid out, so large, so orderly and so full of people.' They might well have done in the Greco-Roman world, but not yet in Europe of the Renaissance. And this alone should take our breath away, for it testifies to settled commerce and order amid chronic and brutal wars.

Then Montezuma took Cortes and a party of the Spaniards to the great temple of Tlatelolco, in the midst of the sacred precinct at the centre of Tenochtitlan; a compound surrounded by double masonry walls, 350 metres on one side and 300 on the other. The pyramid at Cholula covered more ground, but St Peters does not, which gives one some idea of the religious imagination of those vanished cultures. Ascending one hundred and fourteen steps to the pinnacle of the pyramid, our chronicler relates, Montezuma took Cortes by the hand and bid him look down at the great city and all that lay around it, as far as the eye could see. He declared that if Cortes had not had a good view of the great market-place before, he could see it better now.

Sitting with the French Colonel's daughter on the Temple of the Moon half a lifetime ago, I tried to imagine what Cortes must have beheld at that moment in time: the glory of Tenochtitlan and its elaborate realm on the very eve of the catastrophe of their utter desolation. The chronicler tells us he was there with Montezuma and Cortes and that 'we stood there looking', because the huge pyramid 'stood so high that it dominated everything'. There were three causeways leading into Tenochtitlan: the causeway of Itzapalapa, that of Tacuba and that of Tepeaquilla. There was also the great aqueduct from Chapultepec supplying the city with fresh water; and the bridges at intervals on the causeways, allowing both the flow of the lake water and the movement of traffic.

Everywhere, he reflected, there could be seen numerous canoes, some coming with provisions for the market-place, others returning with cargo and merchandise to the edges of the lake for onward traffic to the many towns that stood around its shores and in the hinterlands beyond. Yet, he wrote, *all that I then saw is overthrown and destroyed; nothing is left standing*. He believed the city to have been a thousand years old. Most of it, however, had been built only in the century before Cortes arrived. It was in pristine condition. This was, for all its Neolithic atavisms, humanity ascendant. It was a world that cries out from Neruda's 'depths' for the most prolonged and patient study and for our imagined protection from the incipient ravages that annihilated it.

There was, upon the pinnacle of Tlatelolco, the great sacrificial pyramid of Tenochtitlan, a ceremonial chamber and inner sanctum of the priests. Into this solemn precinct Montezuma led Cortes and his captains on that day in November 1519; after he had pointed out to them the splendours of his realm. It was a small tower containing two altars and a high ceiling adorned with very rich wooden carvings. Above the altars were the giant figures of two ferocious gods: Huitzilopochtli, the god of war, and Tezcatlipoca, the god of the underworld. Around them were smoking braziers, filled with copal, the Aztec incense. There the priests 'were burning the hearts of three individuals whom they had sacrificed that day to those two fierce and insatiable idols.

'All the walls of that shrine were so splashed and caked with blood that they and the floor too were black. Indeed, the whole place stank abominably', the chronicler remembered decades afterwards, as if still his nostrils reeked with that offensive and disturbing odour and the grotesque sight, as of an abattoir. This, however, was the holy of holies within the highest temple of that city of beautifully ordered markets and wondrous gardens, superb causeways and astonishing wealth. Like the cannibalism of the mild and courteous Tlaxcalans, that bloody precinct gives us cause to inquire whether or to what extent human civilization has *always* been built on sanctified human sacrifice – whether of the Aztec kind or gross subjection and war down the ages?'

Imagine you are there upon the highest altar, a witness like the chronicler to the conversation through native interpreters between the high lord Montezuma and the presumptuous Catholic adventurer, Hernan Cortes. Your nostrils are dilating, your senses reeling, your conscience recoiling in horror. Half dazed, you overhear Cortes declare 'Lord Montezuma, I cannot imagine how a prince as great and wise as your majesty can have failed to realize that these idols of yours are not gods but evil things, the proper name for which is devils.' The other responds in hardly suppressed anger, 'If I had known that you were going to utter these insults I would not have brought you here. These are our gods and we hold them to be good. You forget yourself!'

Here we have an exchange between two worlds in collision, in which religion is at the centre of conscious misunderstanding. Already, on strategic grounds, there was profound mistrust and circumlocution; politeness veiling acute misgivings and coiled violence. That mistrust would erupt, that violence uncoil explosively, ending over a year later with the wonders of the city in smoking ruins and the pyramid itself being demolished as a demonic abomination. That the two worlds were, even then, colliding biologically in ways that would prove even more calamitous to the peoples of the Americas, neither Montezuma nor Cortes was even remotely aware. Neither had a germ theory of disease, nor any notion of epidemiology or immunology. Fate ruled both.

'These gods of ours', the Aztec told his guest, through Cortes' Aztec mistress 'La Malinche', 'give us health and rain and crops, good weather and all the victories we desire; as witness the breadth and power of my realm. We are, then, bound to worship them and sacrifice to them and I beg you to say nothing more against them.' So it went at the very portals to the altar of the gods of war and the underworld. Cortes, descending with La Malinche from the high place, conferred with his captains on their options. In fear of the Aztecs, who outnumber them hundreds to one, they will, by deft stratagem, take Montezuma as a hostage; thus holding at bay for a time the growing fear and anger of the Aztecs, whose religion and freedom alike they presumed to judge.

Spaniards hostile to Cortes arrived off Vera Cruz and Montezuma, through couriers sought to treat with them, thinking, perhaps, to find allies. Cortes was too wily and adroit. He marched to the coast, dealt summarily with Narvaez, the new arrival; then returned in force to Tenochtitlan, with thirteen hundred foot soldiers, ninety six horsemen, eighty cross-bowmen and eighty musketeers, reinforced by two thousand Tlaxcalan warriors. With these, arriving on St John's Day in June 1520, he imagined he could hold in mastery the lord of the Aztecs and all his forces, in their artfully constructed city. They, for their part, withheld the gift of food from the Spaniards, who demanded an open market or they would not answer for the consequences.

Exasperated by the arrogant presumption of Cortes and his men, the Aztecs rallied their forces from the Tacuba causeway and marched upon the quarters in which the Spaniards were housed, driving back with heavy loss the third of his command that Cortes sent out to pacify them. And so began the first great battle of Tenochtitlan. The chronicler recounts that the Spaniards 'were struck by the tenacity of their fighting, which was beyond description...some three or four soldiers of our company who had served in Italy swore to God many times that they had never seen such fierce fighting, not even in Christian wars, or against the Great Turk, nor had they ever seen men so courageous as those Indians, charging with closed ranks.' Now all are faded ghosts.

In that first battle, Cortes' men fought their way against thousands to the summit of the great pyramid and there set fire to the sacred and blood-soaked halls containing the Aztec idols of war and the underworld – Huitzilopochtli and Tezcatlipoca. Montezuma being captive, the Aztecs elected a new master and commander, Cuitlahuac, who now led a redoubled assault on the aliens from across the sea. He, the Aztecs taunted their enemies, was a brave leader and would not be deceived by false speeches, as the good-natured Montezuma had been to his cost. With great loss, then, the Spaniards were driven from the city and 'those of us who escaped,' the chronicler confided in old age, from Guatemala, 'did so only by the grace of God' from a relentless onslaught.

All were wounded, he went on, who survived by then. Only twenty three horses now remained of ninety six; while all cannons, muskets and powder were lost and almost all the cross-bows. That was a defeat to remember; the largest ever inflicted on Europeans by Native Americans. Think of that. But Cortes then, even with a depleted force, inflicted in open country a calamitous defeat upon a huge host of Aztecs, 'all the flower of Mexico', it was said, 'from all the towns around the lake, who came in the belief that this time we should be totally destroyed.' Never, thought the chronicler, 'had there been seen throughout the Indies so many warriors assembled for any battle.' Over nine hundred Spaniards now lay dead and over a thousand Tlaxcalans with them.

Smallpox had begun to spread among the Mexicans, but Cortes was bent on retaking the city Tenochtitlan for his God and pride. He marched against it again, with his and 20,000 Tlaxcalan warriors; sending emissaries to the new Aztec commander, young Guatemoc, warning that 'war is easy to stop at the beginning, but very difficult towards the middle and the end'. But Guatemoc made no reply, save to strengthen his defences and gather into Tenochtitlan all his vassals for the war. It was the spring of 1521 and the town-littered hinterland of Lake Texcoco now saw war on a scale as large as Hannibal's campaigns in Italy and equally destructive; while smallpox invisibly snaked its way among those myriad walled towns with gardens, killing silently.

Cortes then besieged Tenochtitlan with his Tlaxcalan allies, cutting off its water supply at Chapultepec. And then he fought a Stalingrad, taking and demolishing the city house by house and bridge by bridge. 'Every building captured was razed to the ground and our Tlaxcalan allies helped us. So we went on penetrating into the city,' wrote our source, who witnessed this. The Aztecs fought ferociously and sacrificed on the pyramid all those they took alive, to the sound of a dismal drum, 'as of a devilish instrument, which could be heard six miles away.' Yet razed and bloodied Tenochtitlan fell at last, after a five month siege. Guatemoc was taken and the brutal idols burned. The mass of putrid dead was not less than when Jerusalem fell to the Crusaders.

The Aztecs had been feared and hated by their many subject peoples. When, therefore, word spread far and wide, as soon it did, that Tenochtitlan had fallen, such people came both to congratulate Cortes on bringing down the Mexican empire and to see for themselves the humbled state of the imperial city with its voracious gods. According to the chronicler, they 'even brought their small children to show them' the ruins of the fallen city, 'pointing it out to them in much the same way as we would say, 'Here stood Troy.'' Ah! Jerusalem and Troy! What fabled antecedents to the calamities of war! But those small children, having been shown the fallen city, would be scythed away before maturity by the ravages of disease. No peace came for them.

A Scene from the Tale of Manntezuma
Image by Catherine Gordon.

Humboldt on the Orinoco

I sat upon the Temple of the Moon with the French Colonel's daughter long ago, while you were in a classy Opus Dei finishing school. I knew little then of what could be seen from the heights even of *that* pyramid in its prime. I knew only hazily of the epidemics that had swept the Americas after 1492. She being French Vietnamese and I the companion of a political scientist on field work about small wars in the plagued and violent isthmus, we spoke more of the realities of the Cold War than of the fall of Tenochtitlan in its time. Afterwards, we returned to the cafes and museums of Mexico City, losing ourselves for a few days in one another's youthful beauty. Only deeper thought and close inquiry yields the wider view and more sober comprehension.

Suppose, however, that you and I had stood upon the pinnacle of Tlatelolco with the elite group around Montezuma and Cortes. When they descend into the city, we are invited to remain behind by an Aztec sage (*tlamatini*). The term means, in Nahuatl, the language of the Aztecs 'he who knows things'. Let's call him Manntezuma.[49] As they depart, he says that he would like to offer us a far wider and deeper vision of the world of the Americas – one that Cortes and his captains would not stay to hear. He is a *magus*, as we might say, this *tlamatini* of Tenochtitlan. And he begins with a ceremony, to set our hearts at ease, after our shock at the blood within the inner sanctum and the human hearts burning in the braziers. He looks up at the Sun, uttering a rarefied prayer to his lofty deity.

Raising both arms, he declaims, three times over, an invocation to the highest god of the Aztecs, Ometeotl, the god of light, whom they called the Lord of the Close Vicinity and Guardian of the Fifth Sun. Then he turns to us, lowering his arms. 'Children of the future', he asks, 'where do you find your truth?' We are lost for an answer. He smiles beneficently. His teeth are white and

---

49   Fenimore appears to have derived this name for his fictional sage from that of Charles C. Mann, the author of *1491: New Revelations of the Americas before Columbus* (Knopf, New York, 2005). It was Yusuf who presented him with this volume at the time of our gathering in New York, the year it was published, at which Irad first briefed us all on the sub-prime situation and argued that we should, through IRI, short the mortgage companies who were making so dangerous a killing from that mendaciously AAA rated and marketed junk. I remember him telling me later that he found it so absorbing he had finished reading it before he got back to Cos from New York. He didn't live to see Mann's follow-up volume, *1493: Uncovering the New World Columbus Created* (Knopf, New York, 2011), but I am certain he would have devoured it, given what he has written in this Section of Notebook III. It deals with the massive circulation of germs, commodities, plants and slaves between the Old World and the New after the European conquest of the Americas. – TCE.

his eyes, when we look into them for the first time, seem to us to be like deep wells, whose depths we cannot fathom. He says, 'Do you not find it in flowers and song?' After the shock and stench of the inner sanctum, we are caught altogether by surprise at this question and remain mute. Then, in a deep voice, he chants softly of the Giver of Life and of the intoxication of song.

He follows this with a hymn to Ometeotl, which he tells us is called 'The Highest Altar', about the need for rituals of sacrifice to keep the Sun burning and the world below it in order.[50] He explains that it had been the teaching of the great *tlatoani* (master and commander) Tlacaelel, who had died not quite forty years before, that the world was an arena for ceaseless battle between the forces of darkness and light. Tlacaelel had organized the Triple Alliance to secure for the Sun a constant supply of the elixir *chalchihuatl* (human blood) that light might prevail over darkness. The epoch of the Triple Alliance is that of the Fifth Sun and it will end when the current master among the sons of Ometeotl, Huitzilopochtli, is defeated by one or another of his warring kin.

Having rendered this account of the religion of his people, Manntezuma looks us in the eye and says with a certain grave irony, 'Cortes, as you overheard, is outraged by these sacrifices; but tell me, does not *his* religion, also, call for the enactment of blood sacrifices, in order to ensure a kind of cosmic order?' Seeing that we are bemused by his question, he continues, 'There are those among us who reflect on these things and discuss the nature of rituals. Perhaps, in time, the meaning of all such rituals will be clarified and religions reconciled. Do you believe that is possible?' Without waiting for an answer, he then announces, 'Come with me now to the western side of the temple, for I will show you things that Montezuma himself could not point out.'

'Long ago,' he began from that lofty point, 'some forty thousand years as you measure it, hardy hunters and explorers came into the remote north out of the Far West beyond the Great Ocean. They came down ancient coastlands now long under water, finding a pristine world of wide fisheries and abundant game. Being intrepid and unhindered, they passed within a matter of fifty generations from the ice-bound north to the Deep South behind us. They found a world which no longer exists, of giant animals and great forests. Then came the Great Thaw, fifteen thousand years ago as you measure it. The Long Ice retreated. A land corridor opened up across the Far North and new peoples came, with new tongues and different features. The old world altered.

---

50   I have not been able to establish to my own satisfaction whether Fenimore composed poems 8 and 10 in Appendix C before, during or after he wrote this Section of Notebook III. The fact that #8 is called 'Invocation' and #10 is titled 'The Highest Altar', unfortunately, tells us nothing, since it could be consistent with any one of these hypotheses. In any case, their close relationship to this passage is one of many reasons why I chose to include his scattered poems under one cover in this volume. – TCE.

'As the climate changed and these new peoples multiplied in the land, the great beasts of the ancient world perished and passed away into the ground. The forests shifted and changed; and then there began the building of the world of fields and food crops. Over those fifteen millennia, peoples of many hundred tongues have terra-formed these wide lands', he went on. 'There are wonders behind you that transcend your wildest imaginings. But in the north, even as we speak, there are agrarian cultures with high mounds and rich crafts; there are numerous and flourishing villages with beautiful orchards full of every kind of nut and fruit tree; as there have been for a long age, stretching across great river valleys all the way to the cold north eastern coasts.

'There the Algonquian speaking peoples of the first light dwell in what they have long called the Dawnland; peoples such as the Wampanoag, Abenaki, Mohican, Narragansett, Micmac and Massachusett. It is these peoples that Cortes would first have met had he landed in the Far North, instead of on our shores. But it is in these lands about us and behind us that the greatest wonders exist under the Fifth Sun. Yonder, to the northwest sits our rival state of Tarasca, with its great city of Tzintzuntzan; to the southeast lies Tlaxcala, which we raid and with which we war in search of sacrificial victims for the gods. A day's march from that resilient realm lies the ancient city-state of Cholula, which we have long reduced to tribute, but which flourishes: a city of priests.

'But we and even the old city of Cholula are latecomers to a land steeped in history. To our northeast is the city of the gods, as we call it, Teotihuacan. It was already in ruins when my people came down from the farming lands in the northwest only seven generations ago and settled in this great and fertile valley, beneath a clear sky. There is a long history around us, only part of which is kept in our books. Alas, Tlacaelel, before my time, ordered that most of the old books be destroyed, for the sake of order and piety. I believe this was an error and have travelled widely in an effort to learn what has otherwise been forgotten – or was never known, even by the great lore-masters. I am learned in languages and have seen what cannot be seen from here.'

We follow his lead to the eastern side of the pyramid, gazing towards Texcoco on the shore of the shimmering lake. We skirt the rancid altar precincts, gazing down upon the vast white-paved grounds of the complex, the market square, the bustling quarters of Tenochtitlan and the great lake with its causeways, aqueducts and bridges. 'Southward', he resumes, when we have come to a halt, 'there are endless kingdoms quite as opulent and populous as ours, with agriculture and writing, mathematics and the keeping of calendars; some of which go back to times even more remote than we compute the age of Teotihuacan to have been. In that direction', he says, with a sweeping gesture of his right arm, 'lie the Mixtec and Zapotec kingdoms with their many towns.'

'Beyond them lie numerous isthmian principalities in a narrow neck of land. But to the east of all these,' and here he gestures with his left arm, 'there runs the great peninsula of Yucatan, filled with the splendid and warlike Maya peoples. Their history has been tumultuous in my lifetime and there are now many self-governing principalities. It is only in recent times that the Maya have been so divided and, even so, they drove the compatriots of Cortes out thrice in the past few years. For two centuries before I was born, the great League of Mayapan united Yucatan; but now Mayapan lies in ruins. Before the building of Mayapan, the Maya had been ruled for many centuries from the great city of Chichen Itza in the heart of the peninsula. It you should see.'

'Chichen Itza flourished for a thousand years. Its temples and public buildings are as impressive as what we have built here. The architecture of the city reminded me somewhat – for I have been there - of Teotihuacan. Its ruins are a melancholy sight. It must have been splendid in its prime. It's great pyramid is not as grand as where we stand. Its other sacred precincts, however, such as the Temple of the Jaguars and the long paved walkway to the Sacred Well, were finely conceived. Its Temple of the Warriors features a thousand stone pillars: a marvel to behold! But to my mind the greatest wonder was their star observatory, lying to the south of the great pyramid. Here they watched the heavens and kept their astronomical records with mathematical precision.

'Working with fine numbers, they calculated the ages of the world. What subtlety of mind that took among their priests! But Chichen Itza was sacked in the Great Rebellion, almost three hundred years ago and now the observatory stands empty and forsaken. A great pity! Chichen Itza also had the finest arena for *tlachtli* that has ever been built. *Tlachtli* is a game which is played all over the middle world and has been for thousands of years. The Maya call it *poc-ta-tok* and play it with great passion. It is a ritual battle between the gods of the sky and those of the underworld. The captain of the losing side is sacrificed on the altar of the winning god. His head is cut off and his skull coated in rubber to be used as the ball for the next big game. Do you understand?

'You can read about all this in their sacred book, *The Popol Vuh*, which I brought back with me from my travels and translated into Nahuatl. There were many ball courts at Chichen Itza, but its great ball court was the largest centre for the game that has so far been built. In area it was more than half the size of the great sacred compound you see below you, with a wall around it eight metres in height and sanctuaries at either end. It was to the sporting passions of the Mayas what the star observatories were to the science of the priests. Can you picture yourselves among the passionate crowds, above the eight metre girding wall, in rows of seats, urging on the players as they strive to win, exhorted by their captains, whose heads are at stake in the high ritual?

'But,' he went on, after pausing for a moment, 'all this is the merest beginning. Our traders have long travelled into these regions. It is far beyond, via the narrow isthmus, down the long coasts, both this side and beyond the immense cordillera that spines the South; and inland along an immense river that the true wonders are to be found. I have been in these places and seen them with my own eyes. Far down the coasts lies an empire larger by orders of magnitude than ours of the Triple Alliance. It is called Tawantinsuyu, the Land of the Four Quarters. It's capital, Qosqo is high in the great cordillera. There lives a ruler who calls himself the Inka. At its centre is a great plaza called Awkaypata, as large and glorious as the temple precinct in which we stand.

'It is carpeted in its entirety with white sand, carried up from the sea-coast. This is raked daily by the servants of the Inka. Monumental villas and temples surround the space on three sides, their walls made from immense blocks of stone precisely cut and fit with artistry as great as any you see here. Across their facades run enormous plates of polished gold. When the alpine sun fills Awkaypata, with its bold horizontal plane of white sand and sloping sheets of gold, the space becomes an amphitheatre for the exaltation of light. Ometeotl himself would feel exalted in such a precinct. I was overawed when I set eyes upon it. It is at the heart of a grand design conceived by the first great Inka, the remarkable Yupanki, who called himself Pachakuti, the World Shaker.

'His life coincided with that of our own great *tlatoani* Tlacaelel and so he was still alive in my youth. But I visited Tawantinsuyu during the reign of his son Thupa Inka, and travelled widely in his vast domain. You cannot imagine how great an empire he rules. It extends over thirty two degrees of latitude, if that means anything to you, and encompasses every imaginable type of terrain, from the rainforests on the eastern side of the mountains to the deserts of the northern coasts and to cities ten thousand feet high in the mountains. Awkaypata is the centre of this empire. From the great plaza there radiate four great highways. They demarcate the four asymmetrical sectors into which Pachakuti divided the empire – the four quarters of his billowing world.

'They are part of a gigantic network of roads and bridges linking up the Inka's domain. They facilitate trade, administration and the movement of his armies. Truly, the Inkas are achieving things that make one think differently about one's own world. Their empire, like ours, is new. The history of that far land, I learned, is incomparably more ancient and wonderful than even the courts at Awkaypata would lead one to imagine. Using their superb roads, I travelled far among the mountains and along the coasts, before crossing the cordillera to journey down the Great River that courses through a land so vast you cannot begin to conceive of its scale. Yet before ever I did so, I visited the ruins of Norte Chico, where towns flourished ten thousand years ago.

'I learned of a great complex of cities such as Huaricanga, on the Fortaleza River that existed five thousand years ago. I saw the ruins of some of these. They were building pyramids even then, not perhaps as large as this, but evidence that they had been working stone for many generations. And this must have been some kind of golden age, for I could find no evidence of warfare among these old cities, not even defensive walls. Here they must have invented sound government. Perhaps these many cities were already united in a realm that prefigured that which Pachakuti and his son have now built? Can you believe such antiquity? Have you heard of these lost cities and their ancient peace? What, in your worlds, coincides with them in age and sound government?

'I travelled south from the Fortaleza to the Rio Supe. There I found, at the mouth of that river, what might be the oldest city in the world. It is called Aspero and it shows, as I now believe, that long ago the first peoples who came to these lands from the Far West came by sea and created a maritime civilization, only later inventing farming. Civilization after civilization followed in the millennia that have elapsed since Aspero was built. When you think about all this, as I did, sitting atop the ruins of ancient pyramids of a different age, or later floating down the Great River, you realize that even those great states which preceded Tawantinsuyu in the mountains – Wari and Tiwanaku – were not, strictly speaking, old. The oldest, I guessed, was in the Far West – distant.

'Wari and Tiwanaku fell into darkness twenty generations ago, after thriving for a thousand years, according to the lore masters, the *tlatanime,* whom I consulted in Qosqo. Before them the realm of Chavin thrived, more than two thousand years ago. Yet even that is as yesterday. The world is old and many kingdoms have risen and fallen since the ancestors came here. And before them, we know, was the world of the giant beasts and the vast forests and the Long Ice.' Manntezuma shivers, as if a chill thought has crossed his mind, and breaks into a soft chant in Nahuatl. 'That is a poem by the great Netzahualcoyotl', he says, 'who was *tlatoani* of Texcoco when I was a child. Does it move you? We are going to die. Do you think much about that and what it means?'

Here he looks first at you and then at me. 'Netzahualcoyotl wrote', he went on, 'that each of us will be erased as if we had been a painting. We will dry up and perish like a flower in the fields. We will come to an end. But let us not talk now of that. Let me tell you first of the wonders of the Great River which, even here among my own people, is utterly unknown and showed me that the world is far wider than I had been taught by the wisest of the wise in my youth. Truly, what I saw is like a New World. For the Inka supplied me with bearers and guides and asked only that I report back to him what I found beyond the mountains. Neither of us guessed that I would discover a Great River and along it cultures and peoples without number and countless wonders extraordinary.

'You will not find it possible to believe this, but the Great River must measure 4,000 miles from end to end and the volume of water it carries is incalculable. Moreover, the farther we went the more thickly populated and the better did we find the land. Far down the Great River, it is entered on its southern bank by the Rio Tapajos, one of its countless tributaries, themselves often mighty rivers. Near its mouth, 400 miles from the sea, I saw houses and gardens lining the river bank for a hundred miles, while inland there could be seen some large cities. We would be greeted as we sailed along by the music of horns, pipes and rebecs. Great parties of people would come in canoes, twenty or thirty to a boat, in their elaborate cloaks and other finery to hail us.

'Most impressive of all were the gardeners of the Endless Forest which fills the whole basin of the Great River. They did not clear the forest, as we and others have often done to make way for fields of maize and cotton, squash, peppers, tomatoes, avocados, cocoa and all the other plants we have learned to cultivate and harvest. No, they have devised ways to replace the wild forest with one adapted to human use. Planting their orchards for countless years, these ingenious peoples have slowly transformed large swaths of the river basin into something more pleasing to human beings. The lowland tropical forests through which I passed must be among the finest works of art in this world of mankind. The key to this art is the creation of deep and fertile soils.

'These would never have accumulated naturally: rich, fertile, dark earth full of charcoal and animal nutrients. They learned, they told me, in many tongues, that if you cut down the rain forest the soil dies; but if you work with the forest, marvels are possible. They have practised agriculture there for many centuries, but instead of destroying the soil, they have improved it. Do those in your countries of the future do such things, or are they as heedless of soils as Cortes is of the customs of others? Ah, my friends, if we stood here for many Moons I could not tell you all I saw, heard and learned on that great voyage. Even to describe it, to map it, to communicate it to my own people, I have had to invent new terms, a new language for unguessed realities.

'I saw a large set of villages on the upper Rio Xingu, on the northern bank of the Great River, linked by a network of wide roads, bridges, artificial river obstructions, ponds, raised causeways, canals. All this was based on the kind of black earth horticulture I have described and, in this case, seems as recent as the works of the Triple Alliance or the wonders of Tawantinsuyu. The Xinguanos have been at work for perhaps four centuries, but much that they do they inherited from others, who seem to have been at work for ten thousand years. And others elsewhere have similar histories. Most lack systems of written characters of the kind to which I am accustomed, so that I could not study records, but had to draw inferences from many careful observations.

'I did not return up the Great River, but heeding traders and taking guides, made my way across the high plains of Beni and there found yet more teeming cities, with their own canals and causeways, temples and archives. It was only three years after I had set out that I came once more to Qosqo, to the golden court of the Inka. There I rested for a year and talked at great length with his multilingual scholars, the *tlatanime*, before beginning the long journey home.' Then he stirred, looking at us with clouded eyes, and said, 'It is time for me to go down from this place. All will soon pass. I have, I now perceive, beheld a universe that is destined to slide into oblivion at the hands of these strangers of your skin and even stranger agents of epoch-ending doom.'

That is where the war I have described began. Yet there never was a Manntezuma. Such knowledge as we have, attributed here to him in this fable, was accumulated by science alone and only long after all that he described had passed from living memory into ruin and utter oblivion. Only late twentieth century archaeology and all its ancillary technologies have brought these vanished realities back to the light. Though, in the sixteenth century, a few attentive observers noted the extent of the calamity, they knew nothing of its prehistory and recorded nothing with precision. Even the scale of population loss was all but buried in oblivion. By the early twentieth century, the scholarly consensus was that there had never been all that many people in 'America'.

The first careful estimates, by James Mooney of the Smithsonian Institution, in 1928, and Alfred Kroeber of the University of California, Berkeley, in the 1930s, suggested a pre-Conquest population for the entire Western Hemisphere of less than eight and a half million. Even that left eight million raw fatalities in the sixteenth century. Incredible! It was the anthropologist Henry Dobyns, in the 1960s, who first pieced together the evidence that the peoples of the Americas had been smitten on an unparalleled scale by European diseases. Two other American scholars, Sherburne Cook and Woodrow Borah, opened a monumental inquiry, published in the 1970s in three volumes as *Essays on the Population History of the Americas*. They shattered the long oblivion concerning these things.

Looking at old census records, registers of births and deaths, financial and taxation records from the Spanish era, they estimated that the population of central Mexico alone, in 1492, had been about 25 million. This was a staggering deduction. The combined population of Spain and Portugal at that time was only ten million. The population for the Americas as a whole they estimated at anywhere between 90 and 112 million: more than lived in the whole of Europe in 1500. We know that, from the arrival of smallpox at Veracruz in 1520, European diseases spread like wildfire in the Americas and killed the Native Americans, as Dobyns expressed it, 'in huge numbers and at incredible rates.' Such a discovery was as ingenious as unearthing the Ice Age.

We know that smallpox reached the Andes up to a decade before the Spanish invaders under Pizarro got there with their horses, guns and steel. We know that plagues in Eurasia had, before then, sometimes swept away up to a third of the population. The Black Death in Europe did so in the middle of the fourteenth century, shaking European society to its foundations. The modern demographers argue that the effects of unprecedented epidemics in the Americas seem to have been far more devastating. Even the initial smallpox pandemic may have killed fifty percent of the population of Mesoamerica and of Tawantinsuyu (the empire of the Inkas) in the early 1520s. Smallpox recurred in 1533, 1535, 1558 and 1565. There was no respite or relief from pestilence.

There were also pandemics of other European diseases: typhus (1546), influenza (1558), diphtheria (1614) and measles (1618). At the same time, proceeding as they had in the Caribbean islands from 1492, the Spaniards killed, plundered and destroyed with a reckless abandon that beggars belief. Within a century of their arrival in the Americas, the population of central Mexico had fallen to about 1 million and that of the Americas as a whole to perhaps 5 million. If the demographers are right, the conquest had caused the greatest destruction of human lives in recorded history. No-one was or could be held to account, least of all the bringers of disease, who knew not what they did, any more than the executioners of the crucified Jesus long before.

Dante's *Divine Comedy* has held a compelling place in the Christian West for eight hundred years. Many seem, however, to favour the drama of the *Inferno* above the theology of the *Purgatorio* or the beauty of the *Paradiso*, suggesting a fascination with the suffering of others that is troubling. In truth, however, there is nothing in Dante that can compare with the 'secret' history of the European conquest of the Americas. The scale of the suffering staggers the imagination and no fiction writer could hope to give expression to more than a small part of it, even in a major story. This was the civilization of the Renaissance in action? This was the march of progress? This was the apotheosis of trigonometry and the bright arc of history trending towards truth and justice?

One response is to baulk at the numbers and deny the scale of things deduced after the fact. How was the higher order of magnitude arrived at by Dobyns, Cook, Borah and others? What grounds are there for accepting that they are right? Just nine years ago, in 1998, a sceptical scholar by the name of David Henige put out a book called *Numbers From Nowhere*, in which he argued that Dobyns, Cook and Borah were hallucinating and that there was simply no hard evidence for pre-Columbian populations of the magnitude they had claimed. Cook and Borah claimed that Hispaniola alone had had a population of at least eight million in 1492 – which died out *completely* within a few decades. This Henige found simply not credible. How could he not?

When I read the original analysis by Cook and Borah, I couldn't credit the numbers. Eight million and all dead by the time Cortes began his conquest of Mexico? They argue their case in great detail, however. And even Henige, since interviewed, confessed that the true figure for the Americas as a whole must have been tens of millions. Las Casas had estimated the population of central Mexico and the Caribbean islands at forty million when Columbus arrived. William Denevan, in *The Native Population of the Americas in 1492*, estimated the total for the Western Hemisphere at fifty to sixty million. In short, the consensus in our time seems to be that the native population was an order of magnitude larger in 1492 than Mooney or Kroeber believed - and *this* many died.

'None of the great massacres of the twentieth century can be compared to this hecatomb', was Tzvetan Todorov's assessment even thirty years ago. The impact in North America was no less devastating than in the more "exotic" regions conquered by the Spanish. The slave trader and torturer Hernando de Soto, with a commission from the Emperor Charles V, landed in Florida in 1539, with six hundred soldiers, two hundred horses and three hundred pigs. Archaeologists have now established, that there were, at that time, flourishing Native American cultures over huge areas of what are now the states of Florida, Georgia, North and South Carolina, Tennessee, Alabama, Mississippi, Arkansas, Texas and Louisiana. All perished in the sixteenth century.

In eastern Arkansas, one of De Soto's party recorded, they found a land 'thickly set with great towns' with earthen walls and sizeable moats. One is reminded of the chronicler's description of Mexico in 1519 and 1520. For four years, de Soto and his band raped, slaughtered, enslaved, plundering and blundering their way across this enormous region. After his death, no Europeans entered these parts again for a century and a half. When they did, they found a wilderness. Diseases brought by the Spaniards and their pigs had annihilated the native populations and there had been no recovery. Whole cultures - those of the Caddo on the Texas-Arkansas border or the Coosa in western Georgia - collapsed in De Soto's reckless, relentless, epidemic wake.

It has been estimated that the Caddoan population fell from 200,000 to about 8,500 in the sixteenth century. That is a fall of 96 percent, which is on a par with the Dobyns and Cook/Borah estimates for the hemisphere as a whole. In the eighteenth century, it fell by 80 percent again, to a mere 1,400. No other demographic and cultural catastrophe in recorded history can match the scale of what took place in the Americas. Of course, it was itself barely 'recorded history'. It has had to be reconstructed from exiguous and often indirect evidence long after the fact – in the late twentieth century. The evidence there, however, points to decades of suffering without any relief or remedy. The scale and muteness of it surely defy all efforts at humane comprehension.

Across two continents, the population did not recover its pre-conquest levels until the mid-twentieth century. The agrarian, urban and trading societies the Native Americans had developed over millennia gave way to the conquistadors' plantations, mines and ranches. Many plants the Native Americans had cultivated – maize, squash, avocadoes, beans, tomatoes, potatoes, cocoa, tobacco, various kinds of nut – became staples all over the world. The rich and balanced diets and agricultures of which they had been the staples lapsed into monocultures and malnutrition. Sugar, bananas, coffee and slaves were imported from Africa, starting in the Caribbean, where the native population had died away. You have ancestors among the owners and traders. Yes?

Was all this an indictment of the sciences of geometry and navigation, the religion and imperial pretensions of the West and the material culture – guns, germs and steel – of 'white European males'? Is it sufficient, with Bernal Diaz, our chronicler of the conquest of Mexico, to denounce the human sacrifice, idol worship and cannibalism of the Mexicans in order to forgive or overlook the catastrophes of that era? Is our current material civilization, with its sprawling urban agglomerations and arsenals of weapons of mass destruction sufficiently 'advanced' to justify the obliteration of what preceded it five centuries ago? How is it even possible to compute such an equation? Can I be expected to take such an equation upon my back and ascend with it?

You live for music and its therapeutic powers, but with you in Yucatan, taking the sun and thought in Cancun and Cozumel, I had a dark dream by night. I was a young baggage boy in the camp of the conquistador Francisco de Montejo, during the wars of the early 1530s. His brother-in-law Captain Alonzo Lopez de Avila had taken a number of prisoners during a raid. One of them was a beautiful and gracious young Mayan woman. I saw her being led past. She looked me in the eye, searing into me her vivid reality as a person. Suddenly there was a jump cut to a terrible scene. Her body was being dragged along the ground and thrown naked to a pack of dogs. They tore at her flesh as if she had been a freshly slaughtered pig. You lay beside me slumbering in the dark.

I heard voices shouting and laughing coarsely and gathered that she had defied – because she was married - the Captain's determination to have sexual relations with her. Left alone, she had taken her own life by hanging herself. He, in rage and contempt, had ordered that her body be taken and thrown to the camp dogs. I had no voice among the soldiers, but had seen many horrors in the course of the campaign, which had been long and bitter and was not proving successful. The Mayas were numerous and fiercely independent. Epidemics had greatly weakened them, but they would not be subdued and our leader had burned and massacred without pity. Baggage boy I was and daily the baggage heaped upon me grew in moral weight too great to bear.

Within the dream, I found I couldn't turn away from the scene of horror, remembering that woman's dark and lustrous eyes as she had been led past me only a few hours before, lithe, long haired and dignified. But, as the dogs tore at her soft flesh, she turned her face to me, her eyes sprang to burning life – as only in a nightmare such eyes can. With your voice, she cried out, "Fenimore!", with a wrenching appeal that tore my heart out. I started from sleep, clutching at my chest and disturbing you in the small hours of a tropical morning. The dream was straight out of Todorov's history of the conquest. He drew it from a 16th century source, Diego de Landa, commenting, 'I dedicate this book to the memory of a Mayan woman devoured by dogs.'

To expunge such nightmares, I want to be someone other than that helpless baggage boy in Yucatan. I would like to enter your ancestral world – from the sugar plantations of Jamaica and other islands to the coffee lands of the isthmus and the oil politics of the recent past– as the 'second Columbus', Alexander von Humboldt: cosmologist, geographer and humanist; whose goal was to reconquer the New World in the name of liberalism and science. Only in that manner can I bear to contemplate it all – songs or no songs. Simon Bolivar declared that Humboldt did more good for America than all of her conquerors – double-edged praise, I'd say. I prefer Ralph Waldo Emerson's assessment of that polymath as 'one of the wonders of the world.'

Humboldt was one of the wonders of the world, who appear from time to time as if to show us the possibilities of the human mind. That was Emerson's estimate of the man. He came from outside and explored your world 200 years ago, when it was still called New Andalusia, after the land of oranges and song that had been fully reconquered from the Moors in the very year Columbus followed the arc of Eratosthenes and stumbled fatefully upon Hispaniola. Sailing, by perverse coincidence, surely, in a ship named the *Pizarro*, after the terrible conqueror and plunderer of the Inca world, he visited Tenerife on his way west and landed at Cumana, where Las Casas had attempted to build a gentle culture and where you went for untroubled childhood holidays.

He was the great *anti-conquistador*, even though he sailed on the *Pizarro*. Truth not gold was all he hungered after. Unlike the conquistadors, he did not kill or plunder, burn, enslave or infect; he inquired, observed, documented, loved and sorrowed. He collected plants and data like an inspired gardener of the Earth, seeking everywhere to understand. Back in Europe after five years, he wrote *Cosmos: A Sketch of the Physical Description of the Universe*, a grand attempt to show how all the sciences cohered, both the physical and the human. His cosmological vision embraced the whole world, including not only the motions of the stars, but the physical geography of the Earth and the nature of human experience. This, surely, is the means for your and my ascent.

Humboldt inspired Charles Lyell to lay the foundations of modern geology. He inspired Charles Darwin to lay the foundations of evolutionary biology. He inspired Franz Boas to open up the sciences of anthropology and comparative linguistics. He germinated – being German - so many new ideas in so many fields that the first half or even two thirds of the nineteenth century became known as the Humboldtian era of science. And through all of it, his humanism and political liberalism were such that he was in the forefront of political and social reform in Berlin, in the years before Germany became a unified - and militarized - state under Otto von Bismarck. He embodied, even more than Goethe, you might say, the aspiration to liberal enlightenment.

Our man grew up in Berlin in the 1770s and 1780s. His family background was such that one day, in 1777, King Frederick the Great of Prussia came to visit. The King asked Alexander's older brother Wilhelm, "Don't you want to become one of my soldiers?" To which Wilhelm, a precocious reader, responded, "No, sire. I want to make a career in literature." The King then turned to the eight year old Alexander, reminded him of how his namesake Alexander the Great had become known as the Earth-conqueror and asked, "Would you, also, like to be a conqueror of the Earth?" "Yes", was the boy's reply, "but with my mind." Both children fulfilled their aspirations, as Napoleon came and went and the vast machinery of modernity began its steely grind.

Even when *Cosmos* was first published, in the 1830s and 1840s, critical reviewers pointed out that it was too ambitious and failed to accomplish its goal. Humboldt's call for a unity of scientific understanding was seen as beyond the bounds of the possible even by the mid-nineteenth century; even for so formidable a polymath as Humboldt. Yet the sciences were all in their infancy at that point in time. How was coherence to be sustained, as the vast engine of inquiry gathered speed? For altogether too many people, from the late nineteenth century onwards, the answer would be turning away from stark, complex science as such to pseudo-science, romantic or nihilistic poetry, historicist ideology, religious conservatism or even fundamentalist religious dogmatism.

Humboldt, by contrast, stood in the great tradition of rational and open-minded philosophy, dating back to the Ionian and Hellenistic thinkers and ascending through the Renaissance and the Enlightenment. In all his travels and all his writing, he was self-consciously the disciple of Immanuel Kant. As he wrote up his voluminous books, in his private library, his very own Vivarium, he was watched over by a bust of Kant. His *Cosmos* was, in many ways, an attempt to build upon the work Kant had written a hundred years before: his *Universal Natural History and Theory of the Heavens.* This is the luminous thread that we must follow; the human mind feeling and thinking its way towards a unified grasp of what is so and how we can know what we are. Humboldt holds the torch.

Transcending anything written in the oldest myths or 'sacred texts', Kant had laid out a synoptic view of the natural world that touched the boundaries of knowledge as they existed in the first half of the eighteenth century. He even reflected upon the idea of 'island universes' (other galaxies) 170 years before Edwin Hubble demonstrated that they exist. He virtually founded the discipline of physical geography and inspired Humboldt to undertake his ground-breaking explorations in the Americas. He went on to do pioneering work on what it means to think, what it means to be ethical and what the prospects might be for a universal, cognitively sound humanism. Yet he lived quietly in Konigsberg with his books. Talk about conquering the world with one's mind!

Humboldt began by sailing to Tenerife. How could I not wish to emulate him, in some sense? Spanish ships had been docking there for centuries, bringing the spoils of the American world back to Spain: Aztec gold and Inca silver. The equipment Humboldt took with him consisted not of horses, guns and swords; but of scientific instruments: thermometers, barometers, quadrants, microscopes, rain gauges, eudiometers (which measure the amount of oxygen in the air). He returned from the Americas laden with incredible spoils of a very different kind to those hauled back by Pizarro: sixty thousand plant specimens and data on almost every aspect of the flora, fauna, topography, natural endowment, climate and human geography of the Americas.

Tenerife, though, made a profound impression upon him. It catalysed his ecological thinking. He suddenly came to see the whole Earth as an island – an island in the cosmos. He was also captivated by the song of the *capirote*, that bird unique to the Canary Islands, as you told me in Toledo. It was so elusive, he recorded in his personal narrative, that he never got to see one, but he was enchanted both by its elusiveness and by its singing, which he came to identify with freedom of spirit and natural beauty. In view of its climate and vegetation, he declared of Tenerife that nowhere else in the world was there a better place to 'dissipate melancholy and restore peace to troubled minds.' Is that why you created Capirote Therapies on the island, in your exile?

Humboldt was imbued with Kant when he arrived on Tenerife and endorsed the philosopher's approach both to knowledge and to justice. On that island, he came to see more vividly than ever that this great sphere the Earth is a whole and humanity a single extended community. No human being and no culture, he decided is, in fact, an island. How curious that he should have reached this conclusion precisely *on* an island. Yet he similarly saw the universal right to liberty, while being surrounded on every side by the realities of the Spanish destruction of the native Guanches, feudal backwardness and oppressive poverty. Inspired by the capirote, he sang to keep his spirits up. But his task was to put the past's ravages into the perspective of deep time.

From his island, Humboldt sailed west, not to reach India, but to map the lands long since seized upon by the Spanish intruders. Again and again, he would pull out his instruments – his quadrants, sextants and chronometers – to keep track of where exactly he was on the great sphere of the Earth. He had better instruments than any that had been available to Eratosthenes and they showed him that current maps were misleading at many points. The Spanish Empire had ruled those parts for three centuries, yet he found himself in uncharted waters. He dropped anchor, at last, off a coastland that no-one could specify, inhabited by robust natives no-one could name. It was the natives, tall and self-possessed, who directed them on to Cumana.

Here Humboldt and his companion found themselves plunged into a world of overwhelming novelty and fecundity that dazzled their scientific minds every bit as much as the gold and other treasures of the Aztecs had dazzled the conquistadors almost three centuries before. They perceived that the native people, whom they had been led by European writers to believe were a degenerate race, were, on the contrary, vigorous and deeply familiar with their environment. Moreover, they were only one among hundreds of tribes that Humboldt soon learned still flourished in the Orinoco and Amazon basins, each with its own language and customs and surrounded by a profusion of plant and animal life that he found it intoxicating to contemplate.

For all that, however, they soon encountered the degenerative effects of the colonial regime and its Catholic imprint. The native tribes had been stripped of their original languages, their traditional folk customs, their indigenous approaches to agriculture and husbandry. They had been made to speak Spanish, taught an infantilizing Catholic religion and forced to grow a narrow variety of crops for export to European markets. Having observed scores of the Catholic missions, Humboldt made clear to the Catholic authorities that he believed they should abandon their catechetic practices, allow the natives to grow crops for their own well-being and profit, grant them their natural liberty, then step back and watch as their civilization rose naturally.

Humboldt was struck by the fact that the natives learned one another's languages with great proficiency, but struggled to master Spanish. From this he drew the perceptive conclusion that the native languages sprang from common roots, to which Spanish was alien. This being so, he thought, the whole of the Americas might have developed differently had a native *lingua franca* been hit upon – perhaps that of the Incas – instead of Spanish being required; which imposed a kind of muteness on the diverse and much-abused peoples of the continent. As for their religion, he was informed by free natives that the Catholic God seemed to be confined to houses as if old and infirm, while theirs thrived in the forests, in the fields and in the mountains of the world.

But his boldest venture on the Orinoco was venturing up it to discover whether it was linked to the Amazon river system via a rumoured waterway called the Casiquiare Canal that flowed, so it was said, between the upper Orinoco and the Rio Negro, which itself flowed into the mighty Amazon. That this was even possible had been denied by armchair geographers in Europe. He was drawn by the legend and not for reasons of geographical curiosity alone, but because he at once appreciated the metaphor of a great flow between river basins, perhaps engineered by human hands, prefiguring a fluid connection between the Old World and the New, between separate and untrammelled cultures, between the diverse fields of the sciences and humanities.

He found the Casiquiare Canal and demonstrated that it did link the two rivers. Alas, he also demonstrated that the metaphor was a chimera. His sweeping humanistic hopes were swamped by a wilderness of insects and cannibals; an alien world of stifling humidity and impenetrable plant growth, defiant of humane and hopeful comprehension. He retreated to the coast and thence to Havana, before coming back to Cartagena and going up the Rio Magdalena to Bogota, before taking the ancient Inca road down the Andes to Quito, going on to Lima, finally sailing up through the Pacific to Acapulco. From there, like a returning Manntezuma, he went overland to Mexico City – long since built on the ruins of Tenochtitlan. Is the Orinoco, then, our valley?[51]

---

51   In editing this section of Notebook III, or at least the final stanzas, I came to realize that Fenimore had drawn upon a book published just before he wrote the above pages: *The Passage to Cosmos: Alexander von Humboldt and the Shaping of America*, by Laura Dassow Walls (University of Chicago Press, 2009). It is a beautiful book, replete with reflections on the life of the mind in German intellectual culture in the century that included Kant, Mendelssohn, Lessing, Goethe, Schiller, Mozart, Beethoven and, of course the Humboldts. The whole book is heavily underscored and annotated in Fenimore's customary manner, yet he drew upon only a small part of it in his highly abbreviated reflection on Humboldt. I was unable to resist reading the whole book myself, having found his copy. Doing so led me to regret that Fenimore had not devoted more space to the figure of Humboldt and perhaps less to that of the fabled Manntezuma. It was, let me confess, the main reason why I chose to give this first section of Notebook III the tile 'Humboldt on the Orinoco'.

The key to what he was uncovering here is made clear only when we reach section iii, which I have called 'Karl and Paula', in which he dwells upon the unravelling of the German Enlightenment in the 20th century. From this point of view, section ii, 'Raneb and Nefesh', looks like a major digression. Yet it seems probable that he was trying to interweave two things here – the line of fable and that of history. He takes his reader (who was, we need to remember, originally intended to be Margarita alone) from the valley of Mexico to that of the Orinoco via a fable and then to that of the Nile, then back to the dark theme of historical catastrophe opened up by 'Circles in the Dust' and 'The Fall of Tenochtitlan' – with the calamitous developments, centred on Germany, between 1914 and 1945. Once I realized that this was the pattern of these sections, I could not help but speculate as to why he omitted to draw upon a passage that he had underlined in Laura Dassow Walls's book, since it prefigures the story he tells in section iii and, above all, demonstrates the crucial role of Jewish intellectuals and the quest for Jewish emancipation in Germany as a catalyst for the German Enlightenment. It was to be precisely the reversal of this process that culminated in the horrors of the Holocaust.

The passage on p. 25 which consist of a description in brief of the intellectual salon in Berlin where the young brothers Humboldt first encountered the wider world of modern ideas:

> *The Christian intellectuals of Berlin gathered in the homes of Marcus Herz and his friend Moses Mendelssohn (grandfather of the composer Felix) to discuss the philosophy of Kant and the poetry of Goethe, Schiller and Lessing. Here was the center of Berlin's intellectual life, where stuffy convention could be defied in the world that the Jewish community, excluded from the common rights of European citizens, had built for themselves. Moses Mendelssohn, who had arisen from poverty and had to educate himself in secret, kept open house on Friday evenings for Jews and Gentiles alike. The Humboldt brothers were introduced to him by their mathematics tutor, who also taught Mendelssohn's two sons, Joseph and Nathan, with whom Alexander formed a lifelong friendship. It was his Jewish friends who made possible Humboldt's American travels, for it was the Mendelssohn's Berlin bank that extended Humboldt a letter of credit when another Berlin banking house withdrew it, just as he was about to board the Pizarro. (p. 25)*

The setting for section iii is also a salon in Berlin in the 1920s, although it isn't Jewish. – TCE.

The Temple at Karnak.
Image by Catherine Gordon.

Raneb and Nefesh

It's over a year since we sojourned luxuriously, or perhaps I should write 'Luxoriously', amid the squalor and old stones of Egypt. We took our time among the columns of Karnak.[52] We visited the shattered shrine of Tell el Amarna and pondered silently the legacy of Akhnaten, the feted monotheistic and iconoclastic Pharaoh. We wandered conversationally and at ease among the tombs in the Valley of the Kings and those in the Valley of the Queens. We drank imported wine from the Ends of the Earth at the Sheraton, Luxor, listening, in the privacy of our suite, to Glass's opera of religious reform. We dined later with friends in Heliopolis, heedless of both Mubarak and the Muslim Brotherhood. And you gave me a gift and made a request for songs.

You made a request for songs based on a book and written into a book. It was Daniel Levitin's book, but not the Book of Daniel and not given in levity. I wish, you wrote within it, that you would compose for me six songs, your own *seis canciones*, inspired by the beauty of our being able to walk so reflectively among such august and ancient tombs. That was in Cairo. To be given a book in Cairo was symbolic. To be given a book concerning the nature of songs and human nature by one's Muse, the mistress of Capirote Therapies, was more than symbolic. It was, if anything can be, a religious gesture. Under the moons that have phased since, even on the secular canals of Venice, I have wondered how to respond – with what manner of nostalgic songs.

The World in Six Songs was and is the book. You asked for six songs of such a kind. You asked for all the world. How am I to give that? And yet I would. Wondering since how it might be done, I have read my Levitin and reimmersed myself in the long chords and choruses of *Akhnaten*.

---

52   This short sentence, I now believe, is highly significant; just as the whole fable of Raneb and Nefesh is disproportionately significant in understanding what Fenimore thought he was doing in writing these Notebooks at all. I believe that he came to remember the great, ruinous columns of the Temple at Karnak as symbolic of what he was creating within the Notebooks. His strangely uniform stanzas – the octavos – and the strict consistency of there being exactly sixty of them in each section of each Notebook make most sense if seen in a ritual and architectural context. He intended them, though he never stated this, to be experienced, to be seen almost as the serried columns in a great temple complex. He was not certain that he could write the songs that Margarita requested and so he never included any in the Notebooks. He did, however, seek to honour her request for a memento of their visit to Karnak and the Valleys of the Kings and Queens of Egypt by constructing an object in which the very shape of the finished writing resembled a colossal Egyptian monument, with the words within each stanza being the equivalent of the hieroglyphs adorning the great pillars in the temple, as clear as when the temple in question was in its glistening and soaring prime. – TCE.

I have set it sonically alongside Schoenberg's *Moses and Aaron*. I have pondered archaism and minimalism, accent, mood and time. I have asked myself questions out of the mind of Egypt, looked for clues in the Pentateuch and the Psalms and even, at times in desperation, thought of emulating the antics of pop song. Do you really want songs from among the tombs? From among the ruins of the first great epoch of human civilization? What would these be for us and now?

I discovered, while researching your request, even before we visited the Veneto this year, that many of the psalms, piously attributed to King David, seem to have their roots and resonance in Egypt of the Pharaohs. Psalm 104, for instance, a quite long hymn of praise to the deity who created the world and casts his light upon it, is said to have been based on a far older Egyptian hymn to Ra. Perhaps, I thought, this is my clue and I can generate a story rooted in this antiquity. Such a story might suggest the kind of songs you asked for on that book in Cairo - five months before the financial crash and the changing of good fortune to vast endowment. You do like stories, almost as much as songs, though you think they're less profound or therapeutic. Yes?

The crucial clue and inkling came at last from the opera. Listening to *Akhnaten* yet again, I was suddenly struck by the opening words of Scene 7, where the Pharaoh sings a duet with Queen Nefertiti. I breathe the sweet breath which comes forth from thy mouth, they sing in unison. I behold thy beauty every day. It is my desire that I may be rejuvenated with life through love of thee. Give me thy hands, holding thy spirit, that I may receive it and live by it. Call thou upon my name unto eternity And it shall never fail. These lyrics weren't made up by Glass. They were borrowed by him from the *Journal of Egyptian Archaeology*. They are the words of a love poem found inside a mummy from the time of Akhnaten himself. Did you have such things in mind?

Late one afternoon I listened to that duet, more than once; and that very evening Tarski, Eleni and some of the other Peripatetica team arrived at Cos for the evening meal and conversation. By prior agreement, after dinner, we all watched *Out of Africa*. Then I was riveted by the fact that in Scene 7, Denys Finch-Hatton asks Karen Blixen can she tell a story and she makes up a charming and moving one on the spot. You will well remember the scene, since we've watched the film together and you love to exclaim dreamily, "I had a farm in Africa, at the foot of the Ngong Hills." For me, however, I believe it was the coincidence of the sevens, as much as the beauty of the Egyptian duet that prompted the following story – set in Egyptian Africa, long ago.

It occurred to me that night while half asleep that there was a breathtaking gold necklace found by archaeologists, early in the twentieth century, in the pre-scientific age of archaeology. Yes, even to archaeology, science has come only very recently. This necklace lay among many treasures in the long lost and extraordinarily well-secured tomb of a Pharaoh of the Second Dynasty of Archaic Egypt. The Pharaoh's name was Raneb and he ruled the unified Kingdom of Upper and Lower Egypt, two hundred years before the building of the great pyramids at Giza. He was a remarkable king, a man of vision and religious insight, who had travelled widely before ascending the already ancient throne left to him by his father, the Pharaoh Hetepsekhemwy. Here was a story.

It was the twenty ninth century BCE and the land of Egypt had already been unified under the double crown for hundreds of years. How do we know this? Ah! That would be a separate, serious and less romantic story. Of course, being as I am, I found myself making up a story that hewed as closely as possible to what 'we' in the charitable sense of the term now know. But for your sake and in search of songs, I allowed my imagination to embroider a Blixen kind of tale around these facts or well-defended hypotheses of Egyptology. I supposed, beyond the facts, that Raneb's enlightened rule and religious reforms opened the way for the Golden Age of the Old Kingdom – when the great pyramids would be built. He occurred as your Egyptian man.

The necklace, as my dream thought conceived it, was a mystery among archaeologists for many years. It was a thing of great beauty, consisting of seven precious stones, held together in a delicate braiding of worked gold. The stones were arrayed so that three of them, each lapis lazuli, were on one side and three, each moonstone, were on the other. The base of the necklace would have lain between the breasts of the woman who wore it. The precious stone at the base, the seventh jewel, was a great pearl. But who wore it? For whom was it made and by whom? There was no sarcophagus containing the remains of Raneb's consort. No story had come down about her. Why would the necklace have been buried in *his* tomb? She is our mystery Egyptian woman.

Our knowledge of the earliest dynasties was exceedingly poor in the 1920s, when the tomb of Raneb was first excavated. The ancient Hellenistic king lists were only beginning to be cross-checked against physical evidence and Raneb was no more than a vague name from the earliest segments of those lists. Of his consort there was, at that time, no record; not even a name. It was only decades later that a separate and stunning find seemed to provide the answer to the mystery of the necklace. That find was the White Wall Papyrus, discovered buried in an ancient vault beneath desert sands. This extraordinary document, when it was pieced together and translated from the ancient hieroglyphics by a team of cryptologists, yielded the story of the necklace.

The White Wall Papyrus was written by a hitherto unknown polymath from the court of Raneb at

Memphis; a man by the name of Urhotep, who seems to have been at once a craftsman, a poet and a sage. He advised Raneb throughout his reign and wrote the Papyrus document in retrospect. It related the tale of Raneb and his consort – Queen Nefesh - explaining the design, making and ceremonial use of the beautiful necklace. The archaeological world was astounded, because nothing else like this had ever before been found from such an early time, when writing itself was relatively new in Egypt, as in Sumer, and was used chiefly for purposes of public administration and accounting, rather than the telling of personal stories of this intimate and sublime nature.

This point deserves emphasis, because in our lifetimes we have become rather accustomed to the discovery of fragments of papyri from the late classical period, such as the Dead Sea Scrolls or the Oxyrhynchus Papyri, which date from between the first and sixth centuries CE. Yet, precious as many of these are; they cannot compare in completeness, to say nothing of age, with the White Wall Papyrus. Specialists infer that its astonishing state of preservation must be attributed to the fact that it was carefully sealed up inside a secure vault, whereas the Dead Sea Scrolls were in caves and the Oxyrynchus Papyri were fortunate to have survived at all, having been thrown into ancient rubbish dumps by those who clearly valued them a great less than we now do.[53]

The White Wall Papyrus told of how Hetepsekhemwy, a great captain of men, held the kingdom together from Naqada in Upper Egypt, when the three hundred year old First Dynasty collapsed. He founded the Second Dynasty and married a Nubian princess. With her, he sailed down the Nile from the uppermost cataracts to the Great Green Sea, as a sign of his lordship and majesty, everywhere inspecting the granaries and the taxation system. They had a son, whom they named Nebra, Lord of the Sun. He was raised at his father's court and educated in both the arts of war and those of government. When he came of age, he was sent on a great maritime expedition down through the Red Sea to the Horn of Africa. Do you believe any of this? It is for you.

---

53   The Oxyrhynchus Papyri are thousands of fragmentary manuscripts discovered in Egypt between the 1890s and 1930s by archaeologists Bernard P. Grenfell and Arthur S. Hunt at an ancient rubbish dump. They date from the 1st to the 6th century CE and include thousands of Greek and Latin documents, letters and literary works. They are now kept in many institutions around the world. A substantial number are housed in the Ashmolean Museum at Oxford University. Early hopes of recovering many of the lost literary works of antiquity at Oxyrhynchus were not fulfilled, but a great deal was found, all the same. The finds include fragments of the long lost poetry of Sappho and Alcaeus, which is of some interest in the light of Fenimore's late poem 'Sappho and Alcaeus' and his apparent sense that his relationship with Margarita bore some resemblance to that between those two poets of pre-classical Lesbos. – TCE.

Nebra made contact with the kingdoms far to the south of Egypt, learning the boundaries of the world he would one day rule. Trading in resins, spices, precious stones, gold and ivory, he sailed as far as an island out in the Arabian Sea, midway between the Horn of Africa and the southern coast of Arabia, the translators deduced from Urhotep's account. It seems certain this island was what we know as Socotra. This alone was a stunning discovery from the White Wall Papyrus, but it was only the beginning. For it was on the homeward journey that things befell Nebra which transformed his life and brought him, by catastrophic chance, into the world of the woman who was to become his consort, the love of his life and the recipient of the mysterious golden necklace.

You see, when Nebra turned for home, laden with luxuries for his father's court, his ships were attacked by pirates off the coast of present-day Somalia, before they could reach the relative security of the Red Sea. The crews were slaughtered, the cargoes plundered, the ships either stolen or scuttled. Nebra, the Lord of the Sun himself, wounded in the fighting, was thrown overboard by the pirates and left to drown. Seizing hold of some flotsam from a scuttled vessel, however, he was able to survive and was finally cast up half-dead, on the shores of what is Yemen today. There, senseless on the sand, he was found by the servants of a princess, the beautiful young daughter of the proud Queen of those parts – the Queendom of Sheba. She was your avatar.

Was there a Queen of Sheba (Yemen) two thousand years before the fabled liaison between King Solomon and the Queen of Sheba? Who knows, but it makes for a good story, doesn't it? The servants of the princess brought Nebra, whose identity was unknown to them, into the palace where the princess took pity on the wounded stranger and nursed him back to health. Concealing his royal identity out of caution, Nebra gave his name as Seti and said that he was the servant of a great lord lost at sea. They believed him, since this is a largely benign tale. In any case, he was alone, harmless and without wealth or trappings that might have tempted plunder by less charitable hosts. And so – as the Papyrus relates – he slowly recuperated in fabled Sheba.

The name of the princess was Nefesh. How did I or Urhotep come up with that name? He, I imagine, was passing down the truth in good faith. I for my part had gleaned the word from Robert Alter's translation of the Psalms, in which I learned that 'nefesh' is the Hebrew word for what, in the King James Bible, is translated as 'soul'. It is a term, Alter observes, more correctly translated as 'breath of life'. This lent it an affinity, I thought, with the poem from the mummy's tomb and the duet of Akhnaten and Nefertiti. Then there was the assonance with the very name of Nefertiti, or that of Nefertari, the legendary beauty who was the primary consort of the greatest of Pharaohs, Ramesses the Great, long after the epoch of Raneb. Did I choose well?

The beauty of Princess Nefesh, as described by Urhotep in the White Wall Papyrus, was exceptional. Unsurprisingly, as if in a tale from the Arabian nights, Nebra and Nefesh grew to love one another as he recovered. They would go for walks together in the palace grounds and eventually for rides in the countryside and would talk for many hours of the wonders of the world and the origins of all things. When he was sufficiently recovered that he felt an urgent need to return to Egypt, he revealed to the Queen of Sheba who he truly was and requested the hand of her daughter in marriage. She, seeing advantage in this, sanctioned their love. Nebra and Nefesh then sailed up the Red Sea coast to Egypt, in a flotilla provided by the Queen of Sheba.

Nebra loved Nefesh exceedingly and they were married in a great court ceremony at Memphis, attended by the Queen of Sheba and the whole upper hierarchy of the ancient nobility of the Red and White Crowns of Egypt. The imagery Urhotep used to describe the young Nefesh, Queen of Egypt, and the pageantry of her marriage to Nebra has no known precedent. But he extols even more than her beauty, her extraordinary character, dignity and intelligence. He seemingly invented new hieroglyphs to make his pictures vivid and give them force. Allowing for the ancient tendency of poets to exaggerate, especially court poets; we must nevertheless infer that Nefesh would have to be ranked with the three most famous beauties of ancient Egypt after her.

I've mentioned two of these already, but, like all beautiful things, they deserve repetition. The first, the most ancient, was Nitocris, the consort of the Pharaoh Mycerinus, in the 27th century BCE, who completed the building of the third pyramid at Giza for her husband, after he died. The second was that Nefertiti, the famous Queen of Akhnaten in the 15th century BCE, who sings the duet with him in Philip Glass's opera. The third was Nefertari, consort of the great Pharaoh Ramesses II, in the 13th century BCE, whom he called "she for whom the Sun rises". Now we know that there were not three but four great beauties of the second and third millennia BCE, each the *non pareil* of her time: Nefesh, Nitocris, Nefertiti, Nefertari; but Nefesh was first.

While still a prince in the court of his father, Hetepsekhemwy, and already married to Nefesh, Nebra made the acquaintance of Urhotep, a young priest in the Temple of Ptah, at Memphis. Urhotep had been singled out by the discerning eye of the High Priest as unusually gifted of mind, hand and spirit. A close friendship developed between the two young men and, as Urhotep's talents blossomed under the prince's friendship and patronage, they came to trust one another more and more. They talked at great length about the nature of the world and the truths of religion, just as Nebra had long learned to talk with Nefesh. By Urhotep's account, they studied the stars, discussed the first principles of things and debated the nature of law and justice.

Urhotep's knowledge of philosophical matters was matched by his skills as a craftsman of precious stones and as a wordsmith. Moreover, he had the insight and wisdom of the later Joseph, so that both Hetepsekhemwy and young Nebra came to trust his grasp of public administration and the arts of government. He and Nebra hunted together like brothers and Urhotep accompanied the maturing prince on military expeditions into the south and into the coastlands of Cyrene and Libya. Moreover, according to the White Wall Papyrus, Nefesh kept them company in all these things, being both literate and articulate, both a lover of fine words and a writer of verse; and being also an accomplished equestrian and huntress. She was regal, our Nefesh.

In all these circumstances, according to Urhotep, when Hetepsekhemwy died, Nebra asked Urhotep to make for Nefesh a special coronation gift: a great necklace with seven stones. This is the origin of the famous artefact found only in the 1920s, almost five thousand years after its making at the Pharaonic court at Memphis. Urhotep took three superb pieces of lapis lazuli, three pieces of moonstone and one beautiful pearl from the Horn of Africa. He told Nebra that moonstone balances the flow of energy in the psyche and moderates the masculine temper. Lapis lazuli, he told the Pharaoh, symbolises deep wisdom and intuition. Pearls, he added, symbolise purity of heart and mind and the emotions being in balance. Of these he crafted the necklace.

According to the papyrus, Nebra himself selected a pearl as the seventh gem, because pearls are of the ocean. He believed that there all life had begun. He knew, also, that his life had been restored from the ocean by the servants of Nefesh and for this reason he wanted a symbol of the ocean to be the crowning piece in the necklace. He called it the stone of healing. It and each of the other stones was cut with the finest skills and set in braided gold, with a clasp shaped in the form of a solid gold ankh, that most polysemic icon of ancient Egypt. It is the symbol of male and female coupling; the Sun on the horizon; it is the Knot of Isis: the symbol for life or the breath of life; it stands for vivacity and immortality and also for acts of purification. It is Nefesh.

Urhotep took great care in crafting the elaborate and priceless necklace, using the finest milled gold from Punt. He gave names to each of the seven stones. The three moonstones he called the Stones of Friendship, Joy and Comfort; these being aspects of the mind in balance. The three lapis lazuli gems he called the Stones of Knowledge, Religion and Love; these being aspects of deep wisdom and intuition.[54] The seventh stone, the pearl, was the Stone of Healing, but

---

54   Fenimore does not spell it out here for Margarita's benefit, presumably because he knew very well that he didn't need to; but according to Daniel Levitin, in *The World in Six Songs*, there are six basic types of song, which characterize all songs around the world since the dawn of human singing: songs of Friendship, Joy,

Urhotep related that Nebra himself called it the Osiris Stone, alluding to the legend of Isis and Osiris, because he saw in his love for Nefesh and her having saved his life, an echo of that already ancient tale. Thus the marvellous necklace was bounded by the Knot of Isis and the Osiris Stone.

Nebra, according to the sage of the White Wall Papyrus, had already decided that he would change his name to Raneb and reign not as Lord of the Sun, but as a servant of Ra. Osiris was the Son of Ra. Nebra wished to be seen not as lord and master, but as servant and steward of the highest deity. His new name proclaimed this, for Raneb meant 'Ra is Lord'. Do you like the story so far? This particular detail is actually true, according to non-apocryphal sources. There is a hint, in this grain of recovered history, therefore, that far back in the 29th century BCE, one and a half millennia before Akhnaten, there reigned a Pharaoh who already conceived of religious reform and of being not master but servant of the Most High and steward of his abundant light.

But back to our story, since that is where I hope to be able to derive songs of the kind you have requested. When the great golden necklace, with its seven precious stones, was completed, so Urhotep's fabulous story continued, Raneb declared that they would hold a great feast far up the Nile at Naqada, ancient capital of the Kingdom of Upper Egypt, before the unification of the Red and White Crowns. It would be called the Feast of the Breath of Life and would be celebrated on the birthday of Osiris. There Nefesh would be presented with the necklace and all the court would behold her beauty and call her Queen and then he would sail with her down the Nile, in the manner of his father long before, back to Memphis, in the north. How about that?

Comfort, Knowledge, Religion and Love. Levitin's thesis was clearly something which Margarita took very seriously, while Fenimore, preoccupied with so much else, does not seem to have taken it altogether seriously until beyond this point in his work. I think, however, that writing this fable was an important turning point for him and that it began to awaken in him – too late, it would seem – an understanding of what truly inspired and motivated Margarita. That's why he went on to attempt, privately, to respond to her request for songs, both by writing the psalms or songs for Queen Nefesh and by writing an increasing number and variety of poems and quasi-songs as a means for distilling his own emotional reflections and ideas.

Levitin wrote: "*The World in Six Songs* is the story of just how music has changed the course of human civilization, in fact the story of how it made societies and civilizations possible. Other art forms – poetry, sculpture, literature, film and painting – can also fit into these functional categories, but this is the story of music and its primacy in shaping human nature. Through a process of co-evolution of brains and music, through the structures throughout our cortex and neo-cortex, from the limbic system to the cerebellum, music uniquely insinuates itself into our heads. It does this in six distinctive ways, each of them with its own evolutionary basis." (p. 39). – TCE.

Raneb, according to the White Wall Papyrus, had a great vision for what he would undertake as Pharaoh. He would renew the grand ceremonial unity of the kingdoms of Upper and Lower Egypt. He would announce religious reforms, which he, Nefesh and Urhotep had long secretly discussed and planned, elevating Ra, the Sun god, above Ptah in the religious pantheon. He would single out Isis and Osiris for solemn recognition, as the guardians of the realm. At this point in his hieroglyphic pageant, Urhotep provided what is by far the oldest account found anywhere of the great legend of Isis and Osiris. He wrote, so long ago, so early in the history of writing itself that the mind shivers at the exquisiteness of his graphical and narrative skills in that epoch.

The beauty of this story, emerging after almost five thousand years, out of the sands of time, is almost as astonishing as the stunning necklace crafted by the hands of Urhotep for the Queen. Osiris, he related, was conceived by the Sky goddess Nut, wife of the Sun god Ra, after she had copulated with the Earth god Seb. When Ra realized that Nut had been unfaithful to him, he declared that her child would not be born in any month or any year. But another of Nut's many lovers, Thoth, looking to help her, played draughts with the Moon and won a seventy second part of every day. He made five whole days out of these parts and added them to the Egyptian year of 360 days. On these days, outside the bounds set by Ra, Nut gave birth to her five offspring.

Osiris was born on the first of these days. So, it's curious, you see: Osiris is acclaimed as the Son of Ra, but in fact, according to the most ancient legends, he was the illegitimate son of Nut and not the Son of Ra at all. He was the Son of Seb, the Son of the Earth, not of the Sun. Now, of course, it is in the nature of such old legends that they do not tie up loose ends or provide quite satisfactory explanations for things. At least, in this case, we aren't told that Osiris was conceived of Ra upon a virgin Nut. We are told something which has a greater ring of truth to it. She had an affair, being a goddess of the Sky, with that muscular and substantial other: the Earth. These things the sage Urhotep owned in his ur-version of the great Osiris myth, almost five thousand years ago.

Nut, by tradition (this is known quite independently of Urhotep, but is corroborated by his telling of the story) had four other children by Seb: two more sons, Horus and Set; and two daughters, Isis and Nepthys. They were born on the other four days Thoth had made available. What was Ra up to that he allowed his spouse the Sky to be so fecund with the Earth that he himself made warm and made swarm with living forms? Was he so lost in the sense of his own radiance that he neglected her? Was he so dazzled by his own effulgence that he was blind to her coupling far below with the earthy and rock-ribbed Seb? It's not as if Seb was the only one, after all. Thoth and many others besides, Urhotep confirms, enjoyed her favours - Thoth and at least some others.

Thoth is a figure worth pausing to reflect upon; and not because of his services to Nut, when the world of human civilization was relatively young. His Grecian name was Hermes, so naturally we don't find him so named by Urhotep. Thoth was the inventor of board games, of writing (so it is commonly said, though we know better), of primary cosmology and subtle thought. He was the originator of what has been handed down over millennia, though chiefly in forms obscured by priests or confused by the uninitiated, of the Great Wisdom. Even in Hellenistic antiquity (the age after Alexander the Great and down to the Roman conquest of Egypt), this body of thought was known as the Hermetica. It lies at the foundation of Christianity and Free Masonry alike.

Not the least among the wonders of the White Wall Papyrus is that, incomplete and inevitably time worn though it is, we have in it not only the Tale of Raneb and Nefesh (to which, pardon me, I shall return in a moment), but the earliest indication of the nature and origins of the Hermetica. In a breathtaking digression, Urhotep intimates that Thoth imparted to a small number of the Wise and Righteous in Upper Egypt, centuries before the unification of the North and South Kingdoms, a body of insights in verse which remained the Venerable Tradition of the Secret Truth down to Urhotep's day. It consisted of forty two poems, collected in the First Book. It was lost in the wars that unified Egypt, but the Tradition was preserved by the learned few.[55]

---

55   This is an intriguing invention on Fenimore's part, especially against the background of his relentless work in the 1990s rooting out mythology and historiographical obscurantism in both European and Asian accounts of the nature and origins of the sciences. He was clearly having fun, in a relaxed mood and making fast and loose with the facts of archaeology and religion, as only someone with his erudition was free to do. This would not necessarily be worth remarking upon here if it was not for his strange reference to the First Book consisting of *forty two poems,* and his statement that these (in the form of the Book) have now been lost, but that their essential content had been handed down over time among a small group of the (Wise and Righteous) few. There may be nothing to this, but in sifting through his papers after his passing, I discovered, leaving aside his Credo (Appendix A), forty two poems, if we include both the thirty five reprinted in Appendix C and the Seven Songs for Queen Nefesh in Appendix B. I could find no evidence of a plan on his part to bring these poems together in a book, much less to attach portentous importance to them. Yet the coincidence between the number of them and this little aside in the Tale of Raneb and Nefesh is arresting; not least because, when he wrote the Tale, he had not yet written most of the poems.

It was Mr Bojangles, Fenimore's long-time research assistant and chief librarian, who, when I raised with him the number of the poems, inquiring whether there might be more, drew my attention to a passage, found in Fenimore's quite early collation of 'Notes on the Philosophy and Cosmology of the Patriarchs of the Christian Churches', to an observation by the second century CE Church Father, Clement of Alexandria, that the sacred knowledge of the priests of old Egypt centred on a

But let's return to our tale and hoped for source of songs. According to the ancient legend, when Osiris grew up, he married his sister Isis. Urhotep makes no comment on this incestuous union, which suggests that it was no late interpellation into the legend, but a primeval component of it. Strangely, to our way of thinking, it was to become a model for Egyptian royalty for millennia. Yet in the legend it is viewed as dignified and unproblematic. Unhindered by the cuckolded Ra, Osiris became the ruler of Egypt – that then favoured section of Seb's great body - and taught his subjects the arts of civilization, especially the cultivation of grapes and grains. The King of Peace, he then left Egypt to Isis and travelled abroad for many years. They, too, lived apart for years.

In his wide foreign travels, Osiris spread the blessings of agriculture and viniculture – bread and wine - wherever he went. On his return, he was hailed by Egyptians as a deity, but his brothers, Horus and Set, jealous alike of his power, his status among the common run of humanity and the love their sisters bore him, conspired against him. They secretly murdered him, dismembered him and cast his *membra disjecta* into the Nile, stuffed into a sarcophagus, fashioned from the trunk of a great tree. It floated slowly down the Nile to the Sea, accompanied by unearthly sounds of mourning, which came at last to the ears of Isis and her sister Nepthys, who were preparing a banquet for Osiris in the great hall of the palace at Memphis unware of his death.

Carried by the currents of the Great River, the sarcophagus of Osiris came at last not only through the Delta and down to the Sea, but far across the Sea to the shores of the Copper Island. There it was found by servants of the Lord of the Southern Shore and, being seen only as a log of uncommon beauty and resilience, was turned into a pillar in the Lord's palace. This reference to 'the Copper Island', presumably Cyprus, is an interesting variation on the later, received version of the story, which describes its landfall as having been Phoenicia and the potentate in question the King of Sidon. In Urhotep's day, however, there was no Phoenicia and no Sidon. The lack of such an anachronism was an early test of the antiquity of the fabled White Wall Papyrus.

---

small library of forty two canonical books. The number forty two was sacred and corresponded to the number of nomes, or administrative districts in Egypt. He (Clement) related that these books constituted the core of all temple libraries and were all attributed to Thoth/Hermes himself. The priests formed a hierarchy and memorized different books, depending on their function. There was a book of hymns; a book about the Pharaoh; four books on the sciences; six books on medicine; ten books of hieroglyphics; ten on education, cults and sacrifices; ten on the laws, the gods and the education of priests. It may be drawing a long bow, but I cannot help thinking that this was the source of Fenimore's playful reference in the Tale to the original Hermetica having consisted of forty two poems in a single book. - TCE

Within the central tale it told, Isis would not forsake her beloved. When she and her sister heard what had been done to Osiris, they flew into a fury against their murderous brothers and vowed before Ra (oddly enough) to find their slaughtered sibling/spouse and restore him to life. Leaving Nepthys to govern the realm in her absence, Isis set off to trace the sarcophagus in which Horus and Set boasted they had sealed the members of their slain brother. Through many adventures she found his body on the Copper Island, gained his release from the Lord of the Southern Shore, then interceded with Ra to allow her to breathe life back into his shattered limbs. The Sun god acceded to her prayers and, through the loving ministrations of Isis, Osiris rose to new life.

They stayed awhile on the Island, then returned together by ship to Egypt and resumed joint rule of the realm for a time, before Osiris was summoned to a higher destiny: to ascend to the right hand of Ra as Lord of Eternity and Reader of the Book of the Dead. Urhotep's version of the story at this point seems to be notably intimate. So much so that it is difficult to know whether the selection of the Knot of Isis and the Osiris Stone for the beautiful necklace were inspired by the uncanny resemblance of the Tale of Raneb and Nefesh to that of Osiris and Isis, or whether the archaic poet went so far as to work into the already old legend of those deities hints of the human story of the Pharaoh and his Queen. Certainly he wrote after Pharaoh Raneb had died.

The last sections of the White Wall Papyrus, when it was found, were too badly damaged to be reconstructed in the 1950s. With new technologies, it might yet be possible to recover more of the immensely old and only miraculously preserved manuscript. It breaks off into more fragmentary text just after the account of the ascension of Osiris to the right hand of Ra. We are left to imagine what else may have occurred in the lives of these two partners of the ancient world, as we call it, after a mere five millennia. Or at least that was the case for many years, until a number of subsequent archaeological discoveries, the richness of which can never have been foreseen and has hardly been surpassed in the annals of the science, filled in many gaps.

The hauntingly romantic Feast of the Breath of Life may, according to certain Egyptologists, have been held near where the great Temple of Karnak would be built by the New Kingdom Pharaohs well over a thousand years after Raneb's death. Some claimed that the Feast was held every year as long as Raneb reigned and always on the birthday of Osiris, but there is no evidence for this in the White Wall Papyrus and sceptics claimed that this was just a poetic fantasy by those who like to fill in the gaps in the evidence with ideas that take their fancy, or will sell popular magazine articles about the exotic past. Of course, given the background story, this notion had a degree of plausibility. Later finds, as it turned out, would lend it unexpected support.

The most tantalizing mystery of the White Wall Papyrus, however, was found, in broken and almost obliterated text, at the very end of the stunning, but sadly incomplete document. It seems that, after a day of sport, feasting and dancing, the evening of the Feast of the Breath of Life was given over to a ceremony, in which *songs* were sung for Queen Nefesh, to the sound of timbrels, flutes, harps and drums, by the finest minstrels of the court and a chorus trained by the priests. Musicologists and historians were agog at this. The very idea of these songs for Queen Nefesh became an instant hit in newspapers and women's magazines, even making it into the pages of *Rolling Stone*. Academic archaeologists disdained amateur speculations, but they had mass appeal, quite naturally.

Popular imaginings leapt far beyond the hard (or rather, fragmentary) evidence, as the White Wall Papyrus story slowly filtered out from research departments of archaeology and Egyptology spread from Cairo to Chicago. What were the songs? And to what music were these songs sung so long ago? Popular theories abounded, but since there was nothing either material or written on which to properly ground such flights of fancy, they were dismissed out of hand by the specialists. For years the lost songs of Queen Nefesh remained one of the more romantic mysteries from the very dawn of history, the answers apparently irretrievably lost in the sands of time. Then not one, but two startling archaeological discoveries broke new ground in the story of the songs.

The first was the extraordinary discovery of the tomb of Urhotep himself, far from where that of his master Raneb had been unearthed. Urhotep's grave, older even that the crumbled Step Pyramid of the Pharaoh Djoser at Saqqara, said to have been designed and overseen by Imhotep, had long gone undiscovered. Urhotep had not been buried in the north, at Memphis, but in the south, at Naqada. His grave had long since been built over by New Kingdom temples and monuments, in the sixteenth century BCE. These had themselves subsequently fallen into ruin and have only ever partly been excavated. Yet there the tomb of Urhotep lay for thousands of years with its deeply immured secrets. It was found in the 1980s, almost by improbable chance.

The unearthing of the tomb of Urhotep turned out to be even more stunning than the discovery of the White Wall Papyrus, thirty years before; though, of course, they complemented one another, just as each complemented the original discovery of the tomb of Raneb. In Urhotep's tomb archaeologists discovered a breathtaking mural, telling of his many works for Pharaoh. Among other remarkable stories, it included what was plainly the complete text of the White Wall Papyrus, enabling scholars to verify many of the more speculative decipherments from the ancient manuscript, but also to see the end of the story. It appears that the Feast of the Breath of Life was held for twenty consecutive years, very much as ignorant speculation had long asserted.

It turns out that the songs sung at the great feast were initially traditional court songs, but that, after a number of years had passed, Nefesh herself instigated a change. She commissioned a song for each stone of her necklace. Here a textual ambiguity arises, because although the mural relates that the songs were composed by Urhotep, it doesn't distinguish between the original songs and the new songs commissioned by Queen Nefesh. Nonetheless, the mural relates, when the seven new songs had been written and performed to the satisfaction of the Queen and Raneb, Urhotep was asked to remake the necklace itself, as 'the Necklace of Seven Songs'. This remaking must have been the most painstaking and skilful work of hand until that time in human history.

In what archaeologists described as by far the most astonishing detail ever unearthed from such a grave anywhere in the Neolithic or Bronze Age world, the mural stated that Urhotep had inscribed the titles and first line of each of the songs, using the finest glyphs, on the *inside of the gold base* which held each stone in place in the necklace. No-one had thought, to that point, to look for any such thing. Yet the mural's statement was verified when the necklace was carefully examined, under expert international supervision, at the Egyptian Museum of Antiquities, in Cairo. Specialists of all kinds were unable to express their wonder that any such thing had been possible. There is, even now, no satisfactory explanation for how it can have been done.

The finding was described as similar in its revolutionary implications to the discovery of bone flutes, dating back tens of thousands of years, traces of ochre for cave paintings dating back 100,000 years; or long Neanderthal spears dating back 400,000 years. Like those finds, this discovery enhanced our collective sense of what it means to be human and of how far back our creative intentionality as human beings actually dates. The fine craftsmanship involved almost eclipsed, in press reports, the fact that the actual lyrics of the seven songs were found inscribed on a large relief within Urhotep's unbelievable tomb. Both, however, were shortly afterwards eclipsed by yet another astounding find: the tomb and memoirs of Nefesh herself in Yemen.

It was just as the Cold War ended, less than a decade after the discovery of the tomb of Urhotep, that the find in Yemen enabled scholars to finally piece together how the Tale of Raneb and Nefesh had ended. Given the violent history and endemic corruption of Yemen, it is scarcely to be believed that a find of this nature was possible. It was made by archaeologists working, with the knowledge and support of the Yemeni government, on the sixth century CE background to the rise of Islam in what the Romans had for centuries called Arabia Felix. They were excavating the site of a fortress that the Jewish king of Yemen, Joseph Hanging Locks, had defended against Christian invaders from Axum, in modern Ethiopia, allies of the Emperor in Constantinople.

Far beneath the foundations of King Joseph Hanging Locks' fortress, the Turkish team found urban remains dating back to the early third millennium BCE. Their sheer antiquity was the big story to begin with. When the team dug further, however, they came upon what turned out to be the third tomb in our story – that of Queen Nefesh herself. This was an extremely contentious claim, until it was revealed that there was an amazingly preserved record of Nefesh's own life, carved in stone so as to outlast more perishable materials. When it was painstakingly deciphered, it rendered an account of her life every bit as remarkable in its own way as the Tomb of Raneb, the White Wall Papyrus or the tomb murals of Urhotep. Do I have your attention with this?

Prior to the finding of the White Wall Papyrus, the romance of Raneb and Nefesh could not even have been imagined – although the necklace was tantalizing evidence, when it came to light. Yet now the tale of that romance turned out to have been written and not by one hand only, but from three different points of view. This third account was the autobiography of the Princess of Sheba and Queen of Egypt, written not in Egyptian hieroglyphics, but in a kind of cuneiform script closer to those found from about a thousand years earlier in Mesopotamia than to the Egyptian characters. It required almost the skills of a new Champollion to decipher, because it was not in any of the known languages of the Middle East. This was the mind of Queen Nefesh.

When the code was broken, however, and that was only in the past few years, it revealed that Nefesh had lived with Raneb for twenty seven years in all. It relates that they lost two children to early deaths from disease, before the birth of their son Nynetjer, who survived to succeed his father. Several times, after the birth of her third child, Nefesh voyaged down the Red Sea to visit her long-lived mother, who ruled Sheba for many years after her daughter's departure with Nebra. She refers to Urhotep and relates that she so loved the necklace he made, which Raneb gave her at the coronation feast, that she composed a song to go with each of its seven stones and arranged for these songs to be sung from then on at the Feast of the Breath of Life at old Naqada.

She composed the songs!? This was itself a revelation. So, according to Nefesh, or whoever wrote the account on the stone tablets in her tomb, she didn't *commission* the songs, but actually wrote them herself. This made headlines in certain women's magazines. Scholars were quick to counter that Urhotep's account may have been merely ambiguous, rather than deceptive. Perhaps he composed original songs and even the music for the new songs. But if so, why had he made no mention of the role of the Queen in the composition of the songs, if she had written the words? Internal evidence from the songs themselves leaves the question of authorship puzzling, as they appear to have been written in different voices and it isn't clear, at times, whom they address.

Sometimes they seem to address Nefesh herself, sometimes Raneb and often the gods. This seems bound to generate controversy for years to come, but the debate is likely to be left to specialists. Popular sentiment and attention quickly gravitated to the more dramatic part of the story from the Tomb of Nefesh: its ending. Long after the songs had been written, it seems the Queen of Sheba faced a terrible rebellion by an upstart commander in her army, whose name transliterates – to the general amusement - as 'Shithole the Usurper'. Taking with her a contingent of Egyptian troops, Queen Nefesh sailed down the Red Sea to the aid of her mother. Before she could reach Sheba, however, her mother perished at the hands of the aforesaid usurper Shithole.

The Usurper stormed the capital, sacked the palace and murdered the Queen and all her household. Landing on the coast not far from where, twenty seven years before, her servants had found the castaway Nebra in his youth, Nefesh marched inland, rallying the people as she went. She took the forces of Shithole the Usurper by surprise near where the capital stands today and routed them. Shithole was taken back to the capital and impaled alive in the yard of the palace he had so recently sacked. The cruelty of this punishment stunned those who deciphered the story, since it seemed to have no precedent in the biography of this beautiful woman. But the incident is recorded without elaboration or comment. She had taken condign and royal vengeance.

The story set in stone then relates that Nefesh found it necessary to remain in Sheba as its ruler, since there was no-one else left of the royal house. For several years she would meet Raneb again at Naqada for the Feast of the Breath of Life, but otherwise they lived apart in these later years. The story goes on to say that, during the fifth of these occasions, Urhotep, feeling the weight of the passing years and looking ahead to his eventual death, requested permission to build a tomb at Naqada and to make it a memorial to the beloved Pharaoh and Queen whom he had served. Two years later, on the eve of the annual feast, Nefesh heard that Raneb had fallen gravely ill. Before she could make arrangements to travel to Memphis to be with him, he passed away.

The still vigorous Nefesh returned mournfully to Memphis and presided over the state funeral of Raneb and over the coronation as Pharaoh of their mature son Nynetjer. She declares in stone, significantly for readers of this threefold tale, that she herself laid the Necklace of Seven Songs (she calls it that) on the chest of Raneb in his crypt and oversaw unprecedented physical security arrangements to ensure that the crypt could never be broken into. After staying in the palace at Memphis for a time, she took a boat up the Nile to Naqada and then far beyond, before taking ship for Sheba and returning forever to her people. She lived to a great age and only twice visited Egypt again, each time for the funeral of a Pharaoh: that of her son and then of her grandson.

The first was that of her son Nynetjer, only ten years after that of his father. The second was that of her grandson Wenegnebti, only seven years after that. She was causing this account to be set down in writing, she stated, in her eighty third year: twenty spring times since the passing away of her grandson Wenegnebti and forty since she had succeeded her mother as Queen of Sheba. Her younger grandson, Sened, was now Pharaoh in Egypt, which was at peace. Her own country, she made so bold as to claim, she had governed as well as Isis had governed Egypt in the absence of Osiris. But now she was dying and would go the Hall of Two Truths to meet Osiris himself, stand before the throne of Ra and be reunited with those she had loved in life, chiefly her Raneb.

One can only wonder at the source of this extraordinary tale. Did the aged Nefesh set it down herself? Was it copied – more or less faithfully – after her death from court records? No evidence has come to hand. In any case, it is a remarkable document. Among other things, it provided unlooked for confirmation of the much later Egyptian king lists, regarding the succession of Pharaohs at the beginning of the Second Dynasty, long ago. What, however, of the songs themselves? There have been several attempts at translation since the late 1980s. The best English one is probably by the Greek American Egyptologist, Dionysus Theokopoulis. However, what may have seemed glorious at Naqada seems less so in his somewhat academic English.

There are reports that the great translator of ancient poetry, Willis Barnstone, is working on a new translation which, like his translations of Sappho, are expected to break new ground in bringing long lost beauty back to life. Theokopoulis rendered them as fifteen-line chants, modelled on Old Testament psalms, without any attempt to artificially impose a presumed song form or melody. No-one, so far, has ventured to put these extremely ancient songs to music. How would they begin to do so? We have no idea how even the Biblical psalms were sung three thousand years ago. All we know is that the songs of Queen Nefesh have been recovered, against all the odds, from the sands of time for our wonderment and reflection – but mute of music.

And with that line, the teller of this tale put down her glass and turned to her audience, like Karen Blixen in *Out of Africa,* as if to say, 'Well, how do you like my story-telling, since you asked for a tale made up out of whole cloth – or rather out of the first things that came to mind on a quiet evening at the foot of the Ngong Hills?' Is it enough that I have imagined a fable in which songs were composed for an avatar of you, or perhaps even by the avatar herself? That she was even more beautiful than the other three great beauties of ancient Egypt? That she saved her country from a rabble-rousing usurper and reigned there for many years as justly and peacefully as Isis ruled Egypt in the days of legend, while Osiris went abroad? Or do you need actual songs?

Bookburning in the Operplatz in 1933.
Image by Catherine Gordon.

Karl and Paula

How am I to write for you six songs of the musical brain while thinking through the relationship between the human capacity for abstract thought and the apocalypse that looms over us all? It's like trying to reconcile the glories of Palestrina with the Holocaust in the Americas. How can the aspiration to rationality and an awakened comprehension of the nature of the cosmos, from the Ionian sages to Kant, Humboldt and Einstein, have culminated in the catastrophes of the 20th century, the accumulation of nuclear arsenals and the colossal congestion of early 21st century humanity on the Earth? Is it possible that the climax of life on this speck of concentrated minerality is a species with a brain inadequate to the challenges its fierce ingenuity generates?

Look at Egypt now! Look at Yemen and Arabia! What travesties of human civilization we see in those lands where I've just set an *Arabian Nights* fable! More broadly, across the Arab and Islamic world, one sees little but narrow fanaticism, resentment, poverty and a religion so coiled up inside bitter fables as to have lost whatever purity there may once have been in the monotheism of the Prophet. Oh for a single book that would, with translucent reasoning, carve away the irrationalities and delusions of all the 'sacred scriptures' and show a clear path forward to humane enlightenment! Isn't that conceivable; in place of the anthropomorphisms, errors and violent incitements of the Bible, the Quran and their various kith and kin, religious and secular?

Yet I am haunted by the image of the burned out ruins of European cities in 1945 and, above all, those of Berlin. That was where – or so it had appeared for a brief while – Enlightenment was coming close to realization. That was the city of the Humboldt brothers and the capital city of a culture steeped at once in natural science and in Kant, Goethe and Beethoven. How are we to internalize the fact that that same city was the capital city of Prussian militarism, which took all these things and turned them into instruments of overweening chauvinism and aggression? How are we to come to terms with the fact that that militarism then recoiled from defeat to embrace Nazism and turn the instruments of science to continental war and genocide? Tenochtitlan?!

If our single book cannot lay all this bare, how can it transcend the ancient sacred scriptures, which already evoke the enigma of the forces of darkness and the need for a messianic overturning of the ways of secular man? Besides, weren't the thousand bomber raids that demolished Berlin and the overwhelming rocketry and tank assault by the Red Army, which sacked it in April 1945, as surely the avenging arm of the Lord God as anything conjured up in the Book of Revelation or the verses of Jeremiah? What, in that light, of the fire-bombing of the cities of Japan and the nuclear destruction of Hiroshima and Nagasaki? Forgive me, but I cannot see either religion or Enlightenment in all this and cannot sing of it. We need, I need, that one, new book.

Has it been written? There was a time in my youth when, stunned by a preliminary sense of the scale of the 20th century catastrophes and the enormities of totalitarian atrocities, I sought among hundreds of books for a candidate to fill this high office. It would have to be a book, I thought, that one could have stood mindfully with amidst the ashes of the Tiergarten and under the ruins of the Brandenburg Gate in April 1945 and so made sense of all that could be seen, eviscerated and ruined by the vengeful turmoil of human affairs. Or a book one could have read on some desolate bunk in a Stalinist labour camp north of Magadan in 1948; or for that matter in the most philistine and witless reaches of Western suburbia in the 1970s. What book arises, then?

Did any such book ever exist? The sacred scriptures themselves, strenuously reinterpreted for the times? Any book at all of philosophy or geopolitics? Some revolutionary tract or other? The novels of Tolstoy or Dostoevsky? I didn't fail to find one for lack of trying. The closest I came, as far as so young and barely formed a mind could judge things at the time, I say again, was *In Bluebeard's Castle*. Yet it long post-dated all those catastrophes. It's great strength was its fusion of religious awareness of a rarefied calibre with literary sophistication, geopolitical seriousness and, above all, a grasp of the significances of both the sciences and music. They say that, in the time of Stalin, a few poets provided the overwhelmed with words at times to grasp at perspective.

"The fully enlightened earth radiates disaster triumphant", wrote Theodor Adorno and Max Horkheimer in 1943 or 1944. "The program of the Enlightenment was the disenchantment of the world; the dissolution of myths and the substitution of knowledge for fancy...Ruthlessly, in spite of itself, the Enlightenment has extinguished any trace of its own self-consciousness...On the road to modern science, human beings renounce any claim to meaning...Enlightenment is totalitarian...To the Enlightenment, that which does not reduce to numbers, and ultimately to the one, becomes illusion; modern positivism writes it off as literature. Unity is the slogan from Parmenides to Russell. The destruction of gods and qualities alike is insisted upon." Hearken!

'The fully enlightened earth radiates disaster triumphant...'. What a line to have written a year or two *before* nuclear bombs were first exploded over human cities! The artillery of the First World War and its relentless slaughter might have seemed enough. The rise of fascism, Nazism and Stalinism;

the aircraft and tanks, the genocide and fire-bombing of the Second World War took all this to a new level of horror. But nuclear weapons created and used in the name of the free societies of the West, used to compel unconditional surrender, then enhanced to unbelievable proportions with the hydrogen bomb and intercontinental ballistic missiles? All these things were the products of 'enlightened' science. They framed the world into which you and I were born, so very recently.

'The disenchantment of the world, the dissolution of myths and the substitution of knowledge for fancy' was surely a research program of great power and nobility. We can see it in the reflections of Kant and his call for humanity to attain its maturity. We can see it, as those two exiles from Germany claimed, writing in New York at the height of the Second World War, in the thought of rationalists from Parmenides to Russell. Vast knowledge has, indeed, been substituted for myth and fancy along the way. Sweeping horizons have been opened up as never before and Steiner was surely correct to declare that we cannot turn back and choose the dreams of unknowing. The question is, how are we to reclaim coherence and meaning in such an enlightened world?

Only two years ago, you and I spent three unforgettable days in Berlin on our way to the Paris conference on Indo-European origins. That was before Egypt and your request for a gift of songs. We were committed to avoiding distraction and chose long conversational walks through the Tiergarten and meditations at key sites over frivolity. This was Berlin rejuvenated after the end of the communist regime in 1989 and so much leapt to the eye as embodying renewal. Not least among these things, we agreed, was a striking sculpture, three metres high, by Gerhard Marcks, of Petrarch. *The Crier* – so it's called. Petrarch the poet stands there looking east with his hands cupped to his mouth, miming 'I pass through the world and cry 'Peace, Peace, Peace."

Petrarch! Poet of the early Renaissance and symbol of European humanism! Ten feet high he stands there gazing east; put there not before but *after* the Berlin Wall was brought down. But in our walks, all central Berlin struck me as a great stage set for an opera. Songs? I think if I could write strong songs, I would like to write them about Berlin's terrible twentieth century drama, embodied in the lives of Karl and Paula Bonhoeffer. Did I make mention of them more than briefly in Grunewald two years ago? Both sprang from the very finest of German bourgeois culture. Karl was an outstanding scientist. Paula was a woman of great moral dignity and personal grace. The family they raised was a model of humanity. War wrought havoc on them all.

As I recall, I only ever related their story in fragments: a little on the Unter den Linden, a little when I took you over to the leafy streets of Grunewald, where the family had lived between the two world wars; a little more during those long walks in the Tiergarten. Here I would like to tell the story as it should be told and imagine Berlin as the setting for an opera by Verdi, with magnificent arias and recitatives – which, alas, I cannot compose and which, alas, he never will. The tale of Karl and Paula has, however, the tragic quality that Verdi captured so inimitably in his great works that I wouldn't nominate any other composer to do the work. Certainly not Wagner! The Bonhoeffers' fate is no pseudo-medieval *liebestod*, but the tragic song of modernity.

An opera can't, of course, be constructed in the same way as a true story. Art doesn't work that way. But since I am writing for you, I can hardly refrain from prefacing my attempted sketch for an opera with the true story of how they first met. It was the winter of 1896. A researcher in brain sciences with the great Carl Wernicke, young Karl was invited to an open evening at the home of the physicist Oscar Meyer. There, he wrote in old age, 'I met a young, fair, blue-eyed girl whose bearing was so free and natural, and whose expression was so open and confident that as soon as she entered the room she took me captive. This moment when I first laid eyes on my future wife remains in my memory with an almost mystical force.' Those words transport me back to Toledo.

The young, fair, blue-eyed girl was Paula von Hase, then eighteen. Their encounter, as described by Karl, could be mistaken for Romeo laying eyes on Juliet at the Capulets' 'open evening', in Shakespeare's famous play; but that would be to misread entirely the nature of the love that followed. There was nothing juvenile, feckless or ill-starred in the love of Karl and Paula. Their families were far from being embroiled in vendettas against one another in streets like those of Verona. Each came from deeply stable, peaceful families with the firmest and healthiest roots in German upper-class culture and the modern Enlightenment. His Bonhoeffer ancestors had been prosperous professionals for centuries. Hers – the 'von' – were of educated aristocratic lineage.

Bonhoeffer means 'bean farmer' and the relentless modern critique of the bourgeoisie, whether by Dickens or Balzac or the ideological revolutionaries, is worth challenging here; since it depicts the bourgeois as a kind of grasping and philistine bean counter. But the Beanfarmers we are talking about here had long since been other than farmers and were far from being philistines. The same was true of the Tafels, on Karl's mother Julie's side. They were prominent in liberal and democratic reform movements and produced many a free thinker and dissenter. Paula's father and grandfather were eminent theologians, her mother, Clara, a countess with a flair for music, whose father and brother were both leading painters. The family was steeped in culture.

It became fashionable among fascists, anarchists, communists and others after the Great War, to deride bourgeois culture, as if it had been to blame for the catastrophe and had nothing to offer a new era. But there was nothing to deride in the culture of the Bonhoeffers and von Hases. On the contrary, if there is to be anything worthy of the name 'culture' in our future, it seems to me that they provide a model for what it might aspire to. The tragedy of the twentieth century was that just such culture, just such people were overwhelmed by the violence of the epoch. Yet they never succumbed to nihilism; they never endorsed the violence; they never surrendered their sense of dignity and integrity. They stood up like strong and beautiful trees in the great Nazi storm.

Dietrich Bonhoeffer was their youngest son. He has become better known than them, but his character and choice of vocation would have been inconceivable without the roots from which he grew - out of them and under their shade and care. Dietrich's friend and biographer Eberhard Bethge wrote, after the catastrophe was over: 'The fullness of his forebears' lives set Dietrich Bonhoeffer the standards of his own. To it he owed an assurance of judgment and of manner that cannot be acquired in a single generation. He grew up in a family that derived its real education not from school, but from a deeply rooted sense of being guardians of a great historical heritage and intellectual tradition.'[56] He - fine Dietrich - was executed by the Nazis in April 1945.

The spirit of the Bonhoeffer household was not dull conservatism, but a richly grounded liberty. Karl's mother Julie Tafel Bonhoeffer, in 1933, when she was ninety one years old, defiantly walked past Nazi thugs in Berlin to buy goods at a Jewish shop. Such were the family's ethics and politics. Julie had a great influence over her grandson, Dietrich. But he had other role models, on both sides of the family. Paula's grandfather Karl August von Hase and her father Karl Alfred von Hase showed him theology as a way of life. Paula herself spent some months, in her youth, living with the Moravian Brethren, a sect whose founder, Jan Hus, had been burned at the stake by the Catholic Church in 1415 for heresy. These were Dietrich Bonhoeffer's roots and inheritance.

---

56   As I remarked in a footnote to Notebook I, when I first befriended Fenimore, in 1984, and we spoke of religious belief and philosophy, the life of Bonhoeffer was one of the most striking stretches of common ground. He had brought with him to Medford his well-thumbed and already annotated copy of Bethge's *Dietrich Bonhoeffer*. Some of our most animated early conversations were about the relationship between Bonhoeffer's unusually independent Christian vision, deriving from the Moravian sympathies of his mother, tempered by the scientific and sceptical worldview of his father; and the religious backgrounds from which he and I had come. There was an afternoon, in a boat on the Mystic River, in the fall of that year, where we cited, almost simultaneously, a remark by Bonhoeffer that 'we should sail our ships quickly out of harbors that have silted up'. We both sensed an electric sense of connection and agreed, with just as much alacrity, that, having sailed out of such harbors, out to sea, one nevertheless had to seek harbourage somewhere. The question for our time, we agreed, was: where, if anywhere, is there a true harbor in the nuclear age? – TCE.

Karl and Paula had eight children in the ten years after they were married. All were born in Breslau between 1899 and 1909. There were house servants, ample space and a country house in a remote, wooded valley which was simple rather than lavish and which shaped the imaginations forever of the older children. Karl was clearly a formidable but also benign father figure. There were clear boundaries around him. His study and consulting room, in the home, were out of bounds for the children. Yet he always spoke quietly, never missed family meals, loved to play games with his children and exerted a moral authority that had a lasting influence on all of them. Paula was a remarkable mother by any standard. Around her figure the household flourished.

She and Karl employed a nurse, a housemaid, a parlour maid, a cook, a governess, a receptionist and a chauffeur. Did this leave her any work to do? Well, of course, it required that she supervise all these household staff and run the agenda for eight children under thirteen, while still in Breslau. In 1912, when Karl was appointed to the chair of psychiatry at Berlin University, the family moved to Berlin and there the children grew to adulthood. Throughout those years, Paula was an indefatigable teacher. She spared nothing in providing whatever could contribute to the healthy development of her four girls and four boys. She prepared them superbly for public school and taught them a great repertoire of poems, songs, games, music and bright theatricals.

In Berlin, the family lived in large and comfortable houses in the city's prosperous western suburbs. The second of these houses was at 14 Wangenheimstrasse in the suburb of Grunewald, (Greenwood), from 1916. It was set in an acre of grounds and must have hummed with activity, given the number of children and servants constantly living there. It was a suburban house, of course, not an island haven on the scale of Cos; but the neighbourhood was full of fascinating people. The great physicist Max Planck lived just down the street. The military historian Hans Delbruck lived nearby. The historian of Christian social teaching, Ernst Troeltsch was not far away. The professor of theology at Berlin University, Adolf von Harnack was another neighbour.

Karl brought such people together in a discussion group. He and Paula also regularly had friends and neighbours over for evenings of singing around the piano and dancing. Similar gatherings were regularly held on Wednesday evenings in the library at Hans Delbruck's house and, as the Bonhoeffer children grew up, they were introduced to this living intellectual culture; to the point where the young Dietrich would walk and talk with the venerable Harnack, as his idiosyncratic interest in theology began to grow. That, of course, was not before the Great War, when he was a small child; but towards its end and in the years immediately following it. By then, darkness had loomed already over the household and the first premonitions of the catastrophe that followed.

Karl was to write in his memoirs, after the Second World War, of how he had been strolling down the Unter den Linden on the evening of the day, in the first week of August 1914, when the British declared war on Germany. He had his three older boys with him, Karl-Friedrich, Walter and Klaus, then fifteen, thirteen and twelve respectively. 'The enthusiasm of the crowds in the streets and in front of the castle and the government buildings of the previous days had yielded to a gloomy silence, which made the scene extraordinarily oppressive,' he wrote, looking back. In the preceding months, from the early summer, he and his learned circle, he recalled, 'did not really believe there was going to be a war.' This was Planck, Delbruck, Harnack, Troeltsch. Quite.

It's proverbial that that last summer before the Great War was unusually beautiful and that few people across Europe had any strong premonition of what was about to fall upon the continent like the apocalypse. There had, of course, been voices prophesying war for quite some time and even anarchic voices expressing a kind of longing for barbarism to shatter the long perceived torpor of rationalized and urbanized life. Yet these wise and deeply educated men, on the eve of catastrophe, had not thought war would come. This haunts me more than anything else. What are the future catastrophes looming ahead of us that we ourselves *do not really believe* are going to happen? How many of us are able to predict events accurately, much less avert their course?

Karl reflected that his circle had believed that the Kaiser, for all his occasional extravagant rhetoric about knights in shining armour and the force of arms, was a lover of peace, at heart. They told one another that the mesh of 'international economic interests...would be sufficient to prevent an armed conflict.' In both respects they were in error. Nor do they appear to have had any grasp of the magnitude of the technological mayhem that was to be unleashed. Moreover, when war was declared, they were all, in their own sober manner, patriots. They had thought well beforehand that 'the encirclement by the Triple Entente was felt to be alarming.' The children thought war sounded exciting. Dietrich stuck pins in a map to mark the army's early advances.

Little by little, the reality of the war struck home. One cousin after another was killed or critically injured, losing a limb or an eye in the appalling slaughter that was going on both on the Western and Eastern fronts. When they had barely reached military age, Karl-Friedrich and Walter were called up, at the beginning of 1918. Russia had been defeated and had withdrawn from the war, but things were grim and America had joined the conflict on the other side. General Ludendorff, the supreme German commander, decided to stake everything on a series of 'hammer-blows' on the Western front to break the resistance of the Western powers. He was prepared, he said, to 'sacrifice one million men' in this campaign to force London and Paris to the conference table.

Karl and Paula's two oldest sons were among those that Ludendorff threw into this campaign. Karl-Friedrich's experiences at the front turned him into a socialist, though never a bitter or revolutionary one. Walter died from shrapnel wounds in April 1918, in the first round of Ludendorff's massive offensives. Both had insisted on joining the infantry, rather than taking a commission. They wanted to be in the thick of it for the sake of their country. With grave misgivings, their parents saw them off at the railway station. Paula ran alongside the departing carriage calling out to Walter, 'It's only space that separates us.' Weeks later he was wounded at the front. He wrote a letter home celebrating the taking of Ypres, but died three hours later.

That was the first hammer-blow, not to the Western Allies but to the favoured and virtuous Bonhoeffer family; the sane and provident parents, Karl and Paula. Ludendorff was prepared he had said to 'sacrifice one million men' to achieve his strategic goals. That had begun. The seventeen year old Walter Bonhoeffer was among the earliest of the sacrificial victims. For Karl and Paula, there would be more, though overwhelmingly in the next war and at the hands of the German government directly. Paula, *mater dolorosa*, was devastated by the death of Walter. When Klaus was called up, in October 1918, she suffered a nervous breakdown from which she took several years to recover. These experiences did much to turn young Dietrich's mind to the world of theology.

Dietrich's governess, Maria von Horn, whom he seems to have dearly loved and who was a devout member of the Moravian Brethren, may have exerted a subtle influence on him in the 1910s. But the immediate impulse to reflection on ultimate things and thus to theology appears to have come from observing his mother's terrible grief at the death of his brother Walter. He used to talk with his twin sister Sabine about death and eternity and in the wake of war he felt a powerful inclination to emulate his von Hase grandfather and great grandfather. The family were sceptical. They told him he would not find the life of a theologian fulfilling, because the Church was a moribund, narrow-minded institution. In that case, he boldly responded, "I shall reform it!"

This is the secondary motif of the opera, of course: Dietrich's sense of vocation and its collision with the forces of the epoch. How is it that he should have found himself so marginal a figure in all that occurred after that, for more than twenty years, while a failed artist, obscure corporal and rabble rouser named Adolf Hitler was able to rise to become the Pied Piper and evil genius of a resurgent German militarism which damned the Jewish leaven in the culture of Europe, brutally abandoned the Enlightenment and wrought havoc on a scale that even Ludendorff would have struggled to comprehend? When he went to his execution, in April 1945, with Hitler's Germany crumbling under Allied hammer blows, what can he have said to his imagined God in silence?

Yet Karl and Paula lived through all of that and saw Klaus, who had been spared in 1918, executed also by the Nazis; as well as Hans and Rudiger, the husbands of their two eldest daughters, Ursula and Christine, and Paula's brother, Paul von Hase; all on account of their participation, at various levels, in attempts to put an end to Hitler's monstrous regime before the Allied powers did so. How was it possible to witness all of this and not be crushed? What version of history, what framework of reason, what residue of old religion can have enabled them, through this wreckage of all they held dear, to hold fast to sanity and love for one another and to avoid bitterness and final despair? Oh, give me the master of opera, Verdi, to put this to overwhelming music!

There is more of the true story to tell before the libretto will make sense. There is the remarkable scene in Rome, at Easter 1924, when the eighteen year old Dietrich, already set upon becoming a theologian and forming a yeasty presence in the substance of the staid German Protestant establishment, visited the immemorial shrines of Catholicism with his older brother Klaus and contemplated the state of European civilization through that remarkable prism. I can call it a remarkable prism in your presence, can I not; since we share a Catholic upbringing, albeit of two different cultural kinds? Dietrich, on the other hand, was not a Catholic at all and his parents not even Lutheran or church-going. His reflections, therefore, on the old religion were very free.

Observing the Easter rituals at St Peters, under the aegis of a Papacy still highly resistant to all the modernizing and dissenting influences that had shaped his own family for generations, the young Bonhoeffer was able nonetheless to feel that here in Catholic Rome one could see at first hand the full continuum of Western civilization from its ancient classical ruins through its medieval transformation, its Counter-Reformation restoration and its defiantly anti-secular enlightenment stance in the modern world. Observing a Palm Sunday mass, he was also struck as never before by the solemnity and beauty of Catholic religious ritual. The Lutheran and other Protestant traditions, he realized, had shallower roots and less strength to endure modernity.

In Rome he beheld what he saw as a sublime blend of the full, complex, richly mature elements of European culture, embodied in the beauties of St Peters and the Easter liturgy. Rome, he decided, was the fulcrum of European culture and European life. Three years later he wrote of it as 'a world in itself'. 'It is hard to overestimate the importance of the Catholic Church's value for European culture and for the whole world', he marvelled. 'It Christianised and civilized barbaric peoples and for a long time was the only guardian of science and art. Here the Church's cloisters were pre-eminent.' It had, he observed, 'developed a spiritual power unequalled anywhere' and therefore no sound reckoning with the modern condition and future of humanity could ignore it.

Yet, rather than inducing him to *embrace* Catholicism, what he saw led him to ask a profound question, which he then devoted his doctoral thesis to exploring: What is the Church? With extraordinary presence of mind for so young a man, he reflected critically that 'it is exactly *because* of this greatness that we have serious reservations. Has this world really remained the Church of Christ? Has it not perhaps become an *obstruction* blocking the path to God instead of a road sign on the path to God? Has it not blocked the only path to salvation?' Here, of course, he was recollecting his Lutheran and Hussite roots, as well as the Goethean and Kantian independence of mind of the modern German Enlightenment. How, then, was he to square this great circle?

With a freshness and urgency of insight drawing upon the full extent of his Christian heritage, this young man in the 1920s was concerned that unless the Christian churches – Catholic and Protestant alike - *thoroughly rethought and revitalized themselves* they would be shipwrecked in the world that was emerging around them. Their response to the Great War had been inadequate and now violently radical forces were stirring that could imperil everything. Both Nazism and Bolshevism were rampant, prompting this son of the cultured bourgeoisie and educated theologians to ask, 'Will our church survive another catastrophe? Will it not be all up if we do not immediately become quite different? Talk differently, live differently...?' This was his calling.

This sense of a calling, this urgency of rooted insight, is exactly what has always made me feel akin to Dietrich Bonhoeffer; just as the wonderful dignity of Karl and Paula has long personalized for me the humanity and richness of the Germany militarism ruined. Yet I have long since concluded that it is indeed all up with the Church and that we do very much need to find a way to live differently and talk differently. The question is, how are we to do that? Dietrich thought the answer was to rethink Christology. I believe the answer is to rethink Cosmology, Biology and Ontology; to understand ourselves at last in deep perspective and to transcend the old religions, whose tangled myths and compromised structures no longer adequately serve our freedom.

When they took him away from Berlin, to Flossenburg, where they killed him, Dietrich took with him just three books: the Bible, a volume of the writings of Goethe and Plutarch's *Lives of the Noble Greeks and Romans*. There is the fullness of the man's intellectual culture, all imparted to him by Karl and Paula without prejudice or dogma. It is not Christianity that I see vindicated by Dietrich's life and grim death, but a certain kind of attitude towards human existence and truthfulness. And these things are even better instantiated in Karl and Paula, because they were *not* killed. They remained as *witnesses* and were not extolled as martyrs. They gave birth and sustenance to a man of integrity and lived to see him murdered by brutes for that very quality.

The challenge before us is not to find a way back to 'Christ', but how to distil and propagate that quality of integrity which we can see in the Bonhoeffer family as a whole, only one of whom declared himself a theologian and hoped to reform and revitalize the old religion for the sake of humanity. Nothing seems more poignant to me in this regard, more emblematic of Dietrich's familial humanity, than his late and ill-fated love for Maria von Wedemeyer. She was eighteen when they met, in 1942; the same age Paula had been when Karl first laid eyes upon her. She, also, was beautiful, intelligent, articulate and confident. She, also, came from a wonderful and well to do family, which was anti-Nazi and committed to revitalizing the moribund Protestant church.

Shortly after they met, her father Hans was killed at the battle of Stalingrad, in August 1942. Two months later her brother Max was also killed on the Eastern front. Within months of their engagement, in 1943, Dietrich was arrested, never to be released. She corresponded with him and kept a diary in the form of letters written to him but never sent. She then came to Berlin and stayed with Karl and Paula, as the tide of war turned irrevocably against the Nazi regime. In the summer of 1944, just before the Stauffenberg attempt on Hitler's life, she visited Dietrich in Tegel prison for the first time. Dietrich hadn't known she was coming and was wonderstruck to see her, but haunted by her departure. She literally embodied everything he had at stake in life.

Immediately after she left his cell, he wrote a poem called 'Loss', in which he describes her as embodying the whole world that he loved and sensed he was about to lose beyond recall. Enclosing the first draft of the poem in a letter to his disciple and friend Eberhard Bethge, he wrote: 'This dialogue with the past, the attempt to hold onto it and recover it and, above all, the fear of losing it, is the almost daily accompaniment of my life here; and sometimes, especially after brief visits, which are always followed by long partings, it becomes a theme with variations. To take leave of others and to live on past memories, whether it was yesterday or last year (they soon melt into one), is my ever recurring duty.' He had no option for liberty past that point.

Everything that had formed the Bonhoeffers was evident in their resistance to Nazism and their fortitude in the face of oppression by the forces of darkness. In May 1943 Karl wrote to Dietrich, after a visit he and Paula had made to Tegel: 'It was a great relief for us to be able to speak to you recently and to see with our own eyes that you are, by and large, physically fit and are withstanding the evil trial imposed upon you with a calm mind and the confidence of a clear conscience.' Six months later, Dietrich himself wrote to Paula: 'You, dear Mother, wrote recently that you were 'proud' that your children were behaving so 'decently' in such a terrible situation. In fact we have all learned that from you both...So it's probably something we've inherited.' Indeed, it was!

It surely is our task now to rediscover a more general such inheritance and build on it a revised civilization for the future. An opera might communicate this to audiences around the world. Its strength would lie less in the pity we must all feel for the terrible fate of that family; than in recognition of their unyielding integrity and love for one another despite everything they were helpless to fend off. Ursula last visited Hans on 5 April, four days before he was taken to the concentration camp at Sachsenhausen and executed. The family persisted in efforts to save the lives of Rudiger and Klaus. Both failed. Christine paid Rudiger a farewell visit, but would not accept his farewell letters, refusing to acknowledge that the struggle had been lost. One weeps.

Karl-Friedrich visited Klaus in jail in the very last days of the Third Reich and found him with a copy of Bach's *St Matthew Passion*. It must be wonderful, the older brother said, to be able to hear the music in his imagination as he read the score. 'Yes', replied Klaus, 'but the words also. The words!' Both Rudiger and Klaus was taken out and shot on 23 April. On 24 April the Soviet security services seized the Kaiser Wilhelm Institute, where Karl-Friedrich worked, looking for nuclear materials and scientists. On 27 April the Red Army took Grunewald, where the Bonhoeffers had spent so many fruitful years. On 30 April, Hitler committed suicide and on 1 May the war ended with unconditional German surrender. Karl and Paula had remained alive.

Imagine, then, the whole of Berlin as the stage set for an opera more spectacular than *Aida*, darker than *Don Carlo* and more profoundly romantic than *La Traviata*! To the left hand side of the vast stage lie Potsdam and Wannsee, with Grunewald nearby. Toward centre stage lie the great boulevards of the city, named for Leibniz, Mommsen, Niebuhr, Pestalozzi, Kant, Goethe and Schiller; all luminaries of the German Enlightenment. Right in centre stage is the Tiergarten, where you and I have walked in intimate conversation among the endless hectares of new grown trees – all planted since 1945. To the right, the Brandenburg Gate, the reconstructed Reichstag, the Holocaust Memorial and between them the Unter den Linden, once more green and open.

That's far too big a stage set, of course, and displays Berlin now, rather than in 1914. It's size is that of truth, rather than fiction. The Metropolitan Opera would find a technological way to provide such a *tour d'horizon* as the overture was being played, don't you think? Or perhaps we can imagine that the premiere is at the Deutsche Oper itself, which is on that very stage? We are special guests at a performance for us. The opera's been *composed* for us. Or at least that's what the program says: '*Karl and Paula*, an opera in three acts by Giuseppe Verdi'. How can this be? But then again, the house is full and everyone has been given a program with the words, 'This opera was composed for you'. No-one else seems surprised that it's by Verdi. We take our seats.

The overture begins with a string-dominated theme of great beauty – Verdi at his pinnacle. But a discordant note is introduced with a brass intrusion, a military march. Such a disruption is almost Mahlerian. There is a great percussive crash, followed by a clashing medley of chords that evoke by turns the Horst Wessel Song and the Internationale. Verdi as we've never heard him before. The opening theme resurfaces and for a few golden moments dances over the brass and percussion. It is accompanied by tantalizing allusions to Bach. But then a dismal and chaotic climax overwhelms these motifs, coming to a terrifying crescendo, before the finale in a minor key closes out the drama with chords redolent of Verdi's great requiem mass for Manzoni.

Then the curtain rises and we see a group of distinguished looking professors standing or sitting. The scene is a drawing room in Grunewald, the home of Karl and Paula Bonhoeffer, in February 1918. Here are Max Planck, Hans Delbruck, Fritz Mauthner, Ernst Troeltsch, Adolf von Harnack and others. Karl and Paula are seated together at centre stage. The gathering begins with a chorus celebrating the wonderful richness of German intellectual life. Planck goes solo with a particular tribute to Karl as a fine embodiment of all that is scientific, enlightened, cultured and principled in modern Germany. Karl sings an aria about the family roots of the Bonhoeffers and his abiding love for Paula and the eight children to whom they have given birth over twenty years.

He sings to the whole group about how he first met her and was so struck by her naturalness and confidence. The two of them then sing a duet about their life together at Wangenheim and the beauty of their children. The chorus echoes them and exclaims at the unusual happiness and virtue of their family life and the wonderful role of Paula as mentor and teacher to her sons and daughters. The scene concludes, however, with a solo by Hans Delbruck, in which he reflects on the fortunes of war and the prolonged bloodshed through which Europe has now been going for more than three years. The Bolshevik Revolution in Russia, he sings, raises profound questions about the future of the old order in Europe. Germany itself faces a severe challenge in the West.

Scene two is a darkened bedroom in the same house two years later. An adolescent boy with very fair hair is sitting under a reading lamp with a book. It is the fourteen year old Dietrich. He begins to sing as if praying about life, death and eternity. He tells his God of the death of his older brother and its devastating impact on his mother, especially when his brother Klaus was then called up at the age of only seventeen. There is then an interwoven set of songs. Dietrich sings of how the death of Walter and his mother's awful grief have made him think of ultimate things and incline him to study theology. Paula then appears, illuminated on her own on the other side of the stage, echoing this story of her grief, but avowing fond hopes for her surviving children.

The four oldest children, Karl-Friedrich, Klaus, Ursula and Christine appear and tease Dietrich about his idea of studying theology, saying that by doing so he would be avoiding the genuine intellectual and moral challenges of the times; that the church is a poor, feeble, boring, petit bourgeois institution. He replies in a stirring song, "In that case I shall reform it!" He sings of how much he loves the family governess, Maria von Horn and is fascinated by her affiliation with the Moravian Brethren. The others tease him further for this. But Paula sings a beautiful aria about her own experience of the Moravian Brethren, how they go back to the reformer Jan Hus who died for truth and how she has taught her children not to be religious but to be good.

The scene concludes with a great chorus of the whole family, their household servants and their learned neighbours, singing in recitative behind and around the Karl and Paula, an adaptation of Psalm 90, said to have been a prayer of Moses himself: 'Lord, you have been our dwelling place in all generations, so teach us to number our days, that we may apply our hearts unto wisdom. Before the Earth was formed and the world, before ever the mountains were raised up, even from everlasting to everlasting, you are the all-high God. You watch over man's destruction; and say, return you children of men. A thousand years in your sight are but as yesterday when they are past, or like a dream in the night.' The couple sing the refrain in unison as the scene ends.

Scene three is set in Rome in 1924, where Dietrich and Klaus have gone to see the Eternal City. The setting is St Peters Square on Easter Sunday. Klaus and Dietrich sing a duet about the wonders of Rome and how it makes a German feel provincial, because it displays the whole continuum of Western civilization. Dietrich reflects that German Christianity, because less connected to the rich humanism of the Greco-Roman past, is more vulnerable than Catholicism to heresy and denial of the goodness of this world. Klaus asks him is he then about to become a Catholic priest and Dietrich responds that he will not do so, because 'Catholic dogma veils every ideal thing in Catholicism without knowing that this is what it is doing.' Is the libretto moving you?

Dietrich nonetheless affirms that Rome is the fulcrum of European culture and European life. Klaus agrees and they sing together of the glories of Western civilization. But Dietrich then sings a solo number 'What is the Church?' He sings that the Catholic Church has been an immense force for culture and goodness in Europe and the world at large, but that its very rootedness in Rome and its vast institutional reach may actually have turned it into an obstruction blocking the path to God. Klaus responds in an ironical coda, 'And, of course, you are going to reform it!' As they duel in these tones, an Easter procession surrounds them in St Peters Square and its Easter Sunday hymns slowly displace the young men's refrains as the two of them recede off stage.

Act Two opens with a brief scene in which Dietrich returns to Grunewald after a year in Barcelona. It is February 1929. His song 'The snows of Grunewald', sung in the winter street outside the front gate of his parents' home is a bright song about the wonderful home to which he has returned, but also his own concern that perhaps his life is too privileged and that he himself is too isolated to be able to play an effective role in the political troubles that are afflicting his country. As he goes indoors, where there are lights and warmth, scene two rotates onto centre stage: a memorial service for Adolf von Harnack, in the summer of 1930. A chorus sings of how Berlin's liberal humanism is dying off. Harnack, the liberal man of God, and his epoch are dead.

Act Two, scene three is set in the heart of Berlin. It is 10 May 1933. The Nazis have come to power. There is a great torchlight procession down the Unter den Linden accompanied by Nazi songs, climaxing with the burning of books at the Opera Plaza, close to Humboldt University beneath the very statues of Wilhelm and Alexander von Humboldt. The Hitler Youth sing a fierce song, 'Into the flames with decadence'. The University buildings are in the background and there stand Karl and Paula Bonhoeffer, flanked by the living figures of Wilhelm and Alexander von Humboldt, watching the book burning. The foursome sing in counterpoint against the Nazi chorus 'What will you do to our children?' A. von Humboldt is the tenor; Paula the soprano.

From the right side of the stage there appears the figure of Micha Ullman, architect of the memorial to the book burning which now stands in Bebelplatz. He sings a mournful aria based on Heinrich Heine's early nineteenth century remark 'Where they burn books, they will end up burning human beings' and painting a picture of the memorial he will build: a transparent glass plate set in the cobblestones of the plaza, showing beneath it a room with *empty* bookshelves. The scene ends, however, with the Nazi SS and Hitler Youth throwing more books on the fire and singing, 'Yes, we shall burn them!' But this is juxtaposed with Dietrich giving a radio address in which he declares that the Fuhrer principle on which Nazism is based is anti-Christian.

Act Three opens with the Stauffenberg Plot, in July 1944, to assassinate Hitler. The setting is a drawing room in the Bonhoeffer home. A breathless Hans comes in with word that the plot to kill the Fuhrer has failed; that Paul von Hase and other senior officers have been arrested and that the family are all in danger of imminent arrest. Dietrich is already in prison at Tegel for other reasons, but he is also now in danger of being implicated in the plot. Dietrich's fiancée Maria von Wedemeyer sings a song of fear for her beloved, recalling their engagement and their letters to one another. Ursula and Christine join her in a trio lamenting the possible execution of their husbands. The scene closes with hammering on the doors and the entry of the Gestapo.

Scene two is set at the Gestapo's headquarters on Prinz-Albrechtstrasse, Berlin. Dietrich, who has been moved there from Tegel, is in his cell reflecting on his situation. He remembers Maria's first visit to him at Tegel and sings a song based on 'Loss'. He takes up his Bible and a chorus sings a song based on his September 1944 poem 'The Death of Moses'. As the chorus sings the last stanza, a guard then comes to the cell door and announces that Dietrich is to be transferred out of Berlin to Buchenwald or Flossenburg, since the Red Army is closing in on Berlin. As he collects his belongings and is led away, the chorus sings the refrain once more about the death of Moses. Dietrich exits stage left with the guard. Both darkness and silence fall over the empty cell.

The final scene of the opera is set in late July 1945. Berlin is in ruins. The elderly Karl and Paula are sitting in their miraculously unscathed house listening to their radio. It is broadcasting a memorial service from London for Dietrich. The chorus sings the hymn 'Hark a herald voice is calling'. The celebrant recites Matthew: 10: 'Think not that I am come to send peace on earth: I come not to send peace but a sword,' then intones 'he saw the truth and spoke it out with absolute freedom and without fear'. Karl and Paula turn off the radio and sing together solemnly Dietrich's own song "What is the Church?" As they conclude the song and embrace one another in mourning, the opening theme is played in a minor key and fades away as the curtain falls on the couple.

A photograph of Aletheia, *taken from a police helicopter, after Fenimore vanished off the coast at The Ends of the Earth.*

Epilogue: Letter to Manuela Saenz

···································· [57]

I do remember – or my brain has created this 'memory' to lend colour and coherence to its confusion – standing under the great, deep blue ceiling, staring up at Atlas the Titan, Pleione and their children, as if seeking to discern something from my chosen stars; like a magus in Ur of the Chaldees, before there was a science of the heavens. But the frescoed fable of the changing Earth began to move around, faster and faster until I became dizzy. The Pleiades, at centre frame, then began to spin away from me like the revolving Earth, as if fleeing Orion the Hunter in the old astrological fable. I fell, at last, in my own Hall; like an exhausted or defeated hunter, among the Ice Age beasts and the ancient ochre signs of the artistic Aurignacians that surrounded me.

Malvine found me there unconscious and covered in vomit, with a head cut and bleeding from hitting the floor; or so I understand. When I came to, she had gathered Mr Bojangles, Othello, Ariel and Theo around me: my faithful household, alarmed at my fall. They carried me upstairs, cleaned me, lay me on the great bed and called my doctor. The party was cancelled, but Tarski and Eleni, concerned, insisted on coming to see me. I remember Eleni sitting by my bedside, holding my hand on the coverlets and exclaiming in horror, 'Fenimore, you look terrible! It's as if you've aged twenty years!' Twenty years – the phrase lodged itself in my brain as I lapsed into a long, dreamless sleep. And that sleep, with various intervals of waking, lasted for several days.

Malvine fed me light meals when possible, like the little Jewish mother she is. My doctor came and checked my vital signs, concluding that there was no evidence of a heart attack, stroke, seizure, severe concussion or any other dangerous condition and prescribing rest from what – by universal consensus – had been for far too long an excessively demanding schedule of work and travel. Or so I gathered when, at last, I rallied and could hold a conversation. Of you I said not a word. How could I have done so, at such a time? And where would I have begun? Nor did any of us guess what I was shortly to discover. For all my attention to truth and regimen, I had been unable to see within myself to detect the enemies within the gates in time to suppress them.

57   There are no opening octavos in this version. They will, in due course, describe Fenimore's return to Cos and his first thoughts and recollections about having returned bereft of his great love and mortally weary, before he collapses in the Hall of Frescoes within hours of his arrival. The existing draft octavos were not up to the standard required to include in this volume.

Naturally, as soon as utter exhaustion eased, my instinct was to read and think, but all around me urged restraint and, overwhelmed still by private melancholy I consented to remain in bed. But I asked them to do something for me that only you had done in recent years and, before that almost no-one since my childhood, except, perhaps, Suzanne on those memorable occasions down by the Charles River long ago: read to me. As if by sombre intuition, or perhaps because Suzanne's reading of those very pages to me had made an indelible impression, I asked Malvine to fetch from The Vivarium and read to me the final twenty pages of Proust's *Time Regained*, in which Marcel reflects on his loss of Albertine to another woman. I did not explain my choice.

His loss of Albertine, if you recall, was coupled with, or perhaps gave rise to, a troubled reflection on the looming danger that he would die before being able to complete his book. The dear little woman obliged me and sat by my bedside for an hour, reading in that inimitable accent of hers, becoming quite emotional at various points, until at last she reached the final sentence. 'A feeling of vertigo seized me...' reverberated in my mind and the phrase, 'If I were given long enough to accomplish my work, I should not fail.' I had chosen the reading well. I must finish my shaped gift. Malvine closed the volume in her lap. I was almost asleep by then and may have drifted off once or twice as she read, but I requested that she leave the book by my bedside; which she did.

It is only now, a fortnight later, that I have taken it in hand and re-read it for myself; in darkened circumstances, having learned in the interim what is happening to me. My attention is riveted by a passage that had never before struck me so deeply. Marcel reflects anxiously on the danger of his body failing him and his work never being written. 'For it is the possession of a body', the passage concludes, 'that is the great danger to the mind, to our human and thinking life, which it is surely less correct to describe as a miraculous entelechy of animal and physical life than as an imperfect essay...in the organisation of the spiritual life. The body immures the mind within a fortress; presently...the fortress is besieged and in the end, inevitably, the mind has to surrender'.

These lines now seem full of meaning to me. I recoil, of course, from the implicit dualism of mind and body, believing that the 'miraculous entelechy' waved aside by Proust (or at least by Marcel) is what we *are* and that all the symbols we assemble in order to organise our thinking are the creations not of some mysterious mind that 'has' a body, but of our cellular brains groping to represent and grasp reality, aided by all the senses. Still, it struck me that what is now in mortal danger is less my body, which I always knew would in time pass away, but the 'imperfect essay in the organisation of the spiritual life' that is my unfinished treatise. It's all ideas, outlines and hints. The most I can do is write a few final thoughts in this book intended always for you.

But then? Must the mind, when besieged as Marcel reflected, surrender? Or should it go down fighting. There is such a thing as choice, isn't there? You have chosen – fatefully. Should I not now do so? When I say – as I have said and as I can hardly turn over in my mind without a sense of bewilderment and paradox – that *I* am about to die, what exactly do I mean; or rather, what exactly does 'I' mean, in the end? Just to write the first person pronoun on the page makes it seem like some external thing, some other 'I', as it were. It is as if the subject in question was no more than an arbitrary fiction that someone else had invented; but that someone is none other than – I. The hand that is writing these lines will simply cease to be animated. It will cease to be at all.

The diagnosis I have been given – and which due to persistent intentionality I am committing to writing - means that I shall soon no longer be able to write. Everything that makes the living motion of my hand possible and prompts it to create these articulate shapes of meaning upon the page will dissolve. That was always going to be so, but many years from now and when all I had in me to create was done and offered to you and to the world with love and gratitude. This will never happen now – but *never*, Margarita. You have renounced our love as mere fiction and anarchic cells, caring nothing for my cellular phenomenology or my philosophical goals, are ransacking my body and will bring down the temple of my being on their own heads all too soon now.

While I was resting, before the week of tests that showed me in stark and luminous images how the 'miraculous entelechy' I am is under siege – or rather, not *under siege*, but already stormed and in the process of being sacked by witless and vandalistic marauders – I asked for other readings at intervals over the six days I was in bed. There was competition for who would get to read and some animated discussion about my choice of texts: the last chapter of *Don Quixote* and the first chapter of *The General in his Labyrinth* - since I had neither the heart nor the energy to explain. Each was chosen with no-one in mind but you. Reject me though you may, I am, in the looming wreckage of all my projects, overwhelmed chiefly by my love for you alone. How could I not be?

I asked for those two very specific readings to summon your presence and to better enable me to turn over in my mind and discover some way to come to terms with the terrible disenchantment of our final meeting. The first took me back to Toledo and that crisp, imperative first note for me that you left behind at the Pintor El Greco. The second took me back to Yucatan in 2006, where you gave me the culminating political book by Gabriel Garcia Marquez and declared 'You have worlds to conquer and I will be your Manuela Saenz!' How could I have intuited at that moment, at the acme of my liberal dreams, that I would end like Bolivar, making my way down my own Rio Magdalena, bereft of you and shorn of all my hopes by the arbitrary cruelties of fortune?

As it happens, no-one in the household had read *Don Quixote* – any more than I had read it when I met you in Toledo. I insisted that the reading must be authentic and so we called in Pablo Daley who, being Chilean by origin, of course, had almost as good a grasp of Cervantes as he has of Neruda. I had Ariel find the big, red-covered copy of the book you gave me when you first arrived at Cos. It is now filled with my underlinings and pencilled annotations; having been read by stages on various journeys in recent years. 'Read to me the seventy fourth and last chapter of the second part of the great story,' I told the painter of my frescoes. Ariel, Malvine, Mr Bojangles, Theo and the aged, white haired Polycarp, who had called in, listened as the painter of my frescoes read.

I wept inwardly, as I have never done, while they sat around the great bed and Pablo read, in his Chilean accented English: 'Since human affairs, particularly the lives of men, are not eternal and are always in a state of decline from their beginnings until they reach their final end, and since the life of Don Quixote had no privilege from heaven to stop its natural course, it reached its end and conclusion when he least expected it, for whether it was due to the melancholy caused by his defeat or simply the will of heaven, he succumbed to a fever that kept him in bed for six days, during which time he was often visited by his friends the priest, the bachelor and the barber, while Sancho Panza, his good squire, never left his side.' Read Cervantes, you had written to me.

'They believed that his grief at being defeated and his unsatisfied longing to see Dulcinea free and disenchanted, were responsible for his condition', so the reading by Pablo proceeded, while I grieved inwardly, 'and they did everything they could think of to lift his spirits...But not even this could bring Don Quixote out of his sorrow...' Those gathered round had no context for hearing this story of Don Quixote's demise as I was hearing it. Even Pablo, who knew his Cervantes well, knew nothing of there being a Dulcinea in my case or of my looming demise. None of them saw me as defeated; much less as dying – only as exhausted by my labours. They asked me, finally, why this reading and I told them that it took me back to my visit to Toledo and Cervantes' world.

Do even you remember how Don Quixote, on his death bed, lamented having read 'too many detestable books of chivalry' and declared 'my sole regret is that this realization has come so late it does not leave me time to compensate by reading other books that can be a light to the soul'? I had Pablo read those lines more than once and everyone present laughed at the humour of Cervantes. Little can they have guessed the weight of meaning they have for me. Who was it who wrote 'the flesh is sad, alas; and I have read every book'? It was Mallarme, I think. I could say as much at this point. Yet these notebooks are the only books of chivalry in my great library. I have read everything that might be a light to the soul, but I have lost you and that is my defeat.

The truth, Margarita, is that, although I am no Don Quixote, I am dying – defeated and without hope of seeing again my own Dulcinea 'free and disenchanted' – though perhaps that's precisely what you are. Yes, I am dying. I learned that within ten days of Pablo's reading, when I arranged for a battery of searching tests. Scans showed that this 'miraculous entelechy', this hall that houses my picturing mind, is filled with unbidden guests, armed against me and my return. The oncologists showed me a body littered with glowing blots against the dark penumbra of the unafflicted general constellation of cells. They informed me that I have 108 tumours in me. They are in my vital organs, in my bones, in my brain. Give me, I told them, the bow of Odysseus to wield.

Lacking both a classical education and Tom's book, they had no idea what I was referring to, or what strange irony I'd seen in the number they'd given me. They declared it was no surprise that I had collapsed twice in recent weeks; that, indeed, it's almost a miracle I'm still alive and able to move around. They confided there is nothing they can do, confessing that the cancer is already so far advanced there is no chance the standard remedies can work. All that could be guaranteed is that the process of trying to fend off the cancer would be traumatic, debilitating, humiliating. It would deprive me of any last feeling of well-being and every last element of autonomy in the determination of my own fate; or so I soon concluded from all that my candid doctors told me.

Oddly, having so assessed the odds, I felt better than at any point since arriving back at Cos. My mind cleared and judgments presented themselves quite apodictically. Two things were apparent. The discovery of the extent of my illness was less shattering than your renunciation of my love on Calle Libertad. There was also, I then conceived, very little time in which to exercise choice about my final priorities. The first thought swept my psyche with certitude at once. The second was like an articulate verdict which followed from the first thought like a court judgement on evidence clearly heard. I could not fulfil my purposes and had to choose what was left to me; and that seemed quickly clear: to substitute for all my serious work these final pages and then to go.

....

It was here – if only I knew that you would recall it as vividly as I do – that we stood that afternoon of your arrival at Cos, as you presented me with Edith Grossman's translation of *Don Quixote*. How strange life is, looking back, and how unexpected! It never occurred to me and I am certain it cannot have crossed your mind, that less than six years later, I would lie stricken in the great bed in this very place with Pablo reading to me the death scene from that masterpiece. Yet, prompted that afternoon by your generous insistence that I read Cervantes at long last, I lay the great red book down on this very desk and invited you down to the second level to see, for the first time, the Hall of Frescoes, which Pablo himself had finished painting only seven weeks before.

In those precious and fleeting hours, I pointed out how the fabulous images of Ice Age creatures were the precursors of writing and of literate thinking itself.[58] Now I am doing my last writing and seeking to give expression to what it means to be a literate being confronting looming personal extinction. Those beasts are extinct, though the images have miraculously come down to us. 'Great works last a long time,' I declared that afternoon, 'and I have set out to write a book that will last a long time and which, perhaps, you will read one day.' I meant, of course, my long envisaged treatise. That was my hope. It has been thwarted. My book will never be written now and even if it was, you have receded beyond the horizon and do not desire to read my promised work.

The painters in Chauvet Cave finished *their* work and then vanished. They may have had what we might anachronistically call a 'theory' about life and animals and even painting, but we don't know what it was, because they left us only the paintings and once their voices fell silent no-one could so much as ask what the paintings meant. Those who saw them could only interpret for themselves what the images and handprints had been intended to symbolize and why they were painted on the cave walls in the order that they were; as if some clear design had been in the minds of the artists. What we know is that five thousand years passed and then a young boy, bearing a burning torch and followed by his wolf-hound ventured into Chauvet Cave to look.

We have no idea what the boy made of them – to say nothing of the wolf-hound, which can hardly have been acquainted with images of great beasts flickering in the light of human fire on cave walls. We can be certain it was not what we see in them. In his time, all the creatures depicted on the cave walls still roamed the Ice Age world. All are now long gone. The boy, the wolf-hound and the torch left their marks within the cave; then they vanished for all time. A landslide sealed

----

58   In a manner showing the unaccustomed haste with which he wrote these pages, Fenimore scribbled into the margin of the notebook alongside this sentence, with an arrow pointing to it, the following classic passage:

> *It was the Egyptians who first symbolized ideas and that by the figures of animals. These records, the most ancient of all human history, are still seen engraved on stone. The Egyptians also claim to have invented the alphabet, which the Phoenicians, they say, by means of their superior seamanship, introduced into Greece and of which they appropriated the glory, giving out that they had discovered what they had really been taught.*

The handwriting was very small and many words abbreviated, but I was able to reconstruct the passage when I realized that the cipher Tac/Ann/XI next to it had to mean Tacitus *Annals* Book XI – given that, a little further on and with more forethought; he draws upon a dramatic story from Tacitus. He must have come across the above passage while retrieving the story and could not resist dropping it in as an afterthought. That this should have happened here only goes to show what extraordinary care he plainly took in writing the rest of the notebooks, since this nowhere else occurs. - TCE

the cave and no-one saw the paintings again for 25,000 years. I would like to believe that you remember our conversations about these things from your first and only stay at Cos and our lingering stroll through the freshly painted Hall; but you have vanished like the Ice Age boy.

No one has ever written a book that has lasted, as those paintings have, for 32,000 years. There have only been books for a small fraction of that time and most do not last for very long. Yet I aspired, at least, to write a book for the ages: one that would extend the human imagination over aeons of time immensely greater than the 32,000 years since the creatures appeared on the walls of the Chauvet Cave. Ever since I studied Heidegger at Harvard, I have felt that his sense of time was absurdly narrow and cramped. I've longed to articulate a way in which others can grasp, in both hands, as it were, how spectacular it is to live in the majestic context of *billions* of years of cosmic and biological evolution. I wanted them to *see* this with awe, like the boy in the cave.

You might say that I aspired, like some Aurignacian Michelangelo, to lay out on the walls of the collective Chauvet Cave in which humanity lives, a vivid representation of the cosmos, so as to impress upon the minds of each and all that there is more than the flux of experience and the shadows cast upon the cave walls by the flickering light of camp fires. There is conscious awareness and a world of ideas that point to *unseen* possibilities; a world incomparably vaster and more wonderful than what they can see with the merely pragmatic eye of the hunter, the utilitarian, the hedonist, the dogmatist, the narrow or unimaginative of all kinds. To begin with art was to touch the hem of possibility and feel uncannily that we can create the world anew.

It would be absurd, of course, to suggest that I was alone in having such thoughts. In various forms, they have been present to countless human beings over time. I've always known that I had company of an extraordinary kind. Nothing seemed more important to me, however, than trying to *master* such ideas and to bring clarity and coherence to a disordered world, or at the very least to achieve it for myself. I dared to hope that might be possible, given my advantages. And what advantages, Margarita! A splendid education, being alive at the high tide of modern science, a circle of learned and idealistic friends and the kind of inherited wealth that gave me the chance to create a quiet refuge far from the world's many zones of conflict, deprivation and stupidity.

Oh, Margarita! Whatever else it was, all this was not fiction.[59] It was – it is, for another few days –

---

59   This is a disconcerting sentence, since it seems plain from what else Fenimore has recorded
      – for example, the second paragraph of this final entry – that he knew Margarita's reference
      to "fiction" was only to her own long deception of both her lovers about the existence of the
      other. It was not a denunciation of his work or his life as some kind of "fiction". I can only

a reality so privileged, so rarefied that it must seem to be a fiction to all those whose more stunted and scrabbling lives do not make it possible for them to see the possibilities that consilience throws into high relief! It shatters me that you, a songbird with such high ideals and a seeker of perfect love, could turn your back on all this. We had agreed to dance the world around and create an unbounded freedom to be. Did I violate that contract? Where did I fail you? If only the answer were simple, perhaps I could come to terms with it. If only you had cast your doubts in my way years ago; before I was so committed to our serene fiction that I could not turn back.

I must end. Setting these last thoughts down has been exhausting. I need to seal this volume and the two older ones in a parcel for Tom and then take carefully premeditated actions. As I pondered my options after the scans had showed how overwhelmed my body is and how perilous my physical condition has become, there came back to my mind a story that I read long ago, when studying classics as a schoolboy. It is related by the Roman historian Tacitus in Book XI of his *Annals* and concerns the manner of death of the wealthy and highly educated Gallo-Roman aristocrat Decimus Valerius Asiaticus. I quietly retrieved the book from The Vivarium and sat re-reading the relevant passage in the alcove where you and I first sat to talk of Atlantis.

In fact, from old habit, I read around it to recover its context, briefly caught up in memories of my youthful studies with old Polycarp. Tacitus recorded that Messalina, the depraved mistress of the Emperor Claudius, cast a covetous eye on the beautiful villa and gardens which Lucius Licinius Lucullus had built more than a hundred years before and which had been acquired by Asiaticus. Lucullus had built a very fine library within the villa.[60] Asiaticus had set about renovating the gardens. The combination was a place of enviable beauty and Messalina decided to make the whole thing of beauty her own. She trumped up charges of treason against Asiaticus, who was arrested and condemned without fair trial or right of appeal. Such was imperial Rome.

---

surmise, therefore, that this statement was a slip of the pen or of a despairing mind betraying itself. It is as if there was a hidden fear within him, in those last days, that he had, after all, been deluded and that his great dream of consilience was no more than a fiction. We, of course, believe otherwise. – TCE

60   This citation from Tacitus with its references to the Gardens of Lucullus and his villa so clearly invokes Fenimore's poem 'Lucullus to Clodia' that it is impossible to believe he did not recall the poem to mind in writing these late lines. Yet he makes no reference here to the poem (#6 in Appendix C), which may have been due to his haste and weariness, or perhaps due to the fact that whereas the poem whimsically invites the 'Clodia' in question to come and share the wonderful villa and library on the Pincian Hill, at the end Fenimore knew that this would never be and left the poem aside as an unfulfilled and empty fantasy. For us, on the other hand, read now in this context, the poem has a sharp poignancy and a deeper resonance than it could ever have had taken on its own, in innocence, as it were. – TCE.

Tacitus relates that when Claudius started to think of acquitting Asiaticus, the artful accuser Vitellius, with tears in his eyes, spoke of his old friendship with Asiaticus and their services to Claudius' mother, Antonia. He took this line only to suggest that the condemned man should be free to choose the *manner* of his death. The insouciant emperor deemed this sufficiently merciful. Asiaticus might have chosen the quiet death of self-starvation, but instead, the historian relates, he 'took his usual exercise, then bathed and dined cheerfully', inspected his funeral pyre to ensure that the smoke wouldn't hurt his treasured trees, then opened his veins and so expired. Tacitus remarks on 'his calmness even to the last.' I read those ancient lines like scripture.

The phrases 'he should be free to choose his death' and 'calmness even to the last' entered into me and shaped what I will now do. For Lady Cancer is coming for my villa and my gardens, Margarita, and I must prepare for my own death freely while I can. The alternative is to face humiliation and lingering uncertainty, possibly imprisonment, torture and a slow death at the hands of this cellular Messalina. While the 'I' can act with calm deliberation, it should – and shall – do so. If I reflected on the calm death of such Romans as Asiaticus, when I was young, I believe it was under the influence of St Augustine, who denounced what he saw as the undignified willingness of Stoics and Epicureans to end their own lives. Now I dissent from St Augustine.

If we believe, as I do, that our humanity consists, more than anything else, in our capacity to bring reality to consciousness and make rational and free choices, then the compelling calm with which Asiaticus accepted his fate and opened his veins comes to make sense, surely. Such a free choice, even if under coercion in his case, glows with dignity. It is of a piece with the need to act, more generally, with calm deliberation in confronting our ends; not only with regard to the manner of death. I've chosen to keep my own counsel, for this reason; rapidly ensuring that the legal papers to do with my will and estate are in order. I wish to spare others about whom I care any needless drama or pointless confusion. You, despite our broken bond, I wish to spare.

It was Ariel reading to me from *The General in his Labyrinth* that gave me the heart, finally, to write this final entry, still as if addressed to you – to you as my own Manuela Saenz. The reading of Tacitus more recently gave me the calmness to do what I had to do with calm deliberation. I say final, because although this set of notebooks can no longer be what I intended - a gift for you alone - I have decided that they will now become a gift for my most intimate friends, whom I have long thought of as my own Pleiades. They will be a posthumous confession of my love for you and will constitute a testament of my hopes and labours. This way all my hand-crafted writing will at least serve some purpose. They will be my last gift to the shining Pleiades'; my good friends.

Ariel read to me from *The General in his Labyrinth*, at my request, without knowing more than generically why I would want, in my evident depletion, to listen to Garcia Marquez. It was you, after all, however, who declared to me in Yucatan that you were my own Manuela Saenz. You know and knew when you gave me the book that the opening chapter depicts Manuela herself reading to Bolivar. Line after line leapt out at me, stabbed me, electrified me, because of associations with you, especially those which stated that 'he had trusted no-one but her' and she 'knew him better than anyone.' 'She was the only person permitted to tell him the truth...his confidante, the guardian of his archives, his most impassioned reader.' That last I'd dearly hoped.

Other lines, however, more aptly fit what occurred outside the Teatro Cervantes: 'The last visitor he received the night before was Manuela Saenz, the bold Quiteña who loved him but was not going to follow him to his death...Only Manuela knew that his disinterest was not lack of awareness or fatalism, but rather the melancholy certainty that he would die in his bed, poor and naked and without the consolation of public gratitude.' Ariel, the true guardian of my archives and confidante of my serious researches, knew nothing of all these secret confessions. They were for you alone as my 'most impassioned reader' and they were always suspended by a thread – my trust in you, my belief in what you finally called the 'fiction' of our love. Now I am Melancholy.

Or perhaps it's time for me to recognize an even more bitter truth: that I was *right* to trust you, that you *did* know me better than anyone else, as Manuela knew the warring Bolivar; and that you were, when all is said and done, the only person who told me the truth: that my grand plan and my work have been a chimera and conjuration, a grand self-delusion and an unsustainable fiction? I have, in fact, suffered from a recurring nightmare since my diagnosis: that I am actually a fictional character – or an historical character like Bolivar trapped in the confused imaginings of others, unable to correct them. In this nightmare, all my work is no more than an amusement for a few passing, distracted readers whose serious concerns are with practical and mundane matters.[61]

------

61   These are surely among the most terrible lines in any of the notebooks. They suggest that Fenimore, before the end, was in a state of despair; a condition very foreign to him in all the years I knew him. Had I been of a mind to "censor" the notebooks, I might have been tempted to delete these lines as unworthy of him. They remain as he wrote them, because they are, paradoxically, the clearest evidence that he was not deluded about his work, but remained scrupulous, sceptical and conscientious right to the end. Whatever his fears before he died, our memories of him and the record that he has given us in this volume assure us that, far from being a 'fictional character', he was very real and authentic. What can have possessed him to see himself in this light at the end? There is only one possible answer; the one he himself provides: the verdict of Margarita in Buenos Aires that their whole relationship had been no more than a fiction, which she could no longer sustain.

Certainly Fenimore was, as we all know, a larger than life character, but his work was no more delusional than that of the great precursors he had chosen for himself: Democritus, whose hundred books

There were many other lines from the early part of that tragic novel that affected me during the two hours that Ariel read to me. The final paragraph in the first chapter memorably evokes the demise of the liberator: 'It was the end. General Simon Jose Antonio de la Santísima Trinidad Bolivar y Palacios was leaving forever. He had wrested from Spanish domination an empire five times more vast than all of Europe, he had led twenty years of wars to keep it free and united, and he had governed it with a firm hand until the week before, but when it was time to leave he did not even take away with him the consolation that anyone believed in his departure.' Your departure deprived me of belief in myself. In closing out these pages I waver as to who I am.

One cannot settle all things in haste or in a shattered state of mind, but I've done what I could to make provision against the dire possibility that at any moment I could be crippled and rendered vegetative by a stroke, or confined to palliation of growing pain and deprived forever of my freedom. I've created a final will, of which Tom and two of the others will be executors. I have left instructions regarding the disposition of Cos and the chairmanship of Peripatetica after I am gone. I have destroyed all our correspondence, in order, as you always desired, to keep our confidentiality inviolate. But I have written to Tom asking that he print a very small, completely private, deluxe edition of these three notebooks for the inimitable Pleiades, my old friends.

There is to be a copy for him and for each of the other members of the original Academy of Lynxes. I hope that, sooner rather than later, Tom will find you and, when he does, his instructions are to give this handwritten original to you, as my parting gesture – something I was in no position to do in Buenos Aires. I always kept the notebooks at Cos, in a safe here in the large study, slowly crafting them for the day when my work was done and you might consent at last to live openly with me. Now all that might have been has become void – except for this. I intend now to take a final walk through Cos in the company of Decimus Valerius Asiaticus, seeking his counsel; share a last meal with my household and then, like him, make a final peace of my choice.

---

vanished in the ancient world, but whose central ideas were vindicated in the modern world; or the great Jewish sage Maimonides, who wrote a three volume *Guide of the Perplexed* in exile in Egypt almost a thousand years ago; Michael Servetus, whose path-breaking book *The Restitution of Christianity* all but vanished at the hands of Calvin, yet planted the seed of toleration and modern Unitarianism; Spinoza, whose *Tractatus Theologico-Politicus* was denounced by Catholics, Protestants and Jews alike, yet went on after its author's death to influence free thinkers and liberals for centuries; or Edmund Husserl, a liberal, a secular Jew whose unfinished reflections on *The Crisis of the European Sciences and Transcendental Phenomenology* were not published until sixteen years after he died. For myself, I see Fenimore as having devoted his life, his energies and his fortune to this great tradition and I honour him for it. The Amor Mundi Foundation will stand for that whole tradition and its place in the human future. – TCE

You know, my very own Manuela Saenz, that Bolivar set off without his beloved and trusted Manuela down the Rio Magdalena through Nueva Granada to the sea port of Cartagena; there to take ship for Europe. I am about to set off alone to take ship at my own Cartagena. Before I get there, I will send these notebooks, with my letter and a copy of my will to Tom – by the old mail, since there is no other means for getting such a parcel to him. Perhaps, in a sense, my whole quest has for years been a voyage down the Rio Magdalena, through 'New Granada' and 'New Andalusia' to the sea; even though I preferred to think of myself as Alexander von Humboldt going in the opposite direction, to land at Cumana and explore the New World for science.

Humboldt found pestiferous insects, cannibals with a taste for the flesh on the hands of their tribal neighbours, impenetrable plant growth and, in all, an alien landscape, on the upper reaches of the Orinoco. Yet he made his way back to the coast and then up the Rio Magdalena into the Colombian Andes and down the cordillera, everywhere gathering data on what was so and making fresh, inquisitive discoveries. Nothing could daunt his spirit of sensitive and intelligent exploration. Every instrument that human ingenuity had by then devised he put to use in his quest for enlightened understanding of the Earth. Was he deluded in that quest? Was the very attempt to bring the whole of terrestrial and cosmic reality to consciousness a grotesque error?

The quest didn't begin with him and it didn't end with him, but after him it ran more than ever into what Husserl was finally to dub 'the crisis of the European sciences', not least in Germany, where engineering and chemistry triumphed only to become the vehicles for militarism on a scale that wrecked Enlightenment civilization. His humane vision was not the one that shaped the culture of the late nineteenth century – or so it might be argued. Yet knowledge grew enormously, of that there can be no question at all. The cosmos that he set out to explore expanded beyond his wildest imaginings until the Milky Way itself shrank, in the 1920s, to a mere corner of the universe. Max Weber, a century ago, called this the disenchantment of the world.

We, if the first person plural can reasonably be applied to humanity collectively when so few of us are scientifically literate or capable of the most elementary abstract thought, have established that Democritus was basically correct in surmising that all of reality consists of 'atoms and the void'. 'We' now know – for all that sceptics depreciate the very use of that word and insist there are only conversations pressed from partisan directions with more or less vehemence – that the universe in which we find ourselves is 13.7 billion years old; that our Earth is 4.5 billion years old, that life on it is 3.8 billion years old; that there has only been life on terra firma for 400 million of those years; and that our hominid lineage has emerged over the past 7 million years.

Those sweeping parameters and all the tools of calculation and insight that have made it possible to establish them have abolished every kind of human myth and creation story, every anthropomorphic deity that was ever deemed to terrorize or look benignly upon our species – as we went forth and multiplied and filled the Earth. They have abundantly vindicated Lucretius' claim that atomism does away with the grounds for superstition. Yet all manner of superstition still abounds upon the Earth and the old religions tenaciously insist upon their dogmas and their dignities under the indifferent stars, while those disposing of the sciences grasp them only as technologies and build arsenals and entertainments that make a mockery of enlightenment.

We can now, privileged by our instruments of advanced geometry and hyper-optics, as Euclid's heirs, infer the existence of galaxies billions of light years from our tiny world, construct through the marvels of our off-world telescopes the very images of spiral galaxies evolving and the gigantic realities of hyper-novas exploding thousands of light years from our small star, or black holes swallowing light and constituting the enigma of event horizons. We can estimate the life cycles of stars and foresee the demise of our sun billions of years hence, swelling into a red giant and then shrinking into a white dwarf for aeons that are purely mathematical. And, as if all these were insufficient, we deduce that dark matter and energy outweigh all that we have yet discerned.

What are we to make of such darkness? What to make of all the worlds we have opened up beneath them, of atoms, elements and cells, of natural selection and mutation, of tectonic plates and continental drift, of wide shifts in climate, mass extinctions and the resilience of life despite all the random shocks that have assaulted it over aeons? Nothing in our religions or our narrow ideologies has equipped us as a species to comprehend what all this means, except in the most superficial and childish manner. It has been revealed with such suddenness that our collective incompetence and bewilderment, sprung from ten thousand years of pell-mell cultural revolution and violent conflict, cannot absorb it or convert it into the civilized wisdom we need.

In my youth, Margarita, I conceived the idea that all this had to be understood and reworked into a symbolic order which would finally bring to fruition the potential of our species for civilized order and exalted, cosmically attuned 'religion'. I was baffled by the savageries that tore apart modern civilizations, east and west, whether in the name of revolutionary 'progress' or racial atavism and genocidal mania. I was oppressed past all capacity for settling into a 'normal' life by the realities of vast stockpiles of nuclear and biological weapons. I was repelled alike by the 'consumer' culture with its bizarre entertainments and by the 'sex, drugs and rock and roll' reaction of the 'baby boomers' of my generation. I wanted none of these things, only to know.

That has been the course of my life and the logic of my friendships. That has been my commitment as a being. Should I have done otherwise? I struck a pact long ago with a small circle of friends, men and women, that we would recognize only the path of reason and the quest for consilient understanding. Even as the findings of the natural and human sciences proliferated like some plague bacillus far beyond the capacity of anyone to master, we believed in the goal of coherence and the harnessing of all these sciences for the good and the renovation of human civilization. Were we deluded? Should we – and I, in particular, who pursued the larger goal more fervently than any of my circle – have done otherwise? Should I have lived a normal life instead?

It occurred to me years ago, before I met you, that if I could at least clarify the genealogy of our methods for understanding and lay out the key ways in which these methods had transformed 'our' grasp of what is so, then that work would in itself be a good in the world. It was only later, after I had met you, that investigation of the archaic epoch of life on Earth led me to understand the importance of biology – more than physics and mathematics - to any theory of reality. That life exists at all is stunning. That it has tenaciously terraformed the Earth over billions of years, overcoming every challenge and elaborating itself in manifold ways, struck me as the single most important truth in the cosmos. I set out to understand, from that point of view, what we are.

No datum so impressed itself upon me in all my researches as the relationship between single celled organisms and light. That relationship led to photosynthesis and the energy so generated made possible the elaboration of single celled beings into multi-cellular life forms. But before that and as a pre-condition for that, it led to single-celled organisms giving off free oxygen, which transformed the atmosphere of the planet. In an oxygen rich atmosphere, cells learned how to exchange genetic information and to cooperate. Both as realities and as metaphors, those two things governed my subsequent inquiries. Three ideas came to sit at the foundation of my thinking: light, giving off free oxygen and exchanging information. These made the biosphere.[62]

Yet there came a time, after aeons of those three realities shaping life on Earth, when the eye became a reality and with it, according to all the fossil evidence we have been able to gather from places like the Burgess Shale, what erupted into the biosphere was the possibility of *predation* – not the exchange of information, but the appropriation of protein. That triggered an arms race

---

62   All these ideas are, of course, set out at much greater length in the early sections of Notebook II, but it is remarkable that, with his failing strength and in his last extremity, Fenimore should have spelled out again the key elements of his naturalistic vision as if for Margarita. These few paragraphs retell with remarkable economy his life's journey and show not only where his relationship with Margarita intersected with its trajectory, but how profoundly it affected him to the very end. Much of his Epilogue addresses her as Manuela Saenz, which is why I have given it the title 'Letter to Manuela Saenz'; but his final paragraph returns to the language of the story he himself wrote for her, set in the Nile valley. This, as much as any other reason, is why I felt it was important to include, in Appendix B, the extra material about the Tale of Raneb and Nefesh that I found among Fenimore's papers.

in jaws, armour, camouflage, fins, speed - and better eyes. All these things occurred beneath the Cambrian seas more than half a billion years ago and they did not slow down in the aeons that followed, except for brief pauses after mass extinctions. Everything that troubles us about our own kind, in other words, already characterized primordial life on Earth - deep under the sea.

This our religions wave away in their anthropocentric conceits about evil being suffered only by human beings or being brought into the 'fallen' world by our unnecessary transgressions. No such thing is true. Rather, we must take to heart that life in and of itself long ago brought forth monsters and the prodigal destruction of the innocent. That is a kind of darkness, I came to think, as profound as the yawning depths of the cosmos and one that, to my deep alarm, makes a certain sense of the irrationalities and monstrous crimes of our kind, so that the Romans – no mean predators themselves – long ago coined the maxim *homo homini lupus* (man is a wolf unto man). We all know, however, that the darkness in humanity runs far deeper than that in wolves.

All these levels of darkness I had set out to fathom when we met, believing still in light, the giving off of free oxygen and the exchange of information. You wanted to believe that music was the answer to all darkness, but your disillusionment with Abreu cast a shadow over your hope. Orchestration and choral polyphony would be the human equivalent to the terraforming work of the prokaryotes. Yes? Dance and song, properly understood, would be the healing therapies for the species. Ah, my songbird of paradise, if I could have one wish, it would be to hear again your singing voice, like that of Nefesh in the high Halls of Memphis, in the days of our youth and our love.[63] Now, however, I must embark alone upon *Aletheia* and go freely, at last, where Nun shall find me.[64]

---

63   Fenimore did not quote quite accurately here from his own verse – the second of the Songs of Queen Nefesh (see Appendix A) – which is clearly what he was alluding to. The relevant lines read:

> *Even in Memphis; Memphis of the kings*
> *In the Halls of the North*
> *In the days of our youth and our love*
> *Dance for me in the high room*
> *O dance for me to my heart's delight*
> *Beloved of my years*

This suggests that he did not have the Psalms folder to hand and was quoting from memory.

64   This final line is the most explicit clue we have as to Fenimore's final intentions and his end. Oddly, given his state of mind, he still could not resist a wry joke. *Aletheia* was the name of his yacht. It means 'Truth', but Heidegger translated it as "unconcealment". "Where Nun shall find me" is a haunting phrase, given what subsequently happened, but is based on a play on the name of Nun, the god of the "primal sea" in Egyptian mythology." 'He was writing, after all, as if to Margarita and we must imagine that he was casting himself, one last time, in the role of the dismembered Osiris. - TCE.'

Afterword: The Truth and the Foundation

I was in London, talking with my literary agent about the forthcoming publication of *Fanaticism and International Law,* when the package Fenimore had sent from the Ends of the Earth arrived in Austin. I learned of his disappearance in the newspapers while returning to Austin via New York. I at once called Cos and spoke with Malvine, who was distraught and informed me that the police were searching for Fenimore's body off the coast, where they had found his empty yacht, but that she could not believe he was dead and still hoped he would be found alive. I stayed an extra night in New York and caught up with Irad. We discussed the situation and called the rest of you. Then I proceeded on to Austin and there I found, waiting for me, Fenimore's three leather-bound Notebooks, a brief letter and his will. I knew, once I had read his letter, that he was dead, but was stunned and, in my own way, as disbelieving as Malvine.

The letter was an apology for the abrupt and unceremonious manner of his departure. Nothing that had happened in Austin and no prior word of his had prepared me for this and I think it was the greatest shock I have experienced in my life. It hit me with the force of an unexpected explosion. You have all since seen the letter, so I won't reproduce it here. As you will all recall from our group discussion about the letter, when we gathered some weeks later, it was less the manner of Fenimore's death than the violent suddenness of it that left us stunned. We had all agreed, over many years, on the principle of free death and there was a consensus that – assuming Fenimore's prognosis to be as grim and inescapable as he believed – he probably made a rational decision to act decisively, lest the choice be taken out of his own hands. But that the disease can have been coursing through him and approaching such a crisis point without any of us realizing it was a terrible discovery.

Having apologized for seeming to desert us without a personal farewell and having explained his reasons, he wrote, of course, that he hoped we would collectively see through the plans that had been made since 2009 to set up the Foundation. He noted that his will had made careful provision for the disposition of his considerable assets and that Cos, since his hopes of living there for many more years had been thwarted, should be put under a trusteeship and used as a combination of conference centre, writer's retreat and facility for Peripatetica seminars. He recommended that, in the circumstances, the Foundation should be set up where it would be more convenient for the rest of us – in Europe or America – and that no thought be given to making distant Cos its centre of operations. He expressed regret that he had been prevented from writing his planned book, but declared that he was confident the rest of us and other enlightened people would step up and do an even better job than he could ever have done. And then he turned to the matter of the Notebooks and his moving request.

When I first opened the bulky parcel that had arrived on my doorstep, I was astonished and mystified. Momentarily, as you know, I leapt to the conclusion that this must be the manuscript of his unfinished, but perhaps substantially written *magnum opus*, though why he would have sent it to me and in this form I couldn't imagine. But those were very fleeting thoughts. Even in the instant they mingled with a sense of bafflement that he had used notebooks of this kind for anything in the 21st century. I inferred in a micro-second that they must be his personal diaries. Then I opened the first of them and discovered that the whole Notebook was written in virtually flawless calligraphy. There was no sign of corrections, of sketches, of doodling or diagrams. This was fair copy; but of what?

Lightning struck out of a blue sky, as I discovered the existence of Margarita at the beginning of Notebook I. It swiftly became evident that the entire notebook was addressed to her, as if it constituted a long letter. This was the case, I then saw, with the whole set of Notebooks. I could not bring myself, at once, to put them aside and spent some time flipping through them to get a synoptic idea of their contents. What soon became apparent was that, while addressed to the mysterious Margarita, the Notebooks were more fundamentally an attempt to explain himself to her as the architect of the treatise he was working on. They thus afforded as clear an account of the development of his thinking as I had seen to that point, yet as you have all seen, in handwritten form and in what I came to think of as 'octavos', eight line paragraphs; as if the whole thing was a kind of prose poem.

This particular feature of the Notebooks was a mystery to me for a long time. One day, in the spring of 2012, as I recall, when I was sifting through my correspondence with Fenimore, looking for anything that would throw further light on how his life had turned out, I came across an email he had sent me in 2001. I was plunging into my work on *The Bow of Odysseus* at that time and we were having an energetic exchange about philosophical problems to do with history, strategy and evidence. In an aside, in the email in question, he mentioned that he had just read that weekend a book of posthumously published essays by Karl Popper, called *The World of Parmenides: Essays on the Pre-Socratic Enlightenment*. He noted his approval of Popper's claim that 'philosophy must return to cosmology and to a simple theory of knowledge.'

Parmenides, he went on, did pioneering work on cosmology and logic, yet had written his treatise on cosmology and logic in the form of a long poem to the Moon goddess; or rather not *to* the Moon goddess but as the transcript of a revelation *from* the Moon goddess. In other words, Parmenides, like any epic poet, saw himself as inspired, in effect, by the Muse. Fenimore had not expressed any special interest in these facts in the email, but the context in which I was now re-reading it made those remarks of his leap off the page. On my next visit to Cos, I located Fenimore's own copy of the Popper book in the Vivarium. It was heavily annotated, as so many of his books are.

Leafing through it, I found that several aspects of Popper's late reflections on the thought of Parmenides had been annotated early by Fenimore (presumably in 2001), but revisited and underscored later (possibly in early 2005, before he had begun work on the first of the Notebooks). Parmenides' work was not simply an epic poem, but a specifically *philosophical* epic poem. I now discovered that it began with a Prologue and had two main parts called The Way of Truth and The Way of Human Conjectures. Popper noted that we have the Prologue or what he called the 'proem' almost complete and also the first part, while the second part has mostly been lost. I was struck with wonderment at this point, by the idea that Fenimore had perhaps quite deliberately modelled his unusual Notebooks on the first great philosophical treatise in history.

But if the work of Parmenides was an inspiration for Fenimore, it now became an inspiration also for me. Under the influence of what seemed to have been Fenimore's Parmenidean conceit, I decided to designate his opening reflections on his encounter with Margarita a Prologue, which in an informal sense they clearly were. Ever since, I have not been able to get out of my mind the idea that in some hidden sense Fenimore is saying more in these Notebooks than is evident on the surface. He was not just echoing Parmenides in some whimsically stylistic sense. He was subtly pointing to something far more profound. I spent some time in the alcoves of the Vivarium carefully reading Popper's book, looking for clues. The clue had to lie, I reasoned, in Fenimore's appropriation of some crucial aspect of Popper's argument.

The central thrust of Popper's interest in Parmenides was that the philosophical position advanced by Parmenides was both extraordinarily original, highly rigorous logically and exceedingly strange in its implications. The key to Popper's approach, which might be considered his own final attempt to set out his beliefs about the cognitive foundations of Western science and civilization, is surely his statement that philosophy *is* cosmology (the attempt to understand the true nature of the universe in which we live) and that 'both philosophy and science lose all their attraction when they give up that pursuit – when they become specialisms and cease to see and to wonder at the riddles of the world.' He was, he wrote, 'a lover of the beautiful story of the Pre-Socratics', because they were the first human beings anywhere to make bold conjectures as to the true nature of the cosmos, rather than simply accept old myths or make up arbitrary stories about how things came to be the way they are. Fenimore was, of course, deeply engaged in the cosmological part of his treatise at that time. The question is, how did this influence his decision to, quite separately, compose the Notebooks not simply as a prose poem, but as a very philosophical one?

Reading Popper's book in a corner of Fenimore's library less than two years ago, filled me with a wave of nostalgia. It brought back vivid memories of conversations with him and some of the rest of you in the Peabody Museum, on Divinity Avenue, on Boston Common or in Beacon Hill twenty five or more years ago. I had not, even on that occasion, brought the Notebooks with me, so careful was I in preserving their confidentiality inviolate; but as I read keenly through Fenimore's annotated copy of *The World of Parmenides*, looking for clues as to the roots of his unique project, I found myself wishing that I had them with me. I realized, of course, that Popper was not going to be the only guide to that project. Clues to and sources for Fenimore's design and creation of the Notebooks would probably be found littered in countless places throughout his vast library. Yet the place of the Pre-Socratics and perhaps of the book I held in my hands had showed up as a striking illustration of how he had used such sources.

Given the common philosophical interests of our group, it seems worth recalling here that Popper was particularly struck by the way in which bold, but paradoxical and surely false conjectures by the Pre-Socratics were *revolutionary* because they were based not on mere observation of elementary facts or undisciplined imagination, but on acute critical reason and the generation of hypotheses open to critical examination and refutation. For example, he referred to the conjecture by Anaximander that 'the Earth is held up by nothing, but remains stationary owing to the fact that it is equally distant from all other things' as 'one of the boldest, most revolutionary and most portentous ideas in the whole history of human thought.' He saw it as anticipating and making possible the heliocentric theories of Aristarchus and Copernicus and as foreshadowing even Newton's theory of 'immaterial and invisible gravitational forces'.

But while Popper admired Anaximander, he reserved even higher praise for Parmenides. Only in reading his essays on Parmenides did I fully appreciate what Fenimore has done in his first Notebook, especially the sections I have entitled 'Dark Matter' and 'M Theory'. Popper extolled Parmenides as 'the first great theoretician, the first creator of a deductive theory: one of the greatest thinkers ever. He built not only the first deductive system, but the most ambitious, the boldest and most staggering ever; and one whose logical validity was intuitively immaculate.' Yet Parmenides, who had made five ground-breaking astronomical and geophysical discoveries, including that the Moon reflects the light of the Sun and that the Earth is a sphere, had concluded that the cosmos is *a solid dark sphere* in which there is no space, no motion and no change.

How could this be so? And how could Parmenides have deduced it? He deduced it simply from the premise that 'What is not is not', so that there can be no 'void' or space between things that *are*. That being so, there could be no movement or change. The crucial thing is what Popper then added:

> *The next step, made possible only by Parmenides, was the recognition by Leucippus and Democritus that a deductive theory of the world, a theory of such power as that created by Parmenides, could only be hypothetico-deductive. So they accepted the existence of motion as an empirical refutation of Parmenides' hypothetical system and concluded from it that both the full and the empty existed: atoms and the void. In this way, the greatest physical theory ever was born from a critically inspired discussion of Parmenides' thought that led to the refutation of his theory.*

This passage was underscored by Fenimore, I feel sure in his early reading of the book – along with much else. He endorsed, of course, Popper's claim that critical rationalism – conjectures and refutations – are 'the only practicable way of expanding our knowledge'. He loved the Pre-Socratics, as Popper had and as we all have, because they uniquely in the world initiated this approach to reality. I'm convinced this was the chief reason he came back to Parmenides and quite possibly why he elected, in about 2005, to model his epic poem on that of Parmenides.

There is a sense, I now believe, in which Fenimore was echoing in his Notebooks all the aspects of Parmenides (and Popper) that I have just described. To an untutored or philistine mind, this could make it appear as if he was just becoming downright eccentric. But the fact of the matter is, once you understand who Parmenides was, what he thought and how he wrote, then recall that the origins of our fellowship lay in our shared love of the Pre-Socratics and the Ionian Enchantment, the relationship between Fenimore's Notebooks and his real work seems a great deal clearer. It could even be that reading Popper first gave him the idea of writing what later became this epic poem to his Muse; though clearly many other influences and ideas were at work in his mind.

Of course, I did not, as I say, discover this – or many other things about the Notebooks – until long after I first received them in Austin. Even so, they at once, by virtue of their mysterious form, raised so many tantalizing questions in those first hours of perusal that it was with some difficulty that I put them aside to attend to urgent tasks. Impressed by their uniqueness in all the circumstances, I locked them in a safe and booked the first available flight to the Ends of the Earth, where I set about trying to establish, from Cos itself, what had happened after Fenimore had sent the Notebooks to me and, apparently, taken *Aletheia* down from the riverside dock at Cos and out to sea. Once I had embarked on that course, there was no turning back and I was to find that the entanglements involved were more complex than I could ever have foreseen.

When I arrived there, Cos resembled an ants' nest that had been violently disturbed. I do not think any of the staff could quite cope with the shock of Fenimore vanishing without a farewell and apparently without making clear provision for what was to happen with them after he was gone. Nor could most of them accept that he was dead, much less that he had taken his own life. The police investigation was still under way while I was there and there was considerable puzzlement among the investigators that none of Fenimore's domestic staff seemed to know about his final illness. What had been shaped into a small community under his guidance, in so few years, had lurched into disarray and urgently required reordering. Based on his will, I was able to reassure them that he had not abandoned them without thought or provision and that he hoped Cos could be kept going as a civilized centre for critical thinking workshops, research and writing.

I was faintly known to some of the staff at Cos; well known to none of them. In consequence, although Malvine was willing and able to assemble the rest of the domestic staff and the staff of Peripatetica Decision Architects, for a reading of the relevant codicils of Fenimore's will, all present were disconcerted that I (along with Suzanne and Monica) should somehow have been appointed its executor. They were not even certain, given that I had come from abroad and lacked citizenship at the Ends of the Earth (to say nothing of residency at Cos), that I could be a legitimate executor in such a case. I sought to reassure them that I had been caught as much by surprise in this matter as any of them and that we had all to work together, cooperate with the quite natural police inquest and do what we could to ensure that all the good work Fenimore had been doing did not go to waste on account of this unforseen development.

I was confident, after that first meeting, that none of them had any inkling of the fact that Fenimore had created the three Notebooks, or that he had sent them to me. I chose, therefore, to say nothing of them. Not only was I myself still far from having absorbed what they contained, but Fenimore's instructions had expressly stated that the circulation of the printed manuscript was to be confined to our circle. There was, therefore, nothing to be gained from making known to two groups of people closely connected to him that I was in possession of a private manuscript that they would not be permitted to see. Besides, with the inquest going on and the police coming and going, it was entirely possible that any word of the manuscript at Cos would lead to a request from the authorities to see it, in a search for possible clues to Fenimore's behaviour and the circumstances of his death.

It would be months before I could find the time to fully immerse myself in reading them, though whenever I was at Treehaven and could seize a quiet hour or two, I would pull one or other of the three volumes from my safe, sit down with it in the library and lose myself in the mesmerising Chancery hand in which it was written. As for preparing a print version, that was a major undertaking; not least because Fenimore had stipulated that he would like the originals to be kept in pristine condition and handed to Margarita, when and if I should find her. That made scanning virtually impossible, since it would almost inevitably have led to the Notebooks being damaged in some way. Nor could I engage a scribe to create the text, since the covenant was that the Notebooks were for our eyes only.

I do not need to set down here the experience I had in designing and printing what you have in your hands. That has all been shared over time and any remaining anecdotes will be better shared convivially when we gather in a couple of months' time, at the Villa Barberini, to celebrate informally the creation of the Amor Mundi Foundation. You will each have a copy of the book at least a fortnight before then. All I will say is that, as I read the Notebooks through and then read them again and patiently typed them up myself, I felt at times as though I was inside a short story by Jorge Luis Borges that had come to life and then grown into something of an altogether different order of magnitude from anything the great Argentinian wrote.

The reading brought back memories of conversations with Fenimore, Monica and Suzanne, in particular, about the fables of Borges over pots of coffee and Canadian pancakes during those Boston winters of the mid-eighties. Visiting Cos in late 2010, hauntingly emptied of Fenimore's enormous personality; I went looking for his own copies of Borges and, with a little help from Ariel, soon came upon them in The Vivarium – along with his annotated copies of the major novels of Gabriel Garcia Marquez and Mario Vargas Llosa. *The General in his Labyrinth* and *The Notebooks of Don Rigoberto* were, I found, especially closely annotated. But it was the philosophical preoccupations of the Argentinian that seemed most germane to what I had been finding in 'The Notebooks of Don Fenimoro' with their reflections on the labyrinth of bewilderment in which so much of humanity wanders.

I would sit for hours at a time in an Icmalius chair on the upper floors of Cos, reading Borges particularly, in order to get perspective on Moneghan. Tales such as 'Tlon, Uqbar, Orbis, Tertius', 'Pierre Menard, Author of the Quixote', 'The Circular Ruins' and, of course, 'The Library of Babel' opened up richly for me all over again, as they hadn't in years. There is a passage, for example, in the first of those stories, which reads:

> *Two years before, I had discovered, in a volume of a certain pirated encyclopaedia, a superficial description of a non-existent country; now chance afforded me something more precious and arduous. Now I held in my hands a vast methodical fragment of an unknown planet's entire history, with its architecture and its playing cards, with the dread of its mythologies and the murmur of its languages, with its emperors and its seas, with its minerals and its birds and its fish, with its algebra and its fire, with its theological and metaphysical controversy. And all of it articulated, coherent, with no visible doctrinal intent or tone of parody.*

It struck me forcefully that I had, committed into my hands by its author, 'a vast methodical fragment' of a remarkable relationship otherwise wholly covered in darkness. What Fenimore had committed to refined, handwritten, epistolary calligraphy was a very personalized distillation of all the work he had been doing for years to master the mythologies, the realities and the metaphysical controversies of this world – the only one we have. He had been doing his serious work, of course, not in order to generate a monstrous Borgesian encyclopaedia of the imaginary, but to overcome precisely the utter confusion which besets the world of the illiterate, the bewildered, the fanatical and the desperately over-specialized. And here, for the love of Margarita, was a poetic form of it, hinting at many other things in the background that can only be guessed at or found in the voluminous draft work he bequeathed to us of his unfinished treatise.

We all dreamed that the completion of his work might be possible. We lament that it has been cut off before he could complete it. But while Fenimore may not have succeeded in his primary ambition, this unexpected treasure, which has fallen into our hands, holds intimate and unguessed beauties. It is all the more touching because it was intended for the one with whom – above all others, including us – he strove to communicate *subjectively*, but without losing his objectivity. We have all conversed with him and corresponded with him; we have all heard him give talks about consilience and the cosmos, about the nature of innovation and the phenomenology of perception. But we have not known him as we see him here: a poet and a story-teller, a rarefied lover and a tragic figure overwhelmed from several directions by things that even his great good fortune and supreme intelligence could not hold at bay. We see him as few of us see others in real life, confronting mortality and electing without fear to keep his fate in his own hands.

He died as he had lived: a sovereign individual. There were, however, unintended consequences of Fenimore's decision to meet his mortality head-on and not linger in the hope of sorting everything out before he died. The first such consequence and by far the most tragic, was the death of Margarita herself. The second, given that Fenimore's body was never found, was the outbreak of a kind of plague of speculation, rumour and conspiracy theory regarding his fate. The third was that confusion arose concerning his unfinished work and accusations were levelled at me and at us; to the effect that we had taken custody of it and were keeping it secret for mysterious reasons, supposedly linked to our plans for the Foundation. I have had to deal with all these problems while sorting out Fenimore's affairs and editing the Notebooks. It has been singularly vexatious, as you can well imagine.

The three consequences, taken together, have caused considerable mischief which is now publicly compromising our plans for the setting up of the Foundation. I have thought it best, therefore, to put together an account of all these matters as a common reference point for our future operations and public statements. They are of consequence for the Foundation, so let me set down the truth here for the purposes of our collective clarity of mind. You each and all know, of course, how ill-founded the speculation has been. You also know the difference between the book Fenimore was working on and this book, although you have not yet (as I write) been able to read it. In a sense, therefore, I hardly need to lay out the truth for any of you as regards consequences two or three. Yet certain details of the case should become our common understanding, so that when – after the setting up of the Foundation next summer – we make public comment on any of these subjects, we will avoid confusion by being consistent in what we state or recall.

I only learned about Margarita's tragic death many months after it had happened, because I made no attempt to trace her at first, believing that she might well find me and that, in any case, there was no immediate urgency. The story of Fenimore's death having appeared in the world's press, it was scarcely incumbent upon me to deliver the news to a woman I had never met or even heard of until the eve of Fenimore's demise. Nor did I relish the thought that she might lay claim to the Notebooks, as of right, before I had been able to put together a printed version of the kind nominated by Fenimore. I can hardly deny that, in making these judgements, I must have been swayed in part by my grief at Fenimore's death and a sense that, whatever had motivated her; Margarita's abrupt abandonment of him had played a crucial role in pitching him off the mountain he had been climbing and into the sea. Part of me, at that early point, I think, was not sure I even wanted to meet her. That changed as I immersed myself in the Notebooks, but I never so much as contemplated the idea that she herself would die before I could find her, much less that she would do so in the manner that she did.

For all these reasons, I did not, therefore, make any attempt to find Margarita in the summer of 2010, or even in the fall. Seldom have I made a more tragic mistake. By the time I realized that Fenimore had left behind no direct means for finding her, but had apparently left it to her to find us; she was no more. But it was some months before I learned what had happened. It was, in any case, only long after the obsequies had come and gone with no word from Margarita that I so much as began to think seriously of where she might be. Even then, other matters intervened to delay any action on my part. I was hampered in my inquiries, when I finally began them, because I felt I was not at liberty to disclose to others what Fenimore had chosen to keep private. I confined myself to acting on the clues that had been left in the Notebooks, thinking that these alone would readily enough enable me to find Fenimore's muse. In this, too, I was in error.

Notebook I made plain that Margarita had been living and working in the Canary Islands for some years; that she had originated in Venezuela and that she had a business called Capirote Therapies based in Santa Cruz de Tenerife. It also recorded that she had family members in Venezuela itself, in Boston (of all places) and in Zurich. Notebooks I, II and III provided evidence that the two of them had met in half a dozen locations around the world over the six years of their relationship. Notebook III made clear that they had last met in Buenos Aires, where Margarita disclosed the existence of her secret lover, a certain Anactoria Lopez. I deduced from Notebook I that this woman might well be the friend who had accompanied Margarita to Madrid in April 2004 and then followed her to Toledo and travelled on into Andalusia. That woman was an archaeologist of Argentine origin, holding a research post at the University of Santa Cruz de Tenerife. How difficult could it be, I thought, to trace the two of them through telephone directories, flight manifests, business registrations and websites?

It was harder, as it turned out, than I had anticipated. I began with discrete inquiries at the Ends of the Earth in late 2010, mentioning Margarita's name casually among a number of others to see what came up; but no-one there knew anything about her. Mr Bojangles and the estimable Malvine had vague memories of a woman visiting briefly some years before, but had never heard of her since and were not even certain that that had been her name. There have, it must be admitted, been a great many visitors to Cos over the intervening years and Fenimore clearly had said no more to his household than to any of us about his love affair with Margarita. Tarski and Eleni told me they remembered a dinner party in late 2004 at which she may have been present, but that was all. Nor could I discover private details about her – a photograph, a letter, an address - among Fenimore's papers or in his computers. It was baffling. He seems to have worked very methodically to conceal all trace of her and of his connection with her. It stood to reason that he must have had means for communicating with her across the globe, but of what exactly these had been I could find no record.

Following unsuccessful web and phone checks, I had a search conducted in the Canary Islands. I was told that Capirote Therapies had closed its doors and that its owner had left the islands in late 2009, which meant *before* the fateful meeting in Buenos Aires. I could find no evidence that it had since opened for business elsewhere. I inquired after Ms Lopez and learned that she had, indeed, been a research fellow at the university in Santa Cruz de Tenerife around 2004, but had left the Canary Islands also in late 2009, when her appointment expired. The synchronicity in the timing seemed significant and I felt impelled to take the inquiry further. I flew to Buenos Aires to make inquiries, but could find neither woman. I lingered there for several days, retracing to the best of my ability, the account Fenimore had committed to writing of his last tryst with Margarita, until I came to the Teatro Cervantes. I stood on the corner of Libertad and Cordoba Streets, where he says they had their final conversation. Then, with a heavy heart, I flew back here. I felt lost in a kind of nightmare of disappearing people, all connected with one another and all keeping secrets about their private lives that I could not penetrate.

Margarita had had a father in Boston called Ycario, a brother in Zurich called Fernando, a mother in Venezuela called Alfreda. It stood to reason that *they* could be found and that they must have some contact with her. I sought for the first, only to find that he had returned to Venezuela to campaign against Hugo Chavez in 2008 and had been imprisoned. I went looking for the second, but found that he had been retrenched as the Euro Crisis broke, in late 2009. He was reported to have gone to work somewhere in the Caribbean, but those I contacted in Zurich were unable or unwilling to provide contact details; nor could I find him listed by surname in the those parts of the Caribbean island and banking labyrinth I was able to access. The mother, also, I could not find and travel in Venezuela was so hazardous for a 'Yankee' like me that after an initial visit to Caracas and exposure to its violence, I thought better of lingering in that tumultuous country and withdrew, once more, to Treehaven.

The case had become baffling and I had many pressing things to attend to. It was, by this stage, well into 2011 and the unresolved difficulties with the staff at Cos – particularly Ariel – and with Peripatetica had led us to agree that Fenimore's advice should be taken. We would set up the Foundation in the northern hemisphere. I therefore abandoned the search for Margarita and concentrated my attention on finding a suitable site for the Moneghan archives and our headquarters while we completed our planning. It was only in late 2012 that I renewed the search. Through a stroke of good fortune, I at last found the mysterious Anactoria. A newspaper story in the Spanish language press of the Dominican Republic was noticed by my assistant Luisa, who knew that I was looking for Ms Lopez. It made reference to the archaeologist as living a reclusive life in Santo Domingo.

I flew there at once and found her living alone in a small apartment. Her life, it was apparent, had fallen apart. From her I learned of the end of Margarita, apparently within a fortnight of news breaking out in the world press of the disappearance and presumed death of Fenimore off the coast of the Ends of the Earth. Anactoria had no idea who I was and declared she had never heard of Fenimore. Grief, depression and alcohol had almost unhinged her and it was with some difficulty and many tears on her part that I coaxed from her the fact that her beloved Margarita had, for no apparent reason at all, and without saying goodbye, committed suicide in late June 2010, during a visit to Greece. Her car, it seems, had been found near a high cliff from which suicides were famously known to leap to their deaths into the sea and she herself was gone. Already baffled by the difficulties of the case, I now felt stunned by its evident unguessed intricacies. It seemed scarcely credible that Fenimore and Margarita should have (a) so abruptly separated after six years of apparent intimacy; (b) that this should have triggered Fenimore's suicide (granted other factors weighing in); and above all, (c), that his suicide would then have triggered hers.

I was incredulous and questioned Anactoria closely. It seemed impossible to believe not only that both the lovers had committed suicide without communicating first with the person they professedly loved most in the world; but that each had done so by casting themselves into the sea without either of their bodies being found. Yet I have not been able to discover any evidence to contradict this bizarre and disturbing conclusion. Moreover, it suggested that Fenimore's own deductions about Margarita's lack of love for him had been erroneous. She had, it seems, loved him so deeply, but so confusedly, that she had ended up destroying his life, her own and that of her other lover in one fell swoop. What can have induced her to cut Fenimore off in the way she did, if she felt so deeply about him? Truly, the human psyche is an enigma – perhaps 4% comprehensible and 96% 'dark matter', as Fenimore might have expressed it, if he only knew of all this.

There was nothing I could do to console the wretched Anactoria and I feared to make things worse by telling her of the Notebooks and what they contained. She herself was so far gone in grief that she did not show any interest in learning more about Fenimore, whose relations with Margarita I had, in any case, described only in the most guarded terms, as a friend of Margarita's from the other side of the world, who had originally met her in Toledo in 2004. I wished her well, gave her my contact details in case she needed help and took my leave. But I had discovered something which truly disturbed me and still haunts me. I feel caught in a nightmare story of the two lovers fatefully misunderstanding one another; the passionate but conflicted Margarita never guessing that her decision to give up Fenimore for Anactoria's sake would precipitate his death and he failing to foresee that his own suicide would precipitate hers.

Apart from that hair-raising and horrific story, worthy of a tragic drama by Shakespeare or even the more bloodthirsty Roman dramatist Seneca, there is the worrying fact that both lovers died in similar ways *without either of their bodies being found.* The second seems to defy the laws of probability, though I suppose stranger things have happened. What concerns me is that a good deal of the conspiracy theory nonsense that has risen like a cloud over Fenimore's death has surely been *due* to the fact that his body has never been found. Should it ever become general knowledge that he and Margarita were lovers and that her body, likewise, has never been found, there will certainly be a whole new wave of such speculation about who did away with them, or even where they have fled without leaving a trace and for what mysterious reasons. Fortunately, we alone appear to know that they ever knew one another, much less that there is any link between their deaths. The evidence is entirely concealed within the pages of this book, to the best of my knowledge. I suggest that we agree to leave it there, in order to pre-empt even more confabulation and confusion than has already been generated.

This brings me to the second unintended consequence of Fenimore's supposedly free and autonomous act of ending his own life, but not leaving the world a corpse to bury or cremate. There seems to be no reason to doubt, going by his final entry in Notebook III, that he intended to put an end to his own life. In my capacity as executor of his will, I found and interviewed his medical specialists, when I arrived at Cos in late June 2010. I was shown scan images of an aggressive metastasis. It was perfectly evident how desperately ill anyone with such a plague of tumours must have been. Still, unable to come to terms with the abruptness of his death, I lingered on at Cos until the police search was discontinued and the official verdict of 'death by misadventure' was entered into the public record. By that time, of course, all kinds of press speculation had been doing the rounds and stories were being written about vast sums of money got – some alleged – by dubious means; of strange foreign visitors to Cos; of a Chinese connection; of submarines, sharks and sinister doings. In no time at all, unable to accept the police verdict and finding abundant colourful material with which to confabulate, people both at the Ends of the Earth and elsewhere around the world began to invent the conspiracy theories by which we have found ourselves besieged ever since.

We have all been inclined to treat these as vexatious but absurd fantasies, of course. Donald Finch and Eleni Tsalanidis, at Peripatetica, couldn't decide whether to laugh or cry over them. They informed me – in the early months, before we had our difficulties regarding the estate - that they had begun to keep a record of all the nonsensical conspiracy theories as grist for the mill in the workshop Peripatetica has long run. Their hypothesis, which seems perfectly reasonable, is that there probably would have been such theories even if Fenimore had died peacefully in his bed, given that he was such an exotic and private character who lived in a palatial residence and had rumoured pasts and rumoured wealth that could provide the material for several novels. But even they were astonished by the proliferation of lush nonsense that sprang out of thin air and the empty boat.

By one account, Fenimore's disappearance had been orchestrated, says Finch, by the Vatican (or the Jesuits or Opus Dei). Other villains conjured up in public bars, tabloid-bestrewn cafes and the wilds of the blogosphere sound like a Robert Ludlum thriller about Jason Bourne. It has been alleged, on who knows what grounds that the Chinese Communist

Party or Goldman Sachs, some shadowy Neo-Nazi group or even al-Qaeda did for our poor Fenimore or spirited him away. And then, of course, there are the right wing cranks that see in his disappearance the all-manipulative hand of the Illuminati. Though I found it in rather poor taste, Finch actually arranged what he called a 'Da Vinci Code party', one hot summer night in the gardens at Cos. Guests came in costumes based on the Tom Hanks film, the film itself was shown on the big screen in The Dionysium, with the wine flowing and abundant finger food being served by caterers. Amid gales of laughter, he recounted to the gathering outlandish stories of how the vanishing of Fenimore had supposedly been contrived by the Vatican and Opus Dei, by the Chinese Communist Party, by vengeful New York bankers or by the CIA.

Other stories again have asserted that Fenimore has gone into hiding to complete a secret treatise that is so explosive that he is in fear for his life even at the Ends of the Earth. Yet others say he has been a Catholic at heart all along and has secretly become a Jesuit in a remote location, repenting of his heresies. It's simply endless and, during my many stays at Cos over the past four years, it has been the subject of both laughter and bemused outrage among all those who knew the man. Somewhat tongue-in-cheek, Peripatetica has offered to run free seminars on the subject, but their work has always been with analytical professionals, not with the *hoi polloi*, among whom such ignorant speculation tends to sprout; so there seems to be no way to bring this epidemic of popular nonsense under control. Fenimore himself, if he were alive, would surely find it a subject of great hilarity and I believe that we, for our part, must leave it to one side with as much equanimity as we can summon and concentrate on finishing the work to which he was committed: the setting up of the Foundation.

After all, it's not as if such plagues of bad thinking and incorrigible ignorance are anything new and it's not as if they can be blown away tomorrow. Our task is to work for enlightenment in a tradition that, as Fenimore well knew, dates back to Pythagoras and has seen the vindication of the Pre-Socratics and Bruno by modern science and critical inquiry. We should set about that work in the spirit of the concluding lines to Fenimore's fine Credo, where he wrote:

> *I believe that I am neither fated nor predestined*
> *But am able to live for possibilities*
> *And move intentionally toward a horizon that is open*

I believe that, in his unfinished writing, Fenimore saw himself as taking bold strides towards that open horizon. I believe, also, that he intended his death out at sea to symbolize the same spirit. He headed out towards the open horizon and surrendered himself at last to the sea, from which life first emerged onto land 400 million years ago, as he wrote in Notebook II.

We should emulate him in spirit. We have a bracing and privileged future ahead of us. Let's concentrate on that and not allow ourselves to be distracted by the ephemeral chatter of the ill-informed. Our line in response to all inquiries about conspiracy theories should, I suggest, be that we know them to be without foundation and have better things to do than to dignify them with our attention.

There is also, however, the third and final unintended consequence of Fenimore's untimely demise. It will, I fear, bedevil us for some time yet with pestiferous press stories and harassment by the paparazzi. Fenimore was known to have published two major books, ten years apart, and it was widely reported that he was hard at work on a third and even more serious book, which, so rumour had it, even before his death, would be published in 2015 and would cause a sensation. With his death, unfortunately, the nature and fate of his unfinished work went straight into the speculative blender along with his wealth and globe-trotting peregrinations. Our press release more than a year ago, announced that reports of Fenimore's forthcoming book could not be gratified, since it remains altogether incomplete and can only serve as the basis for future inquiry by others. We hoped that that would give the quietus to speculation. Alas, somehow the rumour mills have got hold of a story that I have that book in my possession, but have withheld it from release because of its controversial content.

Given that Fenimore's will and letter explicitly specify that his Notebooks are strictly for our private use, I have felt somewhat hampered in addressing these persistent rumours. I can hardly come out with a statement to the press to the effect that I have in my possession a 750 page hand-written manuscript of Fenimore Moneghan's private reflections on his work, on life, love and the nature of the cosmos while insisting blithely that it is not for public consumption. The firestorm of speculation and intrusion that this would inevitably ignite would soon prove intolerable. Yet it is often the case that what is kept secret, for no other reasons than the fact that it *is* kept secret, prompts the most feverish and paranoid imaginings. The common mind feeds on such imaginings and drinks up lurid novels that cater to the appetite. We are, to some extent, therefore, caught between the proverbial rock and a hard place. It would be ungracious of us to rebuke the deceased Fenimore for putting us in this position. How was he to guess what would happen? In any case, the truth is that the clamorous mob has no right to Fenimore's private papers and we should hold a firm line in stating that there is nothing in the swirling rumours and nothing we have in our possession that could satisfy them. I suggest we simply wait for the speculation to blow over.

The truth is that Fenimore is dead, but also that he was a great friend of ours and a fine human being. We shared a philosophical vision with him and we shaped an institutional vision with him. He has committed to us his most intimate thoughts and the outlines of his synthesis of the sciences and humanities. He has given to us the greater part of his ample resources to pour into the creation of the Foundation. The religions which our vision and his thought set out to challenge and transcend all have their martyrs. Let him, then, be ours; not with an eye on any life beyond the grave, but with a commitment to life within the circles of the world. As long as we live, we will all feel his presence among us. As we build the Foundation and extend its work across the world, we know he will be with us in spirit. We have this volume to remind us of that fact. We have only begun the labor of pulling together the details of his work and we know that there will be no sudden blinding flash of insight that will bring an end to these labours; only patient and scientific work over many years. That work will come to the world's attention in a whole new way when we open the Foundation's doors.

Let me conclude with a modest solemnity. Fenimore's last entry in Notebook III, as you now know, requested that, when we gathered to bid him farewell, we recall the pleasures of The Mahlerium and listen to Max Bruch's Concerto for Violin and Orchestra in G Minor Opus 26, because G Minor was Sappho's chord and also the angelic mode of high monasticism. I did so at Cos, on behalf of all of you, soon after my arrival there in June 2010. I sat in The Mahlerium listening to the Bruch several times over. I then found myself reciting, as if from a long-buried memory, a poem of Catullus that some of you may recall Fenimore reciting at a soiree in Boston many years ago, about death and ceremony. It was written by Catullus after he had got to Italy too late to see his brother before the latter died and had been cremated. Perhaps that is why these lines came back to me, strolling around the starkly disinherited halls of Cos:

> *Multas per gentes et multa per aequora vectus*
> *Advenio has miseras, frater, ad inferias*
> *Ut te postremo donarem munere mortis*
> *Et mutam nequiquam alloquerer cinerem.*
> *Quandoquidem fortuna mihi tete abstulit ipsum*
> *Heu miser digne frater adempte mihi*
> *Nunc tamen interea haec, prisco quae more parentum*
> *Tradita sunt tristi munere ad inferias,*
> *Accipe fraterno multum manantia fletu,*
> *Atque in perpetuum, frater, ave atque vale*

Such were the cadenced words of Catullus, two thousand years ago. I can almost hear Fenimore reciting them in the lounge on Tremont Street. My own, rather free paraphrasing of them, for our present and future purposes would be as follows:

*I have come across whole countries and over the sea, brother, full of misgivings, to offer
you the last gift to the dead and to address in vain your mute ashes. It seems that the roll
of the dice has deprived us of you unjustly, luckless, brave comrade-in-arms. Still, here and
now let me utter such things as are, by ancient tradition, offered up at such sad obsequies:
accept my grieving fraternal commemoration within your emptied house – hail, brother,
and forever farewell.*

That *ave atque vale;* that 'hail and farewell', were the heaviest and most meaningful I have
ever uttered. Let's bear them in mind ourselves as we set off, neither fated nor predestined, for
a horizon that is open and for all the possibilities that await us.

Tom Emerson
Villa Barberini,
March 15, 2014

Editor's Postscript: Catastrophe, Kabbalah and Conclusions

Thomas Emerson's quiet confidence that the fever of conspiracy theory would dissipate, as we now know, proved to be tragically misplaced. The brutal climax to that fever was accompanied by magazine stories that competed with one another in their rather crass puns – 'Academy of Lynchings' (*The Atlantic*), 'Barbarism at the Barberini', (*Time*), 'Truck You, Amor Mundi' (*Rolling Stone*) – and drew attention to the violence without being able to get to the bottom of what had caused it. 'Cause', of course, is a rather dubious word to use in such a case. How can we attribute 'causation' at any given point along the virtual 'burning fuse' that began with Cardinal Bolzano – if 'began' is the right word – and ended up with violent intrigues being hatched in the Beka'a Valley?

Yet burn it did and the massive explosion that resulted is a matter of record. As of this writing, it seems doubtful that the nascent Amor Mundi Foundation will ever recover from the mass killings and there is considerable legal confusion over its status and its assets. As we go to press, there are reports that at least one surviving member of the Academy is at work with lawyers and consultants to attempt to retrieve the situation. But there is very tight security around the operation and there has, as yet, been no public announcement. Rumours continue that a second member of the Academy survived the disaster at the Villa Barberini and that Fenimore Moneghan is not dead, but in hiding. There are even sinister suggestions that the whole episode was in fact orchestrated by Moneghan from the shadows in order to eliminate his erstwhile colleagues and claim the entire revenues of the Foundation for himself.

There are, naturally, endless variations on this dubious hypothesis. According to one that has come to our attention, Moneghan foresaw what was coming and stepped into the shadows ahead of time, from where he has now taken the surviving lynxes under his protection, as they prepare to strike back against the forces that have attacked them. This fantastic confabulation has a 'white' version, in which Moneghan is a knight in shining armour who will stride forth in the years to come to strike down both his enemies and those of civilization; and a 'black' version, according to which Moneghan and Irad Kripke are engaged in a war from the shadows against one another. In one variant of this black legend, it was not Hezbollah, but Kripke (the Jewish financier) who arranged the truck bombing at the Villa Barberini, then, from a hidden base, sent assassins to Rome.

The killings in Rome have, inevitably, been the subject of wild speculation themselves. Some claim that they were the work of al-Qaida or other Sunni extremists (even ISIS has been mentioned in this context), given the trademark brutality of the executions. Others point the finger at 'Opus Dei' or reactionary forces within the Vatican opposed not only to the Amor Mundi Foundation, but to the whole OCD project. Others again see the hand of the CIA in the matter, removing traces of a covert operation gone wrong. It has to be admitted that the events in Rome are especially, disturbing simply because no-one has claimed responsibility for them. This gives free rein to speculation. And, despite our commitment to Bianca Ruggiero, we cannot be certain that the publication of this book will put an end to that speculation. It certainly does not provide an answer as to who made the murderous raid on the offices of the Amor Mundi Foundation. Brandom House is, after all, a publishing firm, not a detective agency.

One of the enduring mysteries of the case and one that has been much discussed in the offices of Brandom House is why Emerson and his colleagues did not take greater security precautions after the Anonymous manifesto went on-line, with its lunatic assertions and scarcely veiled threats. In hindsight, of course, the threat looks far more dangerous than it can have appeared at the time. It is important to remember that Emerson, Ruggiero and the others had been aware for several years, before the summer of 2014, of the conspiracy theories that were abroad about Moneghan's disappearance, the manuscript and their own work. Yet during that time there had not been a single violent incident. Why should they have taken greater notice, therefore, of an unhinged YouTube video, which, in any case, seemed to be directed primarily at political and institutional powers vastly larger than the Academy of Lynxes? Our conclusion is that they simply did not take Anonymous seriously. It never so much as occurred to them that such a video would prompt terrorist forces to target them for assassination. Sadly, we now know better.

Quite apart from conspiracy theories, violent or otherwise, our own work on this book has, in the past few months, brought about quite a different development: serious pre-publication interest in the actual ideas contained in the Notebooks and their relationship to the drama of what has taken place around them. There has been a remarkable response to our circulation of the galley proofs of this volume to gauge its likely reception, elicit early reviews and, let it be said, open the way to a market in literate circles. The atmosphere of violence and conspiracy theory, after all, threatened to overshadow the book's serious content and authentic story. We wanted to create a different and more sober atmosphere for the book's release. Among those to whom the manuscript was sent was Professor Lilith Zohar, who holds a chair in Hebrew and comparative literature at Stanford University. She has scheduled a major conference next year, under the rubric 'Alpha and Omega: Fenimore Moneghan's Posthumous Notebooks in the Light of *l'Affaire Moneghan*.'

This development has, somewhat perversely, been deplored by Donald Finch (the 'Tarski' of Moneghan's notebooks) as a distraction from and betrayal of the scientific spirit of Moneghan's work. Finch, a serious philosopher, when he learned of the approach to be taken at the conference, expressed exasperation at what he frankly called 'the slide from cabals to Kabbalism'. In interviews with the *New York Times* and the *Jerusalem Post* (reprinted or excerpted in various other newspapers), he denounced what he describes as the mythologization of his friend and colleague. 'Fenimore Moneghan was a serious and scientific thinker', he declared, 'whose whole purpose was to show that the modern natural sciences provide an adequate account of reality and that the endless wallowing around in esoteric waffle and pretentious semiotics is an egregious waste of our time, when there are so many urgent and practical tasks to get on with.' His vehemence is, perhaps, explicable, in part, by the series of traumatic events in the past five years that have disrupted his world. The evidence in hand, moreover, would suggest that he knew only part of Moneghan's work, being unaware of the Notebooks or the poetry. After reading his outburst in the world press, we sent an advance copy of this manuscript to him at the Ends of the Earth. We have not heard from him since.

Having, she wrote to us, raced through the manuscript at one sitting, Professor Zohar urged publication and requested permission to circulate it much more widely with a view to arranging the conference in question. Our concern, naturally, was that the manuscript would very quickly be posted on the Internet in a pirated version, undermining our market. To our relief, those who have it in their keeping have so far kept it under wraps and it is not yet in electronic circulation. The response to it, however, has been enthusiastic, with many papers being proposed for the conference and expeditious publication being urged from all sides.

There will be seven key themes at the conference:

Moneghan, Emerson and the Death of the Author
The Empty Boat and the Genesis of the Moneghan Myth
Moneghan as Tzadik: Secrecy, the Kabbalistic Tradition and the Privacy of the Notebooks
Cosmology and Astrobiology in Moneghan's Worldview
Autopoiesis and Consciousness in Moneghan's Writing
Capirote Therapies: Freedom and Song as Motifs in the Notebooks
The Temple Complex: Moneghan's Octavos as a Prose Poem Parthenon

The idea of the 'death of the author' is a commonplace in contemporary literary criticism. It is given an unusual resonance in this case by the fact that both Fenimore Moneghan and his friend and literary editor Tom Emerson are in fact dead. Yet no-one disputes that they were, between them, the authors of this book. Or at least no-one to whom we have shown the manuscript has disputed it to this point. As for the empty boat, this also is not in dispute. The *Aletheia* was found empty, in the sense that Fenimore's body was missing. Apparently, this is to be used as a point of departure for discussing the speculative frenzy about Moneghan, his ideas, his colleagues and his money which followed from that discovery. We gather, however, that it is also being seen as a metaphor and questions have been raised about Moneghan's intentions in so arranging his demise that his body was not found on a boat with a Greek name meaning *Truth* or (literally) *Unconcealment*.

The most mysterious theme, though, is surely the third. Professor Zohar has informed us that she had no sooner laid eyes on *Darkness over Love* than she intuitively sensed what an elaborate game its author had been playing. She has informed us that Moneghan occurs, throughout the Notebooks, as a self-appointed modern day version of a Jewish *tzadik*, which is to say a sage or 'righteous one', who passes down the 'secret tradition' – the so-called Kabbalah (sometimes spelled Kabbala, Qabbala, or Cabbala) – from one generation to the next over the centuries. She says that the whole framing of the Notebooks, beginning with the setting in Toledo, then delving into cosmology, the nature of life and the nature of being and ending with the taking up of the *tzadik* into a transcendent dimension, points to their being a Kabbalistic exercise. She says that there are many questions in need of answers about Moneghan's intentions, his death and the existence and identity of Margarita. Moneghan even refers explicitly to Maimonides and other Jewish thinkers right from the outset, as if dropping clues, she argues.

The idea that the Notebooks constituted a secret Kabbalah written to Margarita had never come up in our conversations with Bianca Ruggiero and it doesn't appear to have been considered by Thomas Emerson, when he was editing Moneghan's work. Yet Zohar, a leading specialist on such matters, is confident in her judgement; and the more she explained her reasoning, when I flew over to Palo Alto to meet her; the more plausible it began to sound. Just what the Kabbalah is has itself been the subject of dispute for centuries, she confesses, but it is a complex set of ideas rooted in Jewish antiquity. Via Judaism, these ideas have gradually spread throughout Western and Middle Eastern culture. Originally, however, she says that the Kabbala consisted of a set of esoteric doctrines explaining the relationship between the eternal and mysterious *Ein Sof* (No End) and the physical universe. Seen in this light, the relationship between Kabbalah and the concerns of Moneghan seems at least plausible, though highly mysterious.

Professor Zohar explained to me, as we sat by the pool-side at the rear of the Sheraton Palo Alto, after a long morning of conversation about her reading of the manuscript and her plan for the conference she proposes; that, even if we ignore the many strands of more esoteric Kabbalah, the fundamental tradition is that the Torah, the elaborate Law of Moses, can be studied at four different levels:

Peshat – finding the simple or obvious meaning
Remez – seeing hints or clues to allegorical meanings
Darash – inquiring into systematic meanings in the light of multiple passages
Sod – coming to understand the secret meaning, deep beneath the rest

These four levels of interpretation, according to Zohar, are called PRDS (pronounced PARDES) from their initial letters. And PARDES means paradise, or more literally 'orchard'. In other words, she suggested – for she herself is a secular scholar and not a religious mystic – life becomes most fruitful and sublime when you are able to discern layer after layer of meaning in things and do not become jaded or cynical about the apparently obvious or banal. Not being familiar with the Law of Moses, I had difficulty in understanding how this tradition had evolved; but the larger point about layers of meaning seemed very thought-provoking and I readily conceded that it appears to have relevance to the Moneghan case.

We ordered a bottle of a very fine, pre-earthquake vinted Napa Cabernet and I think I will always associate its aromatic scent of anise and red cherries with the stream of conversation that followed. Lilith explained that according to medieval traditions, the secret wisdom of the Kabbalah goes all the way back to the Garden of Eden. It has been handed down from that remote past as a secret revelation to elect Tzadikim (righteous people). These are only a privileged few; elect and often obscure. Moneghan's attempt to go back to the beginnings of things and make living sense of the realities of the cosmos was not literally a continuation of the old Kabbalistic tradition, she said; but a highly imaginative attempt to achieve the same effect while casting it firmly within the authentic revelation of the natural world by the physical sciences. It was written in a form and style which strongly suggest he sought to build a bridge between the truths of the sciences and the immemorial experience of human beings attempting to share meaning in a bewildering world.

The facts that the attempt was directed at one other person and written as a kind of prose poem were strong clues as to Moneghan's basically Kabbalistic intent, she argued; since there is a tradition that a Rabbi should not teach Kabbalah openly or to groups, but should pass it on only to a single prized student. When she said this, I felt my hand tighten around my wine glass. I could no longer resist the Kabbalistic air around the manuscript that I had myself edited for publication. Prior to this conversation with Lilith in Palo Alto, I had had no knowledge of the Kabbalah; but going over and over the story itself and then listening to what that dark-eyed and softly spoken mistress of words and their secret meanings had to say, I have become intrigued. I realized that there might well be more than one layer of meaning in *Darkness over Love.* In fact, I came to appreciate for the first time that there just might be four layers to it: the simple or obvious, the allegorical, the systematic and the secret. When Moneghan wrote his carefully structured Notebooks in regular paragraphs, he was planting an orchard. He was attempting to set out the map of PRDS for his prized student and show his beloved the way to Paradise.

This thread to the conversation was so rich that we talked well into the afternoon. I realized in the course of those hours that, even as the editor of the manuscript, I had done no more than skim its surface. Lilith, specialist in deep reading, gave me, before we parted that afternoon, a book called *The Genesis of Secrecy: On the Interpretation of Narrative*, by Frank Kermode. In Kermode, whose book I had read by the time I arrived back in New York the next morning, I discovered the idea of *midrash*: a Hebrew word for the means by which a story is either rewritten or explained by a commentator in such a way as to make old meanings clear to a contemporary audience. The word *midrash*, Kermode explains, derives from the word *darash* to probe or examine. It can take the form of fictive augmentation and change or commentary. Its purpose is to "penetrate the surface and reveal a secret sense; to show what is concealed in what is proclaimed." Lilith, I realized, had filled me with puzzlements about what I had been handed by Bianca Ruggiero and had, I thought, faithfully edited.

If Moneghan had seen himself as a kind of *tzadik*, what was the secret meaning beneath his already unusual text? What had I missed in Emerson's commentary? Had his editing of the text, his addition to it of titles, comments and the long appendices of poetry and a credo actually altered it in subtle ways? What kind of *midrash* version of the original had I, in fact, received? What is the relationship between the poetic and private text put together by Moneghan and the events of his real life? Given that he surely cannot have planned the text with the knowledge that he was going to die at the end of it, what is the meaning of his demise in the context of his writing? How can the work of Emerson in counter-terrorism, the stunningly successful investment strategies of Iced Rowanberry Investments, the creation of the Amor Mundi Foundation and the cascade of conspiracy theories that brought catastrophe down upon the Academy of Lynxes be reconciled with Moneghan's whole project? As I contemplated all these things, my head began to spin. I and my colleagues had committed ourselves to publishing the true story and the real manuscript, but after my day with Lilith and my reading of Kermode, I was no longer certain what those things actually meant.

At one point in his book, Kermode asked: "Why, in fact, does it require a more strenuous effort to believe that a narrative lacks coherence than to believe that, somehow, if we could only find it, it doesn't?" Later in his book, at the beginning of a chapter titled 'What Precisely Are the Facts?', he wrote:

> *If so many causes act in concert to ensure that texts are from the beginning and sometimes indeterminately studded with interpretations; and if these texts in their very nature demand further interpretation and yet resist it, what should we expect when the document in question denies its own opacity by claiming to be a transparent account of the recognizable world?*

When I read these lines, I was struck by the fact that I was about to publish a book which met all these criteria. It was a book that required and yet resisted interpretation; one studded with interpretations in any case (those by Emerson) and yet purporting, in our Brandom House reproduction, to be a transparent account of 'the recognizable world' of the Moneghan affair and the circle of ill-fated intellectuals who called themselves the Academy of Lynxes. Was this pure coincidence, or simply a discoverable feature of the world as it is and of all books?

It was, in any case, a disconcerting realization. On reflection, however, and after reading through the manuscript with fresh eyes back in Poughkeepsie, I found myself drawn into a rather satisfying hermeneutic circle. Fenimore Moneghan may or may not consciously have seen himself as a *tzadik* handing down the secrets of the Kabbalah to a prized student. But the manner in which he wrote lends itself to this interpretation for those steeped in that literary and mystical tradition. The manner in which he wrote suggests that he understood all this and believed that interpretation and meaning are central to the human experience of reality – whatever 'the facts' may be. He believed that there is, indeed, a 'recognizable world', a world of fact, but that to live within it we must construe it in ways that make sense to us. From start to finish, in his Notebooks, this is what he was attempting to do. He knew that his sense making could not be purely 'objective'. It was anchored to his sense of Margarita as a presence in his life, from the time he first met her in Toledo; and the Notebooks were his attempt to make sense of the world in the context of his relatedness to her.

When we read Moneghan, of course, at one level, we immerse ourselves in his account of his relationship with Margarita and his account of his own life. This is Peshat: the simple or obvious meaning of the Notebooks. In doing so, however, we cannot help seeing or looking for – and, indeed, finding – hints and clues as to how love, meaning and relatedness in general work; or indications that Moneghan was pointing beyond his personal experience to larger truths about the 'recognizable world'. This is Remez. We also cannot help taking note of the fact that his Notebooks are set out in a very formal structure, which even in itself appears to imply that there are formal structures to the realities he is pointing to, both in the world of fact and in the world of meaning. It is left to us to discern what exactly those formal structures might be. This is Darash. Then there is the fact that he took the trouble to express himself at all and in such a manner, covering so much ground, that there must be a deeper meaning to the undertaking. We search for it, as Emerson first searched for it. We discern Moneghan's anguish, his doubts, his humor, his irony and through all of them his deeper meaning, or rather *the* deeper meaning, beyond any insight or intention of Moneghan himself. This is Sod.

All that said, when I came to the conclusion of Kermode's book, reading it as I was in the context of this book, I found that I had come to a different conclusion than him. He concludes with a chapter titled 'The Unfollowable World' and argues that, although as human beings we are addicted to narrative and want to believe that stories are coherent and that the world as a whole has a coherent story, this is an illusion. He wrote:

> *...we interpret always as transients...both in the book and in the world which resembles the book. For the world is our beloved codex. We may not see it, as Dante did, in perfect order, gathered by love into one volume; but we do, living as reading, like to think of it as a place where we can travel back and forth at will, divining congruences, conjunctions, opposites; extracting secrets from its secrecy, making understood relations, an appropriate algebra. This is the way we satisfy ourselves with explanations of the unfollowable world – as if it were a structured narrative, of which more might always be said by trained readers of it, by insiders. World and book, it may be, are hopelessly plural, endlessly disappointing; we stand alone before them, aware of their arbitrariness and impenetrability, knowing that they may be narratives only because of our impudent intervention, and susceptible of interpretation only by our hermetic tricks. Hot for secrets, our only conversation may be with guardians who know less and see less than we can; and our sole hope and pleasure is in the perception of a momentary radiance, before the door of disappointment is finally shut on us.*

I think this is a view of reality that Fenimore Moneghan would have rejected. He seems to have been convinced that a coherent narrative of the nature of things *could* be both constructed and imparted. His Notebooks were intended to show that, although they were not intended to be a definitive narrative. Indeed, he did not think that a definitive narrative was the goal; but a *coherent* narrative certainly was. That the world is complex, he allowed. That it is unfollowable unless you understand a great deal, he believed. But that it is unfollowable or impenetrable in principle, he denied.

What, after all, do we see in in his Notebooks but an attempt to gather by love into one volume, in perfect order, an account of the world with all its congruences and conjunctions? We know that, while creating his Notebooks, he was at work on a systematic treatise of a scientific and philosophical nature. This demonstrates that he did not believe the world to be impenetrable at all; only that coming to understand it required arduous thinking. The fourth and fifth themes of next year's conference will, presumably, address at least some of these considerations. It is plain, for example, that he saw cosmology and evolutionary biology in highly scientific terms and did not accept that any other, mythological or fanciful account of the cosmos or the nature of life should govern our thinking. It is clear, also, that he was at work on a theory of life and consciousness that would have accounted for both the existence of a being able to do exactly what he was doing and, therefore, by extension, the numerous experiences and capacities of human beings in general. So Kermode's claims are at odds with Moneghan's beliefs and commitments.

Yet there will be those who might argue that Kermode's judgements are borne out by the strangeness of the events which occurred around Moneghan and arguably made nonsense of his hopes and beliefs. He did not anticipate the aggressive cancer that assailed him in his final months. He did not foresee the breach with Margarita or have within himself sufficient reserves of self-belief to withstand it. He did not have any sense, as far as we can judge, that the chosen manner of his death would trigger uncontrollable irrationalities with catastrophic consequences for the people he cared about most. Even though he had helped to create a company, in Peripatetica Decision Architects which fought conspiracy theory, cognitive biases and illusions, both it and his wider work were overwhelmed by conspiracy theories precisely because of his decisions. Likewise, his colleagues, not least among them Thomas Emerson, thought they understood the world, but were caught violently by surprise in the midst of their work. In a manner that Kermode would have recognized, we can see within the pages of this book that Emerson could see what Moneghan could not, while we can see what Emerson himself could not. Doesn't this force us to conclude with Kermode that the world is, indeed, unfollowable?

We at Brandom House do not believe so. That the world be followable does not require that any given individual be able to foresee all contingencies or all the consequences of their own actions. It requires only that those of us who are *witnesses* to such contingencies and consequences be able to interpret them in a coherent manner and account for them without doing violence to the facts. This is particularly important in the case of violence, in fact, having been done. There is no solution, to date, to the criminal violence perpetrated in Rome against Bianca Ruggiero and her unfortunate colleagues and security guards. That only makes fidelity to fact and reason the more important and does not, by any means, justify arbitrary or fanciful deductions – of which there has been a plethora over the past few months. Similarly, the difficulty of interpreting the relationship between Moneghan's strictly philosophical work and the poetics of his Notebooks does not justify wholly whimsical responses to the Notebooks. There is a good deal that we will never know, owing to the destruction of manuscripts and the killing of witnesses. Yet there are some things that we know and these ought to be taken as a guide to at least provisional understanding.

In any case, the sixth and seventh themes of the conference that is being organized open up other ways of looking at what Moneghan wrote and may have intended. The sixth, according to Professor Zohar, will explore the question of song and the absence of song in the Notebooks as a key motif in Moneghan's writing. Apparently, even on a first reading, there are those in the music therapy community who believe that the true message of the Notebooks is the importance of song in human well-being. Several papers from quite divergent viewpoints have been proposed: a radical feminist reading, according to which Margarita is the unsung heroine of the piece and was misunderstood by Fenimore to the end; a sceptical reading, in which it will be argued that Margarita never existed, but was entirely a figment of Fenimore's fertile imagination for the purposes of writing his long poem about the place of music and song in human reality; and a musicological one, which will explore the implicit musical variations in Moneghan's poetry as a key to his therapeutic thinking.

The seventh theme, in which the *structure* of the original Notebooks, rather than the poems included by Emerson, is in centre frame, will look at the symbolic significance of the *aesthetics* of the layout of the Notebooks. The fact that there is such symmetry in the work – Prologue offset by Epilogue, three Notebooks each with eight sections, making a total of twenty four sections; but above all eight lines in each paragraph (or stanza, as some scholars are insisting they be called) and exactly sixty of these 'octavo' stanzas in each of the Prologue, Epilogue and twenty four chapters – has prompted several specialists to pick up on the passing remark by Emerson regarding the Temple of Karnak. It was a professor of classics and art history right here in New York who first raised the suggestion, drawing upon her own expert knowledge of the Parthenon, that that celebrated monument of classical architecture (rather than the Temple at Karnak) may have been what Moneghan, consciously or unconsciously, had in mind, when he set up his 'Parmenidean' epic prose poem the way he did.

Like Lilith Zohar's observations about the Kabbalah, this claim about the Parthenon struck me as so novel and unexpected that I made a point of meeting the scholar who had put the idea forward (via Zohar). Given that she is at New York University, this was not difficult. We simply met in Greenwich Village. She informed me that the Parthenon suggested itself because it is so iconic of just the kind of symmetries we see in this highly unusual manuscript. The French poet Alphonse de Lamartine, she pointed out, had declared, in 1832, that the famous Greek temple was 'the most perfect poem ever written in stone on the surface of the earth'. When I pointed out that there was no mention of Lamartine in the book, she responded with a smile, 'No, but there is mention of Le Corbusier, isn't there? And Le Corbusier proclaimed that the Parthenon is 'the repository of the sacred standard, the basis for all measurement in art' and didn't Moneghan proclaim himself, in one of his most exuberant love poems, 'Your Architect', a very Le Corbusier in spirit?' She then went on to point out, with extraordinary energy, that 'the more we have discovered, the more enigmatic the Parthenon has come to seem and the more inadequate appear the simplistic meanings ascribed to it.' She seemed to be saying that the same may turn out to be true of this book. We'll see what she has to say at the conference.

We are very fortunate, in the interim, in having Emerson's commentaries, because he knew Moneghan as well as anyone and had the opportunity to read the original Notebooks carefully and without distraction. At numerous points, he was able to provide corroboration or correction; to discover among papers in Moneghan's archive, since destroyed, documents which threw new light on what had been going on in Moneghan's mind during the years in which he worked on the Notebooks. The most obvious such documents are the Credo, the dozens of poems and the Songs of Queen Nefesh.

We have reproduced his original Appendices, containing all these things, along with his commentaries, for this precise reason. We also have Moneghan's earlier books and those of Emerson as strong guides to their lives and thought. We have records of our long conversations with Bianca Ruggiero. There are still those, at the Ends of the Earth, who knew Moneghan and worked with or for him. But above all there are sound principles of reason and interpretation. We have drawn upon all these in producing this edition of *Darkness over Love* and can vouch for its transparent authenticity. It is not a book or an interpretation of a book which has arisen through any 'impudent intervention' on our part. Nor has it been subjected to any 'hermeneutic tricks' on its way to the press. On the contrary, it is intended to act as a corrective to the many and pernicious false interpretations that have, over the past few years bedevilled the work of Fenimore Moneghan and his ill-fated colleagues. It is to them that this edition is dedicated.

N. Herman
Poughkeepsie
New York
24 March 2015

Tom Emerson's Appendices

Appendix A: Fenimore's Credo and its Context

Among the more substantial sets of documents in Fenimore's archives, when I came to review them and then remove them to the Villa Barberini, was a disturbingly large set of folders of studies in religion and philosophy. Some of the folders contained notes and papers dating back almost to his school years. The pages were yellowing and at times, since the notes in some cases had been scribbled down in pencil, they had faded and were not always easily legible. Most dated from the years of his doctoral studies and afterwards. The range of his interests was remarkable, but it was not merely eclectic. His core concern, for many years, was the relationship between religious myths as stories around which human action was organized and abstract truth as a corrective to claims of revelation, prophecy or divinely ordained authority. He was keenly interested in the roots and logic of apocalyptic beliefs and millenarian cults. Above all, however, he was interested in the relationship between intellectual argument in the Christian tradition and the claims of modern philosophy.

This is not the place to make a catalogue of all his studies, notes and papers on religion, much less on the broader subject of philosophy. As you know, such a catalogue exists. An impressive one had already been created at Cos by Ariel Kurzweil before Fenimore died. Since taking custody of the archive just over three years ago, I have duplicated that catalogue at the Villa and have been able to correct or update it in a number of ways. It will be a vital resource for the Foundation in the years to come. For the present, I want only to draw attention to a piece of writing which is clearly informed by Fenimore's studies, but appears to have existed in only a single copy before its reproduction here. I found the original in a folder labelled: 'The Catholic Creed in Newman and in Rahner'.

It is a thick folder, containing a dozen or more long essays on John Henry Newman's nineteenth century treatise on the development of Christian doctrine, on the dogmatic pronouncements of the First Vatican Council of 1870, on Karl Rahner's *Foundations of Christian Faith* and on the key documents of the Second Vatican Council. At the front of this folder, in a plastic sleeve, was the single typed copy of what looks to be a draft post-Christian creed written by Fenimore at some point in his reflections on the modern Catholic Church. It has the same number of lines and the same rhetorical cadence as the Apostles Creed or the Nicene Creed, but it explicitly repudiates and replaces the dogmatic claims enunciated in those ancient litanies. I don't recall Fenimore circulating it among us and the fact that he tucked it away in this obscure folder clearly suggests that he thought of it as little more than a sketch. Yet it has a completeness and economy to it that are striking and poetic. I confess that, when I first read it, I felt a kind of shiver run down my spine.

Like so much that we have discovered since Fenimore died, this private articulation of belief sat 'below the waterline' in terms of his published work. It is evident now that that published work, impressive though it was, can only be considered the tip of the iceberg of his thinking and his vision. By bringing it to the surface and finding a place for it in this book, I hope to provide something that we can all share and use as a reference point in the years to come. Certainly, it should not have been allowed to remain tucked away in an unpublished and perhaps unread folder. I believe that if you measure these twenty brief lines against the full body of his work and against the reflections in his Notebooks, you will agree with me that they are as clear and moving a distillation of what he held to be true as one could hope to find. Whether they can be propagated in the public sphere in the time to come, I am less certain. That is something for us to discuss in our colloquies in the summer.

The Credo does not, on the other hand, exist in isolation, even though it was left on its own in a plastic sleeve. It clearly was placed there by Fenimore because he saw a relationship between it and his work on Newman and Rahner. It is clear that, far from viewing either of them with hostility, he regarded each with great empathy. He shared many of their concerns and ideals. He did not share their Christian beliefs, but he devoted a lot of effort to trying to understand what they meant by those beliefs and how to make sense of the more obscure tenets of their creed. He had, after all, been raised a Catholic and educated by Jesuits, including a particularly gifted mentor in Father Polycarp Irons, who appears to have introduced him to the work of Rahner when he was still an adolescent.

Very early in the first of several essays on *Foundations of Christian Faith*, Fenimore underscores a passage from Rahner's book which seems to have been pivotal to what he was trying to grapple with:

> *For a Christian, his Christian existence is ultimately the totality of his existence. This totality opens out into the dark abysses of the wilderness which we call God. When one undertakes something like this, he stands before the great thinkers, the saints and finally Jesus Christ. The abyss of existence opens up in front of him. He knows that he has not thought enough, has not loved enough and has not suffered enough.*

The essay in question is titled 'The Abyss of Existence and the Wilderness of God'. Rejecting, step by step, the Biblical language of revelation, eschatology and salvation, Fenimore presses for a translation of Rahner's existential commitments into a transparent language fitted for the 21st century. At one point, he cites an aphorism from Nietzsche's *Human, All-Too-Human* about Christianity as a piece of musty antiquity, which concludes with the words, "…how gruesomely all this is wafted to us, as if out of the grave of a primeval past! Can one believe that things of this sort are still believed in?" His answer is that they will be clung to until something existentially more profound displaces them. His Credo has to be seen in this context I think.

Here it is, at least for our consideration and discussion:

Credo

I believe that all deities are idols of the mind,
That blood sacrifices to them are an abomination,
That dogmas are obstacles to enlightenment.
I believe in the plurality of worlds,
But know of none that can compare with ours
In its abundance of life
Of a kind that has arisen,
Through countless changes and catastrophes,
Out of the primal waters of the Earth
I acknowledge that I am of this world
Though a brief sojourner in it:
I have sprung from it and will pass back into it.
I recognize that my existence,
Both sentient body and sapient mind,
Is possible only within the natural order of things
Capable of mimesis, metaphor and music,
Of reason and responsibility,
I believe that I am neither fated nor predestined,
But am able to live for possibilities
And move intentionally toward a horizon that is open.

Appendix B: The Seven Songs of Queen Nefesh

The Tale of Raneb and Nefesh seems to have been made up by Fenimore in its initial form during or soon after he and Margarita travelled up the Nile in early 2008. But it was clearly revised more than once before he wrote it into Notebook III and we can see even from its finished form that he was still thinking of other possible twists and turns as he committed the tale to flawless penmanship. In particular, he had become ambivalent about who actually wrote the Songs of Queen Nefesh – was it Raneb or Urhotep, or was it actually Nefesh herself? When were they written in their final form? What was the motive behind them? Perhaps the thought that Nefesh wrote the songs – according to the account in her tomb in Sheba – was no more than a wry witticism to tickle Margarita's fancy? In any case, the songs themselves clearly did not exist at that time; or at least not in a form that he wished to include in the Notebook III.

We know that he had been studying Alter's *The Psalms* and that he had become deeply engaged by Glass's *Akhnaten*. But we also know that he was increasingly preoccupied by the question of his love for Margarita and its relationship to his work and his abode at Cos. Above all, however, what most clearly prompted him to write lyrics for these specific seven songs was reading Daniel Levitin's *The World in Six Songs: How the Musical Brain Created Human Nature*. Or rather, the fact that Margarita gave it to him as a gift in Cairo, during their sojourn in Egypt. I only realized this when I chanced upon Levitin's book in The Vivarium, while staying at Cos in early 2011, attempting to resolve my differences with Ariel Kurzweil and with Peripatetica. The annotations in the book, in Fenimore's inimitable hand, pointed clearly to the process of composition. What was electrifying, however, was the inscription inside the cover.

There, in a hand I had not seen before and which struck me at once because it so obviously was not Fenimore's, was a dedication in Spanish:

Yo quiero que escribas para mí
seis canciones del 'cerebro musical'
que evoquen

nuestra entrañable visita
a los Valles de los Reyes y las Reinas[65]

Margarita
Cairo
14 Abril 2008

---

65   *I would like you to write for me six songs of the 'musical brain' that evoke our entrancing visit to the*
     Valleys of the Kings and the Queens. - TCE

So she truly existed! Here she was expressing herself in just the manner one imagines from Fenimore's pages! They had been to the Valley of the Kings and the Valley of the Queens in Egypt and afterwards she had given him this book, which I was holding in my hands, with the request that he write for her "six songs of the musical brain" evoking their time together there! I am led to conclude, therefore, that he wrote these songs, giving them an Egyptian mythological setting, in response to her request. But perhaps he did not have them to hand when writing the second section of Notebook III. The internal evidence is somewhat unclear on this point. He could not, in any case, have included them within the octavo structure; so this alone would have kept them to one side.

Of course, there are seven songs, not six; which is a curious twist. I think it is explicable on one or more of several grounds. The six kinds of song that "created human nature", according to Levitin, are: songs of Friendship, Joy, Comfort, Knowledge, Religion and Love. He wrote a song under each of these rubrics. The seventh song Fenimore called 'The Song of Healing'. The simplest hypothesis would be that he wrote a seventh out of sheer playfulness, as if to show that Levitin's categories were a little arbitrary and could be added to or varied. As he himself hints, it could be that the idea arose from the mere fact that Scene 7 of *Akhnaten* and Scene 7 in *Out of Africa* prompted the writing of the Tale in the first place. Another possibility is that he preferred the number seven, with its many resonant associations and its primary quality to the number six. A third possibility is simply that, having written that the Necklace of Queen Nefesh had seven stones, he was stuck with the number seven and had to improvise. This third explanation perhaps has more power than the others simply because almost certainly the Tale was written before the songs and the necklace in the Tale has seven stones.

But why did he make his seventh song a song of *healing*? I think our clearest clue is that the song itself draws upon the myth of Osiris and Isis. As he explains in the Tale, this pair was the greatest mythic couple in Egyptian religious lore. Isis healed Osiris, bringing him back to life after he had been killed and dismembered by his treacherous brethren. Inside the Tale, Raneb is healed by Nefesh, after he is left for dead by Somali pirates and cast upon the shores of Sheba. Like Osiris and Isis, Raneb and Nefesh went on to rule Egypt and bring a new and higher civilization to it. It is impossible not to speculate about the autobiographical thread in the composition of the tale. Clearly inspired by his love for Margarita, it nonetheless places that love implicitly in the context of the Isis and Osiris myth at a crucial point in the relationship. Ironically, of course, Fenimore was to be torn apart precisely by his love for Margarita and his body went out to sea never to be recovered. All we have, in a manner of speaking, are his *membra disjecta* – the tale and the songs themselves.

In any case, I have saved the seven songs from oblivion – if only on account of that last poignant line in Notebook III - and print them here, along with a brief reflection on them, which Fenimore appears to have drafted as if to frame the songs for Margarita. It is written with a wry conceit as if the songs really had been composed in ancient Egypt, found on the walls of the Tomb of Urhotep and translated by Dionysus Theokopoulis, as in the Tale. There were quite a number of cases where words or whole lines had been crossed out and replaced. I have not attempted to set out the actual manuscript, which would be of little interest; but have simply reproduced, to the best of my ability, what seems to have been the last version Fenimore was able to write. It is quite possible that he was not satisfied with either the reflection or the songs, but they do seem to me to complement the Tale of Raneb and Nefesh rather nicely. I hope you will all agree and that we might even have a round of recitations at intervals – in our own 'Halls of the North', in the words of the Song of Joy. Here, then, are the Seven Songs of Queen Nefesh, accompanied by Fenimore's rather 'magical realist' commentary.

First Song: The Song of Friendship

O Seshat, whose mysteries form characters
O Thoth, whose stone this is
Sing through me and move my hand to make
An ode, an ode of Naqada
A song of the companionship
Between the divine Horus, your servant Raneb
He of the red crown and of the white
And his consort Nefesh
She who is breath and life
An ode, an ode of Naqada
An ode to the two companions
In the valley of the great river
Where they walk, O Seshat, under the eye
Under the outspread wings, O goddess
Of the falcon; the wings of the falcon

Second Song: The Song of Joy

Rejoice, rejoice, my beloved
In this day of days
For the harvest is ours and the garden of life
Even in Memphis; Memphis of the kings
In the Halls of the North
In the days of our youth and our love
Dance for me in the high room
O dance for me to my heart's delight
Beloved of my years
Rejoice, rejoice, my beloved
In this day of days
When Raneb, your hunter has returned
Like an arrow leaping from the bow
Out of the lands above the cataracts
To the place of our youth and our love

Third Song: The Song of Comfort

Lord Ptah, creator, master of those who make
Lord Ptah, high god of Memphis
O Ptah, spouse of Sekhmet
She of the fearful ravages
She, the lioness of the hunted day
Intercede with your beloved, O master
That she will spare our blood and our seed
O send us the priests of Sekhmet
Healers of the cankered flesh
The priests of Sekhmet, your beloved
She, the lioness of the hunted day
She of the fearful ravages
O Ptah, spouse of Sekhmet
Lord Ptah, high god of Memphis
Lord Ptah, creator, master of those who make

Fourth Song: The Song of Knowledge

Sing, Thoth, sage of the night sky
Sing of number and form
Sing of Atum, spirit of the pre-existent
Afloat in Nun, the primal sea
Sing of Neith of the seeded ocean
Sing of Ra and the coming of day
Sing, O Thoth, sage of the night sky
You, Thoth, keeper of the Hermetica, sing
Tell of Geb and the parting of waters
Tell of Nut and the wideness of the world
Tell, O Thoth, of those who are aloft
Over the formed and founded Earth
Tell of the Sia, the thought of Ra
Tell of Ma-at, the order of Pharaoh
Sing, Thoth, sage of the night sky

Fifth Song: The Song of Religion

Behold, Nebra, called Lord of the Sun
Does homage to the great god Ra
Raneb bows to the Sia of Ra
Bows to the wide horizon of his light
Let the temples ring with a new song
Let the cult of the bull
The cult of Apis, the bull god
Give way to the worship of Ra
The cult of Apis give way
Let blood give way to the great light
Let there be obeisance to Ra the Creator
Bow to Him who rises out of the Atum
Bow, all, before the Sia of Ra
Do homage to the great god Ra
In the name of Raneb, servant of Ra

Sixth Song: The Song of Love

Arise, my beautiful one, my lord Min
Arise as Horus, the falcon
Arise as Ra out of the sea
For I am Neith, goddess of the primal waters
Arise and come in to me, my lord Min
Arise, swift falcon, on wings of urgency
As the Sia of Ra, come unto me
For I am the companion of your heart
Who walked with you even over the ash
Even over the first lands
Who came up with you out of the south
In the day before days
In me is the salt and water of life
In me is the fullness of your desire
Arise, O my beautiful one, my lord Min

Seventh Song: The Song of Healing

I have healed you with my breath
With my hands and those of my sister Nepthys
Have I brought you back from the House of Death
For you are my beloved
You are my beloved, even from the womb
The womb of our mother the Sky
Seeded by our father the Earth
Therefore are you remembered
From the sarcophagus of Set
From the pillar in a pagan palace
From the shattering of your limbs
I have brought you back, with my hands
Isis has brought you back
With the perfume of her breath
For you are her beloved

Fenimore's unfinished note on the songs

These are the songs of Nefesh, as translated into English by Dionysus Theokopoulis. The first three are the moonstone songs, beginning with the Song of Friendship, which invokes Seshat, the goddess of writing and Thoth, the god of time, number and wisdom. Is it Urhotep's voice we hear in these lines, or that of Nefesh? Who can say, since each claimed to have authored the songs and now both their mouths, long since stopped with dust, are forever silent.

Who, in the Song of Friendship, is addressing; who addressed? It almost sounds as though these are the words of Raneb himself to Nefesh, perhaps after returning triumphantly from a great hunt among the wild fauna of the upper Nile. There is an indirect piece of evidence here that the songs – or at least this one – were composed sometime after Raneb had become Pharaoh, since it refers to looking back to 'the days of our youth and our love', as if these are seen as passing, though not perhaps yet passed beyond recall.

What made my heart leap, when I first read the Song of Joy, is the line about Raneb returning to Nefesh 'like an arrow leaping from the bow'. This reads like the reverse of Rilke's injunction that lovers should let each other go as the arrow leaps from the bow.[66] But of course, we now know, from the tale of Nefesh herself, that there was, in the end, no remaining; that she had her own destiny. Still, the joy here is unmistakable, even after the passing of five millennia. To think that the glories of Memphis, so vivid to the writer of the song, have vanished – except for a few evocative fragments like this!

------

66   It took me some time to trace this allusion to its source, but Fenimore seems here to be referring to the first of Rilke's *Duino Elegies*, where the poet wrote:

> *Isn't it time that in love we freed ourselves from the loved one and trembling endured as the arrow endures the string, collecting itself to be more than itself as it shoots? For there is no remaining, no place to stay.*

This passage, in any case, is underlined in his copy of David Young's bilingual edition of *Duino Elegies*. But what is striking is that, a German scholar of many years standing, he most heavily underscored the words in German: "Sollen nicht endlich uns diese ältesten Schmerzen fruchtbarer werden?" Young's translation of this sentence, which Fenimore did not bother to underline, is "Shouldn't these ancient sufferings of ours finally start to bear fruit." That line seems to have made a deep impression on him, but it isn't clear when he read and underlined it. I could not help, however, finding in all this a hint that Fenimore longed very much for a "remaining and a place to stay" with Margarita. – TCE.

The third moonstone song, the Song of Comfort, is an appeal to Ptah, the chief deity of Memphis in the time of Raneb. Ptah's spouse, Sekhmet, was the goddess of plagues and diseases. Physicians were known as 'the priests of Sekhmet' and this song, Theokopoulis points out in his learned commentary, calls upon Ptah to intercede with his fearful spouse and send healers, not diseases to the land of Egypt. The names of the gods have changed over the millennia, but this has always been part of their role in the human imagination – warding off disease.

Epidemic disease blighted human civilization from the time of the earliest agrarian cultures, right up into the nineteenth century. Our respite from such epidemics is under pressure. The microbes are fighting back. We know from the famous stories in *Exodus*, about the plagues of Egypt, which so afflicted the Pharaoh's kingdom that he agreed to let Moses and his people go. That tale is set about one thousand six hundred years after the time of Raneb and Nefesh, but already in their time it is clear that plagues afflicted the most civilized parts of the human world.

The three lapis lazuli songs are the Songs of Knowledge, Religion and Love. The Song of Knowledge again invokes Thoth, whom the Greeks would later call Hermes. As Theokopoulis notes, 'Hermetic' lore would be passed down through the books and councils of the erudite, via Greek commentators and the Church Fathers, such as Clement of Alexandria, to the mythology of the secret societies of the modern world: the Rosicrucians, the Illuminati, and the Freemasons.

Urhotep stands early in this tradition and looks back, already, on an immemorial past. Indeed, he is so much earlier than any other source for Hermetic lore that the articulation of these ideas in his songs, if they are his, is a source of profound wonder. As Theokopoulis exclaimed, in his best known essay on the subject, finding this lyric on the wall of Urhotep's tomb was rather like finding 100,000 year old ochre painting materials in the Blombos Cave, in South Africa, recently. Both discoveries force us to radically reassess long standing assumptions about the antiquity of human insight and art, respectively.

It is remarkable, for example, to see – or, as it were, hear – a 29th century BCE Egyptian poet or Pharaoh (or Queen of Arabian origin) evoking 'number and form', or 'the spirit of the pre-existent'. We tend to think of such abstraction coming only with Pythagoras and the Pre-Socrates, or even with Plato, two and a half thousand years later. Yet we know that Imhotep, some two hundred years after Urhotep, was a great architect and, by all accounts, a great sage more generally. He designed and oversaw the building of the fantastic Step Pyramid of the Pharaoh Djoser, with its immense, elaborate and lavishly colored enclosure – now so mournful a ruin, as we saw at Saqqara. And Imhotep was accounted a learned sage, also.

Theokopoulis's commentaries help to illuminate a little of what the Song of Knowledge means. He tells us who Atum, Nun, Neith, Ra, Geb, Nut, Sia and Ma'at were, in their time. Of these gods, the key ones, he observes, are Atum, Ra and Sia. Atum was the god of pre-existence, floating in Nun, the primeval ocean. This is a brilliant, intuitive insight on someone's part; surely not original to Urhotep, but perhaps going back into the forgotten and unrecorded millennia of Egyptian history, even before the Red and White Crowns were united. It carries over, thousands of years later into metaphysical ideas of a "God" who is wholly prior to the material world and constituted its First Cause by some act of creative will.

This was Atum, the mystery of pre-existence. Then life arose in Nun, the primal sea. Ra, the sun god, was the creator of the world. Sia, the 'thought of Ra' comes closest to what the Greeks and their Christian adepts, two and three thousand years later, would call the *Logos* – the Word or Mind of God. It's a curious word, *Logos*. It can be translated several different ways, with quite strikingly different implications. It has traditionally (as in the King James Bible) been rendered 'the Word'. But it can mean 'reason', 'discourse' or 'thinking', whence theology (reasoning about the gods), dialogue (discourse between two) or biology (thinking about the nature of life).

I'm playing Glass's *Akhnaten* all over again as I write this down for you. I've also been reading John Richardson's *Singing Archaeology*, a study of Glass's opera and its relationship to the archaeology of the greatest and most uncanny religious reformer in Egyptian history. Remember how, during our visit to the ruins of Tell el-Amarna, we murmured to one another, looking out over the Egyptian desert, about the boldness of Akhnaten's attempt to overthrow the pantheon of traditional gods in the name of a new monotheism and how, when he died, the old priesthoods reasserted their power and destroyed his vision and his city?.

Who would ever have thought that a far earlier Pharaoh, Raneb, as long before Akhnaten as Akhnaten was before Jesus of Nazareth – more than fourteen centuries – could already have pushed for such reforms!? Yet the Song of Religion, the second lapis lazuli song, celebrates religious reforms wrought by Nebra when he became Pharaoh, just before 2800 BCE and declares his name change from Nebra to Raneb – servant of Ra. 'Let the temples ring with a new song', the poet writes – almost five thousand years ago, at the dawn of what we think of as 'recorded history'!

But the following lines sent shivers down my spine:

> *Let the cult of the bull,*
> *The cult of Apis, the bull god,*
> *Give way to the worship of Ra.*
> *The cult of Apis give way!*
> *Let blood give way to the great light.*

This is the song of Nebra's religious conversion from the bull cult and blood sacrifices to recognition of Ra and the 'great light'; but as I read them in the Theokopoulis translation, I couldn't help sensing a spine-tingling link between these supremely ancient lyrics and my own song for you about the slaying of the Minotaur in the Labyrinth at Knossos and even more wonderfully the opening lines of my credo:

> *I believe that all deities are idols of the mind*
> *That blood sacrifices to them are an abomination*
> *And that dogmas are obstacles to enlightenment*

It seems hardly credible that such affinities should extend over so many thousands of years, despite all the idolatries, violence and follies that have come between. Yet we should remind ourselves that five thousand years is actually only a short period of time, even in the annals of human evolution, to say nothing of the evolution of the brain and the eye over so many hundreds of millions of years. True insight runs very deep.

The sixth song, the Song of Love, clearly appears to be the voice of Nefesh addressing Raneb as her beloved. It has something in it, Theokopoulis goes so far as to say, of the Biblical Song of Songs, so long attributed to Solomon, but almost certainly written by a woman. It seems almost flagrantly; how shall one put it, not so much phallocentric as *phallocantical*, to coin a word. It is as if Nefesh is seeking to sing Raneb to arousal. Hers is the love not only of Raneb as a partner, but of life itself and the mysterious carnal processes of its renewal.

Theokopoulis writes that the meaning of the lines about walking over the ash and over the first lands is uncertain, but that he has provided a literal translation. He surmises that 'first lands' may mean the lands of pre-Dynastic Upper Egypt and that the ash in question may be an allusion to the wars of conquest, but allows that we cannot know what else they might be referring to. The following line about coming up out of the south, he comments, may allude to the way in which Nefesh and Raneb came up the Red Sea from Sheba; but this would seemingly be at odds with the interpretation he has provided of the preceding lines.

We can't be sure what the original author might have had in mind, but when I read the lines:

For I am the companion of your heart
Who walked with you even over the ash
Even over the first lands
Who came up with you out of the south
In the day before days

I am irresistibly reminded of the ancient foot prints in the fossilized volcanic ash at Laetoli and of the deep past of human evolution. Obviously, no-one in the 29th century BCE had the first idea about human evolution or the scientific ability to find and date foot prints from 3.6 million years ago. Yet 'over the ash', 'first lands' and 'out of the south', when read in this song almost make my hair stand on end. It reminds me of the poem I wrote for you called 'Fire and the Wheel' and enables me to feel an uncanny connection with civilized minds going back thousands of years.

But what was the music that went with these seven songs? On what instruments would they have been played? This we don't know, but this is, I suspect, what you would most like to know. Theokopoulis remarked, in a short academic note on the subject some years ago, that:

Given the astonishing series of discoveries over a number of decades that have brought this wonderful story to light out of the sands of time, we cannot exclude the possibility that the future will yield an even more remarkable find: instruments and some guide to their use in association with ancient songs of this kind and even – but this would be miraculous – with reference to these very songs themselves. For the present, however, all we can do is exclude certain possibilities, based on what little is known of music in that remote epoch – and perhaps compose our own music to go with the lyrics we have stumbled upon in the exotic tombs of the royal couple and their poet.

I say remote, because we all tend to think of the 29th century BCE as "remote". Yet we now know that the use of drums and flutes dates back at least tens of thousands of years and that human beings have probably been 'singing' in some sense for hundreds of thousands of years. We should remind ourselves, also, that the 29th century BCE was not – in the minds of those who lived at that time – an "early" epoch in history. That is merely our perspective, looking back. Agrarian and even urban civilization had existed in the Nile Valley and across much of the Near East by then for at least seven thousand years and even longer. And the human use of music was far older than that.

Perhaps we could create music to bring these ancient, romantic songs to life...Biblical psalm settings – breath of Isis/breath = Nefesh (breath of life = 'soul'/psyche/Psyche)... Solo voice and choir? Chant?[67]

---

67   The manuscript is very incomplete at this point. Fenimore seems to have jotted down a few ideas, but never got around to further developing them. – TCE

The Song of Healing, as it was named by Urhotep himself, in the finest, most delicate hieroglyphs on the gold base of the Stone of H...Osiris Stone - - song of the pearl... invokes myth of Isis and Osiris...[68]

---

68   This is where the hand written manuscript that I found in the Alter folder ends, apparently in mid-sentence. There is no date on the pages, but we can infer from internal evidence that all this must have been written not only subsequent to the tour of Egypt by Fenimore and Margarita in April 2008, but subsequent to his writing of the fair copy of the Tale of Raneb and Nefesh in Notebook III. Notebook III, however, was not commenced until early 2009 and it seems doubtful that he would have left the songs and notes unfinished had he begun them before or while writing the Tale. Given how much was written in Notebook III after the Tale (Section ii) and that Fenimore can hardly have written this during either the month he was abroad, in April 2010, or the six weeks after he returned, that means the songs themselves and the notes must have been written somewhere in the twelve months between early 2009 and early 2010 and almost certainly in the latter part of 2009. We know that he had been working on the Alter commentary before Cardinal Bolzano visited in July 2009, since he mentions this, but there is no evidence that composition of the songs had begun at that point. For what it is worth, I suspect he intended this composition as a stand-alone gift for Margarita in October 2009, but halted when she aborted that meeting and never got back to the project before she broke off their secret relationship at Buenos Aires, in April 2010. - TCE

Appendix C: The poems and songs for Margarita

Among the many tasks that fell to me in preparing this volume and putting Fenimore's papers in order, was that of seeing the relationship between the crafted prose of the Notebooks and the poems and songs created, it seems, alongside them, more especially the second and third of them. From internal evidence in the Notebooks themselves, it was clear that he had been composing verse with growing frequency in an attempt to give what he came to see as a more musical expression to his thoughts and feelings. He never included these in the Notebooks, however, because – so far as I can deduce – he believed that they would remain too open to revision. The prose he annealed before committing it to the page and wrote out in that practised, stylized longhand of his. The prosody he seems to have felt would throw out the symmetry and rhythm of the prose; would possibly want reworking and should, therefore, be kept to one side.

Nor were the poems collected in any one place. They plainly were not composed in a premeditated sequence or intended to form a closed set. Rather, they were found within the interstices of Fenimore's thinking as he both worked on his treatise and crafted his Notebooks. The first, for instance, 'We Karyotes', appears to have been a quite whimsical composition that occurred unbidden while he was deeply immersed in thinking through and studying the science of the origins of life on Earth, the slow evolution of single-celled life-forms, long ago; and the terraforming of the Earth by the oxygen given off by the earliest single-celled beings. I discovered it by chance among his papers on that subject. Others seem to have been written episodically, as various stimuli prompted him and not as part of any overall design. On the other hand, it is striking that there is a closer and closer thematic and substantive congruence between the verse and the entries in the Notebooks the further the latter progress.

The connecting thread is the fact that more and more of the poems, like the Notebooks themselves, implicitly address Margarita or reflect on the nature and possibilities of love and intimacy. What remains puzzling is that, while he seems to have intended to give the Notebooks to Margarita as a gift once he had finished both them and his treatise, it isn't clear what he intended to do with the poems. Perhaps he intended to do likewise with them; perhaps he shared some of them with her when they met, without leaving a record of this. Or perhaps he remained undecided at the point when she broke off the relationship and his hopes deserted him. In any case, they are here brought together in a sequence and between two covers for the first time. They are numbered and arranged, as far as I was able to discern this, in the order of their composition. In a number of cases, there are clear and quite strong parallels between the Notebooks and the poems. Assuming that you read the poems after having read the Notebooks at least once, you will see these consonances.

If the poems that I have gathered together here are added to the seven songs of Queen Nefesh, which seem to have constituted a project in their own right; there are 42 in all. This is a not a large number of poems for a poet to have left; but Fenimore was not, of course, a poet in the conventional sense. While we knew him to appreciate poetry, we all knew him and thought of him primarily as a master of reasoning and the history of the sciences. Had there been a larger volume of verse, it would not have made sense to include it within these covers. Since, however, all of them were plainly written in the same meditative and creative mood that had him create his Notebooks and since, like them, they constitute a reflection on the meaning of life and of human life in particular, it seemed to me that they have a natural place as companions to his reflections in prose. They are, perhaps even more than the Notebooks themselves, a cry from the heart that tells us most about who Fenimore truly was. Insufficient to form a book on their own, they are a fitting complement to the book that we now have as a *memento mori*.

1
We Karyotes

How would life be?
Would it still be erotic,
Had it made you and me
Simply prokaryotic?

Not very, I'd say –
Endless self-replication;
No cellular play
To exchange information

So, second my motion
As life bobs and floats
On the Archaean Ocean,
"We're eukaryotes!"

Will you carry oats,
If they come from me,
As we play wild motes
On a billion year spree?

I'd love some from eu,
If eu sent them my way,
To refresh and renew
My own DNA.

We Karyotes

This poem may be unique among love poems in casting the lover and his beloved in the role of single-celled organisms some billions of years ago and imagining this as conferring creativity and exuberant freedom. Its keynote, of course, is the idea that the ability to exchange information, to communicate, to cross-fertilize makes a world of difference to our lives. This was a theme that went deep into the heart of Fenimore's great project in life – the clarification of information and communication between human beings about what is the case. It was also, as we now know, at the very centre of his most intimate and private reflections on what it means to love and to be with another in the world. In each domain, he was troubled by doubts about what is even possible, but in both cases he was committed to pressing the inquiry forward with the utmost integrity. This book and these poems are his testament. – TCE.

2.

Nutcracker Man

Paranthropa went looking for Nutcracker Man,
Boisei, in the Oldowan Woods;
She hadn't in mind a particular plan;
Just to get him to give her the goods.

Her Nutcracker man, a promising youth,
Sat gazing aloft at the Sun,
Delighted and even astonished, in truth,
On account of the thing he had done.

She found him, at last, by the Olduvai stream
She cooed to him sitting alone
He turned to her slowly, as if in a dream
And showed her a curious stone

"I can see", Paranthropa then teasingly laughed,
"That I've caught you down here again knapping!
I admire, I suppose, your neat handicraft,
But you should be out hunting and trapping!"

Boisei was cut and, in some disbelief,
Exclaimed, "Oh, you're clueless, by Jimbo!
You'd be more impressed by my almond-shaped leaf
If you weren't such a Palaeobimbo!

I had thought that the genius of my chips and cuts
Would light up your mind and connect us;
But I see all you want is fresh meat and rich nuts.
Well, look here, I'm now Homo erectus!"

Nutcracker Man.

Like 'We Karyotes', this is a funny poem, written with a wry and whimsical sense of humour. Yet it expresses an ultimately pessimistic sense that intellectual and artistic creativity are undervalued; their deeper significance and the potential for further development that they embody unappreciated by the 'practical' and 'down to earth'. It reads like a mocking rebuke to an imagined female companion who sees even very basic worldly goods or wealth as more impressive and important than the spark of genius and the longing to remake what is inherited or 'given'. It's hard to believe that such mockery was directed at Margarita, though perhaps that was a passing mood Fenimore experienced at some point in their relationship.

It might, on the other hand, have derived its inspiration precisely from the fact that many women other than Margarita are like Paranthropa. The brief recollection in Notebook I of the abortive romance between Fenimore and Nathalie Morton in 1983-84 could be a clue to the ultimate inspiration for the poem. I remember Nathalie, although dimly, after all these years. Fenimore was deeply wounded by her decision to break off the relationship because of his desire to study philosophy. It's tantalizing to consider that his feelings about what he saw as her philistinism and superficiality all those years ago may have surfaced, twenty years later, in this wry little poem. What we don't know is whether he ever shared it with Margarita. I would like to think that he did so and that they enjoyed a good laugh at its witty barbs. How could either of them have known that she would never get to see his exquisite hand axe – the leather-bound notebooks he spent so much labour and creative intentionality in 'knapping' for her alone. – TCE.

3.

After the Ice

This book, my love, will take your mind
Down many roads, into the past
Allow it to and you will find
How wonderful and truly vast
The Ages were before our own:
The Age of Ice, which slowly warmed,
The immemorial Age of Stone,
When first our arts and dreams were formed.

Our arts? The ways we symbolize
The patterns that we seek and find,
With sapient, exploring eyes,
Our questing and uncanny kind
Our dreams? Our visions and our cares;
The metaphors we make our own;
Upon which, as on unseen stairs,
Our minds ascend by thought alone.

Immerse yourself in Mithen's pages,
Leaving mythic tales behind
Explore the world's defining Ages;
Learn the truth about our kind.
For truth you'll need and insight deep
To comprehend our world in time
And, to that end, I hope you'll keep
This weighty tome and simple rhyme

After the Ice.

This poem seems certainly to have been written for and given to Margarita by Fenimore, along with a copy of Steven Mithen's *After the Ice: A Global Human History 20,000-5,000 BC* (Weidenfeld & Nicolson, London, 2003). The internal evidence of the poem alone suggests this; but tantalizingly, there is other evidence as well. We know from Notebook II that, in April 2007, Fenimore and Margarita visited Paris and Berlin together. Fenimore was in Paris for a conference on linguistics, archaeology and the origins of the Indo-European languages. His notes from that conference have survived. It's clear that among the things he was most taken by during the proceedings was the work of David Anthony, whose path-breaking book *The Horse, the Wheel and Language* was published by Princeton University Press that year.

Fenimore had received an advance copy and read it very closely, making detailed notes before flying to Paris. In seeking among Fenimore's papers for materials that might throw more light on his assignations abroad with Margarita, I came across the Paris conference papers and his notes. It was among them, scribbled on the back of a page of notes summarizing David Anthony's thoughts on 'How to Reconstruct a Dead Language', that I discovered a hand written draft of 'After the Ice' with the personal notation 'pour M demain' (for M tomorrow). The M has to mean Margarita, but he can hardly have meant 'tomorrow' at the time he was making the notes. My surmise is that he had the notes with him at the conference and was going over them the day before he met up with her and the poem came to him in the wake of the conference. Alternatively, since we know (from the poem as well as the Notebooks) that he gave her a copy of the book, he may have written the poem earlier, but have been re-reading it the day before he met her and scribbled the little notation on that occasion. – TCF.

4

Fire and the Wheel

I've loved you from the beginning,
With the simplest of gestures;
With inarticulate cries;
With unself-conscious mimicry

I've loved you since the first fire-wielding,
When we yelled together at encircling beasts;
Feasted on fire-roasted insects and nuts;
Huddled round the flames in awe

Was that Eden, that long ago aeon;
As the hand formed and the inner eye,
The larynx and Broca's brain;
Before ever we sang to one another?

Or was Eden the time of hand-axes,
As all this came together
In our hearths and hunting
From old Andalusia to the Chinese rivers?

What years those were of wide-exploring!
Eurasia was ours with new spears!
Exulting in our uncanny craft,
We wondered at what we were.

Our long days fell like forest leaves;
They endured like evergreens.
Our fire-circles lit the long nights;
Changing our dreams

Were those shimmering years,
Those many hundred millennia
Before our love made music,
Truly our Golden Age?

Did you feel loved then,
As the wide seas rose and fell?
As the ice advanced and retreated?
As the giant forests shifted, again and again?

Or was it only later, only later
That sentiment came and crooning;
Coaxed by oxytocin out of the flicker
Of long light under the waxing Moon?

Was I a caricature to your mind
Of all that was possible – possible –
For a singing hominid under the Sun?
Was I stone in need of shaping?

Ah! We buried each other many times,
Again and again with grief and ochre,
Over ages under the ageless stars,
From Jebel Qafzeh to Beringia.

Remember the times, sheltered from
The harsh climate shift in the north,
When we relished our little piece of Africa
In Andalusia? Those idyllic coasts and caves?

But your love transformed me:
Your call for songs and stories;
Your playing to me on bone flutes;
Your vivid art of changing forms.

We shook the shackles of the ancient trees,
Hailed the Sky God with high hands;
We took to the open horizon;
Pitched bold camp on the stark steppe.

There, at last, you carved me into shape!
Your love cut antler into a figurine;
And I, deer hunter, roamed forth Gravettian,
Making long lasting legends on the plains.

You wove me a coat of wool,
Dyed in wondrous new colours,
Finer than any cured skin and
I revelled in your homespun beauty.

Even that was a long age of ardour
Under the high wheeling stars;
Rich with rumour of far mountains,
With mammoth hunts and possibilities.

Then the revolution came at last: the Wheel,
The mastery and mustering of horses,
The making of wains and war chariots,
The being of bright burnished bronze.

Ah, sky gods! The Wheel and the horse
Brought an end to our long cycles!
Ah! My lover with golden hair,
The Wheel set us rolling, riding, racing

In the chariot of the Sun, did it not?
Since then, everything has gone in a flash:
A riotous blur of songs and innovations;
A nightmare of blood and terror.

I've loved you from the beginning.
Let's not now go under the Wheel.
All our myths are confused.
I long only for your beauty.

Fire and the Wheel.

I have juxtaposed this poem with 'After the Ice' because they seem to have a certain thematic kinship, but dating 'Fire and the Wheel' has proven problematic. Some elements of it, especially the last few stanzas, appear to be inspired by David Anthony's work, but that means little more than that the poem was probably written sometime after Fenimore read _The Horse, the Wheel and Language_, in early 2007. The opening stanzas, on the other hand, when I went looking for possible sources, came to appear as though they had been inspired by a remarkable book by Frances D. Burton called _Fire: The Spark That Ignited Human Evolution_, which was not published until 2009. There seem, also, to be echoes in a number of stanzas of Clive Finlayson's _The Humans Who Went Extinct: Why Neanderthals Died Out and we Survived_, also not published until 2009. I found both these books in the Vivarium, read and annotated in Fenimore's usual fashion. The poem may, therefore, have been written as late as the end of 2009. Yet there is nothing in Fenimore's marginalia in either book that points to the poem and his reading has always been so wide that we cannot exclude the possibility that he wrote the poem before reading either book and that they only look like his sources (for a few of the poem's many ideas) in retrospect. - TCE

5.

Circles in the Dust

You went under the wheel, Archimedes;
Pondering spheres and a theory of gravity;
Absorbed in the beauties of geometry;
Drawing fine circles in the dust.

Did you forget yourself, old man?
How could you think that a Latin sword,
Fired with rage at your machines
Would be withheld from your circles?

Or had you given up on the City,
Now swarming with the legions of Marcellus?
Had you given yourself over to pure thought –
Drawing those perfect circles in the dust?

You'd made mockery of Rome's big ships
And elaborately prepared siege engines:
With your artillery and hydraulic tricks,
You used its vessels to ladle the sea into your wine-cups.

You transcended the factions of Syracuse;
In the chaos of the Punic War;
Your mind was elsewhere, deep thinker;
Divining the workings of the real world.

Had you high hopes of Alexandria at that point?
Remembering conversations with Ctesibius,
Knowing the catalogues of Callimachus;
Reckoning with Aristarchus regarding the Sun?

You went under the wheel, Archimedes;
Pondering spheres and a theory of gravity;
Absorbed in the beauties of geometry;
Drawing fine circles in the dust.

Circles in the Dust.

'Circles in the Dust', as a meditation on the fate of the thinker, is almost a companion piece for 'Nutcracker Man' and their juxtaposition is a neat illustration of Fenimore's acute appreciation of the remarkable progress made by human ingenuity between the first finely knapped hand axes and the engineering feats and revolutionary conceptual daring of the Hellenistic scientists in the age of Archimedes. Yet rather than celebrate the brilliance of Archimedes, we find him brooding with a kind of worldly sense of fatalistic irony on the manner of Archimedes' death. If Fenimore himself were still alive and we read this poem, we would, I suspect, treat it in a rather detached way, as not much more than a reflection drawing upon the antiquities section of the Vivarium. Fenimore's own death, however, lends the poem (and a number of others on similar themes, as we shall see) a haunting and disturbing character. It is as if Fenimore had anticipated being cut down himself, or at least felt compelled to ponder such a possibility, and put himself in the dust there with the ill-fated Archimedes.

The classical sources for the poem are well known: Polybius, in his history of the rise of the Roman Empire, Livy in *The War with Hannibal* (which only very briefly touches on the episode) and Plutarch in his *Life of Marcellus*. Here is Livy's summary of what happened, drawing on earlier extant accounts, as he notes: "The city was turned over to the troops to pillage as they pleased, after guards had been set at the houses of the exiles who had been in the Roman lines. Many brutalities were committed in hot blood and the greed of gain, and it is on record that Archimedes, while intent upon figures which he had traced in the dust, and regardless of the hideous uproar of an army let loose to ravage and despoil a captured city, was killed by a soldier who did not know who he was. Marcellus was distressed by this; he had him properly buried and his relatives inquired for – to whom the name and memory of Archimedes were an honour and protection."

However, it became clear to me in the course of my researches that the classical sources were only deep background material for the poem. The immediate inspiration for writing it was a book published in English in 2004 by Springer, Lucio Russo's *The Forgotten Revolution: How Science was Born in 300 BC and Why It Had to Be Reborn*. Fenimore was enormously impressed by Russo's book and corresponded with Russo about the core argument in the book, which was very close to his own abiding concerns even in his own first two books: the relationship between science and civilization and the conditions under which a scientific culture comes into being or decays. There seems to me to be no doubt that, in writing this poem, perhaps as early as 2004, when he read Russo's book, Fenimore saw the death of Archimedes as symbolic of the death of Hellenistic science as Russo describes it:

Starting with the year 212 BC, which witnessed the plunder of Syracuse and the killing of Archimedes; Hellenistic centres were defeated and conquered by the Romans. During the second century BC, scientific studies declined rapidly. Alexandria's scientific activity, in particular, stopped abruptly in 145-44 BC, when Ptolemy VIII (Euergetes II), who had just ascended the throne, initiated a policy of brutal persecution against the city's Greek ruling class. Polybius says that the Greek population of Alexandria was almost entirely destroyed at that time; Athenaeus gives a lively description of the subsequent diaspora of the city's intellectuals; other sources give a few more details. Our information is not enough to reconstruct the causes of the persecution.

Since Fenimore covers some of this history in Notebook II, there is no need to enlarge upon it here. It does seem, however, as though 'Circles in the Dust', whether it was written on reading Russo or several years later, was a meditation by Fenimore on the fact that the untimely death of Archimedes was only the beginning of a violent assault on the whole circle of advanced thinkers of whom Archimedes had been prominent; an assault that had deep and long lasting consequences. – TCE.

6.

Lucullus to Clodia

I've built a house upon a hill –
The Pincian over Rome.
It's aspect's great and, if you will,
We'll make it our sweet home.

It's really quite a marvellous place,
With statues in the garden;
With trees and nymphs and lots of space
And patios and, pardon,

A library you'll not believe:
The finest books in Greek;
All catalogued. We can retrieve
Our choice and softly speak

Of any poet we desire
Within a leafy arbour;
Til, stirred by an Aeolian lyre,
The longings that we harbour

Can issue in unbridled passion,
Upon the upper floors;
Where, in the most exotic fashion,
We'll recline behind closed doors.

I know you've other interests, lass,
Like gambolling and drinking;
But aren't these just a little crass?
Is it not time for thinking

Of all the subtler things in life
And all that we might share
Were you to play my Pincian wife?
Come see. The house is there!

Lucullus to Clodia.

It's very difficult not to sense a little autobiography in this poem, with Fenimore longing to have Margarita join him at Cos in an open and conjugal relationship. Yet it would be an error, I think, to read too simple and straightforward a meaning into it in this way. Fenimore no doubt delighted in comparing Cos with the famous Gardens of Lucullus on the Pincian Hill in (originally just outside of) ancient Rome, during the late Republic. Lucullus had established the most fabulous library ever built up to that time in Rome and was known to be fluent in Greek and to have made the acquaintance of Greek scholars in Alexandria and elsewhere in the East during his wars. Clodia, on the other hand, was a notorious woman whom Lucullus was foolish ever to have married. It beggars belief that Fenimore would have written this with Margarita in mind, except, perhaps with the idea of teasing or amusing her.

7.

Cave and Woman

Your tousled gold emotions,
White breasts and active thighs;
Your tongue's unfeigned devotions,
The fervor in your eyes

Have summoned forth my darkened heart
From deep within its cave,
Where it had painted ochre art
Depicting it as brave.

It chanted long its lonely song
And dwelt beneath the ground
Where ghosts of night and mourning throng
And hope cannot be found;

But somehow, down from unguessed light,
Your laughing passion thrown
Has cast to me a line of sight
To love that I might own.

So kiss me, kiss me, soft as breath
Beside the ancient stream.
Withheld by you from senseless death,
I live once more and dream.

Cave and Woman.

This is a disconcerting poem, since it is difficult to relate it to what we know of Fenimore's life. The most sense I can make of it is that, until Margarita appeared in his life, love had somehow always disappointed him, but she lit up his horizon in a new way. The idea, however, that he had been living a darkened life in some kind of emotional cave before that, or that her love was saving him 'from senseless death' is exceptionally difficult to place biographically. The Fenimore we knew was full of energy and purpose and gathered people around him in constructive undertakings. The terrible irony, of course, is that, in the end, it was precisely a kind of "senseless death" that Margarita seems to have pitched first Fenimore and then herself into by withdrawing her "laughing passion". It might be possible to argue that the poem should not be read autobiographically, but only as an aesthetic contrivance. Nonetheless, given the way things played out, this poem, like a number of the others, makes an unsettling impression. – TCE.

8.

Invocation

Ometeotl, Lord of the Close Vicinity,
See that the Fifth Sun has drunk deeply today
Of chalchihuatl, the elixir of life,
And will shine out in the darkness.

Invocation.

This is the briefest of all the poems and plainly, like the next few, derives from Fenimore's work on the Tale of Manntezuma. That fable dwells chiefly on matters of history, archaeology and humanity; but the poems point to Fenimore's underlying interest in the theology of Meso-American religion before the Conquest and the strangeness of mutually uncomprehending cosmologies, with their different logics of sacrifice. Characteristically, he has no difficulty in feeling and exhibiting empathy while withholding belief. – TCE.

9.

Aztec Verses

He goes his way singing, offering flowers
And his words rain down
Like jade and quetzal plumes.
Is this what pleases the Giver of Life?
Is that the only truth on Earth?

From whence come the flowers that enrapture man;
The songs that intoxicate, the lovely songs?
Only from Ometeotl's home do they come,
From the innermost part of heaven

Not forever on earth; only a little while here.
Be it jade, it shatters.
Be it gold, it breaks.
Be it a quetzal feather, it tears apart.
Not forever on earth, only a little while here.

Like a painting, we will be erased.
Like a flower, we will dry up here on earth.
Like plumed vestments of the precious bird,
That precious bird with the agile neck,
We will come to an end.

10.

Hymn to Ometeotl

Ometeotl, Cosmic King,
To you, Great God, these gifts we bring:
These hearts that beat with chalchihuatl,
Won for you in faithful battle

Lord, who rules beyond the sky,
Accept them, on your altar high,
As offerings that will feed the Sun,
Lest light and order be undone

Since time began, before the stars,
The strife between your sons that mars
The beauty of the truth you know
Has cast in tumult all below

As each, in turn, has quenched the light,
In reckless and remorseless fight,
With only intervals of peace,
In which one rules and warrings cease.

In Huitzilopochtli's strong domain,
We flourish, Lord, and will remain
The servants of the bright Fifth Sun
And nourish it, as must be done.

For sacred hearts in copal burned,
Sustain that Sun. Your priests have learned;
That this high ritual must not falter,
Here upon the highest altar.

Hymn to Ometeotl.

Read in the context of the Tale of Manntezuma, this is an intriguing composition on Fenimore's part. It projects the imagination of the reader empathically into the mental world of the Aztec priests making their human sacrifices on the pinnacle of the great temple pyramid in Tenochtitlan. But for our small circle, the poem has a unique resonance. It's final line echoes the title of Patrick Tierney's book *The Highest Altar: The Story of Human Sacrifice* (Bloomsbury, 1989), which you will all recall was the reading and subject matter for our winter solstice soiree at the end of that memorable year; a soiree held, as I recall, at Irad's place as a farewell to him, before he headed off to New York to test his MIT credentials working for Bankers Trust. The Soviet bloc had been tumbling down and we were all attuned to the unfolding rebellion within Romania that was, a few days later, to climax with the overthrow and execution of Nicolae Ceausescu.

There is no doubt in my mind that, when he wrote this poem, Fenimore was thinking deeply about the need for an authentic cosmology able at once to engage the imaginations of human beings and to displace the many ancient cosmologies that, like the Aztec cosmology, exhibit a floundering human effort to comprehend our place in the cosmos and come up with religious rituals of a dark and destructive nature, the intent of which is to somehow 'align the stars' or 'appease the wrath of the gods', as in this case. Such thinking was at the centre of his most serious work, including his critical analysis of the ritual and cosmological basis of the Biblical religions. Yet, at the same time, he never repudiated the idea of 'sacrifice' as a human gesture and it is difficult not to see this mystique of sacrifice at work, also, in this poem – especially given what happened to Fenimore and Margarita well after it was written. – TCE.

11.

Manntezuma's Farewell

I will descend the steep and sacred stair
In peace of heart and meditated prayer;
With open eyes I'll go to meet my fate;
But you, since now the hour is late,
Must bravely venture over there
To enter yonder dark and bloody gate.

Manntezuma's Farewell.

As in several of the fables he invented within the Notebooks, Fenimore dances here with the grimmest and most apocalyptic realities without losing his sense of grace or balance. Manntezuma foresees the catastrophe that is about to descend upon his world, but far from sending his interlocutors back to a safe and cheerful abode, he points to the sacrificial chamber as to the gate to Dante's *Inferno* and tells them that that is where they are destined to go. As the fable makes clear, Fenimore clearly did have Dante in mind and this puts the whole idea of passing through the *Inferno* in a different light. – TCE.

12.

Dance me on down from Toledo

Come and dance with me down from Toledo,
By the light on the bridge we have made;
To a land with a non-Christian credo,
Where flamencos and tangos are played

Dance me speechless to high, snow-capped mountains
From which orchards and pastures are fed,
Then the cypresses, arches and fountains
Of Alhambra, the Isle of the Dead.

There the rich Andalusian muses
Sing softly to all who can hear,
Though a pallid, blue past still confuses
The mind and the heart and the ear.

For vengeful and dark Catholic violence
Five centuries since overthrew
And condemned to the grave or to silence
The voice of the Moor and the Jew.

But dance with me down from Toledo,
By the light on the bridge we have made;
To a land with a non-Christian credo,
Where flamencos and tangos are played.

Though golden al-Andalus perished,
Suppressed by the scepter and cross;
The ballads and songs Gypsies cherished
Plucked songlines from ruinous loss.

The spirit of Araby lingers
In the genius of Spanish guitar;
In flamencos for feet and for fingers;
In Tarrega and in Falla

Those flamencos and songlines in flower,
The soul of Granada reborn,
So offended the fascists in power
That they murdered poor Lorca at dawn

Still, dance with me, down from Toledo,
By the light on the bridge we have made;
To a land with a non-Christian credo,
Where flamencos and tangos are played

From there, let's dance on out of reason,
With our hearts full of Lorca's deep song;
Until beauty has come into season,
And we know that that's where we belong.

While we dance, let's sustain that illusion,
With whatever good faith we can find.
May our steps take us wide of confusion;
May our love keep us blissfully blind

For to sing and to dance in our yearning,
To share our deep song face to face;
To glide into each twist and turning
Is to live with both freedom and grace

And so dance me on down from Toledo,
By the light on the bridge we have made;
To a land with a non-Christian credo,
Where flamencos and tangos are played

Dance me on down from Toledo.

If any poem written by Fenimore has a claim to being nominated as the signature poem of his love for Margarita, this poem is probably the one. It takes Toledo, where they first met, as its point of departure; explores Fenimore's long standing concerns with religion, philosophy and political violence; embraces Margarita's love of Spanish guitar music and dance. It has it all. Tragically, its evocation of Alhambra as 'the Isle of the Dead' was to become all too apt and now both are gone. – TCE

13.

Macondo Mambo

Melquiades, up and dance!
Come on, baby, take a chance.
Let's really go bananas!

Turn a trick, but watch the peel;
Show us, baby, how you feel;
And go, go, go bananas.

Hey, the Colonel's got the beat;
Amaranta's on her feet;
The cast has gone bananas.

Let the soldiers march and shoot;
It's Carnival, who gives a hoot?
It's time to go bananas.

Dance on down to Buenos Airs!
Coups and counter-coups, who cares?
The world has gone bananas.

Let it go in old Havana
At the forties Tropicana,
With Prado's sweet bananas

Or head to Franco's Barcelona,
Now the solitary owner
Of all your old bananas

Roll those writer's saucy hips,
Let's hear mambo from your lips,
Til we all go bananas.

Melquiades, dance with me;
The country's heading out to sea.
It's time to go bananas.

Macondo mambo.

This is Fenimore having a shot at Gabriel Garcia Marquez, not as a writer, but a fashionable 1970s Leftist and partisan of Fidel Castro. It can be securely dated to his work on the opening pages of Notebook III, in 2009, and plainly draws upon Gerald Martin's 2008 biography of Garcia Marquez for many of its details. Melquiades, of course, is the magical character in _One Hundred Years of Solitude_, who leads the reader in and out of Latin American history and its reflection in everyday life in the mid-20th century. The bananas trope, of course, is a play on the fact that the novel was set in Colombia, the original 'banana republic' and the novelist's homeland, though he spent much of his adult life elsewhere in the Spanish world. Sceptical though he may have been of Garcia Marquez's politics, Fenimore loved the figure of Melquiades. This is registered in the poem, in which the poet's humane despair at the condition of the world is coupled with the refrain, 'Melquiades, up and dance!', 'Melquiades, dance with me.' It is interesting to juxtapose the mood and language of this poem with 'Dance me on down from Toledo', e.g. the shared allusion to Franco and the contrasting dance rhythms. – TCE.

14.

The Dream

Shadows, gloom, a red and white veined dark;
Muffled voices, murmurings, running, fear;
Horses gallop on a sunless plain; stark
Clash of angers; then – ah! ah! – the spear!

A wounded leg, a pallet and a chill;
Fevered tossing, winter heart and hut;
Lamed and lingering, flickering hope and will;
The limb and life-force fester quickly. Cut

To memories of a settled hearthside scene:
The eye, by fire, enlivening the hand
To carve from unknown bone a figurine –
A likeness hoped and longed for more than planned.

And then, above my fevered form, there swept
The kiss, the breast, the eyes – but – glassy stone;
Mute, I watched agape as those eyes wept,
For I was gone. The kiss stood there alone.

Thought, sharper than spear thrust; start –
Dream died and woke a succoured heart.

The Dream.

This is one of the most staccato and unusual of all Fenimore's poems and appears to record and reflect upon an actual dream he must have had. I found it in fair copy together with the following poem, 'Lara', in a folder simply titled 'Notes on Dream Theory', which included a good deal of interesting material not immediately germane to this book. The imagery struck me at once as alluding to the Indo-European world described in such archaeological and linguistic detail by David Anthony and the dream itself may have been triggered by just such imagery around the time of the 2007 conference.

The poem is complex, but the dramatic penultimate stanza suggests the poet experienced himself as having died and being helpless to respond to the tears and kisses of his beloved. When I read these lines, I was transfixed; for I did not encounter them until after I had finally tracked down Anactoria Lopez and learned of Margarita's fate.

Among Fenimore's many gifts was a capacity for seeing the links or associations between things that most of us overlook. Yet we know that he failed to foresee the impact of his death on Margarita. Indeed, it is quite clear from the Notebooks that he failed to foresee the specific circumstances of his own demise until just before the end. We cannot, therefore, attribute foresight or proleptic vision to the author of this poem. We know better. Yet the poem is there and its key lines rise up before our eyes to haunt us. You will all appreciate, I believe, that it is was considerations such as this which compelled me to include the poems in this volume, once I had found them and been able to read them in the context of Fenimore's secret life. – TCE.

15.

Lara

Is it you who stands over the table of my years,
Flanked by masses of white lilac, cyclamen and cineraria?

Is it you who stands out for her casual beauty
Among a crowd drawn dimly by my poetry and science?

Is it you whose presence fills the unceremonied silence
In which only the flowers stand for singing and for psalms?

You are conversing with my brother, the watcher,
Learning of the long, coincidental meanings of our lives.

Ah! You exclaim in wonder at that late learning:
Is that really true? How astounding! How foreordained!

But have you guessed how my candle burned -
How my candle burned on the table of our winter's night?

Kiss me with that last kiss prescribed in the ritual!
Kiss me amid the white lilac, the cyclamen and cineraria!

Lean over me, shielding me with your whole being:
With your head, your breast, your heart, your loving hands.

Feel what a love ours was: how free, how pure,
How true to song and void of mere passionate necessity.

It transcended all around us in soaring scope:
Trees, clouds, sky, crowded streets – the wide world.

We made everything high and ravishing our own:
The open horizon, the myriad forms of beauty, the very Sun.

Cry freely now – abundantly – for the riddle of life
The riddle of death, the beauty of genius, the winter of love.

But don't stand over me unable to live, in pitiful misery,
Thinking you can't go on, with your hair standing on end.

Above all, do not vanish somewhere, forgotten as
A nameless number on a list that has been mislaid.

This I want for you after flowers and psalms:
A long life, rounded with the joy that I have been yours.

Lara.

This poem is heart rending in the light of how things turned out. The final stanzas, in particular, read starkly as a posthumously crushed hope. It's clear that Fenimore must have written the poem long before the end and without any premonition, one assumes, of what was to happen to him and Margarita. They are a poetic reworking of the last pages of *Doctor Zhivago*, concerning the death of Yuri and the fate of Lara. Preoccupied as he was, in general, with the great existential questions of meaning, mortality and love, Fenimore projected himself here into the character of Yuri Zhivago, as a voice from beyond the grave, calling out to his beloved Lara not to despair, not to vanish into Stalin's GULAG, but to see life through rejoicing in the great and authentic love they had shared. In the novel, of course, no such poem exists and Lara, though she does rejoice in the love they had shared, does later vanish, "a nameless number on a list that was later mislaid" in Stalin's brutal GULAG archipelago.

We all know that Fenimore had loved the tale of *Doctor Zhivago* since he was very young. It might almost be said to have defined his sense of what romantic love was about; as well as pointing him to that creative combination of science, philosophy and personal integrity that Pasternak embodied in his most famous character. I remember, as if it was yesterday, that soiree at Tremont St, in the winter of 1987, at which Fenimore read to us some of his favourite passages from the novel and then asked Monica, especially since her surname is Sventitsky, to read the same passages from the Russian original "just so that we can revel in the music of Pasternak's native tongue". That's how he was, our Fenimore. The soiree had been organized because Fenimore had just read Ronald Hingley's biography of Pasternak and had discovered to his delight that Pasternak had, at one time, been a keen and gifted student of Neo-Kantian philosophy at the University of Marburg. This poem, written some twenty years later, shows just how much he had taken Pasternak to heart all those years and nurtured his "Zhivagoism" quietly, even while doing so much else. – TCE

16
The Poet's Bell

My love for you does not disperse
The virtues of myself or soul,
But rather the entire reverse:

It prompts me to express in verse,
My spirit's heartbeat, with the goal,
That thus my love will not disperse.

In doing so, I must rehearse
Both rhyme and metrical control,
Or bring about the mere reverse

Of music beauty and, what's worse,
Disordering the part or whole,
Imply my love could thus disperse.

In these brief stanzas, then, immerse
Your self and play the critic's role;
Then turn - and play the charmed reverse.

This simple villanelle, though terse,
Might, like a poet's bell, then toll
Of love that, rather than disperse,
Regathers sound from each reverse

The Poet's Bell.

This is a villanelle and it's a tribute to Fenimore's understated skills as a poet that he could even write one of these poems, which are an especially demanding and strict form of verse to write. He has observed the strictest form and hammered out a quite exquisitely crafted little commentary on the challenges posed by living at Cos to work on his treatise while attempting to sustain a deep intimacy with Margarita. The final stanza, with its image of a bell oscillating and tolling that "regathers sound from each reverse" offers a delightful metaphorical echo of Fenimore's experience of time passing and of having to regather himself and his love for Margarita each time they part. As with many of the other poems, it seems to have been written as an almost incidental reflection, with no thought of publication. It is not clear whether he shared it with Margarita. But it does seem to have had an interesting religious and philosophical association in Fenimore's mind. I found two copies of the poem; one under the glass top of Fenimore's large desk in his study at Cos and one being used as a bookmark in a copy of Hannah Arendt's *Love and Saint Augustine.*

The fact that a fair copy in typescript had been placed under the glass on his desk makes plain that this poem had a greater than usual personal significance for Fenimore. But if you read the poem only under the glass, in isolation, you miss its deeper rhetorical significance, which is his implicit dialogue with St Augustine about love and estrangement. The draft of the poem, when I found it, sat between pages 22 and 23 of Arendt's book, in which she is discussing Augustine's argument, in the second book of his *Confessions* that the desire for the things of the world – including the love of another human being – estranges a person from himself and causes the 'dispersion' of the self. Augustine appeals to God to gather him in from the dispersion by which he was torn asunder. He had written of his youthful desire for sexual love that it had debased his capacity for authentic love. He had quoted St Paul's first epistle to the Corinthians as declaring that "a man does well to abstain from all commerce with women". It's clear that Fenimore was disinclined to agree with either the apostle or the saint. He was not, however, prepared merely to dismiss their ascetic claims with disdain. He had created Cos precisely in order to concentrate his energies and resist dispersion – and then Margarita had appeared. – TCE.

17.

Dwelling Place

Lord, you have been our dwelling place in all generations, so teach us to number our days, that we may apply our hearts unto wisdom.

Before the Earth was formed and the world, before the mountains ever rose up, even from everlasting to everlasting, you are the all-high God. You watch over man's destruction; and say, return you children of men. A thousand years in your sight are but as yesterday when they are past, or like a dream in the night.

Lord, you have been our dwelling place in all generations, so teach us to number our days, that we may apply our hearts unto wisdom.

You bear the generations away as with a flood; they pass away like imaginings in the night hours; like the grass in season; they are swept away by your anger on account of their iniquities. Even the fortunate live but three score and ten years, four score if they are strong, but even so they live in labor and sorrow and soon pass away into the ground.

Lord, you have been our dwelling place in all generations, so teach us to number our days, that we may apply our hearts unto wisdom.

O satisfy us early with your mercy, that we may be glad and rejoice all our days. Make us glad in the days in which you have afflicted us and in the years wherein we have seen evil. Let your work appear to your servants and your glory to their children. Let your beauty be upon us and fulfil the work of our hands. Yea, bless the work of our hands.

Lord, you have been our dwelling place in all generations, so teach us to number our days, that we may apply our hearts unto wisdom.

Dwelling Place.

This is a reworking of Psalm 90 and it could derive from any one or more of several points in Fenimore's last years. We know that he studied Robert Alter's translation of the *Psalms* very closely. We know that he wrote at least the outlines for an opera libretto about the Bonhoeffer family's fate in Nazi Germany, which features an aria based on Psalm 90 and we know that he was thinking about psalms and music in writing both the Tale of Raneb and Nefesh and the subsequent Songs of Queen Nefesh. I have not been able to ascertain which phase of his work prompted this poem, but it seems safe to say that it must have been written in 2008 or 2009, when all of these things occurred. – TCE.

18.

You walk away

You walk away – love's happiness and pain
How shall I call you, call you back again?

My past, my life, my bliss, retreat behind that door
I hear your footsteps slowly die away
And fear that they will die for ever more

You walk away – love's happiness and pain
How shall I call you, call you back again?

I want to breathe you in as one breathes air,
Be absorbed and lose myself within
The beauty of your snow-white care

You walk away – love's happiness and pain
How shall I call you, call you back again?

I'm tortured by a sense of loss and cry
In anguish to the blank and heedless walls
Always the question, why, why and why?

You walk away – love's happiness and pain
How shall I call you, call you back again?

But then at night unearthly powers
Wake me to your presence in a dream
Your presence from past days and vivid hours

You walk with me, beloved, once again
And hark I call you 'Life' – and bitter pain.

You walk away.

This is a creative reworking or paraphrasing of a poem by Dietrich Bonhoeffer. The original was written by Bonhoeffer when he was in the Nazi prison in Berlin, at Tegel in 1944. It laments the sad endings of visits to him in prison by his young fiancée, Maria von Wedemeyer. It must have been composed at the time, in 2009, when Fenimore was at work on the opera libretto 'Karl and Paula.' We can see in it, perhaps, more the pathos of the opera than the condition of Fenimore's relationship with Margarita. Yet his ability to empathize so deeply with Bonhoeffer and to rework the original with feeling has to have sprung both from his profound immersion in the horrors of 20th century totalitarianism and his profound love for Margarita, whom he saw only once or twice a year and had again and again to watch walk away. Finally, of course, she walked away never to return and Fenimore, like Bonhoeffer, went to his death alone. – TCE.

19.

The Death of Moses

On Nebo's mountain peak where few have trod
There stands the prophet Moses, man of God.

Absent is his gaze and tired his faithful hand,
As he surveys, below, the Promised Land

'You shall glimpse all this but from afar',
His God informs the prophet standing there

No more shall you witness the idolatry
Of those who, by my grace, shall soon be free

You have seen enough of Israel's toil and sorrow
Behold below the land of its tomorrow.

And Moses sighed 'Now fallen is my stave.
Oh fateful God, make ready now my grave.'

The Death of Moses.

This is a companion piece to both 'Dwelling Place' and 'You Walk Away'. All three were clearly being worked up as set pieces for the imagined opera. Like 'You Walk Away' this is a reworking of a poem by Dietrich Bonhoeffer – TCE.

20.

Your Architect

Your love is enough for my heart
And your wings for my freedom

Your love has called to me
From the Parthenon and Mount Athos
It has had me hail tyrants
With visions of clearance
It has built Ronchamp for the Sun
It has drawn me through darkness.

Your wings have flown me to La Plata
They have created a spectacular residence
A jungle of courtyards and gardens
Cantilevered roofs to shelter my longings
Inspiring me to pitch my freedom
Outside the given ground

Your love is enough for my heart
And your wings for my freedom

I yearned to rebuild Paris,
But your love took me elsewhere:
It had me hurl myself into New York;
It had me scorn the Ossete in his lair;
It had me leapfrog every setback
And take my exuberance to Chandigarh.

Your wings, Margarita, are our secret
They free me to swim towards
The star we steer by
Each stroke an act of worship
Of light, of air, of sea -
And the hope of a right ending.

Your love is enough for my heart
And your wings for my freedom.

Your Architect.

This poem was inspired by the life of the great Swiss/French architect Le Corbusier. We can date it securely, because it so closely adheres to details of Le Corbusier's life to be found in Nicholas Fox Weber's superb biography of the architect, which was published in 2008. Fenimore's copy, as Ariel pointed out to me, is dated 18 December 2008, so it is overwhelmingly probable that the poem was written in 2009. In 2008, he and Margarita had visited Egypt and seen the Valley of the Kings and the Valley of the Queens. She had asked him to write songs for her. He had completed the design for two thirds of his treatise and the composition of the first two of his Notebooks. Later that year, IRI's big short had been vindicated and it had become clear that several billion dollars would accrue to it. When the pair visited Venice and the Veneto in April 2009, their relationship must have been at its apogee and all manner of possibilities were occurring to Fenimore, as we know from his sweeping proposals later that year about what we might collectively accomplish with such resources. The exuberance of this poem surely comes out of this context of love and optimism. – TCE.

21.

Proust and Prolexia

I suffer from prolexia –
An insidious disease:
When it comes to orthographic tasks,
My brain finds them a breeze.

This bothers me, as it may mean
That I am none too bright;
For Da Vinci, Einstein, Edison
Could barely read or write.

Dyslexic savants, it appears,
Prefer to think in pictures,
Leaving logocentric souls
Like me in mental strictures.

I learned all this, I hate to say –
Was it my loss or gain? –
By ploughing through (you guessed): a book
On reading and the brain

It is a book you'll not forget,
It's called Proust and the Squid.
Its thesis may redraw me yet;
Revealing all that's hid

Proust and Prolexia.

This quirky bit of whimsy belongs in the same category as the early poems 'We Karyotes' and 'Nutcracker Man'. The only clues to its composition, since I have been unable to find a context for it, are that *Proust and the Squid* is a book by a specialist on reading and dyslexia by the name of Maryanne Wolf, first published in 2007. The full title of the book is *Proust and the Squid: The Story and Science of the Reading Brain*. The immediate inspiration for the poem may well have come from Wolf's remarks in her eighth chapter, which begins with the sentence: "Thomas Edison, Leonardo de Vinci and Albert Einstein are three of the most famous people said to have had dyslexia." This sentence was underscored in Fenimore's copy, as were passages stating that da Vinci's notes were: "written from right to left, in reversed 'looking glass script'... full of misspellings, syntactic mistakes and strange errors in language" and "Albert Einstein... was mediocre at any subject that required the retrieval of words, such as a foreign language. He once said...that words did 'not seem to play any role' in his theoretical thinking, which came to him through 'more or less clear images.'" – TCE.

22.

Staying Seine

I've been at a table, not far from the Seine,
With Marcel and a bottle of wine
I'd been there before, again and again,
But this evening he helped me refine

My take on old memories I cannot forget
And a doubt which insistently asks
If your voice and your beauty are those of Odette,
Or if she's merely one of your masks

I sat at a table at Les Deux Magots
And I glided like some kind of Swann
On the waters of memory (swiftly they flow):
The current that life moves upon

With binocular vision, I plucked from its banks
Red flowers one might call Odette-me-nots;
They're bright blooms of gratitude, perfumed with thanks -
Better far than mere fabled forget-me-nots.

They're for you, from this café on old Saint Germain,
Where I mused on Odette with Marcel;
On the poignant aromas of unassuaged pain;
And on pleasures one cannot foretell.

What fortunate hours of privileged repast,
A la recherché du temps perdu.
Now, cleansed and reordered, my psyche recast,
I can be far more present to you.

Staying Seine.

Suzanne has confirmed to me that she introduced Fenimore to the pleasures of Proust very much as he has described the experience in Notebook II; but this poem, which must surely have been written either during or subsequent to Fenimore and Margarita's sojourn together in Paris, in April 2007, demonstrates that he had taken the French master's phenomenology to heart. As with 'Lucullus to Clodia', however, there must be some question as to how literally we should interpret this poem in autobiographical terms. That Fenimore the poet would compare Margarita with Odette de Crecy, the demi-monde beauty from *Swann's Way*, if taken literally, would imply that he feared she was toying with him and involved with another.

We now know that, in a sense, this was true, but also that Fenimore was surely oblivious to that fact until Margarita acquainted him with it in Buenos Aires in April 2010. In any case, what the poem fairly clearly states is that, having consulted Marcel on the subject, he feels reassured that his fears are derived from past disappointments in love and that, having put them in 'binocular' perspective, he is free to be 'far more present' to Margarita. That, I am sure, was the mood in which the poem was composed. Perhaps it was even written during the language and archaeology conference in Paris, just before the two of them met 'as if by chance' on the Pont Alexandre III to spend five days in Paris and its environs before flying to Berlin. – TCE.

23.

So That You Will Hear Me

So that you will hear me
My words,
Like lithe chameleons,
Are changing shape and tone.

Before you touched them
My words were murmured darkness
And cold stone

But you soothed my psyche
Persistently making murmurings light:
Lamps over the muttered.

Now I want my words
To say what I want
To say to you
So that I will hear you say
That you want to hear me say them.

I want my words
To form a necklace of pearls
For your hidden self
For your heart's throat.

That You Will Hear Me.

This and the next two poems are what the literary critic Harold Bloom might have called 'strong misreadings' of three early poems by the Chilean master Pablo Neruda, or more precisely of the English translation of Neruda by W. S. Merwin. They form a kind of musical trio. This first one makes the case that the poet is determined to find the words that will not only express his feelings for Margarita, but will evoke in her feelings of recognition and mutual affection, so that she will love to hear his words, his poems and will take them to heart. The second 'Leaning Into the Long Afternoons' is a song of joy and an annunciation that he is diving deep to bring the things of greatest beauty to the light for her – to adorn her being and delight her heart. The third, 'We Have Lost Only a Possible Twilight', is surely a heroic attempt to express and to believe that their long distance romance has a profound richness that others do not see, but which keeps open for each of them a wide horizon of dazzling possibilities.

When I asked Ariel and the estimable Mr Bojangles to direct me to anything Fenimore had kept on Neruda, they came back with multiple editions of several of his works, as well as biographies and studies of his residence at La Isla Negra. One book was the key to these three poems: a Spanish language edition of Neruda's first famous book of verse, _Twenty Love Poems and a Song of Despair_. It had been given to Fenimore, as a signed dedication inside the cover made clear, by Margarita in Yucatan, in October 2006, during their sojourn in Mexico. However, in writing his variations on (at least) three of the poems, he worked from the slim bilingual Penguin edition translated by Merwin, first published in 1969 and reissued with an introduction by Cristina Garcia in 2004. The three poems printed here are based on poems v, vii and x in that edition. Fenimore did more than paraphrase Merwin. He imposed very different meanings on the poems in each case and made them his own, arguing with Neruda as he had argued, in his villanelle, with St Augustine. – TCE.

24.
Leaning Into the Long Afternoons

Leaning into the long afternoons, I look seaward,
Full of memorious musing

Out there, in the wide, turbulent currents,
My nefesh swims and dives;

It sights and brings high to the light to show you
Sparkling, many-colored things of beauty

It revels and frolics, like a dolphin of the deep
In the green and the blue of your regard

And when the gulls circle closer to the stars
It sighs with wonder and sings

Over the ancient, darkling sea, of its desire
To harvest you a necklace made of suns.

25.

We Have Lost Only a Possible Twilight

We have lost only a possible twilight.
No-one can see how our hands link at night,

Or how clear is the sky of our mutual longing
Arcing over worlds and across all time

We can see, through this window, a fiesta
Of possibilities, looming like mountains.

We have our piece of the Unconquered Sun:
It is the coin of our ancient realm.

I remember your laughter, catalyst of conquest;
Your musical capirote punishments

You have urged me to sing beyond my horizons
Ploughing up the Moon to find meaning

We are writing the book of time and meaning and
When I dream, it falls open at tantalizing pages.

26.

Losing Neruda

I lost Neruda in the cold -
Misplaced him in the rain;
But look! I found a thing of gold –
No – better – think again:
I found the truth of things.

Is that claim simply far too bold?
Can any human brain
Think that and not be merely sold
A bill of goods in vain?
The truth of things?

Yes, the ruth, sooth and tooth of things;
The root and the stem and the grain;
A sense of their seeds and their springs
And all that that brings in its train:
The simple truth of things

They are, it's only we who ache,
Bewildered, to belong;
We who, for our longing's sake,
Make poetry and song.
That's the truth of things!

But ah! What plenitude is there,
For those with eyes to see,
With opened selves to build and care
And less to have than be!
Such is the truth of things.

Yes, the ruth, sooth and tooth of things;
The root and the stem and the grain;
A sense of their seeds and their springs
And all that that brings in its train:
The simple truth of things

This came to me one winter's day,
When, hearing quite alone
Sinatra's 'If You Go Away',
I saw that I had grown
Into the truth of things

But, truly, it was not the song
That had me feel so true
It was the sense that I belong,
Affirmed, through loving you
In the truth of things

Yes, the ruth, sooth and tooth of things;
The root and the stem and the grain;
A sense of their seeds and their springs
And all that that brings in its train:
The simple truth of things

Losing Neruda

After reworking some of Neruda's verse, Fenimore appears to have recoiled from what he took to be Neruda's obscurity and misogyny. This poem is constructed almost as if it is intended to be sung and its mood is one that, I think, he hoped was consistent with the hope he had expressed of writing words that Margarita would hear and take to heart. It rhymes, so to speak, with his villanelle, in declaring that his love for her, far from being a distraction from his quest for truth and authenticity, is the embodiment of those very things. Yet, embedded in the heart of the song is a precise reference to another and famous song, Sinatra's rendition of the much recorded Jacques Brel lyric 'If You Go Away (Ne Me Quitte Pas)', which famously expresses an anything but hopeful plaint of longing for the beloved – who seems unresponsive and set on leaving. Tempting as it is, we should not over-interpret this poem, in hindsight, in the light of Margarita's final actions. As the next poem shows, Fenimore's attitude toward their separateness and their recurrent partings was anything but simple or mournful. – TCE.

27

Consuela, my love

Consuela, Consuela, Consuela, my love,
Remember our valley, the clear sky above.

I remember our autumn,
Our fall in the South;
The light in your eyes,
The love in your mouth;

But you asked, lovely bird,
What I could not deny
"Let me wing on my way,
Give me freedom to fly!"

I was awed by your spirit,
In love with your wings;
And said in response:
"We are made for such things!

Your hopes must be fertile,
Your nefesh set free;
So go with my blessing
And fly far from me."

In response, you delivered
An exquisite blow
That shaped down the grain
How the future might go:

You'd now be my muse.
I was struck to the bone!
You had shattered to sharpness
The starkness of stone

You opened a clearing
Beneath the bright sky,
Where I'll not knap alone
To no point 'til I die:

A clearing for planting
The hopes of the heart in;
Where new autumns loom
For us two to part in

Consuela, Consuela, Consuela, my love,
Remember our valley, the clear sky above.

Consuela, my love.

This poem gives what may be the clearest and finest expression to Fenimore's elegiac mood as regards the mutual liberty with which he and Margarita lived. The sentiments expressed are, surely, quite beautiful, hearkening back as they do his early trope about the creative intentionality entailed in knapping stone into hand axes; acknowledging the transformative nature of partings and hailing the possibility of "new autumns" looming "for us two to part in".

I am tempted, also, having spent so much time studying Fenimore's fable about Raneb and Nefesh, set in the Nile Valley, and having taken note of Fenimore and Margarita's own visit to the Valleys of the Kings and Queens, to see his use of the expression "remember our valley, the clear sky above" as an evocation of these things. There is also, unless I am mistaken, drawing on hints here and there in the Notebooks, an allusion to the poetry of Rilke in this idea of the valley and the clearing.

Finally, of course, given that Fenimore saw his Notebooks themselves as his great gift to Margarita, his own 21st century version of Boisei's ingenious hand axe, the second last stanza is particularly poignant: Margarita has opened a clearing "beneath the bright sky, where I'll not knap alone to no point til I die." Yet, in the end, perhaps, he feared that this clearing itself had closed with a violent suddenness that was unendurable. Rather than abandon his hand axe, however, he struck the last flakes from its edges and delivered it to me so that we, if not she, might receive it as a gift. – TCE.

28.

The Bell and the Choir

There are hymns to be heard
On the Isle of the Dead,
Or such is the word
That is still being spread:

Neither brimstone nor fire,
As threatened of old;
But an angelic choir
With voices of gold.

The singing will start
With a high, ringing bell
And conclude with a chant
That will solemnly tell

Of salvation history,
Wonders made plain,
And of life's inner mystery,
Its glory and pain.

Our labors well done
Past the portals of night
We'll rejoice in the One
And repose in His sight

Oh, if life would end so,
On that Isle in the West,
Under Evenstar's glow,
Then I'd go to my rest.

But we all should beware
Of the Sirens of death
And resist going there,
While still we have breath;

For in truth all the Muses
Of rest and delight
Demand that one chooses
The noon, not the night.

The bell and the choir,
The chanting of story,
To be heard all require
The world's 'passing glory'.

So I'll not dream of songs
On the Isle of the Dead,
But proclaim what belongs
To the living instead.

For I am a being
Of flesh and of bone,
Not a soul that is fleeing
To star and to stone.

It is here, it is here
And not in the West,
That what touches the ear
Can make it feel blest.

It's through metaphors drawn
From our love of the world
That our souls are reborn
And our hopes are unfurled.

And so we conceive,
With extravagant eye,
An eternal reprieve
For all those who die.

Too often this tends
To a fervid belief
That the visionary bends
To delusion and grief.

So, though we must die,
Let us love while we may,
The light in the sky,
The sensations of day.

Let life be renewed
By the joys that we find
In what saints have construed
As the 'world' of our kind.

Our religion should nourish
The flowers and trees;
The creatures that flourish
In the skies and the seas.

Our solemnest vow
Of our purpose and worth
Should centre on how
We have sprung from the Earth.

Nor should we yet long
To flee from this green,
With the thought we belong
In places unseen.

For indeed we do not,
But have gardens to tend,
On our aqueous plot
At the Milky Way's end

Let's cherish, then, all
Of the gifts of the Muses
No longer in thrall
To the One who refuses

To grant us surcease
From predation and strife
Except through release
From the pleasures of life;

And with Orphic intent,
With sublime orchestration,
Spend all we've been lent
In the brilliant creation

Of a culture profound
With its halls full of song,
In which will resound
The cry, 'We belong!'

Ah, that is an Isle
Of cypresses high
Where I'd live well awhile,
Then peacefully die.

The Bell and the Choir.

This is the longest of the poems I found among Fenimore's papers (unless, of course, we think of the three Notebooks as a single long poem). It is one of the simplest and clearest in language and meaning of all of them and lays out straightforwardly his repudiation of the old religious doctrines of a 'hereafter' or a world 'beyond the grave'. The sheer simplicity of the language makes this poem a kind of commonplace retort to the claims of all those, but especially Jews, Christians and Muslims, who profess belief in an apocalypse, in a world shattering transformation that will usher in a 'better' world and open the doors of 'paradise'. It almost reads like a response in a conversation to someone having held forth the hope for 'salvation' from the sorrows and temptations of 'Earthly life'. Make of such a life what you can, Fenimore is saying, because there will be no other. It reminds me, more than most of his poems, of the first conversations I had with him, strolling through Cambridge Common or in the precincts of Emerson Hall, about pragmatism, language and natural religion.

Like so many of his other poems, this one was not set apart by him as if he intended it to last. I came across it in a set of papers he had written more or less roughly over a period of many years on the relationship between religious belief in an apocalypse and the modern ideological myth of 'the revolution'. There were three versions, the earliest of which was both shorter than this one and in a different stanzaic structure. It had been written, as far as I can judge, almost on the spur of the moment, in the middle of a reflection on three seminal works by Norman Cohn: *The Pursuit of the Millennium, Europe's Inner Demons* and *Cosmos, Chaos and the World to Come: The Ancient Roots of Apocalyptic Faith*. A second version, still not as fully worked out as this one, turned up in a typescript version alongside his notes from Geza Vermes's *The Authentic Gospel of Jesus*, juxtaposed with Vermes's reflections on the implicit 'rules of eschatological behaviour' that can be gleaned from the sayings of Jesus and the epistles of St Paul.

There are indications in this second version that he was flirting with turning it into a very different poem, laden with direct evocations of the apocalyptic language of the Book of Daniel, the Essenes and the synoptic Gospels and seeking to confute such language. But he seems to have abandoned that idea, simply turning away from the vision of wars and cataclysmic upheavals with which the literature of apocalypse is filled and omitting it, except in the form of the subtlest and most oblique of allusions, in the third version of his poem, as reproduced here. He refers to 'the extravagant eye' and 'fervid belief' that can 'lead to delusion and grief', but he leaves to one side the element of apocalyptic violence which is supposed to usher in the 'world to come'. Instead, he repudiates even the gentlest version of the myth – angelic choirs with voices of gold and a divine clarification of 'life's inner mystery, its glory and pain'. I think he saw this as the stronger argument. In any case, the third and finished form of 'The Bell and the Choir', written out in long hand with some corrections and then in a fair copy as typescript, sat towards the end of the same collection of notes. – TCE.

29.

Thanks for the Thread, Ariadne

Thanks for the thread, Ariadne
Ariadne, O thanks for the thread
Without you, I'd be dead, Ariadne
So thanks, O thanks for the thread.

I was sent on a boat to old Knossos,
Like many a poor youth before.
The elders had decided to toss us
Into Minos's cavernous maw

I was feckless and dumb like the others
And would therefore have gone to my grave;
But you urged me to think of my druthers,
Think quickly, be cunning and brave.

You had no time yourself for King Minos;
Did not like your old man at all;
So you gave me the eye to align us,
Then slipped me gold thread in a ball

Ah! Thanks for the thread, Ariadne.
Ariadne, O thanks for the thread.
Without you, I'd be dead, Ariadne;
So thanks, O thanks for the thread.

You knew – I did not – Ariadne,
Of the dark in the Minotaur's maze
Unassisted, the brute would have had me
And gnawed on my entrails for days;

But I laid the gold thread that you gave me,
As I stole through the cavernous black;
Then, knowing the trail laid would save me,
Slew the monster and found my way back.

Ariadne, O Ariadne,
Ariadne O,
Thanks, thanks so much for the thread.
Ariadne, O Ariadne,
It's not me, but the bull that is dead.

Thanks for the thread, Ariadne.
Ariadne, O thanks for the thread.
Without you, I'd be dead, Ariadne;
So thanks, O thanks for the thread.

That Minotaur won't kill again,
I hit the horned beast to the max.
I broke his skull and spilled his brain,
With a handy old ritual axe

Let's make our escape, Ariadne;
Run off to some balmy Greek island;
Then, after we've laughed and you've had me,
Come back to Athens, to my land.

Thanks for the thread, Ariadne.
Ariadne, O thanks for the thread.
Without you, I'd be dead, Ariadne;
So thanks, O thanks for the thread.

Ariadne, O Ariadne,
Ariadne O,
Thanks, thanks so much for the thread.
Ariadne, O Ariadne,
It's not me, but the bull that is dead.

Thanks for the Thread, Ariadne.

This is clearly meant to be a song, but there is no indication by Fenimore of the melody. The closest he came was to scribble in the margin of the original, after the stanza which concludes 'Slew the monster and found my way back', the single word 'saxophones'. From this I deduce that he imagined the song as a having a jazz accompaniment, at least from that point. The language of the verse is that of a jazz club, rather than a literary salon, of course. The mood is mock heroic, almost adolescent in temper, as if it represents the sentiments of a juvenile Theseus genuinely grateful for the help of the young lass Ariadne in defying her 'old man'. Yet Fenimore must have been playing here with feelings that ran rather deep, if we assume that the poem is autobiographical and that Ariadne is a stand-in for Margarita. The poem seems to date from about late 2009, which would place it at the time when Fenimore had returned from meeting Margarita in Italy, was at work on problems of ontology, writing Notebook III and drawing up in consultation with us the early plans for what has become the Amor Mundi Foundation.

It is tempting to interpret the labyrinth in the poem as the enormous conceptual challenges he had been wrestling with in working on his treatise, but it is hard to see how 'Ariadne' could have rescued him from those. I believe the more plausible interpretation is that Margarita's love, presumably reconfirmed in Venice, had convinced him that the gift he was creating – the Notebooks – would be well received by her when he finally emerged from the labyrinthine task of creating them. Since we know that he had, by then, long since seen creative intentionality as linked with the archaic making of hand axes, we can interpret the 'handy old ritual axe' in this song as the very idea of the 'shaped gift'. With this idea, the poet declares, he has been able to shatter the skull of the monstrous Minotaur in the labyrinth and find his way out again. He can, in other words, see the light at the end of the tunnel (the exit to the maze) and feels ready to run off with Ariadne to 'some balmy Greek island', to laugh and make love – and then to take her with him to Athens, where 'Athens' surely stands for the life of the mind, embodied in his treatise, the life at Cos and the future work of the Amor Mundi Foundation. – TCE.

30.

Lullaby for Junius

Little Lumpkin Junius
Sit lala on my knee
And I will sing a song to you
Of how to human be

Little Lumpkin Junius
Oh apple of my eye
You'll need to transform everything
Then bid it all bye-bye

You see, my dandled darling one,
To sing the thing quite plain,
The loving world I've placed you in's
Completely in the brain

Your Papa's conjured up a world
Of memories, hopes and dreams
To play with Little Lumpkin in
But little's what it seems

You'll find, as you reach out for it
That much of it recedes;
You'll have to make it all again
Consistent with your needs

But sing lala with Papa now
And grin and clap your hands;
There's time enough, when you grow big,
For making future plans

Little Lumpkin Junius
Sit lala on my knee
And I will sing a song to you
Of how to human be

Little Lumpkin Junius
Oh apple of my eye
You'll need to transform everything
Then bid it all bye-bye

Lullaby for Junius.

This is an enigmatic poem; one that I discovered on a loose leaf, like most of the others, folded inside Fenimore's copy of Rainer Maria Rilke's *New Poems*, in the bilingual edition with translations by Edward Snow. It had been inserted near the end of the volume, alongside Rilke's existential poem 'The Solitary'. Both that poem and one a few pages later called 'The Child' are heavily marked in Fenimore's hand, as is a poem a few pages earlier in the volume called simply 'Lullaby'. This looks like a very private reflection on how he might have related to the son he never had and the three Rilke poems may all have helped to inspire it. The curious thing is that the poem addresses a child that does not exist about a world that's "completely in the brain", i.e. not the physical inheritance and beauties of Cos, to which such a child might have been the heir, but Fenimore's understanding of the cosmos gathered from a lifetime of study, reflection and experience.

There is something going on in this poem that runs deep beneath its surface and becomes more unsettling the more I think about it. The refrain 'you'll need to transform everything, then bid it all bye-bye' is, read superficially, simply an observation of the fate of being human, which entails having to acquire skills, remake one's environment to suit oneself but then confront mortality. Yet there is a disquieting sense; one I find I cannot shake off, that Fenimore lived this out far more fully than most of us. He built Cos at the Ends of the Earth, drawing the whole continuum of human culture and experience towards himself. He set about transforming that continuum to his own ends in the form of a set of hand written Notebooks that would make the world itself, in time and space, a beautiful gift to his beloved. He passed this gift, instead, to us and, having done so, he 'bid it all bye bye' – heading out to sea in *Aletheia*.

But that is only the first layer beneath the surface. Consider the stanza which declares that he has 'conjured up a world of memories, hopes and dreams, to play with Little Lumpkin in, but little's what it seems'. Given Fenimore's commitment to bringing forth truth, this stanza disturbs me more than I can say. I find myself haunted by those few words, 'but little's what it seems'. It seems little? No, it seems very large. Little of that large vision, however, is what seems to be on the surface and, as the next stanza states, 'you'll find, as you reach out for it, that much of it recedes'. Throughout my preparation of this book, I confess I have had the recurrent, uneasy sensation that I am addressed as 'Little Lumpkin Junius' by this poem and that it is telling me that I am under some kind of illusion; that the true meaning and the substance of what Fenimore (as 'Papa') has 'conjured up' is somehow eluding me; that little in Notebooks is what it seems. What do you think? – TCE.

31.

Fusion

Hold me now, as Astor would
His sweet bandoneon
And let us dance as if we could
Just tango on and on

Dance with me as Frida did
With Tina - Ashley Judd,
As if we're both in Mexico
With tango in our blood.

Press yourself right into me
With fire in your eyes
Set every vital passion free
As Gardel's voice denies

That we will ever be apart
Or subject to confusion
But will be blended heart with heart
Achieving deathless fusion

I'll dance upon Jean Jaures street,
Tu Buenos Aires Querido
And then we'll fly with winged feet
To Granada from Toledo

Kiss me, kiss me, long and deep
For life and dance are flying
The time will come when we must keep
Appointments, each, with dying.

Oh hold me, then, as Astor would
His sweet bandoneon
And dance with me as if we could,
In fusion, tango on.

Fusion.

'Fusion' was certainly composed before Fenimore's break with Margarita in Buenos Aires, in April 2010, but I don't know how much earlier. It is obviously a piece for the occasion, but tragically it was to be unfulfilled, for reasons we can still only guess at. It clearly follows, as it were, in the footsteps – or the dance steps – of 'Dance me on down from Toledo'. This is signified explicitly in the fifth stanza. It shares the same passionate sentiments of that earlier and longer poem, but there are two elements in this poem that are absent from the earlier one. The first is a sense of urgency, the sense that 'life and dance are flying', that the hour is approaching all too fast 'when we must keep appointments each with dying'. The second is the extraordinary metaphor of being held by Margarita 'as Astor would his sweet bandoneon', his piano accordion, if you will, in any case his musical instrument, so that, in that manner, the two of them could 'in fusion, tango on'. In other words, at the very point where Margarita was about to abandon him, Fenimore longed in effect to become her musical instrument – or so this particular, late poem suggests. That each of them was indeed about to keep an appointment with dying we now know and knowing that renders this poem, like a number of the others, almost unbearably poignant. – TCE.

32.

Ovid's metamorphoses

Everyone, it's safe to say
Is clear where fabled Rome is;
But few in our – or Ovid's – day
Could tell you much of Tomis

'Twas on the Euxine.
Who-xine?
Puke-scene!
A place of little promise

But there it was that Ovid went,
Punished for an error;
Well, went is not quite right – was sent
But Augustus, the Emp-error.

He was sent to the Euxine!
Who-xine?
Puke-scene!
A place of cold and terror

The pretext was The Art of Love
A book that Ovid wrote,
Which was declared, from high above,
To be pernicious smut

So, off to the Euxine!
Who-xine?
Puke-scene!
For the Boss had had a gut

Full of Ovid's frivolity,
Obscenity, jollity;
Toying with morals
For poetic laurels

Off, off to the Euxine!
Who-xine?
Puke-scene!
It's the Boss that wins such quarrels.

When the Boss man and poet
Tangle in quiet,
It's over, you know it –
The promiscuous riot

The poet is off to the Euxine!
Who-xine?
Puke-scene!
On a very much simpler diet

But there Ovid, alone, in a place very strange,
Cut off and deprived of his pleasures
Reflected and learned and started to change
And harvested poetic treasures

On the Euxine!
Who-xine?
Puke-scene!
In hexameters – Homeric measures!

Yes, though out in the dreary Euxinian cold,
The poet refused to stop writing,
He compressed what he felt in elegiac mold,
Letting beauty do all of his fighting.

From the Euxine!
Who-xine?
Puke-scene!
And the beauty is lastingly biting!

He wrote the Metamorphoses,
Or rendered it complete;
And sang, with fabled Orphoses,
In face of love's defeat

On the Euxine!
Who-xine?
Puke-scene!
This the Boss could not delete!

And so we read our Ovid still
To conjure transformation;
We love him for his magic quill
And exiled lucubration

Upon the Euxine -
Who-xine?
Puke-scene! -
He achieved transfiguration.

Ovid's metamorphoses.

After his collapse at Treehaven, as he himself recounts towards the end of Notebook III, Fenimore spent some days recovering. During those days, while he first related something of the story of himself and Margarita, he also re-read Ovid's *Metamorphoses*. He declared that he had never before so acutely felt the shock of mutation as in the loss of Margarita, so that Ovid's tales of mutation and mutilation resonated with him more profoundly than they had ever done before. When he had the energy, he would read aloud to me from the Charles Martin translation, or occasionally, for the sake of linguistic variation, the Arthur Golding translation of more than four hundred years ago. At the time, I assumed that he was reading Ovid simply for diversion or consolation. I knew nothing of the Notebooks, awaiting completion back at Cos; much less that they were – or are, you might say, since we now have them in hand – his own echoing and reworking of Ovid's *Metamorphoses*. Fenimore was not seeking distraction in reading Ovid. I should have known better, since Fenimore never had been one to seek distraction from the existential challenges of life.

Moreover, I already knew that he planned to visit Istanbul and the Aegean on his long way back to the Ends of the Earth. It might have occurred to me at the time that Istanbul is very near where Ovid lived out his life in exile from Rome and completed his two greatest works, *Metamorphoses* and *Fasti*. He was reading Ovid before visiting that part of the world where Ovid, alone and in exile, nonetheless finished two works which were to be become immortal and to make an enduring impression on Western culture long after he was gone. And why was Ovid exiled? It was for writing about the art of love and for having committed some mysterious error, the nature of which has never come to light. I think he felt the irony of his situation with piercing acuteness and was gathering his energies to emulate the Latin poet by completing his own long, creative poem, despite being exiled from his love and for his error in regard to Margarita's other love. His last poems all grew out of his reflections on this situation and his last reading of Ovid. The first of them was this wry, demotic ballad about Ovid being sent packing to the Euxine (the Black Sea), but rising above it in his poetry. – TCE.

33.

Orpheus among the Stones

Clear the dark and let the green emerge!
And be that there is Orpheus.

Upon the carven space of sunlit green
Then pluck the lyre of ages

And so recite the litany of trees
Until they form a temple

Summon into it the flocks of birds
To form a winged chorus

That circling round will rouse the very stones
And so the Earth enliven.

Then sing a song in tune with all that is
Within that hallowed place

Until it be for Orpheus and his spouse
A clearing for the sacred act of love

Orpheus among the Stones.

Among the most famous passages in Ovid's *Metamorphoses* is the opening of Book X "The Songs of Orpheus". It commences with the fabulous story of how Orpheus lost his great love, Eurydice, when she was bitten by a snake and died. He travelled to the Underworld, where he sought to charm the gods of Hades to relent and allow his beloved to return to life and re-join him in the upper world. They relented, on condition that he leave ahead of her and not look back until he had exited the 'valley of Avernus' – which led down to the Underworld – 'on pain of revocation of this gift'.

At the last moment, at the mouth of the valley, he could not resist looking back to assure himself that he had not been cheated; that she was really following him out through the valley. With that, he lost her a second time and forever. Distraught, he wandered alone in the upper world until he came to a hill with an open space on its summit. There he played upon his lyre, summoning trees to him until he had drawn around him a grove, filled with beasts and birds. There he sang many songs of love, suffering and the mutation of beings at the hands of the gods. This poem by Fenimore transparently derives from Book X of the *Metamorphoses* and there can be no doubt that in his mind the Margarita he had known, or thought he had known, was his Eurydice. – TCE.

34.

Sappho and Alcaeus

Ah! Sappho, Sappho, glancing back at me,
You know I know, your eye and posture tell;
That, though you drink from Anactoria's well,
It's only I who understands; that we

Sibling seedlings, sprung from Orpheus' head,
Uniquely draw from Heliconian springs;
That only I, when all your girls are fled,
Will share with you an ecstasy of strings;

Of summoned forms, of new, exquisite sounds,
Aeolian moods exhaled upon the lyre;
Mixolydian passions without bounds
That, come a thousand years, will still inspire

Every light-filled mind that knows the Muses;
That longs to touch the trembling hand and face
Of absent loves; which contemplates and chooses
Evocative recall, by Arion's grace

Here, upon Terpander's music isle,
We've lived and loved and, see what songs we've made!
But – ah, your gaze! – I'd linger yet a while,
Before the light and longing falter, fade.

Sappho and Alcaeus.

Having discovered that Margarita had a lover by the name of Anactoria, Fenimore took up a story almost as old as the myth of Orpheus, but historical, not legendary: the life of the great Lesbian poetess Sappho. Since he provides an account of his sojourn in Istanbul, his meeting with the exotic Cleis Scamandros and his visit to the Cyclades, in the last section of Notebook III (before the Epilogue), I don't need to go over the same ground here. But this poem and the next are not in Notebook III, even though they arose from the same context, so they call for a little explanation. Alcaeus was a contemporary of Sappho and both were brilliant poets. There is a famous classical painting of Alcaeus, who is seated, holding a lyre, with Sappho walking away from him, but glancing back at him as she does so. I don't know whether Fenimore was already familiar with his image, found it in one of my books on Greek art, was shown it or had it described to him by Ms Scamandros, or came across it in a piece of souvenir ware on one of the Greek islands, but he has used it to great effect in this poem.

He seized upon the astonishing coincidence that the most famous lesbian lover of Sappho had been called Anactoria, while Alcaeus had longed for the love of Sappho because they shared a passion for music, poetry and song, or rather poetry as song, as rhythmic words put to music. As if arguing with the absent Margarita, he asserts, through Alcaeus, that she knows - she has to know – that what they have had together cannot be replicated and that what they have created, with their shared 'ecstasy of strings' will forever inspire 'every light-filled mind that knows the Muses' and longs to be able to 'touch the trembling hand and face of absent loves'. It seems that, at that moment, sitting, by his own account, overlooking the great volcanic harbour of Santorini, Fenimore was able to look back over the brief years in which he had known Margarita and see in them enormous riches, which he could not quite bring himself to believe she had left behind. It was if he could see her face looking back at him from the West, across the caldera of Santorini, as he wrote. – TCE.

35.
Cleis Scamandros

Dark Cleis sat across the room from me
She shared her table with some learned Greeks
My eye was caught by flowers in her hair
And then I caught her eye

That night we dined and spoke of Sappho's verse
She led me deep within the labyrinth
She told me that the Popes burned Sappho's books
And saying so she sighed

"Come to Mytilene", she then breathed
"You can join me on a boat, if you so choose
I'm going to research the ancient songs
Of the only mortal Muse"

We climbed through cypress groves up from the port
To where they staged the comedies of old
And sat beneath the trees with Lesbian wine
At noon in flowering spring

She murmured, then, 'Eressos' in my ear;
And, once there, told of Lilley's play
Of Sappho's silence, Phaon's spotless vow
And urged I learn these lines

The evening was beguiled in her soft lounge
Where after drinks she put some music on
An opera: "Gounod's Sappho", she announced
And asked me of my loves

I lost myself in wine-enchanted talk
Of all the great Dembowskis of my life
Their beauty, their intelligence, my loss
She lay and urged me on

Tell me more, she breathed, of your desire
Of why these long haired lovelies turned you down
And whether they have quite put out your fire
Oh tell me everything!

I told her of the greatest of my loves
Of Catriona, Nathalie, and Weili Wu
And then I spoke of Buenos Aires and you
While she removed her clothes

In retrospect, she'd played me like a lyre
And how could mortal man resist such hands?
The conversation turned to her desire
To sate my pent up needs

Her long hair tossing, wild and open mouthed
She told me that she thirsted for my seed
And fell on me with reckless, ardent kisses
My manhood stood up well

For all my recent weariness in Austin
For all my chaste and funerary vows
I could not flee like Phaon from her snare
We coupled then til dawn

Those hours on Lesbos will not quickly fade
The taste of Cleis lingers on my tongue
But when, at last, the Sun had risen high
She washed and bade me leave

Be quick, she urged, your craft will leave at noon
White flower petals rain upon my heart
I've swallowed all your loss and grief and fear
But now you must depart

And so I left bright Sappho on the coast
Of bitten mouth, of shouts and twining limbs
Of copulation fraught with life and force
And took to sea again

Cleis Scamandros.

This is the last poem that Fenimore wrote, to my knowledge. It is written in a kind of Swinburnean imitation of Sapphic metre, with three long lines (in pentameter) followed by a short one (a trimeter). By Fenimore's account, he met Scamandros in Istanbul, at a party Yusuf organized. Yusuf has confirmed that this was the case. What happened after that is a matter of some conjecture. The account provided in Notebook III is not at all the same as the account in this rather remarkable poem and even the Notebook account seems to be a kind of embroidering of whatever did occur, making it into a story to suit the purposes of the narrative at that point. According to this poem, they took a boat to Mytilene, on Lesbos, and then went across the island to Eressos. According to the Notebook, they flew via Athens to Mykonos and spent a few days relaxing, partying and discussing the lost songs of Sappho, before Fenimore went on alone to Santorini to collect his thoughts – and write his two poems. According to Yusuf, Fenimore simply spent some time with Scamandros in Istanbul, then flew to the Cyclades on his own, perhaps only to Santorini.

The seventh stanza is probably the key to the poem. Scamandros was, in reality, someone with whom Fenimore found himself able to talk in depth about the life of Sappho, the complexity of human love, the writing of poetry and the beauties of language. He found himself, as he expressed it, lost in wine-enchanted talk 'of all the great Dembowskis of my life', among whom he was reluctantly now numbering Margarita. He makes a brief reference to Mathilde Dembowski in Notebook II. She was the great love of Stendhal and the inspiration for his initially ill-fated and obscure, but later classic book *Love*. She did not return his passion, despite his assiduous courtship. In a poetic turn of phrase that seems to blend Stendhal with Bartok, Fenimore here suggests that the four great loves of his life all eluded him ultimately. Yet his use of 'all the great Dembowskis of my life' suggests something far closer to Stendhal's mood than that of *Bluebeard's Castle*. It implies that he has learned from his loves and at the poem's end is ready to take to sea again. When he did so in actuality, however, it would be on *Aletheia* - for a voyage from which there will be no return. – TCE.

Brandom House Appendices

Cardinal Bolzano before the gates of Cos.
Image by Catherine Gordon.

Appendix D: The 'Burning Fuse' Documents

Document i: *Cardinal Bolzano's letter to the Pope – Late 2011*

This, Your Holiness is an updated copy of my letter of August 2009, concerning my visit to Doctor Fenimore Moneghan in July that year. You have expressed interest in the public speculation that has arisen since his disappearance last year and also the quiet preparations, which we understand are taking place, for the establishment of the Amor Mundi Foundation. Most of what follows consists simply of my original letter, following my journey to the Ends of the Earth to meet with Doctor Moneghan. I have appended a few brief remarks concerning the recent developments, which centre on the discretion and purposefulness with which his associates have gone about creating a new organization, based on his work and ideas. I note the significance and timing of this organization basing itself here in Italy, at a villa rather poignantly named after one of the more notable sons of the Counter-Reformation Church.

Doctor Moneghan's work, as you know, Holy Father, has been developing step by step for many years. Even in his doctoral studies, it was evident that there was a certain relationship between his concerns and those that animate our own great labours within the Congregation. Yet he undertook his own work quietly and unobtrusively in America and China as we laid the ground work for Opus Civitas Dei, here in Rome and around the world. We had heard that he was preparing a major work and that it had set itself the ambitious aim of resolving the long dispute in the modern world about the relationship between true religion and science. I travelled to the Ends of the Earth over two years ago to gain a deeper understanding of his progress and intentions. Now, it seems, the release of that book by his colleagues is imminent. It will be his third and with it there will come the establishment of a foundation to work behind the scenes with the intention of bringing about of a true *novus ordo saeclorum* – a new order of things.

Naturally, as the great Etienne Gilson expressed it, to the extent that there can ever be such a new order of things, it can only be an order patterned after the City of God. He wrote, some sixty years ago, in his Foreword to a new translation of *The City of God*:

> *The desire of the world-wide unity which fills the heart of man will, in all likelihood, never die...Generation after generation has honestly attempted to gather all men within the walls of an earthly city modelled upon the heavenly Jerusalem. They have studied everything except the Christian faith in order to find a common bond, but they have met with failure... If we really want one world, we must first have one Church, and the only Church that is one is the Catholic Church.*

Yet, Holy Father, our labours to this end have been beset with troubles in the modern world. Indeed, the great question with which the Congregation has had to wrestle since its foundation has been the relationship between the science and technology of the modern world and the future of true religion. It was your great insight, when your predecessor, His Holiness Pope John Paul II, appointed you Prefect of the Congregation thirty years ago, that the 21st century, the beginning of the third millennium since the Master walked the Earth, must bring a breakthrough in the relationship between the City of God and the City of Man – a breakthrough grounded in a resolution of the kind that we believe Doctor Moneghan to have been attempting; hence our interest in his work.

It was to you that your great predecessor handed a certain letter from Professor Ginzburg, in 1979, and asked that you consider how the Holy See might most charitably and openly respond. It was to me that you handed the keys to the office that long ago had been the cell in which Giordano Bruno was incarcerated at the Sant' Uffizio and said that I should think within its walls about how you might best answer the challenge put to you. But you already knew what kind of answer you wished me to find. For you recited to me, as you gave me that instruction, the words of the Psalm:

Will your wonder be known in the darkness; your bounty in the land of oblivion?

You brought to me the files on the banning of the works of Erasmus, the condemnation of Servetus (even if it was not we but John Calvin who had him burned at the stake), the burning of Bruno, the trial of Galileo, the censorship of Descartes and Spinoza. You urged me to immerse myself in the papers that had given rise to the creation of the *Index of Prohibited Books* and to follow that trail down through the files on the drafting for your predecessor His Holiness Pope Pius IX of the *Syllabus of Errors*; and the long struggle against Modernism by the Holy Office. You particularly drew to my attention, with a pained expression, the declaration, less than a century ago, by the venerable Rafael María José Pedro Francisco Borja Domingo Gerardo de la Santísima Trinidad Merry del Val y Zulueta, when Cardinal Secretary of the Holy Office, in 1929, that Mother Church continued to fight a "heroic rear-guard battle against that instrument of the Devil, the wicked printing press." "It is your task, Monsignor," you told me, "to play the role of the Advocatus Diaboli in this grave matter and to help me and the Holy Father to overcome centuries of fear and censorship, in order that the fullness of truth enable us to find a way out of the darkness and into the light which we should be for all nations."

Without question, Holy Father, that light can only be the light of Christ and of true religion. Yet, as your courageous predecessor declared, we must not be afraid to engage with modern science and philosophy; to be open to what is so and in the words of the Apostle, to test everything, but hold fast to what is good. As he remarked to the Pontifical Academy of Sciences on the centenary of the birth of Albert Einstein, the Galileo case created an unfortunate rift between the Church and the world of modern science and Galileo himself had been made to suffer a great deal at the hands of the Church. His Holiness, may he rest in peace, expressed the hope, on that memorable occasion, that "theologians, scholars and historians, animated by a spirit of collaboration, will study the Galileo case more deeply and, in loyal recognition of wrongs, from whatever side they come, will dispel the mistrust that still opposes, in many minds, a fruitful concord between science and faith." That was more than a year before he charged you with the ancient office of Prefect of the Congregation for the Doctrine of the Faith. It was another year again before you handed me the keys to Bruno's cell and gave me my instructions. The labour is long, Holy Father, but it is a labour in the vineyards of the Lord, for truly there is much to be learned here and a great harvest to bring in.

Nevertheless, the assignment you gave me has seemed at times overwhelming. How can I complete it? The archives themselves have long been in (how can I express this with due delicacy?) diabolical disorder, Your Holiness. Yet the work has moved forward and, as it has done so, remarkable things have occurred in the world that could hardly have been hoped for, despite all our prayers. Your most constant counsel to me was to remember always the study of the Word as the guide to all that is written. You would say that we, in the modern world, are again faced with the challenge that confronted the Apostle in Athens. 'Did he not challenge the Epicureans and Stoics on the Hill of Mars?' you would ask rhetorically. 'Did he not declare to them that the Unknown God of their own inscriptions was among them; and is that in which all nations live and move and have their being, as certain even of their own poets had said?' Think on these words, you advised me, and remember the clarion call of the Holy Father that modern human society suffers, like its ancient, pagan predecessor, from a growing despair about the human future and needs to recover hope – hope grounded in the human person and not in technology or the accumulation of endless material possessions. The human person, you admonished me, quoting his words, is "the only ontic subject of culture" and the way forward has to lie less in having more than in being more. With that, you would shepherd me back to my task among the endless files of the secret archives.

I was only seven years into my work when, by the blessed intervention of Our Lady of Fatima, the Soviet bloc crumbled without there being a terrible war. A transformation came to Eastern Europe, beginning with our faithful brethren in Poland. There had been a moment during that extraordinary year when we believed that Communism might fall in China, as so many idealistic and articulate young people called for peaceful change and brought into Tiananmen Square something which might by rigorists have been viewed as an idol – the more so as it was actually named the "Goddess of Democracy" – but which represented at least their fumbling attempts to demonstrate a commitment to beauty, truth and freedom. We were overcome with sadness and dismay when they were crushed by the tanks of the Communist Party. But the Lord works in mysterious ways. For that very spectacle seems to have triggered in Eastern Europe a revolt against Communist power and in this case tanks were not sent in, but held back. Nor did it end with the fall of the dictatorships in Eastern Europe. For within two years the Soviet Union itself had ceased to exist. Not since the days of St Augustine had there been so remarkable a demonstration of the defeat of the City of Man due to its own vices, while the angels of the Lord and the prayers of the faithful pointed to a better possibility. And so it was that we conceived and created Opus Civitas Dei – the great work of renewed evangelism in a world freeing itself from the yoke of totalitarianism and yearning for meaning and truth.

It was at around that time, as you will recall, that Moneghan's work came to the attention of the Congregation, with the publication of his first book, *Continental Drift*. It was our common perception and that of the Holy Father that the continents had, indeed, been drifting for some considerable time and that not Western culture alone, but global civilization had reached a profound watershed in its history. With the United States at the zenith of its power and prestige, we sensed the beginning of an era in which the Holy Spirit must more than ever guide us into the ways of wisdom and peace. That was the context in which your own works, *Co-Workers of the Truth*, *A Turning Point for Europe* and *A New Song for the Lord*, were prepared. We made a file note about Moneghan and received reports about his prior studies from America, but it was many years before we followed this up and during those years he undertook work in China. By coincidence it may seem, it was at the very time that we discovered him, immediately after he went to China, that I began my work on the Congregation's files on Father Pierre Teilhard de Chardin SJ, with your particular encouragement. Teilhard's own scientific work in China on human origins and natural history, during the 1920s and 1930s, deeply informed his later writings, notably *The Divine Milieu* and *The Phenomenon of Man*. Yet we, Holy Father, as you were among the first to point out, persecuted him and refused him the right to teach or to publish on philosophical or theological subjects. So little distance had we moved since the time of Bruno and Galileo.

I was deeply troubled as I pondered the words of our own Holy Office, dating from 1962 and approved by his Holiness Pope John XXIII, that the writings of Teilhard de Chardin "are replete with ambiguities or rather with serious errors which offend Catholic doctrine" and with files dating back many years before that condemning his thinking and preventing him from having his work published. Surely one of the great moments in the complex movement inspired by the Council was the rehabilitation of this man in the 1960s, by Henri de Lubac and you,

Holy Father. I took it as a sign of the capacity of the Body of Christ for renewal that, in the very year in which you were appointed Prefect of the Congregation, there appeared on the front page of *L'Osservatore Romano* itself the words:

> *What our contemporaries will undoubtedly remember, beyond the difficulties of conception and deficiencies of expression in this audacious attempt to reach a synthesis, is the testimony of the coherent life of a man possessed by Christ in the depths of his soul. He was concerned with honouring both faith and reason, and anticipated the response to John Paul II's appeal: 'Be not afraid! Open, open wide to Christ the doors of the immense domains of culture, civilization, and progress.'*

What a shift that signified within twenty years! Yet we knew that there was a great labour ahead of us and that that attempt to reach a synthesis had only begun. We had to go on.

The opening of the archives to scholars in 1998 was a symptom of our growing confidence that the dialogue could move forward and that a synthesis was and is possible. Your own work of 2000, *Spirit of the Liturgy*, gave expression to this hope:

> *And so we can now say that the goal of worship and the goal of creation as a whole are one and the same—divinization, a world of freedom and love. But this means that the historical makes its appearance in the cosmic. The cosmos is not a kind of closed building, a stationary container in which history may by chance take place. It is itself movement, from its one beginning to its one end. In a sense, creation is history. Against the background of the modern evolutionary world view, Teilhard de Chardin depicted the cosmos as a process of ascent, a series of unions. From very simple beginnings the path leads to ever greater and more complex unities, in which multiplicity is not abolished but merged into a growing synthesis, leading to the "Noosphere", in which spirit and its understanding embrace the whole and are blended into a kind of living organism. Invoking the epistles to the Ephesians and Colossians, Teilhard looks on Christ as the energy that strives toward the Noosphere and finally incorporates everything in its "fullness".*

The Omega Point was Teilhard's name, as you know, for the end point towards which the cosmos is moving. The Noosphere – the ecosphere become alive with consciousness and reflection – was his vision of the state towards which our labours and sufferings are tending and of which our often misbegotten utopias are anticipations. He lived and wrote in the light of the great Jesuit motto "finding God in all things." Yet we – here at the Congregation, the Holy Office, the Roman Inquisition, quartered in these very rooms where I now write – had suppressed that man for half a century. How could this be, Holy Father?

Even as I pondered these matters and began to conceive of a book of my own about Cardinal Bellarmine and the condemnation of Giordano Bruno for espousing beliefs that are now commonly accepted among the world's leading cosmologists, there came the shattering attack on the United States by al-Qaeda on 11 September 2001. Who can forget the apocalyptic image of the World Trade Centre burning and then crumbling to smoking ruins in the heart of the world's greatest trading metropolis, Holy Father? So little had our attempt to reach out to the other monotheistic faiths availed in healing ancient enmities! How is this to be done? How, from within our present darkness, are we to find a way to converge on Teilhard's Omega Point with Jews and Muslims, to say nothing of all those of more diverse and divergent beliefs? And where are we to concentrate our efforts in a world no sooner relieved from the fear of nuclear war among the superpowers than beset by terror and jihad against the infidels, Christians and Jews of America - in the name of God? Those were the circumstances, were they not, in which we sought to draw American interlocutors into the vision of Opus Civitas Dei? With little enough effect, to be sure; but the effort has been ongoing.

It was in this immediate context, in early 2002, that the Sant' Uffizio learned, from sources in Munich, of the imminent publication and German translation of Moneghan's second book, *The Horsemen and the Abacus*, about the Mongol conquests early in the second millennium and their impact on Asian civilizations. But we learned something else. He had left China, moved to the Ends of the Earth and was building there a refuge from all distraction, called 'Cos', in order to work on a philosophical treatise which would attempt a grand synthesis of science and philosophy. With your Benedictine background, Holy Father, you responded warmly to this idea and spoke of how St Benedict himself, 1,500 years ago and more, had retreated to Monte Cassino, after the downfall of the Roman Empire in the West and the rise of the Gothic Kingdom in Italy, and founded the greatest refuge of the spirit that the Western world had known up til that time. It was at this point that we saw a possible connection between Opus Civitas Dei and Moneghan's work, but some years passed before we attempted to make contact. During that time, he and his circle seem to have been very active and to have entered into financial arrangements in American markets which have now made possible the creation of the Amor Mundi Foundation.

It was only seven years later and four years after you yourself had become Pope that you sent me, finally, to the Ends of the Earth the summer of 2009. I was to meet with Moneghan and initiate a dialogue with him about the progress of his work, his relationships with his American friends, his perceptions of China and the bearing of his ideas on Opus Civitas Dei. Setting up the visit required some careful negotiation. When we first made contact, there was caution at Cos, but finally there was an invitation to come for the winter solstice festival held annually there and to attend a performance of Shakespeare's *The Tempest* on the solstice itself. That had seemed an interesting and agreeable arrangement, but was held back by work to do with release of your book *The Spiritual Meaning of Advent and Christmas*. As a result, I only departed for the Ends of the Earth in mid-July. This happened to coincide with the announcement by Father Lombardi, on your instructions, that no-one would any longer dream of asserting that Teilhard de Chardin is a heterodox author who should not be studied. We were not sure whether Moneghan would take note of this, but thought that, having been educated by the Jesuits, when a young man, he may well both learn of the declaration and appreciate its significance.

In any event, I needed to prepare myself to meet this man. Perhaps because of my own studies for years past, I had had – I have to confess this now, Your Holiness – nightmares about him as Bruno's ghost or a kind of mocking secular avatar of Teilhard de Chardin, who would hold me to account for the sins of the Holy Office. You knew that I had misgivings. You invited me to walk with you in the Vatican Gardens for counselling. You took me to the Pontifical Academy of Sciences, reminding me that it had been built originally as a villa for the relaxation of your predecessor Pope Pius IV. "Think of Cos", you suggested, "as something along these lines and feel at ease." Then you took me into the Vatican Palace and tried to buttress my self-confidence by conducting me through the grandeur of the Sistine Chapel and the Raphael Rooms: the Room of Constantine, the Room of the Signature, the Room of Heliodorus and the Room of the Fire in the Borgo. You urged upon me the immense dignity and tradition of the Catholic Church and reminded me that I would be going to the Ends of the Earth as a representative of this majestic past and not as a confused or rootless individual. Yet, Holy Father, I confess that the magnificent frescoes of the triumph of Constantine at the Milvian Bridge and the Donation of Constantine to Pope Sylvester filled me more with misgivings than with immense dignity. Similarly, the scenes in the Room of the Fire in the Borgo - of Pope Leo's fleet defeating the Saracens in battle - left me ambivalent.

Am I correct, however, in surmising that you intended something more subtle than triumphalism in taking me through these overwhelmingly splendid rooms? Unless I mistook your eyes, your tone of voice and the significance of your gestures, you intended not that I take into myself the wealth, the power or the secular pretensions of the historical Church but its humanity – its glory and its folly and the supreme irony of its Renaissance art treasures. You pointed very directly to the unforgettable secular frescoes in the Stanza della Segnatura – the School of Athens and Parnassus – and said, as a Benedictine to a Jesuit, "Remember and give the good Doctor Moneghan to understand that we have never forgotten Plato and Aristotle, Pythagoras and Euclid; and that we have gathered here, also, the Nine Muses and even the Tenth Muse, Sappho, as well as Horace and Ovid for the beauty of their work. We wish to talk with him of beauty and the Noosphere." Those words gave me heart and with them I packed my bags and took the long flight to the Ends of the Earth to encounter, as I supposed, a formidable embodiment of apostasy and secularism, immersed in writing a treatise that I hoped – but could hardly bring myself to believe – might be something other than a polemic against religion.

How, I wondered on my long flight over sea and desert, will I be able to find common ground with this man? At least we had a common link through the Society of Jesus.

Nothing – with the possible exception, Holy Father, of your inspired initiative of taking me through the Raphael Rooms – had prepared me for what I found when I got to Cos. The setting itself is evocative and imaginative: a spacious and exquisite Palladian residence set within walls of glistening stone that stand on a the wide summit of a hill overlooking on one side the River that runs through the City at the Ends of the Earth and on the other side vast public Botanical Gardens. The walls are pierced by a major and a minor gate, both facing westward, in the direction of the Botanical Gardens. Over the rather imposing arch which spans the main gate are the letters COS and beneath them a mysterious and striking formula – which Moneghan explained to me, but which still disturbs me. The overall inscription looks like this:

$$\text{C O S}$$

$$\underline{\Omega} = \mathrm{I}$$

Having spent some considerable time before my visit immersed in the files on Teilhard de Chardin, I could not help seeing the symbol Omega as evoking his eschatological theory about all of Being moving towards the Omega Point at the End of the World. To find myself at the Ends of the Earth encountering such an inscription was, therefore, astonishing. But that this Omega should then be equated, apparently, with the individual in residence struck me as a terrifying kind of arrogance, more characteristic of a pagan monarch than of a scientist or philosopher. To my relief, I learned presently that what I had taken to be the first person pronoun was, instead, the Roman numeral I, in place of the more common Arabic figure 1. The formula is a cosmological one and, so Moneghan informed me, indicates that 96% of the cosmos is made up of 'dark matter' and 'dark energy'. He attempted to explain it to me, but I was unable to follow him when he declared that it means the cosmos is 'flat'. We have known since the reasonings of Aristotle that the Earth is round. How, then, can the cosmos be flat? Looking back, I do not know which reading of the equation is actually the more disturbing. It is some comfort, at least, that I have been told and therefore now know the true reading.

I did not enter the grounds by the main gate but by the smaller gate – the garden gate, which has a bell suspended over it that peals as the gate opens and closes – a sound, I think, that I will always remember in the context of what followed. For the grounds that I stepped into when I passed that gate made it seem like the portal into another world – a world, I saw at once, bordered on its inner side by a wide ring of symmetrically planted Italian cypresses, still youthful but fast growing. I had not anticipated anything quite on this scale, or quite so

Vitruvian, when I prepared to go to this remote periphery of the civilized world. Above all, despite everything that I had heard of the Ends of the Earth and even read of Moneghan's work, I was insufficiently prepared for the metaphysical air of his establishment. It was as if the atmosphere subtly changed between the urban boulevard that ran along outside his gates; and the hedgerows and flower-beds, cottages and pergolas, pathways and great enclosures for horticultural and zoological purposes that surround the three or perhaps four level villa. The villa itself is immediately impressive for its assured lines and planes, its ample tinted glass, discrete verandas, elegant porticoes and soaring reflective surfaces. If I had thought that I was about to meet a modern Bruno, I was at once forced to recognize that the master of this house was no upstart monk or insolvent academic radical. He was an aristocrat of the spirit, proud and self-possessed.

He was somewhere aloft when a small, dark featured woman who seemed to be his housekeeper and who introduced herself to me as Mrs Steinschneider, showed me into a sitting room, delivering my bags to a male of African appearance who took them to where, I was given to understand, I would be accommodated during my stay. Whether because he was otherwise busy or because he wished to give me ample time to absorb the measure of his freedom and well-being, Moneghan allowed me some fifteen minutes to sit and contemplate my surroundings. The room had something of the elegant Bustamante about it: austere dark woods, tasteful rather than ostentatious classical and modern sculptures and vases, off-white slatted blinds deflecting the exterior light downwards, a long, low table adorned with learned and beautiful books and an exquisite chaise longue. They chanted to me in an undertone, as if they were a well-drilled choir, concerning the figure who was about to descend from somewhere over my head and, I began to fear, treat with some condescension the claims on his time and his attention of the Holy See. Yet I was agreeably surprised when a man taller than I had expected, leaner and more athletic than a scholar of his years is likely to be, with dark, but greying hair and relaxed, self-assured eyes stood in the doorway, extending a greeting of unmistakable warmth and solicitude. He asked was I travel weary and, when I had shaken his hand, put an uninhibited arm over my shoulder and declared with some ebullience, 'Let me show you around.'

And so, Holy Father, I became for the first time acquainted with Cos. Within it there is a library and research centre of a kind I have never seen elsewhere – and you know me to be an ardent bibliophile and a pilgrim to great abbeys and libraries throughout Christendom. But this is a private library of a grand nature. Even now, I almost shudder when thinking less of its 120,000 volumes than of the physical beauty of their setting and even more their evident use and maintenance. He told me, with a quiet smile, uncanny in its serenity, that he had dreamed of building the Total Library of which Jorge Luis Borges wrote seventy years ago;

but had chosen instead to create what he called the Intentional Library – in which there would be none of the endless volumes of gibberish that filled the library conceived by the fantasist of Argentina. I believe he has exercised severe judgement in excluding gibberish, Your Holiness. As your appointed Advocatus Diaboli for the printing press, I was lost in wonderment. 'It is my intention,' he told me, 'to hold within these halls all and only those works which can serve as foundation stones for a rethinking of human civilization in the era that has just begun.' And it was, Holy Father, ordered as no library is ever ordered – indexed with precision and cross-referenced to his inquiries. Long familiar with the disorder in our own archives, I was awestruck that such manifest coordination was even possible. Yet to all appearances it was the work of but two or three amanuenses – one of them Jewish, one Chinese, one African – working under his instruction over less than a decade.

Nor is the library – which he calls The Vivarium, Holy Father, after the establishment of Cassiodorus at the end of the ancient world[69] – the only such wonder at Cos. The Mahlerium, as he calls it, is a delightful musical auditorium, containing within it a collection of music that seemed as extensive and ordered as the books of The Vivarium. There is the theatre (which he calls The Dionysium), where I could have seen *The Tempest* performed had I arrived only a month earlier. There are guest suites – nine in number – on an upper floor, in one of which I was very comfortably accommodated throughout my stay. But above all there is the Hall of Frescoes, which astonished me, despite my long acquaintance with the frescoes of the Vatican, those of some of our finer Renaissance villas in Italy and those in the great abbeys of Europe. It astonished me because the frescoes are not drawn from any imagery known to Biblical or Classical history or mythology. Across the long and broad ceiling is a wide set of stunning evocations of the entire life-cycle of the Earth from its molten formation to its final end, amidst which sits – rising over the centre of the Hall – a vivid depiction of eight or nine brilliant stars against the deep darkness of the cosmos and numerous lesser or more remote stars. But around the walls, starting from the western entrance and coming back to it, were what I initially took to be reproductions of 20th century neo-primitive paintings. I thought vaguely of certain works by Picasso and Kandinsky. They were in fact stylized but largely faithful reproductions of the

---

69   Cassiodorus (485-585 CE) was a wealthy Roman aristocrat who served the Gothic kings in Italy after the downfall of the Roman Empire in the West. Fenimore describes him and his work in the first Notebook. Throughout his career, it seems, he made great efforts to bridge the cultural divides separating the Greek East from the Latin West, Romans from Goths, and Catholics from 'heretics.' In his retirement he founded a monastery called The Vivarium on his family estates in the south of Italy and wrote major books on education, religion and the future of the world. It's easy to see why his example appealed to Fenimore Moneghan. - NH

images from the Chauvet Cave – paintings of extinct prehistoric beasts: horses, lions, bison, rhinoceroses; and red ochre hand prints.

I have never seen anything quite like this Hall, but when Moneghan explained to me why he has placed these Ice Age images there, I understood that I was in the presence of a philosopher steeped at once in Plato and in the modern sciences. He reminded me of the famous 'Cave Simile' in Plato's *Republic*, then placed the frescoed images, Your Holiness, in the context of the study of signs and the philosophy of meaning, but he also explained the science behind their dating and the geological history of the region of France in which the Chauvet Cave is to be found. That, however, was only one of the strands of our conversation that day and in the remaining days I spent at Cos.

The point that he laboured chiefly to impress upon me throughout was the sense of being within what he called Deep Time. 'Look you', he exclaimed to me, pointing to the great ellipse of images around the ceiling of the Hall; 'our Earth came into being 4.5 billion years ago and will endure several billion more – an immensity of time – before it is burned out by a red giant Sun. But these stars', – and here he pointed like Adam touching the finger of the Lord in the Sistine Chapel – 'are the Pleiades, which were first examined through a telescope by Galileo. The Seven Sisters, they were called by the Greeks, along with their parents Atlas and Pleione' – and he named the seven one by one, then added – 'but there are actually eight of them, since Asterope is a double star. They are at least 400 light years from here and wandered free from the nebula in which they were formed between 75 and 150 million years ago, when the dinosaurs were still kings of this planet. They constitute what is called an open cluster. That cluster will be dispersed by gravitational forces over the next 250 million years – long before our world is burned to a cinder.' Forgive me, Holy Father, if I say that in such a setting and in such company, I had great difficulty in summoning an appropriate sense of the antiquity and majesty of our Mother Church.

I found that this man could discuss with me both the Psalms and Dostoevsky almost as readily as he could hold forth on cosmology and evolution. Moreover, he felt no apparent need to argue with me about matters of doctrine, though I could not gain from him assent to the dogmas of the faith. He delighted in showing me his butterfly enclosures and aviaries, his apiaries and flower-beds and his fish-ponds – all cared for as well by his groundsman and gardener, Theophrastus Forrest, as The Vivarium is by his amanuenses. Everywhere within the grounds of Cos I was struck by the profusion of natural light, the amplitude of space, the Palladian sense of proportion, the atmosphere of quiet and reflection, the simplicity and grace of manners. Nothing was worn out and nothing vulgar. It is evident that the entire compound has been built very recently – in fact, the site was apparently only cleared and excavated in 2002 and the building not completed until early in 2004 - and it was intended to last for many years to come. Nearby he showed me the offices of the business he chairs. It is rather charmingly called Peripatetica Decision Architects. It is a consulting company whose analysts roam widely, delivering services in the clarification of practical reasoning for both government and commercial clients. It is housed in a golden seven story office block on a great boulevard south from Cos and stands opposite the City's largest synagogue and the Ends of the Earth headquarters of the IT company Oracle.

I gained the impression that Moneghan sees all this as the beginning of a great work that will preoccupy him for the rest of his natural life. However, at the centre of his work – and of our concerns – is his attempt to write what he freely described to me as 'a guide for the perplexed in our time'. It is clear that Cos has been set up chiefly to facilitate this work. He had been, as of 2009, immersed in it, one way and another, for five years and told me that he had laid out a detailed design for the first two parts of what was to be a three part treatise. He was then at work designing the third part. He indicated that he had been somewhat detained in this latter part of the work by the occurrence of the great financial crisis in the United States and deliberations concerning the setting up of the 'Amor Mundi Foundation' – of which we had heard some reports.

While listening intently to all he had to say about these things, I attempted to elicit from him a clearer account of his philosophical findings and of the schedule for completion of his treatise. There came a quiet winter's afternoon at the Ends of the Earth, two or perhaps three days after I had arrived, on which we fell to talking of first and last things and the relationship of his work to ours. We were seated in an alcove within the precincts of The Vivarium, on curious chairs that he declared he had had fashioned for him by a skilled craftsman for use around the villa. Ornate lamps glowed over a low table on which Mrs Steinschneider had laid out for us strawberries, honey cakes and coffee.

I sought to draw out from him the extent of his continuing affiliation with his education by the Jesuits and with the long labours of the Church in a fallen world. I may have gone too far in recalling the prodigious labours of St Ignatius and the way in which the Society of Jesus had turned the tide against the Calvinists after the Council of Trent, by becoming the leading educators in Europe; but he listened more than he responded. I asked of his acquaintance with the great writings of Augustine and inquired as to how familiar he was with the proceedings of the Vatican Council. He spoke reflectively and without apparent constraint. Then I described to him, in at least broad outlines, the nature of our vision for Opus Civitas Dei and sought his response. It was slow and measured, but the gist of it was that he sees the writings of St Augustine, the history of the Society of Jesus and all our theological concerns as part of a vastly bigger picture. When I attempted – no doubt inadequately – to stir in him a sense of the majesty as well as the humanity of Mother Church, he gave me a most unnerving smile – I would almost call it Mephistophelean – and proceeded to recite to me three sentences from *The Brothers Karamazov*. They were from that famous passage in the book called 'The Grand Inquisitor'.

He plainly had long since taken them to heart. He recited them in sequence and verbatim, as if he was reciting from Holy Scripture:

> *And so it will be to the end of the world, even when the gods have vanished from the earth: they will prostrate themselves before idols just the same.*

> *I tell you, man has no more agonizing anxiety than to find someone to whom he can hand over with all speed the gift of freedom with which the unhappy creature is born.*

> *Look round and judge: fifteen centuries have passed, go and have a look at them: whom have you raised up to yourself?*

I think that he could have recited the entire Grand Inquisitor parable by Ivan Karamazov and discussed it with me learnedly. I confess that I was stumbling and uncertain in my response. Truly, at this point, the ghost of Bruno seemed to stand at my shoulder and I felt more than ever overwhelmed by the task you have placed upon me. I attempted to respond by reminding him that there has been enormous change since Dostoevsky wrote and that even Dostoevsky himself allowed that Ivan's parable of the Grand Inquisitor was a kind of caricature. I hoped, I said, that he would agree with me and talk of how his new Foundation could collaborate to greatest effect with our Opus. He then did something totally unanticipated, which left me speechless. Rising from his seat, stepping towards me, bending down from that great height of his and then imitating Alyosha Karamazov in the novel, he kissed me gently on the lips as if I had been the atheistic Ivan Karamazov. He enacted the text, Holy Father, as if I had been in the place of the atheistic party! At least, that was my immediate reaction to his remarkable behaviour. Then he resumed his seat, took a sip of his coffee and said, with perfect seriousness, 'How, then, shall we change the world?'

What is one to do with such a man? His gesture had very clearly been theatrical and not homoerotic. It was suffused with irony and literary criticism. I didn't know whether to protest, to laugh or to retreat in confusion. Seeing my evident discomfiture, he said, without a hint of mockery or condescension, 'I have always been intrigued by the fable of the Grand Inquisitor and by Dostoevsky generally. Please accept my apologies for such a histrionic intrusion into your personal space.' He assured me that there was more of Ivan than of Alyosha in him and that he knew I was simply a servant of the Holy Office and not the Grand Inquisitor in person. It was only then that I remembered the story more precisely and realized with a shock that he had seen himself as imitating Jesus kissing the Grand Inquisitor, not Alyosha kissing his brother Ivan!

With that I was galvanized into challenging him and he gave me the rest of his afternoon break in animated debate about the Church in the modern world and the existential interpretation of religious symbols and dogmas. I say the rest of his afternoon break, because he is a man of immensely disciplined routines and he did not make more than a marginal exception for me, save to allow me the freedom to enjoy the wonders of The Mahlerium and The Vivarium during the long hours in which he was absorbed in his studies – or what he calls his ontological exercises.

As you know, Holiness, I have long accustomed myself to rising early to say the office and to reflect before taking breakfast. Yet I discovered that Doctor Moneghan would be up, every morning without exception, fully two hours before I was and would have completed four hours of work, sustained by fresh fruit and muesli before, at 8.00 AM, he took two hours of exercise and ablutions: running, swimming and resistance work. He would then work for three more hours, take a light lunch and relax for two hours with staff, attending to household matters or responding to correspondence. Between 3.00 in the afternoon and 7.00 he would again work, which meant a working day of ten hours, broken by two periods of two hours each. At 7.00, he would sit down to a full meal with his household and any guests who happened to be in residence or to have been invited for the meal. At 8.00 there would invariably be music for two hours, in what appeared to be a well-thought through long cycle. Then he would retire at 10.00. This, Mrs Steinschneider assured me, has been his unvarying routine for years and is altered only when he undertakes foreign travel, is away at his coastal retreat sailing or hiking, or has very pressing Peripatetica business to attend to. He has neither wife nor children and seems to be totally committed to his philosophical work.

Truly, Holy Father, this is not the ghost of Bruno, but an individual who is the heir to all that Bruno stood for. He believes that, despite his public burning four centuries ago, Bruno has won and the Church has been compelled to admit its folly and abandon its erroneous cosmology, its erroneous biology and its inadequate Aristotelian ontology. He did not scruple to suggest that our dogmas impress him in any way. He is, in this sense, a quite unforgiving and formidable adversary. Yet he exhibited the most generous magnanimity in stating that he loves still the high and stern idea of the Catholic Church and admires its long resistance to the tide that has run so strongly against it. 'We do need', he declared, 'a great new unity and there is so much that the secular world has done badly and so much of the human spirit that it has failed to exalt'. He does seek a common language and he seems astonishingly free of cant and cynicism. He extolled Plotinus, Origen and Augustine as heroes of the spirit, yet cheerfully taunted me with the mocking dictum of Nietzsche that 'Christianity is Platonism for the people'. Truly, it is stimulating to have been under his roof. He is one of those with whom we can have a fruitful dialogue, even if he does not, perhaps, have the ultimate simplicity and humility of a saint.

Here is a man, Your Holiness, who has inherited a fortune - made, I understand, by his grandfather and father in industrial plastics - but has liquidated it to reinvest in what he calls 'knowledge industries for the time that is coming'; who has gained for himself an enviable education and complete freedom; whose business interests both at the Ends of the Earth and in the midst of it appear to be thriving to such an extent that he and his colleagues consult with governments and are on the point of creating a multi-billion dollar foundation; a man perhaps fifty years of age who yet seems to be in prime physical condition; who has built for himself an estate and an enclosure which seem like a fantastic combination of a Benedictine monastery, a Renaissance villa and a modern research institute. He is tall – fully a foot taller than me, Holy Father, but then you know that I am a small man – and lean. His eyes are a kind of sky blue and full of light, which can sparkle with vast amusement and joy. Yet they can freeze like a winter sky when he spells out mathematical formulae or talks of grave matters. His voice is resonant and he does not chatter, but converses in what I can only call a well-formed manner. It is rare enough, as you know, to encounter a person who speaks in complete sentences without pauses, hesitations or digressions. But this one speaks in complete and well-formed paragraphs. And he listens, Holy Father, as if he had not two ears but four or even six. He listens and understands. Above all, he thinks – constantly and without quarter or easy presumption.

The day I was leaving, he bade me farewell in the sitting room where we had first met. Mrs Steinschneider showed me all the way to the garden gate, where the Archdiocesan limousine awaited me. She opened the gate for me and the bell tolled, with its uncanny hint of quieter, more ecclesiastical days and a sense of angels. As I was about to pass through the gate, she asked me a most unexpected question: 'Is he as great as Plato?' What was a man of the cloth to say, Holy Father, to such a question from a woman I would not have expected to be so much as aware of Plato? She could sense my confusion, I think and to my further surprise she broke into a gentle laughter. 'I always ask that question, Your Eminence, of distinguished visitors and they always look surprised, like you.' 'I am really not qualified to say, Mrs Steinschneider,' I finally responded, 'but he is an impressive and very learned man. Who knows what the world will say of him if he is able to complete the great book he has set out to write? But Plato lived long ago, when philosophers were few and the sciences in their infancy. Your employer is attempting something that I think would have been beyond the abilities of Plato and will very likely prove to be beyond the abilities of Doctor Moneghan. By the grace of God, however, he will do good work and that will be enough.'

This was the man I met at Cos more than two years ago. Now he has departed the scene, abandoning Cos and giving up his life in a most un-Christian manner, without publishing his treatise. His colleagues have, as you know, proceeded in his name to set up the Foundation of which he spoke: the Amor Mundi Foundation. They have done this not at the Ends of the Earth, but here in Italy. I take it as an encouraging sign of their willingness to cooperate with us in the Opus that they have made this move and that they have done so within two years of my visit to Cos. That they have chosen for their headquarters in this country, Holy Father, a rural retreat in the Po valley by the name of Villa Barberini seems like a direct allusion to my conversation with Doctor Moneghan, that summer's day two years ago in his curious Greek armchairs under the beautiful lamps. What better indication could there be of their disposition towards Mother Church than the fact that they have quartered the Amor Mundi Foundation in a villa named for the illustrious family of your predecessor Pope Urban VIII, Maffeo Barberini, and his nephew, the Grand Inquisitor – therefore also your predecessor – Cardinal Francisco Barberini, whose unfortunate clash with Galileo long ago, set the tone for relations between science and religion for four hundred years? I think they know very well what they are doing.

Indeed, even the naming of their foundation – Amor Mundi – shows the profound Jesuit influence on their thinking, since it was for love of the world that God sent his only Son to dwell among us and to suffer among us for the sake of our sins; and because the Jesuit motto has always been 'Find God in all things'. I believe, therefore, that when it is finally shared with the world, the treatise of Moneghan will lend itself to the same great concerns as Opus Civitas Dei and to the great work of bringing unity at last to this troubled world of mankind. The Foundation will be well-endowed, but will work quietly, I understand – much as we are doing – according to a carefully thought out plan. I believe that we should make contact with them as soon as it can be arranged and that we should ensure that copies of the new treatise are procured for the Vatican Library at the earliest possible time. While it is clear that it will not take an orthodox theological line, we should not place ourselves in the position that we did vis-à-vis Bruno and Teilhard of attacking the author and his work. There is too much at stake and we have taken that path too often in the past – as you yourself have so often said to me, Holy Father. We need, instead, to create an opening for this work to be drawn into the great dialogue about the sciences and the liberal arts, beauty and the Noosphere, the unification of the human world and the flowering of true religion.

Roberto, Cardinal Bolzano
Stanza della Giordano Bruno
Sant' Uffizio 11
Vatican City
3 December 2011

Document ii: Cable from CIA Station Chief in Rome – Early 2012

TOP SECRET CIFRES NOFORN NODIS[70]

D/DNI D/CIA
D/NSA D/NSC
D/DHS

REF: OP COG[71] - File X-42-666/9/0047-SU11

SUBJECT: SECRET LETTER TO HIS HOLINESS THE POPE RE MONEGHAN

ATTACHED = SPECIAL REPORT RCVD ALBAN HILLS/CASTEL GANDOLFO[72] LATIN ORIGINAL: AMOR MUNDI ET MATER ECCLESIA TRNSLTD AT STN RQST CNTXT: VTCN VIEW MONEGHAN/OP COG

PLS PROTECT ABSOLUTELY [RPT: <u>ABSOLUTELY</u>] CLASS CIFRES DUE HIGH SENSITIVITY: PROTECTION <u>VITAL</u> PRVNT POSS CONTROVERSY.

SOURCE LONG-ESTABLISHED/TRUSTED PROTÉGÉ/CONFIDANTE PPBXVI[73]: EX TURIN 78-79. SANT' UFFIZIO EX RATZ APPMT PREF 81[74] ACCESS AAA: POC RE OVRHL SECRET ARCHIVES INQUISITION 1998-2008 – KEY PART OP COG

BRIEFING: OP COG STRONGLY [RPT <u>STRONGLY</u>] CONFIRMED BY ATTACHED ALBAN HILLS BRFNG: RELNS HOLY SEE VWD TRMS WWII, AFTRMTH ITALY, HEIGHT COLD WAR, END-GAME SOV BLOC, GWOT/IRAN/EU CRISIS/PRO-MONTI. OP COG BLVD INTEGRAL LONG VIEW POST-PPBXVI: POSS VATICAN III END DECADE – REF FILE X-42-666/9/0031-SEGNATURA

HUMINT LOMBARDY BACKS SIGINT NSA: EMERSON SOUND [RPT <u>SOUND</u>] MONEGHAN WORK + AMOR MUNDI FDN EXPCTD ALPHA DCLRN MID 2014 MONIES – EST. 3BN US$ - ZURICH/LICHTENSTEIN SECURE POSS INT POTUS[75] RE ELECTION

RIENZI
COS, ROME
05/18/2012

70   The classification TOP SECRET needs no explanation. CIFRES has proven indecipherable, but appears to be a code name for a certain level or perhaps stream of TS material. NOFORN means No Foreign dissemination, while NODIS means No Distribution. The latter is puzzling, given that the distribution list shows the report to have gone to many places across the intelligence system and that the security system put in place after 9/11 encouraged wider sharing across agencies, but there it is. Perhaps NODIS excluded chiefly the FBI? - NH

71   This acronym, central to the significance of the memo, seems to be a compression and translation of the term Cardinal Bolzano uses in his report: Opus Civitas Dei: translation Opus/ Operation **City of G**od (COG). - NH

72   Castel Gandolfo, the Papal summer palace is in the Alban Hills, just outside Rome. - NH

73   This plainly is an abbreviation for Pope Benedict XVI. - NH

74   This extremely compressed set of characters appears to record that the source (Bolzano) had been close to Joseph Ratzinger for many years and had been appointed to some unspecified position – it would seem as an assistant to Ratzinger – when the latter became Prefect of the Congregation for the Doctrine of the Faith (CDF) in 1981. Sant' Uffizio (Holy Office) 11 is the address of the CDF, just off St Peter's Square in the Vatican. - NH

75   POTUS = President of the United States, i.e. Barack Obama running for re-election in 2012. - NH

Document iii: MSS briefing to the Chinese Politburo – Mid-2012

The big socialist country of China has always been a major target for the peaceful evolution methods of the Western capitalist countries headed by the United States. Since the founding of the People's Republic of China and after the failure of their armed intervention on the side of the reactionary forces during the war of national liberation, each American administration has pursued the same goal, whether under Republican or Democrat presidents. The phrasing and the front organizations used to this end may vary, but the underlying strategy remains the same: to cultivate so-called democratic forces within socialist countries and to stimulate and organize political opposition using fanciful terms like 'democracy', 'civil liberties', or 'human rights'.

They also try to win over or split off wavering elements within our Party with the intention of undermining its unity and weakening its grip on political power. All this has been conceived and coordinated since before the Party even took power. It was part of the agenda of the Central Intelligence Agency and its secret monopoly capitalist masters from the time that organization was set up in 1947. It remains more than ever their agenda now and we must be on our guard against its machinations.

This conspiracy against the Party and the socialist future of China has taken five paths over the decades since 1949. It has engaged in: This conspiracy against the Party and the socialist future of China has taken five paths over the decades since 1949. It has engaged in:

1. Ideological and cultural infiltration
2. The cultivation of pro-American forces
3. Putting out feelers to the top Chinese leadership by every means available
4. Targeting future leaders
5. Offering economic and technological aid to us in order to make us dependent on them

When they attempted to stir up counter-revolution in 1989, using black hands from Taiwan and broadcasting open sympathy for the so-called 'democracy movement' in their media, the Party responded with stern measures and restored order. But their efforts to subvert the People's Republic have been unrelenting. The latest plot came to light in 2008, when they supported the so-called liberal reform movement and its Charter 08 manifesto. We have kept track of all these activities and have now received clear evidence that something we believed many years ago was, just as we had suspected all along, yet another Western plan to undermine socialism and extend the hegemony of the capitalist West. It came in the form of an internal CIA document which confirms our belief that, within three years of the Tiananmen Incident of 1989, they had infiltrated agents into our country to begin a long term project aimed, as before, at changing China by creating, as they have said in as many words in the past, 'new modern people with a different belief system'.

And what belief system would that be? The deep involvement of the Jesuits in this plot is evidence enough of that. It was Jesuits who first infiltrated this country, undermining and spying on the Ming Dynasty. They never give up! In the years during which the Party was striving to mobilize anti-Japanese resistance and lay the foundation for liberation, the reactionary fascist Jesuit 德日進 (Dérìjìn)[76] came and went for years unhindered. After the revolution, the Jesuits continued to spy on us from Hong Kong and try to subvert the People's Republic with their lies and propaganda, their superstition and loyalty to outside powers. The notorious Dulles brothers, even though Presbyterians, placed a member of their family in the Jesuit order – as if we would not notice! – and the Vatican acknowledged his work when he was very old by making him a Cardinal. Who can believe that these services were not bound up with the machinations of the CIA? This Moneghan was educated by Jesuits and probably recruited then to do what he is doing now. This Bolzano is a Jesuit and it can hardly be a coincidence that he was sent to meet Moneghan in 2009. It is not for nothing that Lenin expressed a grudging admiration for the Jesuits and even said that good Communists should learn from them. They are relentless and work in the darkness. A sure sign of this new conspiracy coming to fruition will be when a Jesuit becomes Pope. Mark our words!

The key figures in the operation during the 1990s – the so-called OP COG of the CIA - were an American citizen of Chinese descent, Poseidon Wang, and another and mysterious figure by the name of Fenimore Moneghan. They came here in the guise of scholars interested in the history of Chinese environmental affairs and the history of Chinese science. It was clear from the start that they knew one another and had some kind of common agenda. We bugged their phones and their apartments, we placed our people close to them at every opportunity and were able, after some years, to position an agent in intimate proximity to Moneghan, but a year later he abruptly withdrew from China. Wang stayed on, conducting mischievous inquiries, for many years after that. It was only in 2005, when he published a book slandering the Party and the state in the name of so-called 'ecological activism' that we declared him an enemy of the Chinese people and denied him any further access to the country. In our opinion, he should have been arrested and prosecuted much earlier for stealing state secrets. His denunciation of the Party for its handling of the SARS problem was scandalous and destabilizing.

---

76   This, we learned, is the name of the Jesuit scholar Father [Teilhard] de Chardin (1881-1955) translated into Chinese and Romanised pinyin. His name, as the reader will have seen, surfaces in the secret letter to the Pope. He did, in fact, spend many years in China, in the 1920s and 1930s. – NH.

But Moneghan, meanwhile, seems to have been on an even more ambitious mission for his secret masters. He travelled to Munich, where Radio Free Europe and the Voice of America had been based throughout the Cold War and spent some time there talking with various unknown people. He then withdrew to the Ends of the Earth and set up a kind of safe house where he proceeded, with a staff and behind high walls to undertake a research project. We knew that he had a Chinese assistant, Bo Zhangliu. We knew that the two of them were already in league with anti-Party elements by 2003 and 2004, because they gave a paper in Madrid in April 2004 with the provocative title 'Web of Possibilities: The Internet and the Prospects for Political Liberalization in China – Hu, Wen and How'. Even more significantly, Moneghan met Bo in Madrid on his way back from meetings in the United States, where he had, we believe, held meetings with other members of the CIA group running this long term operation. There can be no doubt that his agenda by then included subversion of socialism in China. In fact, our awareness of this helped inform our advice in 2005 that Wang be arrested and prosecuted. We still believe that would have been the best course of action. Indeed, in the light of what we have just learned, it is a great pity that we did not get the chance to interrogate Wang. We might have found out a great deal.

We noted that, after 2005, Moneghan took in as a long term guest a bad element and dissident by the name of Qiu Xiaoli. Visitors came and went and several years passed, but we were not able to make sense of what he was up to, until 2007, when he visited Europe with Qiu and made contact with the Chinese dissident movement in exile. At that point it became clearer than ever that whatever he was doing, he was up to no good. We believe that he may have been the CIA's main conduit, in fact, to the counter-revolutionaries who prepared Charter 08 and hoisted Liu Xiaobo as some kind of supposed national hero. The disgraceful award of the 2008 Nobel Peace Prize to Liu Xiaobo was plainly part of the CIA's overall peaceful evolution strategy. That was as clear as day. What remained obscure was the actual role of Moneghan and his carefully camouflaged links with American intelligence. Above all, we wanted to know what he was doing at the Ends of the Earth. What was the detailed research project that every rumour and report indicated he was immersed in?

From that point onwards, we kept an even closer eye on Moneghan, but we were still unable to make sense of his secret research project. Then something truly mysterious happened. In June 2010, he simply disappeared from the Ends of the Earth. There was no sign that he had completed his research project. In fact, the press there and the authorities declared that he was presumed dead, but his body was never found. This aroused our suspicions at once. Our agents in the Chinese community at the Ends of the Earth reported that a funeral ceremony was held, attended by many people, including several visitors from the United States. They were unable, however, to get names or identities of those visitors. It did not take much thought, however, to deduce who they must have been. We believe that Wang was one of them and that several others were there who had been working with Moneghan and Wang under academic cover for some considerable time. But it was only this year that we began to understand the enormous scope of what they were up to. And that is because our trusted source within the CIA was able to supply us with a cable from their station in Rome showing that those American visitors have billions of dollars at their disposal and are working in the shadows to create some kind of 'foundation' that we believe to be the core of a Western plot of unprecedented scale to undermine not only our Party and state but all other sources of opposition to their future hegemony.

How could a small group of 'scholars' acquire billions of dollars? What was this foundation they were so secretly setting up? Why did Moneghan disappear into the shadows just as they began this work? Our agent's work enabled us to drag all this into the clear light of day. They had not, of course, made billions from research work, which is an absurd idea. It had come from the CIA and the big financial capitalists on Wall Street. That was obvious and should not have surprised us, but the scale of it took our breath away. Nor should it have surprised us to discover that the CIA was in league with the Vatican in this nefarious scheme. They have been in secret league ever since the CIA was created. In fact, American intelligence developed deep ties with the reactionary forces in Italy during the Second World War, beginning in Sicily and New York. Both the Mafia and the Vatican, the twin reactionary octopuses of Italy, joined forces with the Americans in the 1940s, in order to protect their own interests and to prevent the victory over the fascist dictator Mussolini from being achieved by the progressive forces in Italy. We have known all this for a long time. Here, however, we can see these old and deep relationships bearing their evil fruit in a plot of gigantic proportions.

We still do not know where Moneghan went in 2010, but we suspect he has been in hiding in Italy since late last year. There had been reports that his colleagues acquired a retreat in rural Italy not far from the city of Mantua at that time. It took us some time to find it, but we now know it to be a luxurious estate near the river Po called Villa Barberini. We have been keeping it under cyber-watch and human surveillance ever since, but whatever is going on there is being protected under a veil of secrecy so cunning that we have not yet been able to learn its true agenda. Where Moneghan was, in the eighteen months between his disappearance from the Ends of the Earth and the setting up of this base at the Villa Barberini, is a matter for speculation, but we suspect he was in the United States at a CIA or NSA facility. In any case, as the attached documents show, the Vatican saw the operation as coming to maturity when the rural safe house was acquired. That was now more than six months ago. Our assessment is that Moneghan has been working with a team of others to complete plans for the operation and that it will get under way in the near future, if it has not already commenced its work. We infer, based on the secret documents from the CIA and the Vatican supplied to us by our agent; that the research project on which Moneghan had been engaged at the Ends of the Earth was a detailed blueprint for the operation.

The presence of both Bo and Qiu at Moneghan's walled compound at the Ends of the Earth is proof enough that that blueprint targets our Party and our country. His earlier dubious work in China and that of his colleague, the traitorous émigré Poseidon Wang, were already evidence of a deep and cunning plot against our country of the typical CIA kind. But the move to Italy shows that this plot is even bigger than was previously thought and the attached documents testify clearly to that fact. We have assigned high priority to breaking the wall of secrecy that surrounds this operation and have directed our offices in both Rome and Milan to focus their energy and resources on identifying the members of the team and finding out what is in the blueprint. We have attached copies for the attention of the Politburo Standing Committee of the secret Vatican memorandum and the top secret CIA cable that covered its dispatch to Washington. They are extremely sensitive and should be very closely protected. They should not be circulated more widely or referred to in public even indirectly. As the next generation of leaders takes the helm, they will need to be aware of this plot and will need to keep a calm demeanour and adopt a patient attitude while we establish its true scope and nature. We stand ready to protect the Party and the country against this new and dangerous conspiracy. We will leave no stone unturned to defeat it and are already at work to do so.

Document iv: Anonymous YouTube Manifesto – Late 2013

Dear brothers and sisters on this Earth of humankind. This is, as we have been urging for some time, the point at which to open your eyes! We hacktivists have come into possession of secret documents which expose a covert operation on a breathtaking scale by establishment forces. It is called Operation Cog – as in Cog and Macog – and is an attempt to undermine your freedom at its very foundation. Its aim is an Omega state in which there is only one power. That is their secret sign:

$$\underline{\Omega} = I$$

Note that the numeral 'I' is Roman, not Arabic, which shows that it is the Roman Catholic Church that sits at the heart of this new bid at Universal Empire. They realized this in China. Now you can see it for yourself. These documents demonstrate that those who tax you tyrannically and have given themselves the 'right' to lock you up without trial or kill you in the name of national security, have far-reaching plans to subvert liberty and dominate the future of human civilization with a hidden agenda.

We have denounced the banking practices that have bankrupted the United States of America, culminating in the monstrous frauds on Wall Street in the 2000s and the lavish use of your money to bail out and enrich the bankers. These new documents show that billions of dollars accumulated during that time have been channelled, by the master-minds of Operation Cog, into the creation of a secret 'Foundation', the agenda of which is to revitalize the power of the Papacy, in an alliance with the dark forces that have taken over the government of this country, and to set a 'new' course for civilization around the world in the name of 'true religion'.

We warned last year that the National Defense Authorization Act – which passed late at night by 93 votes to 7 in 'your' Senate - had declared the entire USA to be a 'battleground' upon which U.S. military forces can operate with impunity, overriding Posse Comitatus and granting the military the unchecked power to arrest, detain, interrogate and even assassinate U.S. citizens with impunity. But we can now see that they intend not only to coerce you, but also to infiltrate your mind and subvert your independence of judgement.

If the passage of that law was, as we warned at the time, 'nothing less than an outright declaration of war against the American people by the military-connected power elite', then this covert operation shows nothing less than an alliance between the secret powers that passed that law and the ancient Roman Inquisition to undertake a new program of thought control and a new kind of crusade against freedom of belief, all in the name of law and order and true religion. The ambitious scope of this plot is astounding. There has never before been a covert operation on such a scale. It literally defies belief – your belief in your freedom and your future.

The new law, as we have warned you, shreds the tenets of the Bill of Rights and will soon unleash upon America a total military dictatorship, complete with secret arrests, secret prisons, unlawful interrogations, indefinite detainment without ever being charged with a crime, the torture of Americans and even the 'legitimate assassination' of U.S. citizens right here on American soil! The new 'Foundation' will manufacture legitimacy for this abolition of your civil and political rights and it will do so in the name of true religion. You will become no more than a little cog in the vast machinery of Operation Cog!

If you have not yet woken up to the reality of the police state we've been warning you about, I hope you realize we are all fast running out of time. Once this becomes law, you will have no rights whatsoever in America - no due process, no First Amendment speech rights, no right to remain silent, nothing. And if this Foundation gets up and running, you will face a wall of authoritative propaganda that will enclose your churches, your schools, your municipal governments and those few media outlets that still have any credibility.

Neither the CIA nor the Vatican want us to draw attention to this Foundation they are creating. We suspect that even now orders are being silently and secretly conveyed under secure cypher and that men with guns, or perhaps more subtle 21st century weapons, are already looking for us, even as we create this message and prepare to release it like a dove of peace, like a carrier pigeon bearing a vital warning. Why will they come for us? They will do so, because they cannot abide the disclosures we are making.

Words, we know, will always retain their power. They offer the means to reveal hidden meanings and, for those who will listen, the enunciation of truth. And the truth is, there is something terribly wrong with this country and something deeply sinister about the secret forces that have been striving for so long to bend it to their will and to extend their power over all those who have defied oppression and Papism since the dark days of old. We know you agree with this. That is why we are putting the truth out there – for your sake and that of your children.

Where once you had the freedom to object, to think and speak as you saw fit, you now have both censors and sensors watching and inhibiting your freedom, coercing your conformity and soliciting your submission. How did this happen? Who is to blame? Those who are responsible will be held accountable. They believe that they can send their minions to hunt us down, but they will fail in the pursuit. They will encounter their nemesis. We shall reclaim our freedom! Rise with us and demand the liberty that is your birthright.

Now that we re-COG-nize what they are up to, we shall all stand together against this outrageous conspiracy to undermine freedom and extend the sway of secret and unaccountable power.

We are Anonymous. We are Legion. United as ONE, Divided by ZERO, we do not forgive Conspiracy, we do not permit Regression. We are coming!!

Music by: Franz Schubert *Death and the Maiden*

Appendix E: A Brief Chronology of the Life of Fenimore Moneghan and its Aftermath

1960   Fenimore Moneghan is born at the Ends of the Earth to Patrick Moneghan and Monica Moneghan nee Waterford.

1966   The Moneghan family company Martin Moneghan Plastics is publicly listed as Ends of the Earth Plastics Inc. It is heavily subscribed and the family fortunes begin to inexorably rise.

1970   Birth of Margarita in Maracaibo, Venezuela.

1971   Fenimore commences secondary education under Jesuit tuition at St Ignatius Loyola College in the City at the Ends of the Earth.

1977   Fenimore taught Year 12 Classical Languages by Fr Polycarp Irons SJ.

1978   Fenimore begins his studies in languages, philosophy and physical sciences at the City University at the Ends of the Earth.

1979   Fenimore forms a relationship with Catriona Campbell, an English Language and Literature major at the City University.

1981   Fenimore completes his undergraduate studies with distinction. He wins a scholarship to go to the Fletcher School, Tufts University, Massachusetts, to study for the Master of Arts in Law and Diplomacy (MALD). Margarita begins secondary studies at an Opus Dei school in Caracas.

1982   Fenimore's relationship with Catriona ends some months after his departure for the United States.

1983   Fenimore meets and forms a relationship with Nathalie Morton, a graduate in Fine Arts from Vassar College.

1984   He meets Tom Emerson, a graduate student in constitutional law with interests in philosophy, history, poetry and strategic affairs. They form a friendship. Fenimore travels with Nathalie Morton to Europe. They see the Veneto, a little of Greece and parts of Spain, including Madrid and Toledo. He completes the MALD and is offered a job at Salomon Brothers in their new bond trading department, but chooses instead to go to Harvard and undertake a PhD in Philosophy. Nathalie breaks off their relationship.

1985   Fenimore at Harvard.

1986   Fenimore and Tom befriend Bianca Ruggiero, Irad Kripke, Poseidon Wang, Suzanne Baker, Yusuf Erdogan, Amartya Menon and Dambisa Mbeke. They discover a convergent interest in the philosophy of science and the future of civilization. They meet regularly and decide late in the year at Bianca's instigation to call their discussion circle the Academy of Lynxes.

1987   Fenimore starts learning Chinese on the side and studying Joseph Needham's multi-volume history *Science and Civilization in China*, in close discussion with Poseidon Wang, who is working on environmental history, the human impact in the Pleistocene and the origins of agriculture. He (Wang) is thinking of a dissertation on Iron Age China and the extinction of China's rhinoceros and elephant populations.

1988   Fenimore commences his doctoral dissertation on the relationship between the theories of ontology in Nietzsche and Heidegger and the findings of the natural sciences. Margarita commences a Music degree in Caracas and begins her association with Jose Antonio Abreu's El Sistema.

1990   Fenimore completes his dissertation and commences a post-doctoral fellowship to turn his dissertation into a book. Margarita completes her Music degree and goes to work with El Sistema.

1991   Nathalie Morton takes up with Bruno Herman, a Harvard MBA who is making a career on Wall St in investment banking.

1992   Fenimore's first book, *Continental Drift: How Existentialism Became Unmoored from the Natural Sciences*, is published. He leaves Boston for China. Margarita undertakes a business diploma in Mexico City.

1996   Fenimore meets and befriends Axel von Darmstadt in Beijing. He meets Bo Zhangliu and engages his IT skills as an assistant.

1998   Fenimore meets Weili Wu at the Suzhou conference. They form an intimate relationship within days. Hugo Chavez becomes President in Venezuela. Margarita goes to Buenos Aires for graduate studies in Music Therapy. She meets Anactoria Lopez and they form an intimate relationship. Long Term Capital Management, a wildly successful hedge fund in Connecticut, blows up when Russia defaults on its debt. Irad Kripke is fascinated by the debacle and begins to think about creating his own hedge fund.

1999   Irad Kripke sets up his hedge fund, Iced Rowanberry Investments (IRI), in Connecticut, with the other members of the Academy of Lynxes as his advisory board. Weili vanishes without trace in Beijing. Fenimore's parents killed in a catastrophic road accident in the Apple Island, off the edges of the Ends of the Earth. He inherits an industrial fortune. The Communist Party attempts to crush Falun Gong in China. Bo Zhangliu flees China and comes to the Ends of the Earth.

2000   Fenimore leaves China. He visits Germany and meets with Axel von Darmstadt, who introduces him to Immerwahr Denker and Giuliano Pippi. He visits Todtnauberg to look at Heidegger's hut. He sets up a temporary base in the City at the Ends of the Earth, while planning Cos. Creation of the consulting company Peripatetica Decision Architects with Fenimore as chairman of the board.

2001   Tom Emerson begins work on *The Bow of Odysseus*. The 11 September assault on the United States takes place. Fenimore acquires and clears the site for the building of Cos. Margarita and Anactoria move to Tenerife, where Margarita forms her company, Capirote Therapies.

2002   IRI announces record returns for its clients. The Academy of Lynxes meets at New Haven to discuss an investment plan. They begin to invest in IRI. Publication of Fenimore's second book, *The Horsemen and the Abacus: The Mongols and the Stagnation of Civilization in Asia after the 13th Century CE*.

2003   The building of Cos begins. Fenimore conceives the idea of writing a *Guide of the Perplexed for the 21st century*. Peripatetica's work grows exponentially. It begins to run its Conspiracy Theory and Cognition Workshop.

2004   Publication of *The Bow of Odysseus* in March. The Academy of Lynxes meet in New York to celebrate the launch and each member is given a copy by Tom. Fenimore flies from New York to Madrid, in early April, where he meets Bo Zhangliu and they give a paper on the internet and political reform in China. Anactoria flies to Madrid to give a paper on the Guanches. Margarita comes with her, but heads off ahead of her to Toledo to relax and look at the Rodriguez guitar shops. Fenimore drives down to Toledo for a few days break. He meets Margarita by chance at La Cubana on his final day. The building of Cos is completed in June and is celebrated with a theatrical production in The Dionysium of Michael Frayn's *Copenhagen*. Margarita visits in October for a Music Therapy Conference. She stays at Cos for ten days. She and Fenimore form an intimate, but secret relationship.

2005   Irad Kripke proposes to the Academy of Lynxes that they short the mortgage companies selling sub-prime mortgage loans. Fenimore begins to create Notebook I, as he works on the design for the first part of his treatise – on cosmology. Fenimore and Margarita meet in Vienna and Budapest. Fenimore's theatrical troupe performs Chekhov's *The Seagull* in The Dionysium. Poseidon Wang publishes a paper on the Communist Party's handling of the SARS crisis and is declared *persona non grata* in the PRC.

2006   First Shakespearean performance at Cos: *A Midsummer Night's Dream,* on the winter solstice. Tom and several of the other members of the Academy are there for the occasion and stay on for a few days. Fenimore and Margarita meet in Yucatan and tour Mexico (October), following the Academy's traditional gathering in New York, at which Tom reveals that he is writing a new book on executive power, law and terrorism, which he hopes will be published by 2010. His title for it is *Fanaticism and International Law.*

2007   Irad attends the American Securitization Forum in Las Vegas in January. It becomes clear that his calculations about the mortgage market are correct and that the financial crisis could be massive. IRI moves to off-load its mortgage assets and short the Wall St banks themselves. Fenimore and Margarita visit Berlin and Paris in April. Second Shakespearean performance at Cos: *Much Ado about Nothing,* again on the winter solstice. Irad reports to the others at the annual gathering of the Academy in October that the mortgage market and Wall St bond dam is set to burst within twelve months. Fenimore concludes Notebook I and opens Notebook II as he starts work on the second part of his treatise – biology.

2008   Fenimore and Margarita visit Egypt together in April. She gives him Daniel Levitin's *The World in Six Songs: How the Musical Brain Created Human Nature.* He completes part two of the treatise design and Notebook II. Vera Burbage oversees the third Shakespearean performance at Cos: *Hamlet,* on the winter solstice, as usual. The sub-prime crisis breaks out in New York and across America in September. IRI reaps billions on its 'big short'.

2009   Fenimore begins design work on the third and final part of his treatise – ontology. He and Margarita spend a week in Venice and the Veneto in April, where he had been 25 years before with Nathalie Morton. He begins writing Notebook III. Vera Burbage and the drama troupe put on the fourth Shakespearean performance at Cos: *The Tempest* on the winter solstice. Cardinal Bolzano visits Cos in July. Fenimore and Margarita plan to meet in Buenos Aires and Rio de Janeiro in October, but she postpones the assignation until the following April. The Academy of Lynxes meet in late October and agree to pour the overwhelming bulk of their profits into a Foundation to do intelligent, lasting good – the Amor Mundi Foundation.

2010   Fenimore meets Margarita in Buenos Aires in April. She declares that the relationship is over. He proceeds to Austin, to Tom's place ('Treehaven') and stays there for over a week, attending the conference on 'Global Warming and International Policy Coordination'. He collapses and spends some days recovering, re-reading Ovid's *Metamorphoses* and talking with Tom. He decides to spend a week in the Aegean before returning to the Ends of the Earth. He flies via New York and London to Istanbul. He stays for a number of days with Yusuf, meets Cleis Scamandros, then flies down to Santorini and rests there for several days, reading, writing and reflecting

He then flies back to Cos, only to collapse again. Tests reveal extremely aggressive metastatic cancer. He tells no-one for several days, writes a final entry (the Epilogue) in Notebook III and puts his affairs in order as efficiently as possible. He sends Tom, by surface mail, his will, a letter appointing Tom, Suzanne and Monica as his executors and the three Notebooks, with a request that Tom publish them in a private edition for the Academy of Lynxes. He then vanishes from Cos. Less than twenty four hours later his yacht is found off the coast, but his body is never found. Rumours and speculation erupt. Tom flies in to sort out the mess and runs into confusion at Cos and Peripatetica – and resistance to his plans. Several of the others then arrive for belated obsequies in early July.

2011   Tom patiently sorts out Fenimore's estate and the Academy members plan for the creation of the Foundation. At their annual gathering they agree to locate its headquarters in Italy and appoint Tom and Bianca to find suitable premises. They find the Villa Barberini and purchase it in the late fall. Meanwhile *L'Affaire Moneghan* has become an international cause celebre and conspiracy theories are rife. Cardinal Bolzano is asked by the Pope for a fresh and updated copy of his letter of 2009 about Moneghan.

2012   Cardinal Bolzano takes a drive through the Alban Hills to Castel Gandolfo with the CIA Station Chief and gives him a copy of the updated letter. The COS sends it to Washington with a highly classified covering cable. The two documents together are sent to Beijing by a Chinese mole in the US intelligence system. An analysis of and commentary on them are sent to the Politburo. A CIA spy within the Chinese intelligence establishment supplies Langley with a copy of the report to the Politburo attached to the CIA cable and the Bolzano letter. The NSA warns that Anonymous has become a national security risk.

2013   Tom and the other members of the Academy convene at Villa Barberini in the late spring and discuss the manuscript and Tom's editing of it at some length. A month later, Bianca, in Rome, announces that the Amor Mundi Foundation will be officially set up in the summer of 2014. The Bolzano letter, Rienzi cable and Politburo briefing are obtained by Anonymous in early November. They write and create on YouTube a manifesto denouncing an alleged conspiracy between the CIA, the American military-industrial-financial complex and the Vatican to take over the world.

2014   Tom completes the editing and printing of *Darkness over Love* in the winter and early spring. The Academy members meet again at Villa Barberini in April and agree on final preparations for the setting up of the Foundation. Tom presents each of them with a printed copy of *Darkness over Love*. After their departures, he remains at Villa Barberini to continue work on Fenimore's papers and the manuscript of the unfinished treatise. On 20 June, in the middle of preparations for a Midsummer party at the villa to celebrate the setting up of the Amor Mundi Foundation, a truck drives into its grounds and sets off a massive bomb that obliterates the villa, killing nine people. Bianca is not there. The bodies are so charred and disintegrated, however, that even DNA identification is very problematic. Hezbollah claims responsibility and denounces the victims as participants in a monstrous conspiracy, as servants of Satan and enemies of Allah and the Prophet. In early August, Bianca flies to New York and meets executives at Brandom House to request publication of *Darkness over Love*. Brandom House review the manuscript, consult their lawyers and agree to publish the book.

As the page proofs are completed in New York, in early November, the offices of the Amor Mundi Foundation on Via dei Cappellari are attacked by terrorists. Bianca is killed, along with three of her staff and two security guards. Brandom House faces threats and adopts stringent security precautions, but decides to go ahead with publication. In early December, galley proof copies of the core manuscript, minus N. Herman's Introduction and Postscript, are sent out to a number of readers, including Lilith Zohar at Stanford.

2015   In early February, N. Herman flies to Stanford to meet Zohar and discuss interpretations of the book and the idea of a conference, to be held at Stanford in 2016 under the rubric 'Alpha and Omega: Fenimore Moneghan's Posthumous Notebooks in the Light of *L'Affaire Moneghan*.'

Author's Quiz: Discussion Points

There are only two novels of which I am aware in which the author sets out points from which the novel might be further developed or points for discussion. The first is Lawrence Durrell's *The Alexandria Quartet* (strictly speaking, therefore, four novels)[77]. The second is Bernhard Schlink's *The Reader* (1995). It is their example that I am following here, in asking readers of the present volume to consider a set of questions.

Schlink asks straightforward questions of his readers. Durrell was far more elliptical. Out of regard for my own readers, I intend to adhere to Schlink's practice rather than Durrell's. However, it's worth noting that what I am attempting in *Darkness over Love: A Complete Fiction* and have offered in a preliminary form in *Darkness over Love: A Writer's Workbook*, has far more in common with Durrell's ambitions as a writer than with Schlink's.

Jan Morris writes of *The Alexandria Quartet* that it 'was an experimental novel in its day'; that 'the four volumes concern the same characters, but several narrators tell its complex tales from their several viewpoints, and they write at different times'; while the quartet 'is often ornately overwritten, sometimes to an almost comical degree'. I suspect that all three of these things might be said of my own novel, at least as it currently stands.

Here, then, are my ten Discussion Points.

1.   Does the essay 'The Evolution of a Story' hold your interest through to the end? If not, what parts of it lost your interest?

2.   Given that I state boldly at the beginning of that essay that I have set out to write something on the 'epic' scale that might become 'a myth for the 21st century', what did you expect the writing to be like, before you actually began reading N. Herman's Introduction?

3.   What were your immediate reactions to N. Herman's Introduction and the dramatic story about terrorism and secret manuscripts and conspiracy theories?

4.   What do you think of the 'Russian doll' narrative structure of N. Herman's account to a 'global readership' of what has happened, followed by Tom Emerson's earlier account of how the original book came about, addressed only to the Academy of Lynxes; followed by Fenimore's even earlier Prologue, addressed only to Margarita?

---

77   The four are *Justine* (1957), *Balthazar* (1958), *Mountolive* (1958) and *Clea* (1960). My own edition is the Faber & Faber paperback omnibus edition of 2012, with a new introduction by Jan Morris.

5. What do you think of the octavo style of Fenimore's notebooks as an idea? Does it work for you? Is the language too stilted? Would you like to see more dialogue? If so, how would this work, as you see things?

6. What do you think of Fenimore, having travelled with him from Toledo to his final hours at Cos? Do you believe that what he was attempting was important? Or does he strike you as being another Don Quixote? In retrospect, do you think that is the significance of the use of Cervantes and the Prologue being set in Toledo itself?

7. How did you find yourself responding to the tone of Tom's commentaries in his Appendices and the humour in N. Herman's Postscript? Can you see how she has constructed the whole thing? What difference does it make to your appreciation of Tom Emerson and his commentaries, or Fenimore and his grand dreams, or Margarita and her theories, therapies and behaviour, that they are all the fictions of N. Herman's imagination?

8. What reactions did you have to the documents in Appendix D, especially Cardinal Bolzano's Letter to the Pope? What did you think of Bolzano as a character? What do you think of his portrait of Fenimore?

9. Did you enjoy the Tale of Raneb and Nefesh and the Songs of Queen Nefesh? Why, in your opinion, does Tom Emerson come to see them as central to the whole story of Fenimore and Margarita? Do you agree with him? Do you think that they have a place in N. Herman's construction of the 'complete fiction' transcending the insights of Tom? If so, what is it?

10. There are twenty missing sections, but their titles are supplied. Given all that you now know and assuming you have enjoyed what you've read so far, which of those titles look most alluring to you? Which sections should Fenimore write into his notebooks next?

Portrait of the author
by his eleven year old niece, Lauren Hawkins.

Acknowledgements

This book is the first fruits of a project whose roots go back a long way and the completion of which is surely still somewhat uncertain and some way off. Within the essay in this volume, I refer to two individuals as having played singularly important roles in stimulating me to start work on it and encouraging me to persevere with it. I refer to them there as the Muse and the Friend. They know who they are and due tribute is paid to them within the essay and has been communicated privately.

But even so, there are others whose encouragement and practical support have been invaluable in making this book possible. These begin with the readers of early drafts or portions of them, such as Jane Monk, Claire Baxter, Susan Mann, Ian Gordon, Sawsan Howard and Robert Horvath. There were many times when I had difficulty believing that I could write literary prose. The inexplicable enthusiasm of these readers for what they could see I was attempting helped me to keep going. I hope they all find that this version exceeds their expectations.

A book, however, is a finished and typeset product between covers. That required the professional work of Ian Gordon and his designer Peter Gamble at Barrallier Books. This is our third collaboration and it will, I think, sit comfortably (even in this 'unfinished' form) alongside the first two: *Sonnets to a Promiscuous Beauty* and *The West in a Nutshell*. It has taken far longer than them to write, but that is chiefly because they each consisted of simpler work written long before and then edited into book form. This, by contrast, is the beginning of a far more ambitious piece of work.

To have been able to draw upon the skills and enthusiasm of Ian and Peter once more has been a great boon. The certainty that a handsome and durable book would be the product of their labours has helped to inspire me to work the story up into this provisional form and send it to press, where otherwise it might have remained no more than a work in progress, somewhat stranded on the long way up the mountain. It will now be a terrific base camp from which to set out on the next stage of the climb. I hope a couple of dozen people will explore that base camp and cheer me onwards.

One of the features of both of the earlier books was the superb art work contributed by the late Jorg Schmeisser. We have been very fortunate, through communication with his life partner Keiko, to have been able to acquire and use two of his etchings for this book, the cover image and the frontispiece to Book I. In addition, however, it has been a delight to have been able to engage the services of the talented Cathy Gordon to create half a dozen drawings for the core of the manuscript.

Such is the quality of these pieces that I find myself dreaming of a book in which every one of the twenty six sections of Fenimore's Notebooks will have a Cathy Gordon illumination to accompany it. And then there is the unexpected gift of a portrait of me drawn by my eleven year old niece, Lauren Hawkins. This drawing came out of the blue and so astonished me for its precocious skill and for the love that evidently went into it that I decided to include it within this book in token of my appreciation. The next thing will be to introduce Lauren to Cathy.

Finally, I should acknowledge both David Speakman and his colleagues at the Peter MacCallum Cancer Centre; and also my ever patient and rational business partner, Tim van Gelder, for their respective roles in making this creative work possible. The team at Peter Mac have worked tirelessly, again and again, to keep me physically viable against a threat of the kind that, in 'reality', overwhelms Fenimore in the novel.

They tell me that I am a somewhat 'freakish' melanoma patient, in having proved so resilient for so long; but without their skilled intervention and cheerful professionalism, it is rather doubtful that I would still be here. Tim, on the other hand, has had to cope both with the many vagaries of my melanoma campaign and my deep distraction from consulting work as I wrestled with how to write (and rewrite and then again rewrite) the novel. To all of them I owe a great debt of thanks. I hope that they, too, see the fruits of my labour as justifying their own labour and patience, respectively.